Judi James was a highly  starting her own school o becoming a management businesses on presentation *Carmine*, was published in

By the same author

*Carmine*

JUDI JAMES

# The Ruby Palace

Grafton
*An Imprint of HarperCollinsPublishers*

Grafton
An Imprint of HarperCollins*Publishers*
77–85 Fulham Palace Road,
Hammersmith, London W6 8JB

Published by Grafton 1992
1 3 5 7 9 8 6 4 2

First published in Great Britain by
GraftonBooks 1991

© Judi James 1991

The Author asserts the moral right to
be identified as the author of this work

ISBN 0 586 20796 1

Set in Bembo

Printed in Great Britain by
HarperCollinsManufacturing Glasgow

# THE RUBY PALACE

# Book One

---

## ENGLAND

# CHAPTER 1

*June 1953, Coronation Day*

The great house in Surrey appeared as a palace to the children, drawing a small sigh from their round-opened mouths and some of the fidget from their skinny white limbs as the rotting grey Humber pulled slowly up the drive.

Elaborately carved, and old beyond any child's comprehension, the house lay cupped in the veined roots of a tall cabbage-green hill like a pale and very ancient fossil. It was at once grand and proud and magnificently neglected – a rich white slab of peeling alabaster that grew mysteriously from the thick dank ivy that curtained it at its base. Its creamy stucco walls had crumbled completely in parts, to expose the rough grey stone underneath. Fat damp mosses clung to those stones, while row upon row of tall windows reflected the blue of the summer sky like well-polished mirrors.

The house even had a name; it was etched into the stonework right above the doorway. 'Rowan Hall' the children read, and beneath the name a date: 1779.

Grandad Gilbert came around the car to release the children from the back, plucking them from their seats like pieces of ripe fruit; his chest wheezing with the effort as he did so.

'Don't ask for nothing and don't take nothing, right?' he warned them. His eyes were as beady as wet black

olives and his brown scalp sweated from the heat inside
the car. 'Use your hankies to blow your noses and if you
gotta pee make sure you ask for the lavatory. Don't wait,
ask! Right?'

But none of the six children could answer him, not
even a nod of the head, they were too busy staring at the
house. The long journey from London had made them
itchy and irritable and their once-splendid party costumes
had wilted like unwatered flowers; they scratched uneasily
in the drizzling rain. The damp of their bodies and clothes
brought out unwanted smells of boiled potatoes and
frying fat.

They stared at a house the colour of fresh mushroom
skins and its endless green gardens that rolled away on all
sides. Their ears heard the breezes that stirred among the
apple trees in those gardens, and when the currents of air
reached their hot faces they smelled of lavender and mint.
Their faces screwed up and they used their hands to shield
their eyes as they looked across the cress-coloured lake,
whose surface of lily-pads heaved gently in the wind.
There were large golden fishes beneath those pads, nib-
bling at the surface and then darting off through the cool
green waters.

The children stared for a while at the view, and then
became bored, except for one girl who remained transfixed by what she saw. Ruby Elizabeth was, at seven
years, the youngest of the group by about a year, but her
legs were the plumpest and she wore the cleanest socks.
Ruby stared unblinking at the house, unworried by her
crushed fancy dress and the fact that her Pierrot hat had
slipped to the side of her head. She stared while the others
kicked their sandals into the gravel and whined about the
rain, and then she adjusted the hat elastic under her chin
and set off to take a closer look.

Wildflowers grew everywhere, and Ruby was
entranced. The drone of feeding bees grew louder, like a
chant, in the background. Purple dog roses tangled with
the fingers of ivy that wove like thread around the wide

doorway, and thicker, uncultivated bushes ran off into the gardens to each side.

There were even flowers carved into the stonework around the pillars of the door. Ruby closed her eyes as the droning grew deafening, and soaked up the perfume of the flowers and the wet earth they grew in. The house was unreal in the damp air, like a photograph or a dream.

A tall, large woman with a peach-powdered face and a nose as sharp as a javelin point emerged suddenly from the gloom around the doorway. Grandad Gilbert caught sight of her and nipped straight back into the car.

'See you kids again about four,' he shouted, and the Humber stirred into life, billowing blue fumes that enveloped the circle of children like a fog. 'OK, missus?' he checked, shouting now. The woman frowned and nodded.

'Hurry!' she called, waving as the car drove off and the fumes cleared. 'You're just in time for the wireless!' The children turned to watch the car grow smaller in the long drive, then turned back again as the woman stepped out of the shadows. 'Single file now, girls first,' she said, 'and don't forget to wipe your feet as you come inside.'

The children followed reluctantly, forlorn now, not irritable, and slippery-wet with embarrassment. The dye from their crêpe-paper costumes had begun to run in the rain on their legs, and their white skin was stained with ribbons of red and blue. Even the boy dressed in newspaper, the one whose mother could not afford crêpe, had black marks on his hands and his face that looked like dirt.

The children shivered inside the hallway of the house, which was as cool and as high as a church. The ceiling had been painted to look like sky and three of them lost their hats bending backwards to look up at it. It was the sort of sky that you would see in heaven; deepest peacock blue with fluffy, pink-rimmed clouds. There were angels playing in the carved plaster mouldings of the ceiling, fat-bellied and golden, like the fishes in the lake outside.

A marble fireplace as tall as a grown man stood to their right and a giant grey dog slept in front of it on a faded silk rug. Any light in the hall came from a long window at the top of the wide central staircase, and it came through the panes in shafts of floating dust and weak sunlight. Everything else was hidden in dark silent shadow.

The woman ushered the shuffling children through a door to their left and the muffled voice of a wireless grew louder and clearer as they approached. The woman placed a finger to her lips and cupped a hand to her ear to show them they should be listening. A maid appeared on tiptoe, her black leather lace-ups creaking on bare boards, and handed each child a paper flag on a stick.

'These bloody Union Jacks are bloody well on upside-down!' Lenny Gold said, pulling a face, but he was only parroting something he'd heard his father call out when the bunting went up in their street at home. Apart from Lenny the children were silent, though their rubber soles squealed badly on the varnished wooden floor. They huddled like goats, long-legged and miserable, out-of-place and suddenly shy.

The wireless was the only new thing in the room and they felt let down by the furniture that was older than at home.

'Sirs, I here present unto you Queen Elizabeth,' the wireless said. It was square and heavy, made of chocolate-brown Bakelite, with bright, greenish lights that glowed above its dials.

'Your undoubted queen,' the voice went on, 'wherefore all you who are come this day to do your homage . . .' A mass of faceless voices somewhere hollered out 'God save Queen Elizabeth!' A wasp buzzed lazily around the vase on the wireless.

'We thought you had television!' one of the older boys complained. They had a wireless at home. He couldn't see why they'd come all that way just to listen. His sister started snuffling and the woman who lived in the house

stopped smiling. 'I wanted to see the crystal coach . . .'
one girl said, and another child kicked her.

The door to the room opened again and the maid ushered in a second group of children. They stared with
horror at the children from the Humber, and the children
from the Humber turned to scowl back. This second
group were different. They had costumes made of sewn
fabric and their knees looked clean and unbruised. Ruby
stepped quickly to one side, suddenly ashamed of her own
group and unwilling to be associated with their obvious
poverty.

Chests puffed out and knuckles began to whiten as the
children forgot the wireless and squared themselves up
for battle.

'Most gracious queen,' the wireless-voice went on, 'we
present you with this book, the most valuable thing that
this world affords.'

'Swankers!' The boy dressed in newspaper took an
exploratory hack at the bare legs of a silver fairy with his
rolled-up paper sword. As his weapon clove through the
air the crowds in Westminster Abbey sang out to the
Father Almighty. A harlequin from the rich group pushed
a blacked-up minstrel from the poor group and a general
shuffling broke out as feet hooked round the backs of
ankles and elbows were shoved into ribs. The maid
frowned and tutted loudly, telling them that they should
be quiet.

Ruby looked away from the fight and out into the
hall, where a movement had caught her eye. A beautiful
golden-haired boy stood there against the bannister,
caught in the powdery yellow ray of light, as still as
though he were one of the carvings. He was like a ghost,
too perfect almost to be real, his chin resting on the crook
of his arm and his eyes half-closed, his head tilted as
though he were listening.

Ruby crept a little closer, afraid to move in case he saw
her and vanished. She had never seen such a beautiful face
before. The boy's skin was pale and quite as delicate as

her own; his lashes were golden-pale, too, and long, so that they left blue shadows on his cheekbones. His lips were red and pouted, like a child's mouth, or like the mouths of the fat cherubs that looked down lovingly from overhead.

The boy, who was not in costume, was older than the others, perhaps as old as fourteen, and taller. He wore a brightly-striped school blazer over a cream-coloured shirt and green silk cravat. His fingers on the bannister were long and slim, and the nails were pink, like seashells.

As Ruby watched silently, not daring to breathe, the boy suddenly straightened and yawned, like a cat in the sun. His teeth were perfectly white, and Ruby could see the outline of his ribs against his shirt as he stretched. She badly wanted to walk over and talk to the boy but he was much older than her and would think she was stupid. Perhaps he would talk like the woman who lived in the house. She spoke like the new Queen and Ruby could barely understand what she said.

The maid walked into the hall banging on a small brass gong, and Ruby jumped. 'Tea!' the maid shouted. 'Tea in the marquee in the garden!'

The children let out loud whoops and broke rank suddenly, each determined to be the first at the food. They darted through the large French windows, whacking the paintwork with imaginary swords, followed closely by a small group of adults, shaking their heads and waving their arms, leaving Ruby alone in the doorway. She moved slowly into the dark hall, touching each cool varnished wood panel with her fingertips and feeling the spongy rugs under her feet. The hallway smelled musty and old, like a church.

Ruby had decided that she wanted to stay in the house for ever. The wanting was so bad as it came over her that it felt like a hard ball, burning in her small chest like heartburn. She wanted to own the house so badly that in her mind she imagined that it was hers – that it had belonged to her all along, and had been waiting for her.

She had never known a wanting like this before, it made her feel small and weak, and her limbs feel heavy, like lead.

'The garden is through there, if that is what you're looking for.' The boy's voice was surprisingly strong, and Ruby turned quickly to face him. He was a whole head taller than her and he smelled of soap and fresh air.

'Are you one of the charity children?' he asked, smiling at her. He swung gently from the stairpost as he spoke, backwards and forwards, hanging by one arm, like a snake, hypnotizing her, smiling at her.

Ruby's face flushed. 'Charity?' she asked. Her voice was hardly heard. She should have cleared her throat. It was a squeak and a whisper, nothing more, whereas the boy's voice had been so strong and so clear. Her whispered word hung in the air between them like a wasp.

The boy nodded and a spike of blond hair fell over his forehead. 'One of the London kids,' he prompted her. 'The ones from deprived families. Is your father in prison and your mother on the gin or something? Hang on though.' He tapped the side of his forehead with one finger. 'Is it deprived or depraved?' he asked, laughing out loud. 'I always muddle words like that. Which is it now – are your lot deprived or depraved, or both?'

Ruby looked at the floor and rolled the edges of her paper skirt between her fingers. She'd never heard either word before. She'd never heard real silence before, either, you just didn't get it in London, not even on a Sunday, but it was there in that hallway once the boy had finished speaking and it pressed on her ears like being underwater.

'Don't you speak for yourself?' the boy asked politely. 'Have you been beaten at home? Mother told me some of you might have been.' He pressed his face closer to hers. 'What's your name then?' He sat down on the stairs so that their faces were level.

'Ruby,' she said, but the 'R' came out as 'W', a habit she had had throughout childhood, and which returned when she was nervous.

'Wuby?' the boy asked, 'Wuby?' and he laughed again, showing his perfect teeth. 'Well, Wuby,' he said, once his laughter had subsided, 'as you are one of our guests for the day then I suppose I should be the perfect host and find something to keep you amused. Now what do you suppose would amuse a little scrag like you then? Chess? Poetry? The piano? Do you play, Ruby? How about "Roll Out the Barrel"? I'd love to see Mother's face as that came tinkling out of the Steinway.'

Ruby stared at the boy in silence, still working her hem between fingers damp with sweat.

The boy raised his eyebrows and feigned a yawn. 'No?' he asked. He snapped his fingers suddenly. 'Horticulture!' he said, smiling at her again. 'I'll bet you're mad on horticulture then.' He leaned towards her and pressed his lips against her ear.

'Flowers, Ruby,' he whispered, 'that's what that means, flowers. I'll bet you like flowers now, don't you?'

Ruby nodded, staring at the floor. She could feel the boy's breath in her ear. It smelled of aniseed. She pulled her head away.

'Do you like roses, Ruby?' the boy asked. 'We have loads of them here, millions of them, in fact. We even have a Ruby rose, now I'll bet you'd like to see that, wouldn't you? A rose named specially after you?' He stood up and took Ruby's hand. 'It's in the rose garden,' he told her. 'Come along now, and I'll show you.'

The boy took Ruby through the hall and led her out into the garden. 'There,' he said, looking up at the sky, 'it's even stopped raining, just for us.' The other children were miles away, it seemed; she could hear their voices only as seagull cries, screeching and whooping somewhere in the distance. They came to a wall with a door in the middle. The boy pushed aside some ivy and turned a rusted key in the lock. The door fell back with a scream of old wood and they were in the rose garden, walking inside, so that the door shut behind them. The boy locked

the door and threw the key into the air and caught it
again, before shoving it deep into his trouser pocket.

There was a spell in that garden, and enchantment.
They had walked through time. The air was different,
damp and heavy and thick with the perfume of the roses,
and the sounds from outside had vanished as the door had
closed. All that Ruby could see and smell were the roses;
huge overblown velvety hybrids that stood before her in
rows, gorged as they were on the sun and the dank soil
until their heads had swollen and dropped with their own
weight.

'What did I tell you?' the boy asked in a whisper. 'Millions of them, just as I said. Look at them, scraggy, just
look at their beauty. Obscene, isn't it? Too much perfume
and too much colour, like a line of old overblown tarts.'
He pushed Ruby closer to the rose beds, she felt his hand
in the small of her back. 'Look at the colours, Ruby,' he
said. 'Scarlet, like blood that fades to purple where the
petals have died; yellow, like an egg's yolk, only with red
veins running through it like the chicken's own blood;
pink, like boiled shrimps . . . and then there's this one,
the most obscene one of the lot.' The boy pulled the head
of the largest bloom towards him and buried his face in
its petals, drinking up the scent till yellow pollen covered
his nose. 'Your namesake, Ruby,' he told her, turning
back. ' "Ruby Port" my uncle called it, his own creation,
the richest rose in the beds.'

Ruby gazed at the flower, at its folded black-red centre
and its lighter, blood-red petals. It was as big as a tea-
plate and heavy with scent that stuck in Ruby's throat.

She put a finger out to touch it. 'I like it,' she told the
boy. It was a lie – she loved it. It was her rose, it had her
name. She had never thought of her name as a colour
before, but now she was seeing it, ruby red, red like port
wine when you hold it up to the light, red like the jewel
she was named after.

'Well, that's all right then,' the boy said, smiling.

In a sudden movement that made Ruby cry out he

twisted the head viciously off its stalk, crushing it in his hand and shaking the crushed petals to the ground.

Ruby watched him, horrified. She wanted to beat the boy, to make him stop, but he was bigger than her and she was afraid. 'You shouldn't do that,' she said.

'Shouldn't I?' the boy asked. 'Why not? There is one thing that you have to learn in this life, young Ruby, and that is the law of ownership. That rose belonged to me, and that means that I could do what I liked with it.'

'You killed it,' Ruby said.

The boy merely shrugged and looked bored. 'Did I?' he asked, looking at the fallen petals. 'Yes, I believe I did – you see, you do know something about horticulture after all.'

There was an uneasy silence between them and the boy pulled a squashed cigarette out of his pocket and lit it with a match.

'D'you live 'ere then?' Ruby asked him, staring miserably at her feet.

The boy laughed. 'Live 'ere?' he mimicked. 'Why, I practically own the place!' The smoke rose out of his nostrils like dragon's breath and he flipped the dead match in among the flowers. 'My father has been in a nursing home since he was sent home injured in the war,' he said, 'so that just leaves my mother, my kid sister and myself. You've met my sister, by the way,' he added, 'she was the one that your friend was busy goosing with his paper sword earlier on.' He nodded his head in the direction of the house.

'I'm so sorry,' he said suddenly, pulling himself to attention, 'I should have introduced myself earlier. My name is Piers,' he announced, holding out his hand. 'When my father is gone, which I fear might be sooner rather than later, I shall be the eleventh Earl of Bicester.'

Ruby took his hand to shake it, but Piers grabbed it instead and held it, laughing. A fat bee moved steadily from flower to flower, droning like the engine of an aeroplane.

Piers looked down at Ruby's bare legs, fat and dimpled like a doll's and shoved his free hand deep into his trouser pocket. 'Do you like my house then, Ruby?' he asked, his voice sounding suddenly thick, as though his mouth were filled with honey.

Ruby nodded, her cheeks burning. Piers let go of her hand and raised her chin with one finger.

'Would you like to live here too?' he asked. His eyes were blue, like the ceiling in the hallway. Ruby wanted that more than anything else. She wanted to stand dreamily in the hallway, as Piers had done, to swing from the bannister by one hand, to hear her shoes squeak across the parquet, to light fires in the hall when it was winter. She wanted to be alone with the roses, to bury her face in the pollen as he had just done, and she wanted to pull her skirts up and paddle in the cool waters of the lake until her calves were white with gooseflesh and the goldfish nibbled at her bare toes.

It was the first time in Ruby's life that she had ever seen anything that was not hers for the asking and the feeling brought out greed and jealousy, emotions that she had never experienced before.

'You'd have to marry me then, to get all of this,' Piers told her quietly. She watched as he blew a smoke ring that rose lazily in the air, and took the stub from his long fingers as he offered it to her and placed it between her lips. The smoke was like acid in her eyes and she blinked, rubbing at them with her knuckles.

'Do you know what being married means, Ruby?' Piers asked, his face turning serious. 'Do you know what grown-up people have to do together, when they're alone?' His fingers were less steady now as he took the cigarette away from her.

Ruby watched him, mesmerized. His long fingers fascinated her and so did his words. The smoke had made her head feel light. Of course she wanted to know what people did when they were married. The day had so far been the most exciting in her entire life, and now this older boy was about to share secrets with her, almost as if they were exactly the same age.

'Do you really want to know, Ruby?' he asked. 'Can you keep a secret?' She nodded. Piers moved closer towards her. She felt hot suddenly, and saw the yellow pollen that was stuck to his top lip.

Piers bent towards her quickly, before she had time to move or cry out, and his mouth pressed against her own. She could feel his teeth behind his closed lips, a hard row that ground against hers until she thought her lips would bleed. She opened her mouth in surprise and his tongue popped swiftly inside, quick and darting, like a snake.

As Ruby coped with the feeling of another live thing inside her mouth she felt Piers's hands fingering her bare legs. They grabbed at her thighs, then pushed quickly upward until they were fumbling through her short paper skirt and into the leg of her knickers.

Ruby felt pinned to Piers, and unable to escape – his soft tongue and his teeth and his long delicate fingers had become part of her own body and bound her to him like rope, as did her own overpowering curiosity. He was changing, getting strange, and she wanted to know badly what it was that he knew about grown-ups. She was sure it was this secret that would eventually lead her to own the beautiful house. People did it when they were alone and married and she would one day have to do it with Piers if she were to marry him.

It was embarrassment that forced Ruby to pull away, and pull away fast. Her Pierrot dress was a sham, home-made by her aunt some ten minutes before she'd left the house. She'd stood in the kitchen, in her knickers and her liberty bodice, and her aunt had pinned the crêpe paper straight on to her underwear. Piers was about to discover her most terrible secret. People who lived in big houses in the country wore proper fancy dress for the new Queen's coronation, not sheets of paper from the sweetshop that had to be pinned on to their oldest vest. Auntie Marge had refused to give her a clean one because she'd said that the pins might hole it.

Ashamed and nearly in tears, Ruby twisted out of Piers's hands, and heard him laugh at her as she did so. Her red skirt tore a little in his hands and a small piece of crêpe paper came away in his fingers. She knew that Piers was laughing at her because she was poor and she was stupid. She rushed towards the garden door but then remembered that it was locked. When she turned back Piers was holding out the key and laughing. She reached for it but he snatched it away, but when she cried he finally gave it to her and she ran out of the garden and towards the house.

Bells pealed out on the wireless and singing voices echoed through the empty hall. Ruby ran right to the front door and pulled it open to stand shaking and blinking in the pale sunlight. She was hot and she was hungry. She had missed her tea, but she would not go back inside, she would wait until the Humber came up the drive to collect them.

The sun moved behind black clouds again and Ruby rubbed at her arms as though she were cold. The sounds of the other children playing games only added to her misery. She would travel back with those children, but she no longer felt herself to be one of them. Ruby had plans now, special plans.

The sun reappeared suddenly, a rich afternoon sun that blinded Ruby and made her cover her eyes. Then she pulled her hands away and looked at the house. It could have been on fire. The sun blazed deep red from every window; bright ruby red, like the flower, like her name.

It was her house, it would be hers, and one day she would be back, but this time wearing proper underwear and good expensive clothes. Her legs would not be plump and bare and she would talk properly, like the new Queen on the wireless. She would not be deprived and she would no longer be blushing. Then she could marry Piers and the house would be hers. Then she could bury her face in the roses and paddle in the lake until the fish nipped at her toes. Then she could invite her own groups of deprived children down from London to listen to the wireless.

The sun-flames guttered in the windows and were gone. Ruby tasted her own blood in her mouth from the kiss she had had with Piers and she spat it quickly into the mud and dust around her feet. Blood, spit and dust. She stared down at the three elements. It was true now, she had made a pact. Her promise to the house had been sealed. One day it would belong to her.

# CHAPTER 2

## 1953

When I was a child I would sit alongside our Billy as he worked the stall in the vegetable markets.

Billy 'King' Edward, the king of the vegetable markets, and I his only and much-loved daughter, the Vegetable Princess, proud of my birthright and the honours it bestowed. I can see myself now, as I sat there in state, my blond hair thick and curly like kale, and shining in the sun like nuggets of ripe corn. My skin was pale as chicory with the soft precious feel of the down of a peach. Two fresh green-pea eyes and a beetroot-pink smile. How could I not be happy? I was my father's pride and joy.

Ruby, Billy called me, although my name by birth was Ruby Elizabeth. I in turn was to call him Billy, for what he said were 'legal reasons'. Never Father or Dad, because his memory of my conception was claimed to be hazy, and therefore my true parentage open to discussion.

'I could've been there and I could've done it,' he told the rest of the family, 'but I ain't admitting to nothing.' I was his cuckoo, planted in his nest when his back was turned, as pale and dainty and pretty, so he told me, as he was dark and ugly, but we lived as father and daughter, for all that. Billy seemed handsome to me then; the whole world that I lived in seemed handsome to me then. But that was in the days before I came to Rowan Hall, and met Piers, and therefore I had no comparison.

Apart from Billy, who was tall and big and always wore a hat, there was Aunt Marge, who was bigger, and who had married Billy's brother just before the war had started. He had gone away in the war – left her, not died – and she worked next to us in the market and lived alone. Then there was her father, Gilbert, who the kids all called Grandad. Gilbert did the fruit, Marge did tins and seconds, and Billy and I did vegetables, the best stuff north of the river. Our stall was the largest, and piled to the sky with stuff. Billy started work before dawn, taking each vegetable from its box, polishing the finer produce on the sleeve of his shirt, stacking the potatoes so that the best and the biggest were at the front, and then arranging the rest like a daily work of art.

He piled peas in front of the potatoes; long fat pods bursting with their fruit, in clusters like fingers, beside fuzzy-topped carrots. There were speckled marrows and foam-headed cauliflowers, and bouquets of deep green spinach that hung from the canopy over our heads.

On those dark mornings the market resembled a silent funfair, with its strings of bare-bulb lights and steaming tea stalls. Billy came in and woke me around nine, but sometimes when it was cold I would wake early, and stand by the oil fire watching the market from our window, steaming the glass up with my breath, and then finger-painting faces in the steam.

I thought we were rich, I wanted for nothing, but then I had seen nothing and therefore thought that I had everything, and that is why my life changed so much on that visit to Rowan Hall. I should have stayed in that market, inherited Billy's stall, and lived with my wealth like my Aunt Marge. She allowed the things that she loved to slip from her grasp, but she stayed with her thoughts instead of running after a dream. She even seemed happy enough, with her tinned soups and her neatly-folded rows of hankies and underwear. We each had our own flat, thanks to the benevolence of the local Council. We were warm and ate well. We had more than other people that we knew. But then I met Piers and I knew that we had nothing. I had thought that North London was beautiful. I thought we were well-spoken and educated. I even imagined my father to be a real king. When I discovered the truth I fought for what I had missed, and during that struggle became a liar, a thief and a murderess.

I should have stayed in the market. I should have been like my Aunty Marge.

William Albert Edward was born in 1928, the seventh son of a seventh son, which he told me was supposed to be lucky, but which in his case could not have been true, because he was given away at four years of age. This is not to say that Billy's parents did not love him, they simply couldn't afford to keep him. Perhaps it was the same with my own mother. Billy said that being given away like that had given him a chip, that he was a surly cuss throughout his youth, and always planning to get back at his father. In the event he never got the chance. His father was killed by one of Hitler's bombs, blown to bits in the Anderson shelter while he was trying to forge clothing coupons by torchlight.

Albert and Edna cared for my father, because they were unable to have kids of their own. Edna drank and Bert spent most of his time out of the house, according to Billy. He claimed that they were his aunt and uncle, although I've never found anyone in our family who will back that theory up. He also claimed that Edna tried to seduce him one night when she was drunk and Bert was away, though from what I can remember of Edna, I should think that story is unlikely. Edna was a keen churchgoer, despite her liking for drink, and right up to her end, Billy would never so much as whisper an oath in her presence.

Half a mile down the Holloway Road, on the corner of Seven Sisters and Enkel Street, there used to be a pub where Edna would drink, called The Two Brewers. Saturday night was Country Night at The Two Brewers, and

Billy and a few of his pals would get dressed up like
cowboys to drink beer and yodel a few songs, and it was
there that he first met my mother. Behind The Two
Brewers there was a yard where the bottles were stored,
and at the end of the yard was a wall that led into an
alley. The wall is still there, it's tiled halfway up with
mottled brown tiles. Billy had my mother up against that
wall, and it was up against that wall that I was conceived.

Nine months to the day after that night Billy was at
the stall as usual, whistling his cowboy songs and winking
at all the women, when one girl that he hardly recognized
stepped up to his counter and placed a bundle of blankets
into the large brass scales.

'Eight pound four ounces,' the woman told Billy, and
walked off into the crowd. Billy remembered the
woman's face, and her name – Lily. He also remembered
that she worked at the factory up at Highgate. Then he
remembered the night at The Two Brewers, and then he
looked into the scales and found me.

It was good fortune that Billy should have treated my
arrival with such good humour and good grace. He never
tried to trace my mother to give me back, and he never
once thought of giving me to the Council to be taken care
of. Instead he brought me up as his own, which, in fact,
I almost certainly was. Even if he had not recognized Lily
I believe that he would have kept me without question,
because he had been given away, and so had I. Billy was
only eighteen then, but he took me home in his arms and
introduced me to Bert and Edna like a friend he'd just
met in the pub. Edna waited three days before asking
when I would be going back, and when Billy told her
that I wasn't, that I belonged to him now, Edna offered
no opinion of his promiscuity but did not speak another
word to Billy until the day that she died.

Bert kept away from the house even more after my
arrival, and died soon afterwards of ulcers, leaving Billy
sole ownership of the stall in his will.

And so our life together began, Billy and myself, the

king of the market and his golden-haired daughter. I became pretty, as my mother had been, and chubby on my Aunt Marge's fritters. I ate sherbet dabs and liquorice that the customers bought me, and I grew to love the vegetables every bit as much as my father.

Other children had two parents and large families and skinny arms and legs that poked out of too-big or too-small hand-me-downs, but I had only Billy, and he spoilt me. Other people wanted new clothes or furniture or more food, but the only thing that I ever heard Billy yearn for that he couldn't afford to buy was a cocktail cabinet that he saw one day in the window of Fuller & Sons, and which he said would look nice in our lounge. I found his yearning for this cocktail cabinet strange, all the more since he had given up drink the night after I had arrived. Billy loved me to death, but he wasn't about to get drunk and let himself get caught like that again.

In that softly-baked summer of 'fifty-three I was seven years old, and Billy still a young man of twenty-five, although his black hair was already thinning, which was why he had taken to wearing a hat. If you took a bus down the Holloway Road and got off just before the United Dairies and took the first on the right, then you would have found yourself walking past some prefabs and into a large, red-brick estate. That estate had been built on a bomb-site and the bomb that had dropped there had been the one that killed Marge's young brother, Stephen, who had been at home with the dog while his parents watched a film at the Roxy up at Archway. They heard the bomb go off, but they thought it was part of the film.

The estate was crummy from the moment that it was built, but we lived there and we liked it because it was modern and it was new. I often thought about Stephen and his dog, and said prayers in bed at night to be forgiven for living on the spot where he died. The winter had been so cold that year that the ground had frozen, and cracks appeared in our walls. Billy said we could live with the cracks, though, because we had a kitchen and a lavatory,

unlike Marge's flat, which just had a scullery and an outside privy. Billy papered the walls of our flat himself, and
painted them all bright orange because he said it was a
cheerful colour and would take our minds off the cracks
that were underneath. My bedroom was the only room
that faced south, and therefore my window was the only
window in the flat that had a view of the market.

On Wednesdays, Fridays and Saturdays the market
never stopped. The noise was like a chant in a church;
repetitious, familiar, building to a crescendo and then
dying slowly note by note. I miss that noise now, and the
smells and the people. The stalls stretched for two streets
and then curled into a bombed-out yard, where the books
and shoes were sold. Our customers were women in
floral-printed aprons with headscarves tied into turbans
and slippers and rolled-down stockings on their feet. In
winter they wore camel coats and hand-knits over their
aprons and in summer you could see their brassieres
through their transparent nylon blouses.

Their days were spent in a constant war with their
children, their husbands, their houses and the prices, and
yet they still had time to cheek the stallholders, especially
my father, who was young and looked healthy and rough.
Marge watched him like a hawk, from behind her tiers of
outsize bloomers and interlocked vests. I never once saw
Marge smile, except when she knew Billy was watching
her.

The war had led people like us to take pride in poverty.
Hardships were hidden by bravery. I was surrounded by
filth and decay but I never once realized it because I never
once heard anyone complain. I think that maybe a child
sets its own sights, and will see all of the magic that it
wants to see, wherever it is born. Perhaps the real cruelty
is not in the poverty, but is showing a child an alternative.
At any rate, I know that I knew no better and wanted no
better until the day I was shown real riches, and that was
the day that I was taken to Rowan Hall.

Did the people who lived in Rowan Hall ever feel like

that too? Did they pine for better things as I pined to own their home? I cannot imagine that they did, for everything that I wanted in life was there, cupped into that hillside.

In my ignorance I was as blissfully happy as a pig in its sty. The greater of life's questions eluded me totally. Where, for instance, did Billy get his money? I never thought to wonder. We had more than others, and yet Billy did the same line of work. No other children had the clothes that I had, or lived in flats as comfortable as ours. I knew of families whose children shared pairs of shoes. No one in our street ever had new clothes, only hand-me-downs and hand-mades or pickings from the jumble, yet Billy and I were always dressed well enough, and I remember the new things he'd buy for me to wear when I grew out of the old. My cast-offs went two doors down, and the kids there hated me for it.

I assumed that God just gave more to some than he did to others, but I was to find out soon enough where the extra money came from, and God, it turned out, had very little hand in it.

Then there was my Aunty Marge. Why was she so strange? 'She was made that way' is the answer I would have given then, but looking back now I suppose she was in love with our Billy. Marge was a great big misery of a woman, always mooning around the place and chewing at her nails. The layers of clothing that she, like all the other stallholders, wore to keep warm in the winter gave her the overall look of a great lumbering cow. I may not have known what it was that I wanted at that age, but I knew with my whole body what it was that I did not want, and that was to grow up like my Aunt Marge.

I thought that her name was short for margarine, and it put me off the stuff for life, because her skin was oily which made her look as though she were made of it. Billy was not a handsome man, but there was a sort of proud, rugged beauty about him, and the thought of him together with Marge would have appalled me more than words could describe.

Besides, Billy belonged to me, and as far as I was
concerned, he was not to be shared with any other
woman. Billy loved me and his vegetables and his music,
and his occasional betting on the dogs, in that order.
There was no room in that list for my cow-like Aunty
Marge.

Billy knew something had happened the moment I got
out of the Humber. My paper skirt was torn, and he said
that at first he thought I'd met with an accident, my face
looked so white and I'd lost all of my smile.

The other kids leapt out of the car like animals, smelling
of the country air, emptying their pockets of all the food
they'd managed to stow away. A couple of silver-coloured
spoons slipped out of Joey Prestwick's pocket, along with
broken Rich Teas and a squashed lemon-curd tart, and
Joey got a clip round the ear for thieving, although I
noticed his mother put the spoons into her purse nonethe-
less.

I just stood to one side, my head hanging. There was
bunting all over the street and Billy was wearing a paper
hat and waving a flag. I knew that he'd done it to make
me laugh. He expected me to be full of excitement and
tales like the other kids, but I wasn't, I was quiet. I looked
at my father and for the first time I felt ashamed of him,
seeing him as he would have looked to the family at
Rowan Hall. I saw a big ignorant man with a loud crude
laugh wearing a stupid paper hat, like a kid. He didn't
make me laugh, he made me cry with embarrassment. I
felt that he had been wicked, keeping this secret of another
world from me for so many years. Why hadn't he told
me that we were poor and stupid and shameful? Why
hadn't he told me we lived and worked in places where
proper people wouldn't go?

Billy looked at me, then he looked at Grandad Gilbert,
and Grandad Gilbert just looked at me, too, and shrugged.
'Been like it all the way home,' he told my father.

'Been sick?' Billy asked. 'Grub too rich? Fall over or
something? Get into a fight? Lose at all the games?' Billy

listed all the potential problems of kids' parties of those days, and I shook my head at each one. I think that he knew when he was beaten, even if it was by a seven-year-old. He gave up asking questions and walked me home in silence, lifting me up to sit on his shoulders, and making no comment when I cried every step of the way.

# CHAPTER 3

God knows how I kept my mouth shut about Rowan Hall, for it filled all my thoughts for months after my visit, but I did, and I was proud of myself for doing so, too. I'd lost a line of vision back there in Surrey, the sort of child's-eye-view that will see the best of everything. In my eyes up till then North London had been a vast thriving city, full of opportunity for Billy and myself. You don't know you're poor till you see something better, and that's what I'd seen, all right, on the day the Queen was crowned.

I'd been spoilt for being pretty, but my prettiness was ugly next to the beauty of that house. I clung on to its memory like a precious jewel, turning it over in my mind in bed each night, reliving each smell and colour and sight, so afraid was I that it might all fade and be lost to me for ever.

My other world turned sour overnight. I saw the dirt and the dust suddenly, and the magical playgrounds that I'd so loved to play in became bomb-sites that were graveyards with rats, and puddles that were deep enough to drown in. The rainbows that I had seen floating in those puddles were just filthy slicks of petrol that the lorries had left behind, and the flowers that grew between the rubble were merely weeds. What I'd thought to be ancient castles turned out to be dark derelict buildings awaiting demolition, and the magic mists surrounding them were just stinking London smogs.

The people annoyed me. I began to hate them for their cheeriness and good humour. They didn't know what I did, they hadn't seen the real world. They behaved as though being poor were an act of heroism. I was ashamed of what I was. I no longer got the joke. I decided to run away.

I got as far as the City Road before Billy found me and rounded me up. I'd run out of bus fare and was standing crying by the public toilets. Billy arrived on a motorbike with sidecar, though to this day I have no idea where he'd got it from. Perhaps he stole it, he could have been desperate enough.

'Come on, nipper,' he said, and loaded me into the sidecar and stuck some greasy goggles on my face. Then he drove me home, with the wind blowing through my hair and chapping my tear-sodden face. He talked to me throughout the entire journey, yelling things that were lost in the wind and the roar of the motorbike. He wasn't angry with me after that, but I could tell that he'd been hurt. He had every right to be hurt, too; he'd done everything for me, after all, yet still I'd upped and run off.

It was Marge who told me that he'd missed the point of my bid for freedom – he'd thought I'd run off to find my mother. Evidently the thought that I was missing a mother had worried him for a long time and he'd even thought of proposing to Marge, his brother's wife, just to provide me with one. In the event, though, he'd had no choice in the matter as the police caught up with him long before Aunty Marge got the chance.

They arrested Billy outside the pub one evening near Christmas. Most blokes down our street got arrested at some time or another, it wasn't anything special, but I'd thought somehow that my dad would be different. I never found out what he'd done, though whatever it was, it had been providing the good life for us for a few years over the odds. Billy had been on the fiddle for years and I suppose he'd got blasé with it, which was why he'd been caught.

I was home alone in our flat that night, though the woman next door was keeping an ear out for me. Someone was always keeping an eye on me in those days and the system seemed to work, too. I knew, because I'd tested it. I screamed my head off once just to see, and the woman from the flats at the back came rushing round some two minutes later, half-dressed, with her brassiere showing and her teeth out. When I told her it was just a test she clipped me round the ear, which was the only time anyone had hit me, until Billy went away, that was.

I didn't even notice he was late home, I was too busy playing fancy dress, and looked a proper sight when Marge and the copper came to get me. I was wearing Billy's best waistcoat and his flat cap on my head, and it was dark in our hall because the bulb had blown. I remember Marge peering through the letter-box at me, shouting for me to open the door, which I couldn't, because I was scared. The copper had held a torch under her face to help me to recognize her and her eyes looked queer, like a monster's.

Marge's staring eyes at the end of that black hallway frightened me more than I can describe. They made me afraid of the dark, Marge's eyes, and to this day I still sleep with a nightlight burning.

'Why wouldn't you answer the door?' she shouted, the minute I finally let her in. She filled the hallway with her bulk, standing with her fat arms folded across her chest.

'Billy told me not to,' I told her miserably, 'not if it was strangers,' and this made her angrier. She raised her great cow eyes to heaven and clicked her tongue in her mouth, and I thought Billy's brother was smart, getting shot of her like he did.

'I ain't a stranger,' she told me. 'I'm yer Aunty Marge!'

She was wearing tartan slippers, the ones with the pompoms on top. Women round our way wore slippers all the time, but I knew these were Marge's best, the ones she wore indoors, and I wondered for the first time how late it must be, if Marge was into her best slippers.

'Where's me dad?' I asked, panicking. Neither of them spoke, and Marge looked away for a bit, as though studying the wallpaper.

'Get yer dressing gown,' was all she said. 'Yer coming with me.' I thought for a moment that I was being kidnapped and I started crying. I don't think Marge meant to be cruel, children just didn't come high on her list of priorities, that was all. I'd got her out of bed, and that was enough sacrifice for one evening, without having to be tactful on top. I was making a noise and I wasn't even grateful that she was willing to take me in.

I must have felt as Billy had done when they'd come to arrest him outside The Two Brewers. I was frogmarched down the darkened street, the copper on one side and Marge on the other, trying to poke my unwilling arm into the sleeve of my dressing gown. When I started to wriggle Marge slapped me round the back of my legs and I felt ashamed that she should have done that in front of a policeman. Curtains were twitching, though, and she didn't want us making more of a spectacle of ourselves than we had to.

Marge lived on the ground floor of a two-up and two-down in Andover Street, between the baths and the funeral parlour, in a row that the German bombers must have left alone out of pity. Each doorway in the row was painted matt dried-blood red and the paint had peeled and blistered as though gone over by a blow-torch.

Grandad Gilbert had moved into the upstairs front when his house had been listed for demolition on account of the rot, and a strange couple they'd suspected of spying during the war rented the back. Marge had ice-cold worn brown lino throughout, and the place smelled of dogs, even though Marge never owned any.

'It's not much, is it, Dad?' I asked Billy that night, even though he wasn't there to hear me, which was just as

well, or I'd never have got away with calling him Dad. I
talked to Billy a lot over those next few months, especially
once I'd realized he wasn't coming back for some time.
It made me hurt a bit less, pretending he could hear me.
No one told me that he'd been sent down for two years,
and for weeks I expected him back every day. Then all
our belongings were brought round in a van by one of
Billy's friends and I saw that another family had moved
into our council flat, and that's when the penny finally
dropped. I thought till then that he'd just gone off for a
bit to serve me right for running away.

Marge forced me to go to Sunday school, which was
something that most of the kids did, but which Billy had
never insisted on. Although I enjoyed all the singing and
the stories, I hated it once I found out why we were there.
We were taught to enjoy being poor, for all the rewards
it would bring us in heaven. We even prayed to God to
make us poorer because our poverty was a sign to Jesus of
the purity of our hearts. There were more camels passing
through the eyes of needles than there were rich men
being allowed into heaven, but then I'd think of Piers and
know that the teaching was rubbish. Piers looked like an
angel already. God would have had a hard time turning
down a face like that. Piers wasn't afraid of God. Piers
would have walked in wherever he fancied, money or
not.

By God's exacting standards old Mrs Cowcross
should've found the door to heaven hanging off by its
hinges. The only one of Grandad Gilbert's sisters who
had married, Mrs Cowcross lived next-door-but-one and
was the poorest person we knew. Her roof had been
bombed but never repaired, which meant the entire top
floor was given over to weeds and pigeons. The weeds
grew out of the windows and holes in the rafters, waving
like beggars' arms in the breeze. Mr Cowcross had been
a sailor, but he'd died at home one day, in a chair that
nobody ever sat in again. His animals had outlived him,
along with his wife. There was an old dog called Boy, a

parrot called Cracker, a tortoise with a hole in its shell, and a half-crazed, ferocious monkey called Johnny. The Cowcrosses had never got round to having kids of their own, and Johnny had been like a son to them until the day he started to turn queer and had to be put in a large cage. Johnny hated that cage and he hated the humans that had put him there even more. He lived in the narrow scullery, in virtual isolation, and old Mrs Cowcross would get to her back yard via the outside alley, rather than pass that monkey in a mood.

Johnny caught me once in the dark, on the way to the lavvy. I'd thought I could outsmart him, but I found out too late I was wrong. I screamed the place down once he had hold of my hair and Mrs Cowcross came lumbering after him, shouting his name till he released me again. 'He'll have to go,' she said sadly, but it was the tortoise who went. Boy bit his head off while we were busy shelling peas on the back step. I saw it happen, but Mrs Cowcross went on talking, her back turned to the scene of the crime. She saw my face, though, and then she went running round to the front of the house and came back with a reel of pink sticking plaster. She'd read of people losing arms in accidents, she told me, so she thought she'd try sticking the tortoise's head back on again.

I used to go to old Mrs Cowcross's when Marge got angry and locked me out of the flat, and it was she who finally told me the truth, that Billy was in prison and would be away for years. She made me swear on the Bible not to let on to Marge that I knew.

In return for those secrets I told her about Rowan Hall and she said she'd been in service at a place like that, right up until the war. I told her of all the things I'd seen, and she told me of what I'd missed; of the vast kitchens they had with open fireplaces, larger even than the one I'd seen in the Hall. She told me they had cellars you could get lost in, where they kept wines and champagnes, and I shuddered to think of all that dark coldness underneath the old white house.

She told me of monogrammed sheets and linen and of the silver services that had to be polished after each use, and of the numbers of guest rooms that were cleaned every day till they smelled of lavender polish, even though they were used only a few times a year.

It was the balls and parties that excited my imagination the most; the guests in their evening gowns turning up in their coaches in the snow, the butler taking their coats and hanging them near the fire so that they would be warmed for later. I saw the drinks on trays being handed round as people talked and laughed, and I heard how they danced until the sun came up again, when they ate a hot breakfast before leaving for home.

The house became real to me again as I listened to the old lady's stories – more real than it had been before, because now I felt I knew its soul, rather than just its exterior. It was like a doll's house in my head, a tiny perfect replica that I could walk through in my imagination and which I owned from top to bottom. I asked Mrs Cowcross how you got to own a place like that in reality and she laughed and said you didn't, not if you were me, you were just born living there and that was all there was to it.

I told her that there was another way, that you could marry into it, but then she laughed more and said that I could knock that idea on the head as soon as I liked because I was the lowest of the low to them, not good enough to spit on their boots.

'You're pretty enough now, but in a common sort of way – you'll go like Marge in the end, I suppose,' she said, and I began to hate her. 'You're an awkward little bitch too,' she said, looking at the expression on my face.

Old Mrs Cowcross died just before Billy came home again and they put all her animals down. The whole lot of them went away so easily that you'd have thought they had never existed – no mark on the place to show they'd been there at all. It was this that made up my mind. Mrs Cowcross was wrong and so was the church. You could do better if you wanted, God didn't mind if you got rich. Mrs Cowcross and her animals weren't blessed, and neither was Aunty Marge, just because they were poor. They were miserable old women who God had forgotten. I became determined in my own mind. I would get the thing that I wanted and I would get it any way that I could. You had to grab things yourself in this life, or else God overlooked you and you died without anything. I thought of the half-bombed house with the weeds that grew in the windows, and I thought of Rowan Hall with its roses and its ivy. I knew what it was that I wanted and I didn't intend to wallow in my poverty in the hope of some sort of afterlife. I wanted the house – my house – and all I needed to do was to work out how to get it.

# CHAPTER 4

## 1961

'Move along, Ruby, you're taller than us, and you know I can't see a thing without me glasses!'

'Is 'e there or not?'

'I was so nervous tonight I couldn't get up enough spit to put on my mascara.'

We linked arms, the six of us, our full, petticoated skirts bobbing like crinolines in the wind, our hair ratted and shaped high, in bouffants. Some candyfloss stuck on the side of my cheek like pink glue and I picked it off quickly, rubbing the patch with my hankie, although I'd said I didn't care how I looked.

The talk had all been of Frank that summer, and I'd hated him long before we'd even met.

Frank was flash, and I didn't much care for flash men. I'd seen the type in the market, sleeves rolled up to show off their muscles as they lifted the crates, always shouting to one another to make sure they attracted all the girls' attentions. I suppose our Billy had been a bit flash too when he was younger, but he'd quietened a lot since he'd come out of prison, Aunty Marge had seen to that.

I'd thought that things would go back to the way they were before once Billy came home, but they didn't. Billy said we'd never get another council place because he'd got a record, but I think it was because he was too afraid to try. Billy wanted to lie low after his little skirmish with

Her Majesty, and this meant keeping well away from anything to do with authority. He seemed happy enough to stay with Aunty Marge, and to put up with her misery and her nagging, just to get what he described as 'a quiet life'.

Grandad Gilbert took ill with his chest around this time, and we all waited for him to die, so that we could have his room. He came downstairs once, when the others were out and I was the only one at home, and I was shocked to see how much he had changed. His black olive eyes were grey and filmy, like Mrs Cowcross's dog Boy when they'd taken him to be put down. Would Grandad Gilbert be taken to be put down too? We couldn't wait much longer for his room. Sharing with Marge was more than I could stand. She smelled like fruit that has gone bad, and the sheets of hers that I had to sleep in before they would be washed smelled as bad. I was sure that the smell left the house with me and clung to me while I was at school.

Grandad Gilbert had shrunk with his illness, and his slippers were too big for his feet. He tried to make for the back door, but got puffed in the scullery and had to sit on the edge of the plank that covered the bath. His hands were veiny, and the skin of his neck hung in big empty sacks.

'Gotta take a pee,' he said, and tried to get up. His lips were a mauve, flat line, and when he took in air his throat whistled and sounded as small as a squashed drinking straw. He paused, tottering, by the edge of the bath. The waxed gingham table-cover slipped suddenly under his fingers, and a packet of foil-wrapped bath cubes fell off the bread bin. One of them must have broken, because a smell of gardenias suddenly filled the air.

Grandad Gilbert seemed to sniff the perfume, then he looked straight at me.

'I don't want to die,' he said.

I looked away, embarrassed. Aunty Marge would be mad about the broken bath cube and, anyway, it wasn't

up to me whether Grandad died or not, it was up to God.
God decided when you went and when you didn't, and I
was shocked that Grandad Gilbert should be arguing the
toss. I'd somehow thought that old people became
resigned to their fate, yearned for it even, yet here was
Grandad Gilbert leaning on the bath and complaining to
me just like he used to grumble to Aunty Marge that his
tea was late.

He was still there on the bath when Marge got back,
and she slapped me round the head because he was cold,
and because of the broken bath cube.

I was ten when Grandad Gilbert died. He hung on right
up till the spring. Marge even got a chair and a blanket
outside for him, so he could sit in the weak sunlight on
the front doorstep. The whole of North London seemed
to turn out for his funeral, and there was a wreath of
yellow letters three feet high, spelling out 'Grandad', on
top of the car that drove him to the crematorium.

I had a new dress to wear, that Marge had found me
on one of the stalls. It was black, with a black velvet
collar, and more suitable for a twenty-year-old, but Marge
said it would just have to do, and anyway, I was tall for
my age.

I was enchanted by the dress once it had been made to
fit me. It hugged me round the ribs and it was tight
around the knees, so I had to walk with little steps, as
though I were crippled, or at least slightly lame. The black
fabric made my skin look pale, too. I was obsessed with
illness and death for about a year after Grandad Gilbert
took his last wheezing breath, and the look of the dress
suited me just fine. I acquired a limp, and I longed for a
plaster cast like the other kids had when they broke bones.
I started a cough, and I bought a handbag mirror from
Woolworths so that I could lie in bed at night and see
what I would look like if I were put into an iron lung. I
wanted appendicitis and tonsillitis and I yearned for a cold
sore on my mouth. Most of all I wanted attention, but
Billy seemed either too busy or too bemused to give it.

I gave up on illnesses the day I found out about sex, as that seemed a much easier way to get the type of attention I craved. By the time I was twelve the black dress had started to be let out to fit me, and Aunty Marge said she was thinking of getting me a brassiere because I was 'developing'. She said this with as much distaste as if I had taken to wetting the bed at night. I was more rounded than the other girls of my age, who had still to outgrow the awkward skinniness of their childhood, and my face, Billy said, had lost none of its prettiness.

I cadged a pair of tan-coloured stockings off the twin brothers who owned the hosiery shop at Highbury Corner, and I wore them for best, instead of socks. When I stopped wearing my hair in plaits the men started to grin at me, and I knew that I would be spoilt again, as I had been as a child. Now all I had to do was wait.

I stood on draughty bomb-sites for hours, staring at the thin waving weeds, thinking of the roses at Rowan Hall. I could smell them if I closed my eyes. I wanted to be away from there. I wanted the life I'd glimpsed so briefly but still dreamed of every night.

'Pedigree roses grow up from dirt and mud, just like weeds,' I told myself. 'I can grow up either way, a rose or a weed. It's up to me to choose.'

A new police constable began patrolling our market around that time. He was tall and handsome and broad-shouldered and had a pink rash on his neck where his starched white collar rubbed. Billy got jumpy when he began to hang around our stall a lot but it wasn't long before we realized that it was me he seemed to be interested in, not Billy and his prison record.

The policeman was old – nearly as old as Billy, it seemed to me, and I was flattered that he should take so much interest in a kid, which was all I was, however grown-up I liked to pretend to be. He was good-looking in a solid sort of way and I'd seen the other girls watching

him with an interest they usually reserved for rogues like
Frank.

'Hello, Goldie,' he said one day and winked, which
made me blush.

'Me name's not Goldie,' I told him, my legs swinging
from the stall.

'Eh?' he asked as though he were deaf. I'd spoken softly
but I knew he had heard what I'd said. He was teasing
me, taking the mickey, and I smiled back because I liked
a bit of teasing. Most kids do.

'I said, me name's not Goldie!' I repeated, only louder
this time.

'What?' he asked. 'With hair like yours? What do they
call you then? Marilyn? Jayne? Diana?'

I was pleased because he'd picked three of my most
favourite stars, but I wouldn't let on I was flattered.

'They're all bleached, if you don't mind,' I said, tossing
my head. 'Mine's natural.'

'Get away!' He ran a finger down one of my curls. 'I
could've sworn it was out of a bottle!' I tried to sniff like
Marge did when she was angry, but the policeman just
winked at me and walked off on his beat. He came by
every day after that, sometimes stopping for a chat, and
other times just winking and putting a finger to his lips
as though to shush me, as though we had a secret that
had to be kept.

'You coming out with me, then?' he asked one day the
following summer.

'I can't,' I told him, sucking my finger. 'I'm too young.'

'You don't look too young to me,' he said, coming
closer and staring down at my bosom, which was twice
its real size, owing to all the padding that I'd stuffed down
the pre-teen brassiere that Marge had bought me. I crossed
my legs, and he put a black-gloved hand over my tan-
stockinged kneecap. My knees were chubby and covered
with light hairs that a grown woman would have taken
off with cream. I was glad that he was wearing gloves
and so probably wouldn't have noticed.

'How old are you then?' he asked. 'Sixteen? Seventeen?'

I was so flattered that it took my breath away. 'Thirteen,' I told him, lying by a year.

His eyes narrowed a bit. 'That's old enough,' he said, smiling. 'My mum was married with two kids by the time that she was your age.'

'You're having me on!' I laughed, but deep down I wasn't too sure. A girl in our class had started her monthly bleeding a year previously, and that was supposed to be the sign that you could start getting pregnant. I went to the library after that conversation, looking for a book on having babies, but there were none on the shelf and I guessed you'd have to ask for them specially, and I was too embarrassed to do that. I could never have asked Billy, either, and I knew my Aunty Marge wouldn't be able to tell me anything. Piers would have known about babies, and he would have happily told me, and I missed him at that time with a feeling that was almost like homesickness.

'Well then?' the police constable asked when I saw him next.

'Well then what?' I said cheekily, playing for time.

'What about our date then?' he asked, looking about to make sure the coast was clear.

'You'll have to wait a bit,' I said, trying to sound confident, although my knees were knocking. 'Till I'm older. A couple of years at least, I should imagine. Your mum never had kids at my age, and I can't go out on dates yet.' It was a bluff, but it seemed to have worked, because he laughed and bounced around on the balls of his feet a bit.

'Two years!' he said, leaning over me. 'I can't wait two years. I'll be off the boil by then.'

Curiosity got the better of me, just as it had with Piers in the rose garden.

'Off the boil?' I asked. 'What do you mean by that?'

He grabbed my hand quickly and placed it on a lump between his legs. 'That,' he told me. 'That's what I mean.'

I thought the lump was something policemen were issued with, but then it twitched under my hand, like an animal, and I screamed and took my hand away. He looked about nervously before shushing me with a finger on his lips as he always did.

'Can *you* wait two years?' he asked quietly.

I had an urge to shake my head. I would die of curiosity before the two years were up, but I sat still, staring at the ground.

'Bet you don't,' he said, and he sounded angry. 'You'll go to one of these scruffy scum-ridden louts around here before long, like they all do. Then you'll get in the club, and before you know it you'll have six kids and a husband in Parkhurst. Is that what you want, Ruby? Same as all the rest?'

I shook my head, and tears ran down my cheeks. It was all so unfair. I wanted to tell him about Rowan Hall, about my real future, and about Piers, but somehow, at that moment, none of it seemed true and I knew that he would only laugh. He made me feel stupid and ignorant, just as Piers had done.

Men had secrets that women didn't know about, but when they found the secrets out they became sluts with six kids and a husband in jail. The secrets were the power that men held over women. I wanted that power for myself, so that I could have the same hold over Piers. My only power was the power to say no, and I used that power liberally over the next few years.

Instead of two years I made the policeman wait three until I agreed to date him, and then I would only see him during the daytime, when we were with other friends. Jack, his name was, but Billy always referred to him as 'that copper', and kept well out of his way whenever he came to the house. I became arrogant, and would have been unpopular with the other girls, except that I was pretty enough to attract the boys, and they stuck with me to gain from that. Six of us became inseparable; Maureen, who had left school early to work at the local shoe factory;

Joan and Kath, the sisters who wore matching butterfly-wing glasses and who hoped to be taken for twins; Sylvia, whose real name was Ann and whose compulsive behaviour – like counting things and not walking on the cracks in pavements – she had inherited from her mother who had had a shock in the war; Shirley, who always wore make-up, even first thing in the morning; and Linda, who could smoke *and* give French kisses.

It was Linda who first started on about Frank, and I ignored her until they all started, and then I got annoyed. I was jealous somehow, which was strange; it was as though I'd lost my friends because their loyalty had moved from me to him. Even Sylvia stopped her counting and pavement-hopping for long enough to spend an evening gawping at Frank, and her mouth with its metal braces went dribbly as she described what it was that she had seen. Frank was tall and handsome, with dark hair and eyes like a gipsy. He was moody, in keeping with the latest fashion, and rarely smiled, but when he did his teeth were white and his smile tinged with a touch of wickedness. I looked around at the others while Sylvia told us all about it expecting them to be as sickened as I was, but I could see from their faces that they were enraptured. Frank had come with the fair, and I couldn't wait for the end of the season when he would pack up and leave with the rest of the sideshows so that I could take my place again as head of the pack.

They spoke of Frank's looks as though mine were second-rate in comparison, and I was determined to meet the man and put him in his place. He must have thought that the only lookers in North London were a gang of pop-eyed, dribbly mouthed girls who giggled as soon as he flexed a muscle. I was sure that I could show him otherwise.

Someone should give you a warning when you're about to mess up your life. We all deserve a second chance, and there should be a sign to give you time to change your mind. No sign came to me, though, as I rushed off to

meet Frank. I wish to God that it had. How could I have
known? It was just a laugh. I wanted to teach him a
lesson. How could I have guessed that I was setting off a
chain of events that would end in one death and the ruin
of three other lives?

Frank's good looks were not to my taste. He had neither
the angelic pale beauty of Piers, nor the solid, honest
handsomeness of Jack. Perhaps this should have been my
warning. Maybe I should have taken just one careful look
at him across the dusty, scrubby fairground and realized
that he was not for me. Not my type, with his sharp-
featured face and scowling eyes. I could hear Billy's voice
in my head, as I used to hear him talking to me when he
was away in prison. 'Hard as nails and as sly as a fox.' I
could hear Billy saying those words as I watched Frank
ride the backs of the dodgems, leaping from car to car,
electricity crackling and sparkling overhead. His features
were in darkness, but I knew how they would look even
before he turned his face into the green fairground lights.

'His hair is like Tony Curtis's, he's got one gold earring,
like a gipsy, his body is like James Dean's, only taller,
he smiles like Elvis Presley . . .' I could hear Maureen's
slobbered litany of the night before in my head. She'd
exaggerated about the earring, though. There wasn't one
as far as I could see. Frank was young, much younger
than Jack and possibly younger than Piers, but he looked
as though he'd lived through ten lives already. His confidence was hypnotic and overpowering. I was both
repelled and mesmerized by him. I watched him jumping
the cars, hoping he would fall so that I could see the
confidence vanish. I wanted to see him humbled in front
of his audience, and there were more people watching
him than just the six of us. All around the rail bar hung
small groups of girls, their eyes glinting in the glowing
green light.

The cars slowed and the music stopped, and the car
Frank was riding pulled up in front of us. Frank leaned
back, holding the car's rail with one hand, and stepped

off just as he reached us. He stood straight in front of us, and I heard Linda snigger and winced with embarrassment as Maureen kicked her to shut up. Frank didn't laugh. I could tell from his expression that he thought we were just another gang of local young tarts, looking for a bit of a giggle. Then he looked straight across at me.

'D'you want a ride?' he asked, motioning towards the empty car behind him. His teeth were white, but they were fox's teeth. Billy had warned me. His voice was too deep for his age, and his accent was so rough that it grated like pumice in my ears.

'What d'you take me for?' I answered. It was the sort of answer that I imagined Piers's mother would have given, haughty and high-handed. To my ears, though, it just came out sounding young and rude. Words come out different when they're said with the wrong accent. If I'd known that I'd be needing that phrase I'd have practised it until I sounded like the Queen. The words rolled off Frank like water off oil, and he even shrugged his shoulders to make sure the last few drops were gone.

'Suit yourself,' he said without smiling, and hopped over a few cars to find some girls who would like to take him up on his offer of a ride.

The others stared at me in amazement. 'I don't think he's at all good-looking,' I said, but we moved in closer to watch him nevertheless.

The others hovered around the dodgems, jiggling in time to the music, their faces radiant like moons that dogs would howl at. I moved on, depressed and embarrassed. You can't walk around a funfair alone, though, it's not the place for girls by themselves. I clutched my bucket bag to my stomach, and my heels wobbled over dried clods of earth. Fat women in cardigans spun in front of my eyes like washing in a tumble drier, their mouths open in a perfect letter 'O', but you couldn't hear the screams they made until the music stopped. I watched a couple climb off their ride, the woman staggering like a drunk and clutching at her husband's shirtfront. A boy pushed

between them, spilling brown ale down the front of the
woman's dress.

I found myself looking for the others again. The dodgems had emptied. The scene of the action had moved on
to the rifle range. Frank and his mate had guns dangling
over their arms and the girls were grouped around them,
bristling with excitement. Frank was one shot away from
winning the biggest prize on the stall.

The doll dangled from a noose that tied it to the top of
the striped awning. It had blond hair and round cheeks
that were pink with rouge, and legs that were dimpled,
like mine. In its hand it held a sign saying 'Fifty points
and I'm yours'. Frank looked at the doll, and then he
looked around the admiring group of girls. He saw me
and I swear that he grinned.

'For the best-looking bird in North London,' he said,
and I felt myself blush. Maureen dug me in the ribs and
I got some dagger looks from the other girls.

The shot went off, echoing into the night. There was
a ping as it hit the tin figure on the shelf, and some of the
girls clapped as though Frank had just felled a tiger. The
doll was cut down from its rope and a hush fell on to the
group as Frank turned, clutching it. He looked at the
doll's round rubber face, and he looked across at me and
I smiled. Then he shouted, 'C'mon, Pearl,' and I thought
for a minute that he was calling to a dog. He looked to
his right, and that was when I saw Pearl for the first time.

Pearl was tall, taller than me, and in the shadows of the
tent her face looked as black as ebony. She walked towards
him slowly, her face turning biscuit-brown under the light
of the bare bulbs, her black frizzed hair tied up in a red
velvety ribbon, her huge onion-white eyes never leaving
Frank's face for an instant.

One by one we folded our arms, our cardigans flapping
like small cloaks around our shoulders. I watched Pearl's
shy black fingers proudly circling the plump rubber arms
of that doll, and I felt a hatred that I had never known
before, not even for my Aunty Marge. I had been humili-

ated once again, and this time on my home ground. I
hated Pearl for winning the doll, and I hated her for her
erect, proud walk that belied the shyness on her face. But
there was one thing that I hated Pearl for above all else.
Frank was right – Pearl was beautiful, whereas I was only
pretty. I would never forgive Pearl for that for as long as
I knew her.

# CHAPTER 5

I tried to forget about Frank after that, but the memory of the night at the fair chewed away at me like a dog gnawing a bone. I'd lost face with the others too, and from that night I felt they were laughing at me whenever my back was turned.

Then Frank suddenly turned up in the market, roaring around those narrow streets on his filthy black motorbike, and my humiliation was complete. I watched him do deals with the traders, laughing with them and slapping their shoulders as though he'd lived there all his life. As a child I had always loved market weekends in winter, with the stalls lit up and steaming in the dark, but now I only felt the cold that chilled me to the marrow, pinching at my fingers and nose with unrelenting spite.

To me Rowan Hall had somehow become forever bathed in summer. Seasons didn't change there, it was perfectly preserved in the sunshine of my memory. I knew it wasn't really like that but my daydreams about the house were all I had. I had never outgrown them like the other dreams of childhood, and I never wanted to, although they brought a sort of sweet pain. I would walk up that drive in my mind, the gravel crunching like crisps under my stilettos. The house was whiter now, and perfect, the plaster whole and intact, like cake-icing. In my imagination there had been no rain and the sun was setting, and as it set the windows blazed up once more, only richer this time; purest ruby red, like pomegranate seeds. It was a ruby palace, my home. I heard the trees sighing in the wind and I shuddered as the chill hit me. Now I visited the whole house, not just the hall and the room with the wireless. I wandered into the study, gazed at all the leatherbound books like the ones old Mrs Cowcross used to have to polish. I could smell the kitchens, the rich, buttery smells of baking. I saw copper pots hanging from the walls, felt the heat from the blackened furnace. I floated through the cellars, felt the dampness of the walls. But I always saved the best till last. I had the key to the rose garden now, because it belonged to me. I stepped inside with my eyes closed and the perfume rose, like voices, to greet me. Piers was there too, waiting. He had been in the hall, swinging from the bannister, but the boy in the hall was a ghost who mocked me as I passed. The real Piers was waiting in the garden, quieter, older, more beautiful, if that were possible. He didn't mock me any more. The rose he had crushed was whole in his hand, offered to me intact.

I was fifteen by now, and Piers must have been over twenty. Most boys round our way were married and bringing up children by that age, and the fear that it might be the same with Piers bit into me along with the memory of that night at the funfair.

Jack knew of Frank and tried to warn me off him.

'He's a wide-boy,' he told me. 'He'll come to no good.' And: 'He's too clever by half, that one. Thinks he's bloody Jack-the-Lad, but we're on to him, I can tell you. One day he'll upset the wrong person and then we'll all see just how bloody big he is.'

Jack tried to pin something on Frank one day in the market, just to impress me. I watched him stop him and at first I thought he was going to arrest him straight out. They talked for a while and I saw Frank grinning and shaking his head, but I was too far away to hear what they were saying. Jack must have asked to look inside a

van Frank had been helping to unload because Frank
shrugged and started fishing in his pocket for the key. He
unlocked the door and went to climb in, but Jack pulled
him back and stepped inside instead. Once he'd disappeared, Frank looked around at his mates and they all
burst out laughing.

Jack emerged from the back looking dusty and angry
and set about finding fault with Frank's precious motorbike instead. He must've spent an hour checking it over,
while Frank just stood by watching and smoking a cigarette.

In the end Jack gave up and Frank rode off smirking.
He didn't mention Frank's name a lot after that, and I was
relieved for that much at least.

Jack had plans to get himself out of North London and
away to somewhere better, and as his score with Frank
turned into something bigger, so his desire to get away
grew into more of an obsession.

At first I thought that it was just promotion and a house
outside London that Jack was thinking of, but I found out
later that he was set on emigrating. His widowed mother
was in poor health, and as soon as she was gone he would
be off, he told me. He'd been abroad in the war, and it
had left him with what he called itchy feet. The Force
wasn't enough for him any more, he told me, and England
wasn't the country he'd thought it to be while he was
busy risking his life for it overseas. The people here were
lazy, dishonest and, worst of all, ungrateful. Immigrants
were coming over here by the planeload, and were busy
snatching London right from under our lazy noses, but
Jack was damned if he'd sit by and watch it all happen.
The rest of us could do what we liked, but Jack was off
to Australia.

The talk of immigrants reminded me of Pearl. I had
not seen her since that evening, and now the fair had
gone. Frank was a local, according to Jack, which was
why he'd stayed on and not left with the fair. He had
relatives up at Tottenham and he'd done a runner when

he was a kid. Nobody knew what he'd been doing since
then, although Jack said he'd stake his life on him having
a record.

Pearl was different, though. Pearl didn't seem to fit in
anywhere. And then I saw Piers's picture in the paper.

The market is full of newspaper, it blows around like
tumbleweed in the summer, and usually we ignored it.
For us it was for wrapping rather than reading. The outside news didn't interest us – we were a closed community
and heard all we wanted to know by word of mouth.
Gossip was our daily news, which was how I'd heard
about Frank.

Billy had tied some sheets of newspaper to the stall by
a length of string, for wrapping the cabbages and the cut
cucumbers. The top sheet was flapping in the wind on
this particular day but it was a picture on the sheet underneath that caught my eye and made me sweat.

The face in the picture was hanging sideways, and I had
to bend my head to see it the right way round. Even
from sideways, though, I knew that it was Piers. I'd have
known his face a mile off, even though it was eight years
since I'd last seen him. The picture was on some sort of
society page and was surrounded by other pictures of
people having a good time at balls and weddings. For a
moment my heart stopped. Was this Piers at his own
wedding? Then I began to think straight again. They
photograph brides at weddings, not just grooms, and
there were no women in the shot with Piers. His eyes still
had that same kind of dreamy quality, and his face was
just as pale and as handsome as before.

It all came back to me then, in a rush. I thought back
to the rose garden, and to Piers's hot mouth that smelled
of toast, and his long, fine fingers working their way up
my paper skirt, and I blushed, despite the cold. I didn't
even hear the motorbike as it pulled up behind me,
although I smelled the blue fumes all right and they made
me start to cough.

'What're you up to, then?' Frank was standing there,

not six inches from my face, talking in such a nonchalant
way it was as though we'd known one another for years.
I folded the paper carefully before answering, taking care
not to put a fold across Piers's face.

The market was quiet. Most of the stalls had shut up
early and Billy had taken Marge home with her chilblains.
I looked for Jack, but he'd gone off duty hours ago. Jack
was down at the library, looking at books on the Great
Barrier Reef.

'You're the one that goes out with that copper, ain't
you?' Frank asked, as though he had guessed who I was
looking for.

I nodded. Now perhaps he would go away. But Frank
stood his ground.

'Why?' he asked.

'Why what?'

'Why d'you date a copper?' he looked genuinely concerned as though it held some meaning for him, the sol-
ution to some age-old puzzle that had been bothering him
for years.

'Why not?' It was the best I could do. Not good
enough, judging by Frank's expression.

'Your old man's done time, hasn't he?' he asked.

'So what?' I was immediately on the defensive. Billy's
record was not something we discussed with strangers. It
was not even something we discussed between ourselves,
come to that. It hung in the air between us, though, the
great unmentionable that ensured that Marge won all of
the arguments, simply with her silences.

Frank shrugged. 'Just thought it might've been a bit
awkward, that's all,' he said, kicking the tyre of his bike.

There was a pause that seemed to last a fortnight.

'You coming out with me then?' Frank asked in a low
voice that had lost all of its nonchalance.

'No.'

And that was it. The magic word. Frank left the stall
and he left the market, and by all accounts he even left
North London. I should have been pleased, but I had no

time to gloat. Instead I was too busy being confronted by my mother.

# CHAPTER 6

It was Marge who spotted her first, though God knows how she recognized her from fifteen years ago.

'Jesus Christ!' we heard her mutter, and Billy and I both looked round, shocked, because we'd never heard Marge use such words before outside a church.

When we turned back we saw a woman standing there waiting to be served, except she hadn't any shopping bag and she didn't give us her order. She just stood there, staring, and offering a wide, tired sort of smile.

At first I thought maybe she was mad, we got lots of doolally types around the market, usually begging or just there to make nuisances of themselves. They usually spoke to you – in fact, you couldn't get them to stop speaking, great thundering streams of endless, meaningless babble. But this woman said nothing, just stood there smiling.

Her hair was dyed black so that you could see a ring of grey around the roots, though she didn't look old and her face was only lined around the eyes. She wore a blue nylon overall under her coat, the sort the factory workers wore, and her feet were squeezed into pointed stilettos.

Billy looked at her, then went back to wrapping some veg, and then he looked back again, as though a thought had suddenly occurred to him. He squinted his eyes and his skin turned pale.

'Gawd save us!' he said. 'Lily.'

The woman nodded, quickly, like a bird, as pleased as Punch to have been recognized, judging by the expression on her face.

'And you must be Merle,' she said, smiling towards me. I should have guessed there was something up by the look of that smile. It was the sort of thin, bloodless, knowing smile that the saints wore in the pictures we'd been shown at Sunday school.

I was relieved that she'd made a mistake. For some reason this woman made my flesh crawl, and I didn't like the expression that was hanging on Billy's face either.

'Sorry,' I said, smiling as kindly as I could manage under the circumstances. 'Me name's Ruby.'

'Merle,' the woman corrected, standing as though her shoes were nailed to the ground. 'After Merle Oberon. I knew you'd grow to look like her.' She looked across at Billy and her eyes went flinty.

'He told you it was Ruby, did he?' she asked, still managing the saintly smile. 'Well,' she said forgivingly, 'I suppose he wasn't to know better. But you'll always be Merle to me.' Then she paused for effect.

'I'm yer mum, Ruby,' she said, running her tongue round my name as though it left a nasty taste in her mouth. 'I've come to fetch you back.'

Naturally these were the worst words that she could possibly have said to me, but at that moment, standing there looking at this short, plain-looking woman with her dyed black hair and her too-small high-heeled shoes, I found myself laughing as though the whole episode was some awful joke.

Billy didn't laugh. Billy just stood there next to me with the blood draining from his lips and the brussels sprouts rolling out of his hands. One large sprout rolled near the woman's feet and she kicked it out of the way as neatly as a centre forward playing for Arsenal. I began to suspect that she was enjoying the whole scene, especially as people had started gathering round to watch.

My mum didn't look like this. My mum was tall and

blond and graceful, despite her lowly class, and possibly
the daughter of some wealthy family, slumming it for a
time until she settled into a good marriage. My mum
would never have called me Merle, not in a million years.

'You can't be me mum!' I shouted for all the street to
hear, just in case anyone listening had been taken in for
an instant. 'You've got black hair!'

When I'd laughed she'd looked upset, but now the
saintly smile had come back on to her face.

'I *was* blond,' she told me and the crowd, 'before I
went grey, anyway. I dye it black because that's how my
*husband* likes it.'

When she said the word 'husband' she looked straight
at Billy, and the saintly smile slipped a bit into a sneer of
victory.

'Ask yer dad, Ruby,' she added, in a quieter voice. 'He
should remember whether I was a natural blonde or not.'

There was an ugly noise behind me, and I looked anxi-
ously over my shoulder. Aunty Marge had woken from
her usual apathy and was struggling to rise to her feet.
Two old women from the newsagent's had her by either
shoulder intent on holding her down before she spoilt
some of the fun.

'Go on, ask yer dad, Ruby,' Lily repeated. 'He knows
I'm yer mum right enough.'

I looked across at Billy and he shook his head, but as
much as to say that he knew when he was beaten, rather
than to let me know that this mad woman was lying. Lily
smiled and at that moment a figure pushed past me,
almost knocking me off my feet.

Marge had slipped the leash and was spoiling for a fight.
She towered over Lily by a good nine inches and the
breath steaming from her mouth and nostrils looked for
all the world like smoke. Lily stood her ground, though,
her jaw set like a terrier.

'Slag!' Marge shouted, but the word sounded a bit weak
under the circumstances.

Lily sucked in her cheeks and pursed her lips confidently. '*You* can talk,' she said in a civilized tone. 'You've been living over the brush with him for the last six years, or did I miss my wedding invite?'

Suddenly I was impressed. Lily had been doing her homework. I could tell that the crowd were impressed, too, by the way they were nodding and looking at Marge.

Marge flew at Lily with the grace of a bull elephant, and although Lily dodged nippily to one side her bag was knocked from her hands and her coat was pulled off one shoulder. Marge grabbed the empty sleeve and began pulling, and when Lily pulled back it ripped.

'That's OK,' Lily said, looking slightly dishevelled. 'Me *husband* will buy me a new one.'

I could tell this was a bluff from the cheapness of her clothes. Husbands with money to burn did not let their wives out in nylon overalls and foam-lined coats, but I was impressed again by her cheek and was more on her side at that moment than on my great, lumbering Aunty Marge's.

Marge gave Lily a look that said she was prepared to kill her if she had to now, and it was probably a good thing that Jack turned up when he did. Jack did quite well, under the circumstances, but I wish it had been a different day and I wish it had been a different constable on the beat. He pushed Marge back to her stall and told Billy to keep an eye on her. Then he spoke quietly to Lily, although I saw he soon shut up and started listening when she began to speak. His hands went to his hips, and he looked over at me once or twice, and all the time I just stood there, wishing I could be somewhere else.

'This woman says she's your mum, Ruby,' Jack said when he'd finished listening.

I suddenly thought how much older Jack looked when he was in an official capacity. Marge had always told me that he was old enough to be my father, and on that day I could see for the first time that she was right.

'She can't take me, can she?' I asked Jack. The thought of leaving Billy left goosebumps down my arms. 'There's

laws against that sort of thing, aren't there?' I said, pleading with him as though it were his decision.

'If she's really your mother then she's got a right to see
you,' Jack said. 'Better ask Billy,' he added when he saw
I was upset. 'See what he says about it all.'

But I was too angry with Billy to discuss anything with
him and it was four days before we spoke again. I knew
it wasn't Billy's fault, but I felt that he'd lied to me about
my name, and, anyway, I had to be angry with someone.
At one point I even found myself wishing that Frank
would come back and pick me up on his motorbike and
take me off to that never-never land that he kept disappearing to when things got a bit too hot around the collar.

'You ought to see her,' Billy said, when we finally got
around to talking again. I loved Billy even more than I
loved Piers, but at that moment I could only feel hate and
shock, as though he had let me down somehow.

'Why?' I said, shouting, my voice as thin as a reed.
'Why go and see her now? She hasn't wanted me for
fifteen years! She didn't want me when I was born. Why
now, Billy?'

Billy looked away, and for the first time I got a strange
hollow feeling that he hadn't been telling me everything.

'It's bad enough for an unmarried girl with a kiddie
now,' he began, 'but it was even worse in those days.
You've got to understand what it was like, Ruby. Nobody
wanted to know.'

'But you'd've married her if she'd've stopped that day,
wouldn't you, Billy?' I asked, and I realized as I said it
that I'd never asked him that question before. I'd always
assumed he would. Always thought that if Billy could
have caught up with her when she went running off out
of the market then I'd have had a full set of parents. Now
I knew the answer without even hearing it from Billy's
lips.

'She could still've found me before,' I said quietly, my
voice thick with tears. 'She could've come for me if she

wanted me that much. She knew where I was. She didn't want me.'

And that was when Billy looked up to face me at last.

'She did come, Ruby,' he said slowly. 'She came for you years ago, and then she came back a couple of years later. She didn't see me, though, and you were at school. Marge told her we'd gone away. That we were living somewhere else and that she didn't know the address.'

So I set off to visit Lily in my best dress, and to be honest I didn't much care for the look of the area that she lived in. The old houses of Notting Hill and Ladbroke Grove were larger and grander than ours in Holloway, but ours had a sort of resilience that was missing where Lily lived. Our wild, muddy holes and dead, fly-blown masonry were like scars that we'd won in the war, but to my eyes the decay in this place seemed to have come from self-inflicted neglect.

A wind blew up, and I clutched at my skirt with one hand and my high-piled hair with the other. It was the beginning of spring, my favourite season, and yet the air around West London had the rotting, depressed smell of those last few days of summer, when everything seems stale and the wind cuts like paper around your bare legs, just to remind you that autumn is waiting and flexing its muscles.

Overhead the sky was low and grey, as if waiting to erupt on to my carefully lacquered bird's-nest. Boys on bikes rode along beside me, whistling between their front teeth, and one of them tried to grab at my skirt. I saw small groups of blacks, hands dug deep into their pockets, heads dug still deeper into their coat collars, hurrying along and keeping out of the way. A boy on a Vespa followed me for a bit, pop-popping along the gutter, trying to catch my eye and, at the same time, not to wobble and fall off his machine. An old black woman watched us from an open window on the third floor of a crumbling house, her big beefy arms crossed over her

chest as she lent on the sill, shaking her head slowly from
side to side. Then the boy on the Vespa saw that she was
watching, too, and raised two fingers into the air and the
woman leaned back as though he'd hit out at her and
pulled the window quickly down.

We had barely any blacks in our area at that time, and
the sight of so many was quite a shock to me. We had
our share of immigrants in North London, though – the
Greeks, who Billy said were sharper than him when it
came to a deal; the beautiful Indian women who came to
our market like peacocks, in their coiled, glittering saris,
even in winter when the hems risked trailing into the
mud; and the Jews, with their long black coats and flying
ringlets of hair, but they were all part of the patchwork.
These immigrants wore another face entirely. I knew there
had been riots in this part of London a couple of years
before, when the Teds had thought it handy to put them
in their place, and their faces still wore a greyness that
could have been wariness or a longing for revenge.

There was a café with steamed-up windows and the
sound of pinballs pinging round tables, and there was a
big old cinema, closed and boarded, but with the name
of the last film, some of the letters missing, still strung
up outside. The rain started then, and I was glad to find
Lily's turning because the streets smelled worse once the
dust and rubbish got wet.

Lily and her husband lived on the fourteenth floor of a
new block that rose with six others like mastheads out of
the gloom. Lily's flat was so high that you could see the
clouds level with the window, so that most times the
ground was hidden from view. When the clouds did lift,
when a wind blew up, and the tower creaked and groaned
like a clipper on the high seas, then the ground looked
like a map of Hiroshima after the bomb.

Lily's front door had flowery nets strung behind the
glass panels, and this cheered me a bit after the lonely ride
in the vacuum-flask lift.

When I rang the bell a budgie started squawking and

then Lily's face appeared, close to the glass and mottled behind the nets. She was smiling, I could see that, even through the curtains.

'Come in, luvvy.'

She was wearing a primrose-yellow nylon wrapover V-neck blouse, the sort with frills down the neck that you always associate with tarts, and a brown jersey skirt that fitted so tight it made her stomach bulge. Her hair was black to the roots now, and she had two kirby'd kiss-curls plastered with setting lotion to each cheek. She smelled of Drene and Soir de Paris, and it was then I realized that, despite everything, I liked Lily quite a lot.

I was like that at fifteen, changing my mind about things in a matter of seconds. I'd been hating Lily for wanting to claim me, and for looking as she did, and not like someone upper-class, but underneath I found I quite admired her, despite everything. In a funny sort of way I liked the way she looked and the way she'd stood up to Marge, which was something I'd been wanting to do for years.

I admired her toughness and her expression which said, 'You're-welcome-but-I'm-not-about-to-beg-if-you-don't-like-what-you-see.' Marge had been no match for Lily, and I didn't suppose that I would be, either. Lily could have taken on seven of Marge and still come out with her kiss curls intact. The only thing was, I didn't want Lily for my mother.

'I like yer hair like that,' she said as I walked past her into the hallway. 'It suits you.' I smiled a bit, making a mental note to change it as soon as I got home.

The lounge was small, but decorated like a palace. There was wallpaper on the walls and a swirly purple fitted Wilton on the floor. There was a red stretch-covered settee that was big enough for three, but which would have only seated one because of the mounds of matching scatter cushions. There were pictures on the wall, of beaches and bending palm trees, and the windows were

hung with orange nets that were frilled down the side like
the blouse Lily was wearing.

There was even a small bar in the corner, strung with
multi-coloured Christmas-tree lights and covered with
miniatures and strings of plastic fruit. It was the sort of
bar that Billy had wanted and I thought it was strange
that Lily should have got the bar and Billy should have
got the baby.

I must have spent a long time admiring the room in
silence, and when I looked back at Lily she was glowing
like a lamp with pride of ownership. 'Look!' she said,
moving to the mantelpiece and bending to click a switch
on the floor. There was a statue of a Spanish lady on the
shelf, her back arched arrogantly and her skirts spread out
into a fan. The skirt lit up when Lily flipped the switch,
and the room was filled with a warm reddish glow to
rival the one coming from Lily's cheeks.

'Shall I play some music?' Lily asked. 'We've got a
gramophone.'

'Don't bother,' I told her, settling carefully down on to
the red settee. 'The radio will do.' Lily was watching me
closely, as though the settee only got used for best. When
she went out to make tea I tried to move the cushions to
give more room for my skirt, but the first one I moved
had a cigarette burn underneath it so I moved it back
again, quickly. There were probably odd stockings and
old newspapers under the others, if our house was anything to go by.

'So, how've you been?' Lily asked when she came back
with the tray. She'd done the whole thing properly, with
a jug for the milk and small tongs for the sugar cubes.

'OK, I suppose,' I told her, summing up the whole of
my fifteen years in a couple of capital letters.

'We've got a lot to catch up on,' she told me, breaking
a Jersey cream in two and dipping half into her tea.

I nodded in agreement, and then we fell silent.

'Isn't your husband home?' I asked, when the silence
got too painful.

'Vic?' Lily looked surprised. 'Oh, no, he's out right now. To tell you the truth, luvvy, I asked him to go for a bit of a walk so that we had some time to get to know one another first.' She dabbed at her lips with a paper serviette. 'It must seem strange for you, knowing that your mum's got a family of her own!' She laughed, and the budgie by the window woke up again and copied the laugh perfectly, which made her laugh some more.

'You've got kids?' I asked. The idea hadn't even occurred to me before; that a woman who gave away her first one would be allowed to have any out of choice.

Lily nodded. 'Three,' she told me. 'Two boys and a girl. The girl's the eldest, a bit younger than you. She's at work, though, part-time. I told her to get back early, so you'd have time to meet her.'

There was a key in the door before I had time to think about my half-brothers and sister, and Lily's eyes spun immediately to my face, narrowed like a hawk's, to see how I took to her husband.

Vic was huge and very very black. He towered like a shadow in the small, cosy room, clutching a carrier bag, with a look of apology on his face.

'It was raining,' he told Lily. 'I couldn't stay out any longer.' His skin looked shiny, like a dark, polished aubergine, then his face split apart into a ripe watermelon smile.

'Ruby,' he said, putting his hand out towards me. 'Pleased to meet you at last.'

I'd never been so close to a black person before. Crystals of rain hung in Vic's black knitting-wool hair.

'Vic used to box,' Lily said as Vic shook my hand. If she thought I was going to be shocked, then she was in for a disappointment. Vic looked like a good swap for Billy any day of the week. Billy was good-looking, in an ugly sort of way, and he was big and even-tempered, too, but Lily's Vic was the handsomest man that I'd seen in the whole of my life. I didn't count Piers when I came to this conclusion. Piers was beautiful, like a statue or a piece of fine music.

'Well?' Lily said, impatient for my opinion. 'What d'ya
think?'

'Well done, Lily,' I said, grinning at her, and Vic burst
out laughing at my cheek, a huge, booming bellyache of
a laugh that started us both off again.

'You got some nerve,' Vic said, when he'd wiped his
eyes on a hankie.

'She should do,' Lily told him happily, 'she's my
daughter.'

Then I remembered Lily's threat in the market, that
she'd take me back home with her for ever, and I stopped
laughing and fell silent. Lily saw my face, and she must
have realized what I was thinking, because she patted my
arm and told me I could come and visit her as often as I
liked, which was her way of saying I was off the hook. I
didn't have to leave Billy after all.

Then Vic sat down beside me, amongst the cushions,
and told me stories that made my eyes pop. In a serious,
deep voice he told me how he'd left his home country of
Jamaica and sailed to England soon after the war, to find
his fortune in Maida Vale.

'But I met Lily instead!' he said with a smile, and Lily
grinned and raised her eyes to the ceiling. 'She told me
about you straight away.' Vic was leaning forward and
whispering as though someone might be listening.

'She's an honest woman,' he went on. 'One of the only
truly honest women that I have ever met over here. That
was one of the reasons I married her.' His head hung
slightly over his hands and he placed his palms together.
'I was young then,' he said in a mournful voice like they
used to use at Sunday school. 'I didn't know what grief I
was letting her in for.' He looked at Lily and she looked
away, embarrassed.

'She's been through the lot, Ruby,' Vic said, shaking
his head. 'She still is, and so're the kids. They won't stand
it much longer. They'll be driven away. I can see that
look in the eldest's face already. It's like we're losing her,
and there's not one thing I can do to change it.'

I didn't know what Vic was talking about, and I was late for my bus.

But Vic had more to tell me.

'They spit at her in the street, you know,' he said, nodding in Lily's direction.

I began to feel uneasy. It wasn't my fault if Lily told everyone she had an illegitimate baby. Was that why they'd invited me here, to tell me how uncomfortable I had made life for them?

'And our kids,' Vic went on, his face looking so sad that at any moment I expected to see huge tears rolling down his black face, 'they don't fit in with no one! We get bricks thrown through our windows, we had shit pushed through our letter-box . . .' He was into his stride now, but Lily put a restraining hand on his arm.

'It's not Ruby's business,' she told Vic gently. 'She only came here for her tea. She doesn't want to know all about our troubles, do you, Ruby?'

I didn't care so much, to tell the truth, not now I knew it wasn't me they were complaining about, but, of course, I couldn't tell them that. Then Lily took up the tale.

'It's not for myself that I worry, anyway,' she said, taking the lid off the teapot and swirling the contents. 'Vic knows that. It's the kids. It's not their fault. They've seen it all – mobs fighting in the street, blacks getting beaten up. They've heard it all, too, all the names and the swearing. They'll blame us for it one day, you mark my words.'

'They're good kids,' Vic said like a chorus.

I wanted to leave. There was no way I was about to feel sorry for Lily's kids, whatever their colour. They hadn't been left in some scales on a market stall. That was rich, expecting me to share grief over three kids who'd been brought up in a nice flat with scatter cushions and two parents.

I stood up to leave, but Lily had a further surprise in store for me. A key turned in the lock as I pulled on my coat, and Vic's face lit up like he'd seen a holy vision. A girl walked into the lounge, straight and proud, but with that touch of shyness that I'd seen on the night of the funfair. The same biscuity skin and the same fine beautiful face.

Lily's smile broke with relief. 'Pearl!' she said. 'I thought you'd be too late. I couldn't have had Ruby leaving without meeting her half-sister, now could I?'

# CHAPTER 7

We eyed one another for a short while, Lily and Vic watching us all the time, wondering what the hell was going on between us. Then Pearl smiled, showing rows of straight white teeth, and I tried to smile back, out of politeness to Lily and Vic, but nothing much happened to my face. The tea I'd just drunk turned sour in the back of my throat and all the friendly cosy warmth seemed to drain out of that room just like someone had pulled out the plug.

If Pearl had any inkling as to what my dark looks were all about, then she made a very good show of covering it up.

'Ruby,' she said, long after the pause had become noticeable. 'Good to see you. I've heard so much about you from Mum.'

Her voice was deeper than I'd expected, and throaty, like actresses try for when they imagine they're being sex kittens. Her mouth was all sort of pouty, too, but it wasn't an act. She just happened to sound and look like that.

Untied, Pearl's hair hung frizzed around her shoulders, making her face look wilder and haughtier than it had done before. She had on one of the low-waisted, twenties-style dresses that were all the rage at that time, and white ankle socks, which I thought looked odd because all my friends were into stockings. I thought of her coming home, just now, in that strange get-up, with people in the street spitting at her and calling abuse. Did she run all the way home from work? I would have worn a plastic mac to protect myself.

Pearl hadn't been telling the truth when she'd said Lily had told her so much about me, because Lily knew nothing to tell. It never occurred to me that Pearl might have been saying it because she was polite and embarrassed. I didn't even know whether she remembered me from the shooting gallery. I just assumed that she did, because I remembered her. I hadn't seen her with Frank since then, but that didn't matter. He'd known her name and called to her in a familiar way to give her the prize for being beautiful, and that was more than enough for me. *Now* I had to get used to the idea that we were related. Suddenly I felt like joining the people in the street that spat and called abuse, because I hated my half-sister. Pearl had got everything. She'd got my mother and Vic, and the lady with the lamp under her skirt, *and* Frank's admiration. I had only Marge and her worn, holey lino. I didn't include Billy and Jack because I was feeling so down, and when you're down you forget about the good things in life and concentrate on the rotten. 'Count your blessings', they used to make us sing in Sunday school, but at that moment I couldn't think of any blessings that I had to count. Pearl had them all.

All my ideas of Piers and Rowan Hall seemed unreal suddenly, and the only thing I wanted at that moment was to get back what I'd lost to this girl. Frank. The moment at the funfair was even sourer now in my mind. I wanted to tell Pearl there and then that Frank had asked me out since, but I knew better than to lose a fight before it had even begun. We hadn't even warmed up yet, Pearl and I, and I wasn't going to spoil it by losing face in an unprovoked outburst. I'd seen what those sort of tactics did to Aunty Marge in the market, when she'd suddenly lunged at Lily.

I left the flat quickly, with Ruby and Vic wondering
no doubt why I'd suddenly turned the freeze on their
beautiful polite daughter, and I ran when I reached the
street so that my face could cool off.

A push bike came quickly up behind me. I could hear
its rubber tyres hissing on the road, and then a little squeal
as the brakes went on, but when I turned round angrily
I found that it was only Jack standing there in his uniform.

'Just got off duty,' he said, and his face was red with
the effort of pedalling so quickly to catch up with me.
'Thought you might like an escort. Not a good place to
be by yourself, not with all these coloureds around. Never
know what might happen.'

So Vic had been right. Even the police would spit at
the blacks, given half the chance.

'I'm OK,' I told him, and carried on walking. Jack
pulled off his cycle clips and followed me, pushing his
bike in the gutter. Every so often he came upon a huge
bank of rubbish that he had to steer his bike around
because he didn't want to wheel it on the pavement.

'Your dad told me where you were,' he said when I
didn't say any more. 'I thought I'd miss you. I thought
you'd have left long since.' We walked in silence for a
while.

'Met your mum, did you?' Jack asked eventually.

I just nodded. I was confused. I was angry with Jack
for being just like the others and hating the blacks, yet
there was I, hating Pearl as much as was humanly possible.

'My step-dad's a black,' I said, and then turned to see
if a flicker of embarrassment crossed his face because of
what he had just said.

Jack cleared his throat. 'Bit of a shock,' he said in a flat
voice. Then he seemed to think for a bit. A sweet wrapper
had caught in the spokes of his wheel so that it made a
ticking noise as it turned, but Jack seemed not to have
noticed. 'Shouldn't make any difference though,' he said
finally.

'Difference to what?' I asked, annoyed by the ticking, wishing he'd take the paper out.

'To us,' Jack said, looking up at the sky as though searching for more rain. 'It's not as if you'll see them much, after all,' he added. 'You don't have to go telling everyone your mum's married a darkie now, do you?'

'I'll tell who I like!' I was mad now, spitting mad. There was half my world ashamed that I should be seeing a copper, and now there was Jack telling me I should keep quiet about my mum marrying Vic. Jack, with his pink neck and pale eyelashes, ashamed of Vic, with his handsome black face and rich, fruity laugh.

'What difference does it make to you who my mum's married to?' I asked Jack, anger written all over my face.

'When we get married he'll be part of the family, that's what,' Jack answered.

We walked home in silence after that, but Jack didn't take the hint. Now that the dog was out of the trap he'd got no intention of leaving it there, and kept up a running commentary about his precious Australia and how much I'd love it out there.

I was still quiet by the time we reached home. Jack had put me on a bus and then cycled along behind it, winking at me occasionally through the window until I moved to sit upstairs. The thought of marrying Jack was like a joke, and I can honestly say that it had never crossed my mind until he mentioned it that day. I realized then, though, that that was why he hadn't laid a finger on me since that day in the market when he had first asked me out. He was obviously saving me until he got me up the aisle.

Jack had changed since we'd started dating properly. He had toned down and got serious, and I wasn't sure that I liked it. It was as though there was one rule for the bits of stuff in the market, and another for a girl he took seriously. He'd stopped making passes and he'd started taking care of me. He still had an eye for the girls, all right, but between him and me all that 'monkey business' had stopped until after we were married.

He'd done a good job in selling Australia to me, though, especially with the stories of the money to be made out there. I was in a trap and I knew it. Sixteen years old, and no nearer to getting Rowan Hall than I had been at the age of seven. I spoke the same, I'd learned nothing at school, and had no prospects, no possible chance of getting out of North London. Perhaps if there were fortunes to be made in Australia then I could get rich out there and come back with enough money to make Piers's eyes pop. I chewed the idea over, then slotted it into the back of my mind. It was something, a bit of a plan. But first I had to get even with Pearl.

# CHAPTER 8

Jack must have taken my silence to be agreement to his idea of marriage, because the following year he bought me a ring, and considered us to be properly engaged.

'He's too old for you,' was all that Billy said when I told him of Jack's ideas, but Marge looked pleased, I suppose because she thought she'd have Billy to herself at last. As for myself, well, I didn't know what I wanted. It was like living life on two levels – my imaginary life at Rowan Hall was becoming more blurred, like the face of someone who's died, who you know that you miss, but whose features you can no longer remember. My life in the market was stale. I was getting nowhere, running backwards, in fact, and running out of steam fast. All my friends were engaged; Maureen to a boy she'd met at the factory; Joan and Kath to real twin brothers so that they were hoping to get their wedding photos in to *Reveille* as twins marrying twins (their mother had promised to burn their birth certificates); Ann who had run off with a sailor on her seventeenth birthday; and Shirley who had got herself pregnant by her sixteenth. That only left Linda, the girl who could smoke and give French kisses. She'd left for Margate, to be a chalet maid in a holiday camp. That was seven months ago, and we hadn't heard from her since. Maureen said you always met married men in those sort of jobs, and I imagined Linda as some man's mistress, in a love nest near the coast.

I saw Jack once during the week, then twice at the weekends, because since he'd taken to calling himself my fiancé he'd started a ritual of tea at our house on a Sunday. The weekly event was a painful one. Jack made no show of pleasure at being there, which was strange since he'd been the one to instigate it, while Billy showed equal lack of enthusiasm as a host. They'd sit at either side of the small room, Billy in his armchair, gazing out of the window, even though it was dark, and Jack on the hard chair by the cupboard under the stairs, stirring his tea with a sigh, and staring at his bootlaces.

Marge would buy slab cake from Broomfield's round the corner, and this sign of goodwill surprised me until I realized how desperate she was to get rid of me. If a few slices of Angel or fruit cake meant that Jack took me away sooner, then Marge would have considered it cheap at double the price. She always broke her cake into pieces, then transferred each chunk on to the side of her saucer before putting it into her mouth. The crumbs would stick to her lipstick and dangle there whenever she talked. I'd never heard Marge talk as much as she did during those teas. I don't know who she imagined was listening. Billy was in a world of his own, gazing round-eyed out the window, Jack was lost on some crime he'd yet to solve, and I was drowning in a bath of boredom and embarrassment.

Marge's voice was like the sea, relentlessly ebbing and flowing, never going away. It was only later, when the clock would strike, and Billy could leap from his chair to turn on the television so that we could all watch *Sunday Night at the London Palladium*, that Marge's droning would finally cease. If it was a singer on she'd watch transfixed, but if it was jugglers or a magician she'd go and make more tea. Either way we got a bit of peace.

'Walk me to the door, Ruby?' Jack would ask once the programme was finished, and we'd talk on the doorstep

instead of kissing, which is what Marge thought we were
up to.

Jack had kissed me briefly a couple of times, but the
last time it had happened he'd gone on a bit longer and
his face had started to get hot. I was a big girl then, full-
bodied and chubby, and I'd felt my breasts push into his
chest in my keenness to find out more about the thing
between his legs that he'd made me touch so long ago.
Jack was immediately on the boil again, after being off it
for so long, but he quickly controlled himself and pushed
me away roughly.

'You got me going there, Ruby,' he said, wiping a film
of sweat off his forehead. I knew nothing about sex then,
really, only about rabbits, which was what they'd taught
us in school. I'd guessed a lot of bits and read other bits
in books, but the thing between the legs had a veil of
modesty drawn across it whichever books you read. I'd
seen statues of naked men at a museum we'd been taken
to by the school, but the thing had looked unimportant
and reminded me of winkles out of their shells. Jack's had
felt much bigger and moved with a life of its own.

They got bigger, according to Linda, like telescopes. I
tried to think of Jack and his telescope, but Frank always
got in the way. I told Lily that I'd got engaged. I don't
know why I did, because it wasn't strictly true, not as far
as I was concerned anyway, but she said that was good,
because her Pearl was going steady too. I hadn't asked
who with, I couldn't. Something was too busy eating
away inside at me, suddenly making me feel empty and
sick.

Piers's father died. I saw it in the newspaper, in the
obituaries. There was a photograph with the obituary,
taken in the forties, of a thin, military-looking man,
except that he had Piers's dreamy, half-closed eyes. So
Piers was now the eleventh Earl of Bicester and the owner
of Rowan Hall. I felt that if I could go there again I could
get my life running back on its tracks. As things were, I

was way, way off-beam. A million miles and a million class layers away from Rowan Hall.

I thought of the place every night in bed. I could still see it all, but in a haze rather than in detail. I longed to see it at night, silvered in the moonlight, tall and white and silent like a church, the roses in the rosary overpowering with their perfume. I walked through that garden in the dark, naked and cool, like a ghost, pressing my nose deep into the centre of each flower until I too was drunk on their scent and the pollen stuck to my nose.

I prayed to God to get me the house, although I was ashamed to hear my own prayers. You should not pray to someone you're not sure exists, and you should never pray out of greed or you will not get into heaven. As time passed my prayers grew more desperate, because instead of Piers I began to see Jack's face, or Frank's, but most often Vic's, barging uninvited into my daydreams and bringing with them a different type of longing. I felt that I was growing up and became frightened that this meant Rowan Hall was slipping away like the skin of a snake; that I'd outgrow it along with all those other childhood fantasies. Yet I couldn't sleep for thinking about Vic.

I think Vic guessed I had an eye out for him, because he took me aside one day when Lily was out in the kitchen.

'You got the same trouble as your mum,' he said, in a good-natured sort of way. 'You like the men.' I tried to look shocked, but I hadn't really grasped what it was he was offering to tell me.

'Be careful,' he said, nodding like a sage. 'It was your mum's weakness too. Look at the trouble it got her into. You're a beautiful girl, Ruby, but don't let it go to your head. You think you got power over men with your looks, but they'll have the last laugh if you're not careful. Our Pearl's a beautiful girl too, but she hasn't got the go in her that you've got. She'll find her man and she'll be loyal to him, whatever grief he might bring her. You want more though, Ruby, I can see it in your eyes. Be careful you don't go wrong, though. Make sure you get what you want, not what your body tells you you need.'

Then Lily came in with the biscuits, and Vic leaned back in the chair again and our conversation was over, back to the polite chatting that it had been before she left the room.

I looked at my body that night, wondering what it was that it needed. It needed food and it needed clothes, and right there and then, as I looked at it in the mirror, it needed a much bigger bra. I sucked in my ribcage which in turn flattened my stomach and made my breasts stand out. Not that they needed any help on that score. They were big in those days and cushiony-looking, another thing that I'd inherited from Lily, along with my liking for men, according to Vic. They called for the sensual satin wired-and-boned half-cup type of bra that Sophia Loren wore in the films, but all I got were the circle-stitched cotton ones that cut into me like a crêpe bandage.

I wasn't stupid. I knew that my body had other needs and I knew that one of the biggest of those needs – the biggest, if stories were to be believed – was sex. I just couldn't believe Vic though, I couldn't believe that sex could take over my entire body, crushing my mind as though it had no thoughts of its own.

I knew that Jack went on the boil, but I sensed that women were different. He was afraid of losing control, whereas all I felt was a twinge of curiosity and excitement. So why the dire warning from Vic? I turned Vic's warning over and over in my mind, like a coin, and the warning became a dare and the dare grew into necessity the more I thought about it.

I was ripe for picking and Jack's thin ring on my finger did little to save me from the wanting. I just wanted to touch Vic, that was all, to see how his skin felt. I wanted to kiss Jack properly too, to pop my tongue inside his mouth as Piers had done to me, to egg him on to the boil again, and to see what would happen when he finally lost control.

# CHAPTER 9

There wasn't much sex around when I was growing up. At least that's what I thought, which just goes to show how wrong you can be when you're young. Even when you're at that stupid age, even when you don't know what's what, what goes in where, and who does what to whom, even then you still think that sex is something invented exclusively for your own generation.

There was tension in Marge, I could see that, like bubbles you saw in the water of the washer on a Friday night when she was washing the sheets. She'd stand over the wash, the steam rising into her face and her neck running with sweat, poking at the washing with a pair of wooden tongs as though it were alive like boiling lobsters and threatening to jump out of the water.

Marge was obviously seething with longing for Billy. On the surface Billy was like all the other men in the market, cocky and full of cheek, winking at the women shopping, but underneath I felt that he'd fallen to pieces since his spell in prison. He rarely went out now so perhaps he'd gone off the boil permanently.

I had thought that the only sex in our street was done by the dogs, but I was in for a surprise. Billy must have been having Marge for years, only I'd been too stupid to notice. It was a shock finding out, both for them and for me. It was winter, and the time of year when it's so cold

that even the dogs have stopped doing it, although that
didn't deter Aunt Marge and my father.

I walked into the house to hear Billy making the sort
of noise that he made when he unloaded crates off the
van. A sort of straining, grunting noise. There were no
other sounds, and I thought he must be shifting the furniture around. Instead it was Marge he was shifting, as I
saw when I opened the door and realized what it was they
were up to.

Marge's great white knees reared up towards me from
the armchair like two huge peeled marrows. Billy's bare
bum was trapped between them, pumping and jiggling
like a fly caught in a web. His trousers and pants lay in
folds around his ankles, and his feet were slowly slipping
back on the linoleum. Marge's head had fallen against the
chair-wing, and her face looked resigned and disinterested
as though she were thinking what to get for our tea.

I meant to leave the room, but I couldn't. They didn't
hear me, or if they did they couldn't stop. I'd seen the
same thing happen with the dogs. Welded together by
lust, they'd hobble through the streets getting pelted by
the kids and hosed with water by the grown-ups, but
nothing would make them stop what they'd started, not
even fear, which you could see in the rolling whites of
their eyes.

Then Marge saw me, just as Billy's bum gave its final
heaving thrust and his toes finally lost their grip and he
slid to the floor on his knees between Marge's legs. He
must have cracked his shins in the fall because he swore
under his breath, and that seemed to annoy Marge more
than seeing me standing there watching them. Her ankles
were tied by her knickers and she still held a tea-cloth in
one hand, as though Billy had caught her in the middle
of doing the drying-up from breakfast. I'd been told to
mind the stall but I'd come in because my eyes were
freezing in their sockets.

I was sick with shame, not because I'd been caught
looking, but because our Billy, the king of the market,

had resorted to screwing that lumbering fat cow with the
dead face, and so brought shame upon us both. A look
of what must have been victory ran across Marge's face
and I wanted to go across and kick her for what she had
done.

'Pay 'er!' I shouted and Billy's head snapped round so
fast I thought his neck might break. 'Go on, Billy,' I
shouted, hysterical now with anger and with shame, 'pay
'er – she didn't enjoy it! Pay 'er like you would any other
old tart!'

Billy's face went red like a ripening tomato, and he
pulled up his pants with hands that were shaking with
anger. He glanced back at Marge and stuffed some
cushions quickly into her lap because she hadn't moved
and her knees were still wide open.

'Ruby!' I heard Billy shouting after me but my back
was turned. I had already seen more than I wanted to.

There was more that I wanted to say, but then talking
about important matters wasn't something we went in for
much in those days. People gossiped about the trivial,
moaned about the weather, laughed about their bad luck,
but when big things cropped up they shut up shop and
kept quiet. There were moods and there were sulks and
there were silences that could last for years, but there was
never any suggestion of resolving things by discussing
them.

Our silence lasted three days, and you could have cut
the air in the house with a knife, it was so thick with
things unsaid. I could see Billy cracking like a nutshell
under the strain of all the things that he wanted to say to
me, but I could only guess at what they were, and,
anyway, I wouldn't have wanted to listen. Marge carried
on as though nothing had happened, but then Marge never
spoke much anyway so her silence was barely noticeable.
We ate our meals like monks in a silent order, not looking
and not listening, each lost in a world of our own
thoughts. Funnily enough, it was Marge who finally
broke the silence.

Billy was out and we were eating tea together, Marge
a poached egg with ketchup running like blood through
the yolk, and me some boiled winkles that Jack had
bought me in a mug. When I was a kid we used to pick
the lids off and stick them on our faces for beauty spots.

'You'll have to leave now, you know,' Marge said, her
mouth stuffed with damp bread and her eyes already on
the Battenburg.

I looked across at her – the first time I had looked at
her since the scene with Billy. I could still see her sitting
there, with her knickers twisted round her ankles and
slippers on her feet.

Some food caught in her throat and she coughed and
slimy crumbs spluttered down her chin and on to the
tablecloth. Marge thumped her chest with the flat of her
hand and carried on with the conversation.

'You don't have to leave yet,' she said in a flat tone.
'You find somewhere first. I don't want people saying I
chucked you out on to the streets. But you must go. You
know that, don't you?'

'We'll go tomorrow,' I said, getting angry. 'Tonight,
if Billy's home in time. We never wanted to come here
in the first place.' I wanted to say more, to get it all off
my chest like Marge and her lump of bread, but she
stopped me with a look.

'I didn't say your father,' she said quietly, 'I said *you*.
It's you who must get out, Ruby, not Billy. You're the
one who causes the trouble. You get out and find somewhere else to live. I can't be bothered with you any more.
I want you out of my house.'

I laughed then, but I felt like killing her.

'Billy won't stay without me,' I said.

'He might,' she told me, and got up to start clearing
the table. A blue-black winkle shell rolled off my plate as
she snatched it away and landed in my lap, on my best
skirt. I picked it up and examined it closely, more for
something to do than from any real interest. It had fine

grooves on it that you could run your nail around, like a long-playing record.

'Look at you,' Marge said, coming back with the tray. 'You dress like a right little whore, showing yourself off to all the men like you do. I've seen the looks you give them in the market. You're just like your mother – I could see her for what she was the moment I clapped eyes on her. She got what she deserved all right, and so will you if you're not careful.'

'What do you mean, "got what she deserved"?' I asked. I was breathing heavily by now, as though her words had left me breathless.

Marge pushed her face closer to mine so that I could smell the talc that she wore as perfume. 'You know what I'm talking about,' she said, her lips pursed as though she were about to spit at me. 'Up the spout at sixteen and then married to a blackie, *that's* what I mean!'

Marge was shouting now, her voice raised to the finely-pitched level where it would reach no further than the surrounding four walls. I'd called her a tart in front of Billy, and now she was furious and shaking and out to get her revenge. She'd been saving this one up for some time, and she was going to give it the best that she'd got. I didn't even know that she knew Vic existed. I was almost glad Marge spoke of Vic as some sort of white woman's curse. It only put him even higher in my estimation. I felt sorry for Aunty Marge at that moment – the woman who sat back in an armchair while a man was having it away with her, one hand on the tea-towel and her stupid head nodding like the dog car ornaments that were so popular just then – and this was probably the only thing that stopped me from hitting her with the tea-tray.

Days went by and the weather got worse and I thought I should die of the cold some days on the stall, when the fruit was rimmed with frost that burned your bare fingers, and the earth on the potatoes grew so hard that digging it off to get the right weight left your nails torn and your

hands raw. I had no other job and so I had to help Billy.
I had refused to work in a factory like my friends, and
found myself longing for the warm chalky atmosphere of
a schoolroom. I should have laughed to find myself thinking like this, because I had hated my years at school and
cursed Billy for making me go. I was only sixteen yet
already suffering from a bad dose of raging nostalgia.

I told Billy that Marge had said I was to get out as soon
as possible, but Billy said nothing, his head well and truly
stuck in the sand. Marge said no more about it either, but
I knew she was only biding her time. I think Billy thought
we were like two dogs fighting over a rag, and that if he
kept his head down we'd get bored with the fight and
just drop it. This particular piece of rag meant too much
to Aunt Marge for her to give up as easily as that, though.
She'd wanted me gone for ages by then and she knew
that if she had relented I'd have turned Billy against her
for good.

'Go and live with your mother,' she finally said when
she saw no sign of my budging. 'You'd make a right pair,
you two. She wanted you, didn't she? Why not go and
live with her till you're married?'

The thought of marriage threw more shivers through
my body than Marge's order to leave. I was engaged, but
I still thought of it as something of a joke. Never once
did it occur to me that I'd be leaving to get wed. Jack
didn't mention it much, but I suppose if I'd been sharper
I'd have realized that that was because he was so sure of
me. Australia was his topic, and he spoke of it like honey,
golden and warm and running with wealth. I suppose,
like Billy, I thought he'd get it out of his system if he was
allowed to go on about it for long enough, but that only
shows how little I knew Jack, and how little Billy knew
Marge and me. I was sure Billy would never let Marge
throw me out, but I suppose I had forgotten that it was
her house we were living in. I also knew that Billy was
unlikely to come with me: he had nowhere else to live,
whereas I did. I had Jack and I had my mother. Lily's was

the obvious choice, but that was somewhere that I knew
I'd never want to live. I had different fish to fry at Lily's.

Winter thawed into spring and, warmed by the first
weak sunshine, I became cheerful again, and thought that
all things were possible. The house smelled stale and so I
opened all the doors and windows to let the new air in.

I'd got fat over the winter, but it was a saucy sort of
fat, firm and 'in all the right places', as Billy told me. My
summer clothes no longer fitted and I noted that men
couldn't keep their eyes off me as I walked through the
market, all straining seams and bulging buttons. Marge
saw their faces and I caught her looking at me out of the
corner of her eye, but it wasn't my fault. I'd just got that
way. The walk was one I'd developed myself, though,
based on a Brigitte Bardot film, but Marge couldn't really
pin that one on me without having seen the film herself,
which she hadn't. Marge had only been to the cinema
once in her life, and that had been during the war, to find
out whether our side was winning or not on the Pathé
News. She'd come out before the film started, happy to
hear that Hitler was getting it in the neck. Two days later
the cinema had been blown up by a bomb.

That was how it was when I went to see Vic. I'd only
gone to find out what was what. I'd never meant to stay
for the main feature.

'Lily's not in, love,' Vic had said, his huge fuzzy head
filling the gap between the door and its frame. He kept
the door half closed, for all the world as if I'd come
collecting orders from the catalogues. It occurred to me
then that he was probably afraid of me, for all his fine
lectures about morals.

'I've not come to see me mum,' I told him, which
sounded a lot bolder than I felt. Under my skirt my legs
were shaking, and I was hoping Vic had no way of knowing that.

Of course I knew Lily wasn't in. I'd been outside for
an hour, waiting for her to go out. Wednesday was Lily's
day for bingo. She'd had her hair newly dyed for the

occasion, raven black to the roots, and teased up into a lacquered mountain so high that the corners of the chiffon scarf barely met to tie under her chin.

Vic never went to bingo with her, she'd told me that herself. He'd gone just the once, like Marge and her pictures, and he'd put up with the looks for her sake, because he knew she enjoyed the occasion so much. But a terrible thing had happened. His number had come up and he'd won the star prize, and even those who had not minded a black man being there in the first place had minded a lot when he'd won the best prize of a holiday at Butlins.

Lily had been thrilled. They had never had a holiday, ever, but Vic had told her he had no intention of going up to collect the prize. Tears had rolled down Lily's face at the thought of the prize going begging, but even that hadn't appeased the crowd. First the whistles had begun, then the missiles: bingo cards, sweet wrappers, then heavier things like glass bottles. Vic had pulled Lily out of the place just in time, and she'd stood and cried for an hour on the street outside, but only about the holiday.

So Lily went alone to bingo now, and Vic stayed in, enjoying his afternoon off. And there was I, trussed up like a turkey, pushing my way past him through the half-open door so that he jumped out of my path like a wild scalded cat.

I'd worn a mac but had unbuttoned it on my way up in the lift. I saw Vic look down at my short, child's-sized sweater, which I'd nicked from Marge's stall before she'd had time to count them from the box. Made from bouclé nylon wool, it was more suitable for a nine-year-old and stretched to just above my waist, as tight as a drumskin. I had no shame, that much was obvious, even to me, but my intentions, nevertheless, were near enough to honourable. I wanted to taste Vic, that was all; just to see what he tasted like. I was saving myself for Piers, but in the meantime curiosity had got the better of me, and I needed to find out if Vic smelled and tasted as good as he looked. To know, too, whether I could have him if I wanted him,

and if all that Lily had got could be mine as well: the
settee and the scatter cushions and the lady with the lamp
up her skirt. It was like waking up and then wanting to
stretch a bit, that was all.

Once inside I felt heavy with relief. The flat was warm
and smelled of fresh-peeled tangerines. There was sport on
the radio in the lounge. Vic would understand everything
because he seemed to me to be wise. We stood for a
minute in the hall, pinned to either wall like riders on the
wall of death.

'Why are you here, Ruby?' Vic asked, suspicion in his
eyes. His voice was as soft as toilet tissue. Things that
you dream about look different in reality, but Vic hadn't
changed. He still looked just as good. I was the one who
had changed. I didn't know what I wanted any more.
Suddenly. Just like that. Sophia Loren had gone and a daft
kid with a big bosom had taken her place.

I felt stupid. I'd belted my skirt up tight at the waist
and my borrowed stilettos put me on a level with Vic's
chest. His cardigan had football buttons on it, which was
like one that Billy wore. I looked at Vic's buttons, and
Vic stared at my thrusting chest.

Then Vic moved closer, and I smelled him at last and
he smelled of chocolate, dark dusty chocolate, which I
thought was funny at the time, but which I realized later
must have come from some cocoa-oil dressing on his hair.
Vic bent down and kissed me, and I could feel that his
hand was shaking when he used it to tilt my chin upward.
His lips were so soft that I hardly felt the kiss, and then
I started to shake too, and Vic pulled away.

'Was that all you came here for, or was there more?'
he asked in a voice that told me that if I wanted more he
was about to tell me I was out of luck, which was fine
by me, because I'd frightened myself sufficiently by then.
Vic had kissed me to show me that I could be frightened,
plus a bit because he fancied me like most men did, I was
sure of that. He was Lily's husband though, and that was
the way it was going to stay.

Then Pearl walked in. She was sniffing and blowing her nose, and at first I thought that she was crying, and that she must have already seen us, maybe through the frosted glass, but then I realized that she had a cold, and that that was maybe the reason why she'd finished work so early. Either way the sniffing stopped the minute she saw Vic and me in the hallway, still touching bodies, and with faces full of embarrassment at being caught doing so very little.

My lipstick was all over my mouth and all over Vic's mouth, and I wiped my own face with the back of my hand. I felt exhilarated and excited, full of power and about to explode. Pearl had no anger inside her to use, nothing to draw on, that was obvious from the confused look on her face. Then I saw it growing. Once the surprise fell away I saw the truth begin to dawn and the anger begin to grow. Pearl's beautiful eyebrows knitted into a frown above her beautiful eyes and her beautiful face crumpled into lines until it became quite ugly.

Vic stepped towards Pearl, to grab her before the anger took over; to stop it before it grew; to explain that it was unnecessary, that what she'd thought she'd seen and what she'd really seen were two different things, but I could tell he was too late. By the time he got to her the anger had penetrated her veins, just as it had mine the first time I had seen her. Vic went on talking, but I knew neither of us could hear him. Pearl stared at me and I stared back at her. Things were even now. She hated me just as much as I hated her.

I left the flat before Pearl could find words to speak, running, taking the stairs two at a time until I frightened myself into slowing down before I fell and got hurt. I was evil, I thought, and would go to hell when I died. The idea appealed to me, and absolved me from any ideas of guilt.

Then I thought of Vic's face suddenly, the face I had seen as I ran out of the door, and remembered the pain in it as he had looked at his daughter. I thought about

Lily, my mother who I had admired, and I stopped feeling clever and started instead to cry with shame at what I had done.

# CHAPTER 10

'Look out for yourself, Ruby,' Jack said to me two days later as we walked towards the chip shop.

'What do you mean?' I asked, annoyed at his tone and feeling a bit guilty at the same time. He wheeled his bike on a bit, gazing silently at the spokes for inspiration.

'Just be careful, that's all,' he said. 'You know what I'm talking about.' He looked from the spokes to the heavy grey sky. 'I'm off on a course for a few weeks, they just told me today as I was going off shift. I won't be around for a bit. I just want you to be careful. You're a big girl, Ruby, but there's a lot you still don't know about.' I turned my head quickly and caught him eyeing my breasts, just like Vic had done.

'What is it I don't know about then?' I asked, as bold as brass, and I could tell my tone annoyed him because his face went red.

'You don't see all that goes on like I do in my job, Ruby, that's all,' he told me. 'You're a good-looking girl and you're not a kid any more. There's some men that will take advantage of a young girl like you who doesn't know what's what yet. You don't know how men think. I get to see a few sad cases sometimes. I wouldn't want to see you ending up like that just because you didn't know any better. You should be careful. Just remember men can't always control themselves, they're made like that, they can't always help themselves. Men try to do stupid things and it's up to the women to make sure they don't go too far and don't take any liberties. Men can go too far without thinking, that's all. Start to act stupid, that sort of thing. If they see a young girl who looks like you do, with your sort of clothing, they get the wrong idea.'

There were times when Jack sounded more like my father than Billy ever did. Shutting my mouth tight to stop myself from arguing, I buttoned the top two buttons of my cardigan to show Jack I'd caught his drift.

I felt guilty about Vic and Pearl, but my stubbornness turned my guilty feelings into anger at them for making me feel bad in the first place. I felt sure that Pearl would have told everyone what she'd seen going on, and that everyone in turn would hate me for it. I didn't dare to go round to their flat, for fear that Lily would kill me. I even thought that Jack's warnings had come because he'd got wind of me and Vic, but I was wrong again there. Jack knew nothing about Pearl and her problems. Jack had got itchy because Frank had come back to our street.

'Ruby!' Frank was standing behind me, chewing on a match and leaning up against the stall, greeting me like an old friend, even though we'd hardly spoken to each other before.

Frank looked taller and his hair was longer, falling over his face in the style that was popular at that time. I wondered whether he dyed it – I'd never seen hair so black before that was natural. He had a dog with him, seemingly coiled around his ankles, a shiny mottled greyhound with ribs that pumped as though it had just been running.

'How're you doing?' Frank asked, and his voice came out deeper and softer, as though only I was allowed to hear the question. As though he'd asked me something personal and private.

The dog's eyes were wet and black, like cockleshells. I straightened up, aware that my hair was brushed flat, and that I wasn't wearing any make-up. I was sixteen years old, but thought I looked twelve still when my face was bare. Until you looked at the rest of my body, that is, which was where Frank's eyes were busy wandering at that moment.

I let him look his fill, keeping my eyes on his face all the time to show that I wasn't embarrassed, and to show that I wasn't ashamed, either, even if Pearl had told him about me and Vic.

'What made you come back?' I asked, trying to make my voice husky like Pearl's.

Frank shrugged, and looked off down the market.

'Work,' he said softly, and this time when he looked at me I had no time to look away and got held fast in his stare. Like a rabbit caught in a trap. He frightened me with that look, not in a way that I was afraid for my person, but for my mind and my soul, as though he could look inside me and know what it was I was thinking. That was the most frightening thing of all, when you had such thoughts as I had. I dropped the brassy smile I'd been wearing to show Frank I didn't care that he was there, and scowled at him instead.

'You're beautiful, Ruby, you know that now, don't you?' Frank asked, and when he said my name things started to curl up inside me like flower petals. 'It's a shame the insides don't match up with the outsides,' he said slowly, coming closer so that I could smell the leather of his jacket.

I tried to look shocked, but he laid a finger across my lips.

'You upset people, Ruby,' he told me. 'You know that too, don't you? A lot of people, if what I've been hearing's true.'

So Pearl had told him about Vic. I didn't care. It was none of Frank's business.

'Does your copper know?' Frank asked, and I felt a sickness come into the pit of my stomach.

I shook my head, pulling my face away from his hand.

'You going to tell him?' I asked, knocking his hand away before he could touch me again.

'I might,' Frank said, smiling, and I hated him for his smile, which was handsome and showed his white fox's teeth.

'I'll kill you if you do,' I said straight, and Frank laughed.

'I like you inside,' he said, looking me straight in the eye again. 'I like you all the way through, right down to the core. Your copper only wants the best bits, the bits he can see, the beautiful bits that look innocent and fresh. He'll never know what he's missing then, will he, Ruby? That all right by you, is it? Going to act the innocent all your life, are you? You'd be better off with someone like me, Ruby. Someone who likes you for what you are, rottenness and all. Someone so much like yourself that they'll catch you out at every turn, that's what you need, Ruby.'

Then it was my turn to laugh.

'You're mad!' I said, although something in his words had made me shake. I looked at his face, and all at once I saw him with Pearl, and I saw him kissing Pearl, like Vic had kissed me, and jealousy hit me like a clenched-fist punch to the guts. Whatever I'd done, Pearl was still there, with Vic and with Lily, and even with Frank, who'd come to make me feel bad for kissing his girlfriend's father. Frank would go back now and tell Pearl how he'd sorted me out for her and put me right back in my place.

'You're marrying Pearl then,' I said to Frank, and watched his face colour with satisfaction in my soul.

'That's what you think,' he replied.

The dog whimpered and looked up at me, rolling its eyes and licking its chops with its long wet pink tongue.

'She's hungry,' I said, patting her head.

'She can't eat,' Frank said, pulling the dog away from me. 'She's racing tonight.'

'Take me out after the race if she wins,' I said, sensing victory. 'Somewhere nice, to celebrate.'

Frank thought for a moment, looking down at the dog's head.

'Where do you call nice?' he asked, not looking up.

I thought quickly, and suddenly it all fitted.

'To the country,' I said, sounding excited. 'For a drive. I know where to go. Leave the journey to me.'

# CHAPTER 11

Frank called for me in a van, which surprised me because I suppose I'd been expecting his bike, and had dressed for the same. I quite liked Frank's bike – it was noisy and flash, just like him, and I wanted the neighbours to hear us and stare as it pulled away. I'd worn my ski-pants and boots, and a plastic three-quarter length jacket to keep the wind off yet not trail in the grease from the chain.

Frank didn't get out because he had no manners, but I'd seen that quite clearly before. Jack would have opened the car door if it'd meant walking through fire to do it, but Frank just pulled the lock down from the inside, and I was left to open it and to climb in by myself. The operation took some time, my trousers were tight and my jacket stuck to the plastic cover on the seat. Frank got impatient, and swerved away as soon as I was ready. His face was in darkness, and I heard his dog snuffling in the back. I thought he seemed angry, and wondered whether it was because the dog had lost its race.

'D'you want to change your mind and go to the pictures or something?' he asked. I watched his face under the stripes of light from the streetlamps, and I watched the stripes getting quicker across his face as the van gathered speed.

I wanted Frank to look at me properly, to see the

trouble that I'd taken for him. My hair was fresh washed
and set into tiny curls with Twink, my make-up was
carefully blotted with powder from the Stratton compact
that Lily had given me for Christmas, and my lips were
painted frosted pink, to match the stuff on my nails. I
wanted Frank to sniff my perfume, too, the new scent
that I'd dabbed behind my ears and then dribbled down
into my bra as a precaution. I wanted Frank to be
impressed by me and the way that I looked. I wanted his
eyes to pop like the men's eyes did on the adverts when
their girlfriends were up to something.

'No,' I answered, disappointed by his attitude. 'I want
to go to the country, like I said.'

Frank looked at me then. 'And do you always get what
you want?' he asked, and winked.

'Most times,' I told him, and he laughed, and the atmosphere in the van seemed to ease a little.

'You might think you do, Ruby,' Frank told me, 'but
you're wrong, girl. Getting your own way all the time
only means that you miss out on things that might be
important later on. Things that you never knew you
wanted until you get to try them.'

'Like what, for instance?' I asked, but Frank just smiled
and tapped the side of his nose as though he knew things
that I didn't.

I got angry at this, but turned round to pet the dog to
show that I didn't care.

'It's a bit like Lady there,' Frank said, tilting his head
towards the dog. 'Now if I spoilt her all the time like
you're trying to do, she'd get fat and lazy and she'd never
run. Dogs like her are made for running, Ruby, it's what
they're best at, and it's beautiful to watch. If she got what
she wanted all the time, she'd just lie around the house
all day. She'd never know what it was that she was missing, and neither would I.'

'Are you saying I'm fat?' I asked, and Frank laughed
again, looking at my figure until even I started to blush.

'You're OK,' he said, smiling. 'It's all in about the right

places. But you're spoilt though, Ruby. I could tell that a mile off. You like your own way, and so far everyone's been daft enough to give it to you.'

Frank shut up then, which was just as well as far as I was concerned, because I didn't like hearing the truth about myself, not when it sounded like that, anyway. I folded my arms across my chest and tried instead to think of the route. I'd got hold of a map of Surrey and I pulled it out of my handbag, spreading it on the dashboard and peering at it in the dark. By all accounts I should have known the way to Rowan Hall by instinct, but I'd decided not to trust my instincts that night and to take a map instead. I wanted everything right, I wanted everything to be perfect when I went back to my house.

We drove in silence, Frank never even asking me where it was we were headed. I only spoke to give him directions and when I did my voice sounded trembly with excitement. When the van stopped at last and the doors were thrown open, the bare roaring silence of the dark country night hurt my ears. Frank jumped straight out of the van and let Lady quickly out of the back, so that she flew off like an arrow, a silvery flickering flame in the distant hills.

I watched Frank walk to the brow of the hill and peer moodily over the edge, his hands stuffed deep into his pockets. The air was sweet and warm and smelled of cut wet grass. Frank lit a cigarette, though, to show that he wasn't impressed.

I walked to the top of the hill too, so quietly that I could hear no footsteps, and as I climbed I could feel and hear the blood beating hard in the veins of my head. I was alive in my own dreams. I opened my eyes slowly and there below me stood Rowan Hall, silver and perfect in the moonlight, its gardens laid out around it like a blanket.

I am still unclear as to my motives for getting Frank to drive me to Rowan Hall that night. I had not thought so much about the place lately, and I believe I may have

hoped that I would lay the ghost to rest by going back.
You grow out of your childhood dreams and fantasies
with time, but Rowan Hall still nagged at me occasionally
and I wanted to see it done with.

I believe I was hoping to find that the house had
changed somehow, grown smaller, less significant, so that
I could laugh at it and cast it from my mind. At any rate
I was unprepared for what happened as I stood on that
hill; for the sudden and violent sense of longing that came
over me as I gazed down at the house. I was overcome,
off-balance for a moment, it was as though the house was
waiting for me. I couldn't breathe, and I clutched at my
throat, my eyes closing as I rocked on my heels. I had
sworn an oath to the house, and my promise had been
like a spell that held me still in its grasp.

'What's up with this place, then?' I heard Frank ask.

'It's mine,' I whispered. 'It belongs to me.'

He laughed. 'What's your name then, Lady Muck?'

I had sealed that oath with spittle and with blood, and
I had broken my promise, I had done nothing whatever
to keep it. I felt the shame I had felt as a child every bit
as keenly now as the pain had been to me then. I had
found out what I was down there in the rose garden –
which was nothing. I was still nothing. Nothing had
changed. I had been seven years old, and I remembered
Piers's hand inside my skirt, his long fingers probing,
searching the seat of my embarrassment. I'd been too
scared to talk in that house, for my voice sounded different. It sounded even worse now because I'd made no
effort to better it.

'I want to go, Frank,' I said suddenly, pulling my coat
about me and shivering in the wind. I could smell the
roses, I swear that I could smell them, even from there.
'Take me home,' I pleaded.

But Frank had walked off.

'What, all this way for nothing, Ruby?' he asked. 'If
this is your house, then we'd better take a closer look.'

'It's not mine!' I shouted. 'Not really, not yet!'

Frank stopped walking and turned to look at me. 'Well, make your mind up, girl,' he said softly. 'Either it is or it isn't.'

'It will be,' I said miserably. 'I'll own it one day.'

'And what are you going to buy it with, shirt buttons?' Frank asked, and I could tell he was laughing at me.

'I'll marry into it,' I said, getting in deeper. I didn't want this conversation, I wanted it to stop. I knew how I sounded, but Frank was goading me on with his mocking attitude.

'Oh, well, I should think they'd love you, Ruby,' he laughed. 'They'll just about bust a bloody gut rushing to welcome you with open arms into the family! What, has your dad been having negotiations for an arranged marriage with Lord whoever-his-name-is that owns that place? What's your dowry come to, Ruby? A large crate of Jaffas? Don't make me laugh, Ruby, I didn't take you for that sort.'

'What sort?' I was angry now. I hated Frank's stupid tone.

'The daft sort,' he told me, 'the sort who are too busy with their noses in the air to make a go of their real lives. The sort of slags who've got their noses stuck in some romantic drivel in *Woman's Own* while they've got six kids snivelling round their skirts! I thought you were a bit special, Ruby, like me, I thought we were the sort to really make something of ourselves.'

'And what are you going to do with yourself then that's so bloody great?' I asked, nearly in tears.

'I'm going to make money,' Frank told me. 'I don't really care how, though I've got plans already. I'll nick it if I have to, to start with, because once you've got it you keep making it, if you're clever.'

'You're going to jail then,' I said, trying to laugh, to make him feel as stupid as he had made me feel.

'Not with coppers like your boyfriend around I won't,' Frank said. 'That prat couldn't nick his chin shaving.'

'Jack's sharper than you think,' I said, quickly. 'He's got your card marked, so watch it.'

'I don't want to talk about Jack,' Frank said, and his voice had gone softer. I knew that he was waiting to kiss me and I felt nervous and uncomfortable and moved away a bit. 'You shouldn't marry him, you know,' he added. 'He's not right for you.'

'Oh? Then who is, you?' I asked.

'I could be,' Frank said, and his words surprised me and made me even more edgy.

'I'd have to be desperate,' I said, and then Frank pulled me to him, so suddenly that I had no time to move.

'No,' he said, looking down on me in the darkness, 'you'd just have to be in love with me, that's all. I'll buy you the house then, Ruby, once I've got my money, if that's what you want.'

I opened my mouth to make a rude reply, but Frank was too close, and nothing came out. His mouth covered mine neatly, like we were made for one another, and as he held me to him and kissed me I felt all the cheek run out of me, and something the texture of marshmallow take its place. Our kiss lasted a few seconds, that was all, and then Frank politely pulled away and pushed the hair back off his face.

'Let's go down there then and see what we'll be buying, shall we?' he asked, and he'd run off before I could stop him, Lady bounding at his heels and the wet grass squelching under his boots.

I rushed to follow him.

'Don't, Frank!' I called. 'They might be at home, they might see us!'

'There's no lights on,' Frank shouted back.

'They might be in bed!' I was desperate by now. I didn't want him getting any closer to the house.

'What, at nine o'clock? Off on their hols, more like,' he said, and he was gone before I could catch up with him.

I'd only wanted a quick look, I'd found out all I needed

to know, yet there was Frank haring off to see the place more closely, and liable to get arrested for trespassing into the bargain. I was terrified of getting caught. I imagined the horror of being dragged inside the house, in front of Piers and his mother, and having to stand there, ashamed, until the local police arrived to arrest us. I began to sob as I ran after Frank, the wind tearing at my hair and my feet slipping dangerously on the long wet grass.

Frank was waiting for me in the garden, but I didn't see him in the darkness and ran into his back. He caught me and pulled me round beside him, supporting me with his arm.

'Do you want to get inside?' he asked.

'What do you mean?'

'Inside,' he said patiently, 'in the house. Would you like to take a look while there's no one there, Ruby?'

I stared at him as though he was mad, though the idea appealed to me enormously.

'Look, Ruby,' he said, pointing, 'there are no lights on and the shutters are closed on the ground floor. That means they've gone away, we've got the place to ourselves. Do you want to take a look or not?'

'You can't be sure,' I said. I was shaking. 'You'd have to break a window – we could get arrested, Frank, somebody might find us.'

Frank saw I was scared then, and spoke more kindly. 'I can get in if you want, Ruby,' he said gently. 'I've done more secure places than this one in my time, and if I guess right, I won't have to break any glass. Now, don't you think we've got a right to take a look about, seeing as how we're going to be buying the place one day?'

I nodded. I was scared, but my curiosity was greater than my fear.

Frank nodded back, and kissed the tip of my nose. Then he was gone, running around to the other side of the house, while I stood alone in the darkness.

My teeth started to chatter with fear as I stood there, and when Lady suddenly emerged from the gloom and

brushed against my legs I screamed and nearly wet my
knickers. The moon went behind a cloud and for a
moment I could see nothing, not even a hand in front of
my face. I started to walk, and the gravel under my feet
seemed to make a terrible crunching noise as I tiptoed as
best as I could to the back of the house. My fingers
touched rough brick then, and I knew, with relief, where
I was. I had reached the rosary, and for some reason I felt
safe. I fumbled around the wall till my fingers found the
rotted wood of the door and though the lock had rusted
the key still turned with some effort.

The door gave immediately and fell back heavily, so
that I had to use all my strength to hold it half-open. The
scream the wood gave out as it fell could have been heard a
mile off and I stopped, not breathing, afraid that someone
might hear and come after me. But there was silence. The
moon returned like a lantern and I stepped inside once
more, into my own private rose garden.

It was as though all the perfumes of the world had been
contained in that enclosed space. The air was thick with
the scent of roses; it hung there like smoke, but invisible.
I inhaled deeply, drinking it in like a drug. 'You should
smell them at night,' Piers had said about the roses, and
now I had. The night had robbed the flowers of their
colour, but it magnified their perfume. There was a still-
ness and timelessness inside those walls that made it like
a graveyard, and I thought at once of incense and of
churches, and of saints praying on their knees.

The roses were grey-purple and tipped with silver in
the moonlight. There were weeds too, many more than
when I had been here as a child, and the ivy that grew
outside the walls had taken control of the insides as well.

A breeze shifted the half-closed roses and I had a fancy
that they were nodding to me, showing their approval.
How long would they wait for me? There was a noise,
then I heard Frank calling my name, and his voice was
soft, like a whisper carried by the wind. He burst into the

garden looking for me. He grabbed at my arm and his eyes looked excited.

'I've done it, Ruby,' he said. 'We're in.'

'I'm not climbing through any windows,' I warned him, 'not in these trousers, anyway.'

'Then it's just as well I've opened the main entrance up for Her Ladyship, isn't it?' Frank laughed, and when we reached the front of the house I saw that he meant it; the main door was wide open, and I saw darkness inside.

'Are you sure there's no one about?' I asked him, still petrified we would be found out.

'Not a soul,' Frank reassured me. 'Trust me, I've checked.'

I stepped inside the house, and my heart was beating fit to explode. There was a thin beam of moonlight from the window at the top of the stairs, enough to see the hall, but not its walls or furniture. The wide stairway stood before me, its polished bannisters winding upward out of view, and the moonbeam formed a shape, like a ghost, that hovered, waiting, at the top.

There were other ghosts in the hallway. I screamed as my eyes became used to the dark, and Frank grabbed at me and pulled me to his chest. 'They're only dustsheets, Ruby,' he said, laughing, and I looked again and laughed at my own stupidity.

There *was* a ghost in that house, but it was the ghost of a little girl, a stranger who had visited there and who had waited for me to return. I could see her in the hallway, watching the blond-haired boy swing from the stairpost. I could watch her walk to the rose garden and rush back again later, her paper dress torn and her face red with embarrassment.

The air smelled stale inside the house, and the dust was thick on the floor.

'They've moved!' I said, and a sudden panic gripped my chest. Piers had not waited for me after all, he'd gone, moved away, and I never would find him. Throwing open the door, I ran into the lounge, and the furniture

there was covered in dustsheets too. There was not a
sound in the place, apart from my footsteps, and the
scratching of Lady's claws on the parquet as she followed
me from room to room.

'They've gone!' I shouted to Frank. Not even the clocks
were ticking. The house was dead inside. I couldn't bear
to think I'd come too late.

'Don't panic,' Frank told me, loading logs and dried
twigs into the fireplace in the hall and throwing a lighted
match in among them. 'There's fresh food in the larder,
so they must keep a skeleton staff. My guess is they've
just moved up to London for the season. They do that in
these places, you know, board them up and move to their
cosy little flats in Town. They don't sell places like these,
they hand them down through the generations. If they
sell up they sell the furniture too, and it's all still here, by
the looks of it.'

He pulled some dustsheets off the furniture. I tried to
stop him but was too curious to see what they hid to be
bothered to speak.

Frank whistled through his teeth. 'Got some tasty pieces
here, you know,' he said. 'The whole family must be
loaded all right. Get a few quid for this lot back in
London. I'm surprised they haven't taken the trouble to
get an alarm fitted with scallywags like me roaming the
countryside.'

'Don't you dare!' I warned him. 'Not one single item
goes missing, OK?'

Frank looked round and shrugged. 'Suit yourself,' he
said. 'Who did you plan on marrying around here,
anyway?' he asked. 'Some doddery old earl with a weak
ticker?'

'There's a son,' I said, and then I told him the whole
story. Frank poked at the fire as I told him, and sometimes
he looked angry, and twice he laughed, and once he just
shook his head knowingly. When I was finished he sighed
and leaned back in his chair, biting at his lip, with his
arms folded behind his head.

'Why d'you want to get landed with that lot, Ruby?'
he asked.

'What lot?' I was wishing I hadn't told him now, I
remembered his comments from earlier on. It was the
house that had done it, had loosened my tongue. I needed
to tell someone, and it was Frank who was there. .

'The upper bloody crust,' Frank said, with a curling
lip. 'Those twerps and deadheads that make up the British
aristocracy. We're just a joke to them, Ruby. Why d'you
think they'd even be interested?'

'I can change,' I said, more to myself than to him, 'I
can become one of them; talk like them if I've got a mind
to.'

'There's more than your accent to alter,' Frank said,
and he leaned forward, making Lady prick her ears with
surprise. 'There's your past you'll need to change too,
your breeding. What are you going to do about Billy,
Ruby? Sweep him under the carpet? He's your dad, Ruby,
your family. That's where you belong, in London, not
out here with this lot. You should be proud of where you
come from, Ruby, not trying to cover it up to impress
this lot of scroungers!'

'You don't know them . . .' I began.

'Do you, Ruby?' Frank interrupted. 'You've told me
about this bloke Piers trying to get his fingers up your
skirt, and then you tell me that he's the man you want to
marry! Why, Ruby? *I'll* get money if you want it. What
makes him so bleeding good?'

'Because he's got class and he owns this house,' I told
him. The fire crackled with little explosions of dry wood
and I said each word slowly and deliberately, so that Frank
would understand. 'I told you, Frank,' I said, leaning
towards his chair, 'I want this house, and I'll do anything
to get it. It *belongs* to me, Frank, and I intend to have it.'

Frank laughed, and I watched the small wrinkles that
appeared at the corners of his eyes. It was dangerous
watching Frank for too long, you got sort of spellbound
by his face and the way that he looked. It wasn't just his

features, either, though they were handsome enough in their way. What fascinated me more were his expressions and the way that he moved his body. There was a great casualness about Frank, a sort of easiness of movement, and if you watched him for too long you found yourself aching to touch him.

'I told you, Ruby,' he said, laughing. 'I'll get this house for you and I'll make you love me into the bargain.'

'You'd never do that,' I said, and I leaned away quickly, nearer the fire. The air in the room seemed to thicken, and I could suddenly hear myself breathing. I tried to breathe naturally but I couldn't. I'd lost the rhythm.

'I can hear your heart,' Frank told me, smiling.

'Don't be stupid,' I said.

'Let me make you, Ruby,' Frank said. 'Let me make you fall in love with me for ever.'

'You never could,' I said, and his smile widened.

'If you think that, then what are you so afraid of?' he asked. 'Look at you, Ruby. If you get much further away you'll be rolling right into the fire.'

'I'm not scared of you,' I said.

'Then come and sit closer.' He patted the arm of his chair.

I got up slowly, reluctantly, crossing to his seat and lowering myself on to the arm. Frank grabbed me and he kissed me, pulling me over his lap, curling his arms round me till I fought to break away.

'What's wrong?' he asked, still holding me by the waist. 'You did it with Vic, so what's wrong with me?'

I exploded with anger then, but he had the strength to hold me till I'd calmed down.

'Ruby, Ruby, Ruby,' he said, shushing me and stroking my hair. 'I'm sorry, I'm sorry. So you two only kissed, I'm sorry, I got you all wrong. I just thought that with Jack and all that you'd be a woman of the world. You've got a bit of side to you too, remember? You act a bit as though you know it all.'

I looked at Frank and I relaxed a little, and he kissed

me again, though more gently this time, and when he'd finished our faces were so close that I could see right into his eyes in the darkness. I could see the fire reflected there, a small orange flame drowning in all that dark wetness, and I felt as though I were turning liquid too, and that my heart was like that reflected flame, tiny and burning in a sea of vast darkness.

'You've never done it before then?' Frank whispered, his lips now pressed to my ear. I shook my head, my pride gone, and only curiosity remaining.

'Do you want to do it, Ruby?' he asked.

How could I answer? I could have no opinion on a subject about which I knew so little. Frank saw my face, and he guessed my dilemma.

'How much do you know about what goes on?' he asked, and I shrugged.

'A bit,' I told him, and a bit was the truth, no one had ever really told me about it. All I knew was what I'd seen that day in the lounge at home, and that wasn't much, just Marge sitting in a chair and Billy jiggling about between her legs.

Frank kissed my forehead and then he kissed my cheek. 'It can hurt a bit the first time, you know,' he said, but I didn't care, and told him so. There was something about the way that we were there, the two of us, with me in Frank's lap and him planting kisses on my face, that made me feel dreamy and unafraid. There was a burning stoking up in my stomach, a sort of knot of excitement, and I believe if Frank had stopped there I would have died of disappointment.

He cupped my face in his hands and he kissed me again on the mouth, and it was a splendid kiss, neither too strong nor too gentle, so that I flung my arms about his neck and set about kissing him back. Frank pulled my arms away though, after a bit.

'Not too quickly, Ruby,' he said, and I wondered why slowly was better.

He laid the palm of his hand across my breast and

squeezed it gently, and I felt a volt of electricity run right
up through my body. I laughed out of nervousness.

'Do you like that?' Frank asked, and I nodded.

'It feels strange,' I told him.

'Now how did your copper ever manage to keep his
hands off these then, I wonder?' Frank asked, and I hit
him gently on the cheek. 'They're magnificent, Ruby,' he
told me, kissing my breasts through my jumper, 'the best
pair of tits in the market.'

I lay against Frank's chest, my legs across his lap, sideways in the chair, like a child being read a story.

'Let me teach you, Ruby,' Frank whispered, 'let me
show you what to do.' He closed my eyes with his fingers,
then he kissed the closed lids, one by one till I shivered.
He kissed my throat, and my neck responded, arching
backwards as I let out a sigh.

'Do you want me, Ruby?' he asked. 'Tell me you want
me, tell me.'

'I want you, Frank,' I said, and the words surprised my
own ears, for I had no idea I'd say them.

'Touch me then,' he told me.

My hand moved quickly to that place on his trousers,
the place where I'd felt Jack's thing when he'd caught me
in the market. Frank's jeans were thicker fabric, though;
the thing was just a lump.

'Do you know what it is, Ruby?' he asked. 'Have you
seen one before?'

I shook my head. I was sweating, my hands were wet
with it. I was going to find out at last, what Piers knew,
what Jack had let me touch through his trousers.

Frank tutted. 'Your Marge should have told you what
was what,' he said, then he smiled. 'Still,' he said, 'I'm
glad she didn't. Makes it more exciting for you, go on,
undo it.'

I moved my legs to the side a bit and undid the button
on Frank's jeans. The zip came down a few teeth of its
own accord, and I pulled it gently the rest of the way,
with Frank flinching in case I caught him. I pushed my

fingers into the top of his pants and slid them down slowly inside.

'Go on,' Frank urged. 'It won't bite.'

There was a mound of hard flesh down there, and I almost pulled my hand back. Frank covered my hand with his own, though, curving my fingers around it, so that I had it held firm in my palm. It was hard and curved and rubbery, like giblets. Frank pushed my hand gently so that I was rubbing it, and I felt it respond, growing bigger in my hand.

'Have a look, Ruby,' he said. 'You should know what it looks like.'

It was a strange-looking thing, and bigger than I'd imagined. I kissed Frank for having it, and then I turned back to it again.

'Play with it, do what you like,' Frank told me in a whisper. 'I want you to get to know it.'

I curved my fingers around its base and it waved and bobbed in my hands. I curled my spine and kissed its tip and licked it, and it tasted of salt.

'Are they all like this?' I asked Frank, curious. 'Are all men's the same?'

'Why, bored already?' Frank said, and I shook my head and laughed.

'No, I love it,' I told him.

'Well, at least that's part of me you love, then,' he said.

I stroked it as I talked, and Frank's eyes closed and he groaned. I stopped immediately, afraid that I had hurt him, but he pressed my hand back again and told me not to stop.

He undid the buttons of his shirt and his bare chest lay before me, covered in black hair, so that I pressed my face against it and ran my tongue down to his stomach. His pelvis began to move slightly in the chair, pushing up towards me in his eagerness for more.

Then suddenly he stopped me. 'Let me show you where it goes now,' he said, and he stood me up before him, and undressed me like a child. When I was naked in front

of him he stared at me silently. 'Your body is beautiful,'
he said. 'You look like a film star.' He told me to lie
down and I lay on the rug before him, watching him pull
off his clothes until he was naked at last above me. He
knelt then, pushing my legs apart first with his hands. I
tried to pull them together; I felt strange in that position,
too vulnerable. 'You have to trust me,' he said, and I did,
and I let his hands work me into position.

'It goes in here,' Frank told me, and he pressed a finger
gently inside me, moving it, pushing, till I squirmed and
all but cried out. Nothing hurt, but it was strange still,
to have something inside you, and moving. I frowned
and bit at my lip, and my back arched with the strangeness
of it all.

'Tell me if I hurt,' Frank said, and I felt a second finger
slip inside me. The gap between them widened, and I felt
myself pulled right apart.

'You see?' Frank held the fingers in front of me. 'You're
wet, Ruby, you're ready for me.'

And it was true. I felt his fingers and they were sticky
with dampness. I almost cried out for him to stop when
he lowered his body between my legs and I felt the head
of the thing I had been playing with pushing at my opening, which was closed completely shut.

'Relax, Ruby,' Frank whispered. 'It will hurt if you
don't. Your body knows it wants me, now let it do the
rest.'

I closed my eyes, and felt him lift my hips a little with
his hands. There was a silence, a pause, he was waiting
for me to look at him again. 'You're like a child taking
an injection,' he said, and I smiled, and opened my eyes
and knew then that I wanted him.

He guided himself in with his hand, pushing gently,
inch by inch, stopping when it hurt me, but never retreating, just pausing before going on again. Once it was all
inside, and my mouth had opened with the shock of it,
then he lowered his body down on me, and his weight
on top of me confused me and made me relax more inside.

He eased it backwards gently then, and I cried out from the feeling of losing it just as I had at first, when I felt it go in. We were slippery with wetness, but even so I felt a grinding that made me cry out again as he slid back inside. He covered my mouth with his own, stifling my cries with his too-tender kiss. My whole body felt like a tube then, with a stuffing and an emptying going on endlessly inside.

The stuffing grew faster. 'I can't wait, Ruby,' Frank said, close to my ear. 'I've got to come . . . Chriiiiist!' The word stretched out for ever, his hips became spasmodic, pushing upward, driving him inside me until I clung to the skin of his back, crying for him to stop.

And stop he did, slowly, running down like an old car. I watched his face so close to my own, screwed up with a pain and a pleasure that I could not understand until his neck seemed to give, and he fell heavily against me, a dead man, for all I knew, and I closed my eyes under his weight.

'Oh Christ, Ruby,' he panted into my neck and, as we lay there, I felt the thing grow smaller inside me. I tried to hold it there, in the warmth and protection of my body, but it fell out in the wetness, and I could have cried for losing it.

Frank lifted himself up and I felt his face with my hands, and it was wet too, but with sweat. I could see the painted ceiling above his head, with its blue sky and its pink-tinged clouds, and Frank looked like an angel then too, not a pale-gold Christian angel like Piers, but the black-haired Roman-faced sort that you saw in Catholic pictures of saints.

His hair had fallen over his face and was stuck there, plastered in curls. 'Did I hurt you?' he asked, and I shook my head slowly. 'Did you feel anything good?' I started to answer, but I couldn't. What I'd felt was strange, but I couldn't call it good. Not good in the way that it had been for him, where he had jerked with the pleasure and I'd ridden along with his throes.

'What makes you like that, Frank?' I asked. 'What's so good that it bends your body in that way and leaves you so gutted afterwards?'

Frank kissed me, and his kisses moved down to my nipples, and he kissed and then sucked at each one, so that I pushed at his head and my spine squirmed on the carpet.

'Relax,' he told me quietly. 'I won't put it inside you again this time. I'll just show you how I felt, that's all.'

He pushed my arms out to the side, like a crucifix, and he kissed down my ribcage to my stomach. I felt nerves begin to play down there when he did that. I was sore inside, but something else was still keen.

I felt his fingers in the hair around my groin, and he pressed his palm against the bone there, and as he pressed it I felt my pelvis rise up in reply, pushing against him till his palm ground harder.

He kissed me there then, and it embarrassed me. I tried to push his head away but he reached up to my face with his fingers and pressed them against my lips as if to quieten me. 'Relax,' I heard him whisper. 'I promise you you'll enjoy it.'

My body relaxed in a sigh, I couldn't fight against him. I felt his tongue working at me, squirming down there, pressing inside me, creating small whirlpools. I found the spot before he did, felt it crying out for him, the pain of longing there surprised me. It had been there always, yet I'd never known it existed. Suddenly it was the heart of my body, it took over completely. I felt Frank's tongue touch against it, and I thought that I would explode, it was what I wanted so much. He worked against it, and I felt myself rising, puffed up with each lick until I felt like an over-filled lilo. My hands clutched at anything to try and hold myself down; I found Frank's head, my fingers grabbed cruelly at the wet curls. I was wanting only, not giving any more. I could cause pain and damage, but there was a point that I knew I must reach. My legs wound around Frank's shoulders, I kicked him on with my heels.

I was high but I had to get higher, then suddenly I was there, the lilo exploded, I whirled and eddied like a length of torn rubber. I shouted, I screamed, I felt Frank's fingers in my mouth and I bit at them, then I landed again, still twitching, and I thought I had reached to the end of my life.

'Good?' Frank asked, and I could tell he was proud. I could hear it right there in his voice. My mind was returning from a journey, I laughed when it reached my skull again.

'Where has it been, Frank,' I laughed. 'Where has it been all my life?'

'It was there all along, Ruby,' Frank said, cockily. 'It was just waiting for me to come along and set the fuse!' Then he looked more serious and kissed me again suddenly. 'Your first time is special, Ruby, don't forget it. You'll never forget what we did together for the rest of your life. You're mine now, Ruby,' I heard him whisper, and we lay back on the floor, where I slept with my head on his chest, the fire crackling gently in the background, and Lady whimpering as she fought in her dreams.

# CHAPTER 12

I lived in a dream during the weeks that followed. Nothing could have hurt me, or harmed me, or upset me. Even when Frank showed me the bit in the paper about how the house had been broken into, I only laughed. I thought that we were clever, you see. I was bursting with my own cleverness and blind to everything else.

They thought we must have been tramps, breaking in like that and taking nothing, just lighting a fire and then leaving. I got a few more facts from that article though, and Frank was right, the place was just closed for the season. They'd be back then, the house wasn't empty. We hadn't been found and I felt that we led charmed lives, Frank and I.

Even Jack had gone away on a course to leave us together, and I liked the feel of Frank and me, it seemed right. I was proud of him and he, I knew, of me.

Frank taught me all I felt there was to know about sex, and I was the keenest pupil.

'You're killing me, Ruby,' he'd laugh when we did it, 'there's only so much a man can take!' But Frank could take it all, I never met another like him. He was ready any time for a bit of our nonsense; only once did I hear him give up, and that time we declared it a draw.

It was an Indian summer. The leaves turned rust brown

and golden but then seemed to cling to the trees as the weather became warm again, with a generous richness that you don't get in spring.

We had sex in the van, driving at night to a parking lot Frank knew, where he had the keys and could let himself in. We'd wind up the windows and get them steamy with our breath, and then we'd start out slowly, because there was no room and you'd think you'd never find a way to do it, but we did, every time, though I'd often set the wipers off with my feet, and once I got stuck on the horn, which frightened us both.

We let Lady out for a stroll once, and tried it in the back, where there was more room, but it didn't work. She was gone for two minutes and then she came back, scratching at the door and whimpering to be allowed in. I started to giggle and Frank shushed me, hoping she'd go away, but she didn't, she started howling instead. So we went back to our cramped front seats, while Lady slept happily in the back.

When the weather turned even warmer Frank picked me up from the market one day and drove me out to the country, near Cambridge. We watched the stars come out as we sipped a flask of tea, and then suddenly he opened the door and pulled me outside.

'Where are we going?' I whispered. There was something about the countryside that always made me whisper, even when there was no one around. But Frank wasn't telling. He just helped me over a fence and then we walked through a field, with him dragging me by one arm.

He stopped right in the middle, where you couldn't see the sides, just wide space and velvet sky, and no one around for miles.

'Lie down,' he said, 'I'm going to have you,' and I was excited by his tone.

I did what he told me and I didn't giggle, like in the car. Frank seemed to fit into the countryside, he seemed to know what he was doing, just like he did in town. I felt all wrong there, I would never have had the nerve, but Frank took control that night and I liked it, it was the best.

I liked the feel of Frank on top of me, and the earth beneath my back. We could have been anyone that night, it wasn't common, like it was in the van. There was just us and the grass, and the moon overhead, and as I felt Frank push up inside me I lay back, strangely quiet, wanting to watch rather than to join in.

I didn't move, just lay there spread-eagled on the ground, and Frank understood. He worked on top of me while I bathed my face in the moonlight. It was all sensation, no effort, I let Frank do it all. I lay there feeling him fuck me, and it was the best feeling in the world. He went on and on, and I was happy to let him. I was in no hurry to come, no hurry to do anything.

When it came it grew slowly, and it was delicious, like a meal. I felt it there, could control it, could let it take over my body. It grew enormous but I held it inside me like a secret. I hardly moved when it took me, just closed my eyes tight and shuddered inside. I felt Frank shuddering too, though, and knew that we'd come together, at the same exact time. It was perfect.

'I love you, Ruby,' he whispered when we'd finished, when we both lay there panting on the black heavy grass. I didn't speak though, I couldn't. I was in a spell in the moonlight and I didn't want to break it. Together Frank and I could have done anything at that moment, and I didn't want that feeling to end, I wanted it to go on for ever.

Perfect things don't last, though, and I knew our time together had run out the day I opened the door to see Lily standing there, pale-faced and alone, without her lipstick and with a headscarf tied around her bouffant.

'Can I come in?' she asked. 'I can't say what I want standing out here in the street.'

I stood back and as she passed me in the doorway she did so in a cloud of Soir de Paris that nearly left me choking.

We stood there in the lounge and she sized me up in silence, her hands folded over her waist and her handbag hanging off one arm. It was a big bag, made of some sort of animal hide, and I guessed one of Vic's relatives must have brought it over from Jamaica, for I'd never seen one like it before.

'Leave him alone, Ruby,' she said, her chin raised.

'Who?' I had to ask, I had to be sure. I thought at first she might have come about Vic.

'Frank, that's who,' Lily replied, and she looked annoyed at my display of stupidity. Lily would never have come about Vic, it wasn't her style. She shamed me more with her silence on that matter, and she knew it.

'I don't know what you're on about,' I said, avoiding her with my eyes.

'Don't give me that.' She was really angry now.

'You're killing my Pearl, Ruby,' she said, 'and I can't just stand by and let you do it.'

'I didn't make him take me out,' I said, and Lily just snorted, like a horse.

'You can make 'em do anything, Ruby, you realize that by now! You're that sort of girl, Ruby, you'll always have your pick. My Pearl is different, though, she's deeper and a bit quiet. She loves Frank, and you don't, so just leave him alone.' She unfolded her arms and her hands shook as she searched for a cigarette. The handbag seemed bottomless, and the search took some time. 'Did he tell you they were engaged?' she asked, once the cigarette was lit.

I shrugged. 'He's in love with me, Lily,' I told her, 'he told me himself.'

Lily looked nonplussed at the news. 'Men keep their brains in their balls, Ruby,' she said. 'You found that out with my Vic and then you decided to try your luck with Frank. Vic's a good man, but even he's only human. Frank's a different case. I knew he was wrong for Pearl the moment she brought him home. He's a type that you get to recognize, Ruby, a lot like your dad Billy when he was younger. Put it on a plate for them, though, and

there's not one of them won't be picking it up for a quick
sniff.'

'Vic didn't touch me,' I said, but I don't know if she
believed me. I didn't have much of a conscience in those
days; you don't when you're younger. That sort of thing
only comes once you can see yourself in the other person's
shoes. The thought plagued me later, though, as it still
does today. Vic was a good man, and I hope that Lily
believed me when I told her.

'Like I said,' she went on, 'Frank's not my pick of a
son-in-law, but my Pearl's been keen on him for years.
Pearl's a lovely girl, Ruby, but she's no match for you.
She's like her father, good-looking but don't know it. She
didn't deserve the life she's landed with; what Vic told
you was true, she gets the lot slung at her for being neither
one colour nor the other, even now. She deserves to be
happy, and I can't bear to see her like she is now.'

'What about me, Lily?' I asked. 'I'm your daughter too.
Doesn't my happiness count?'

Lily looked at me out of the corner of her eye at that,
and I could tell I hadn't fooled her for a minute.

'You've told me that Frank loves you,' she said. 'I didn't
hear you say anything about you loving him, though.' I
watched her, silently. 'You just wanted to play, didn't
you? Well, you've had your fun, Ruby, and it's time to
let him back where he belongs again. He'll go back to
Pearl OK, he loves her really.'

'Frank's his own man,' I said, my voice wavering. 'I
can't tell him what to do.'

Lily looked at me hard for a second then shook her
head slowly and stubbed out her cigarette on Marge's
lino. She walked towards the door, pushing past me as
she did so.

'Pearl loves Frank, Ruby,' she said, retying her scarf.
'If I thought for one minute that you wanted him I would
never have come here today. But you don't, do you? You
don't give a toss about anyone but yourself, do you? I can
see what you're like, Ruby, you don't have to tell me. I

was the same myself at your age, until I had you. I know how it feels, Ruby, believe me, I know.'

And she was gone in the rain without giving me time to answer.

Frank was proud of me, and proud of himself, come to that. His pride shone through him, there for anyone to see. He was proud of being my first man, and proud of what he'd taught me. He told me often that he loved me in those days, and I was sure then that he meant it, despite what Lily had said.

'Have you had many women then, Frank?' I asked him the next time I saw him after Lily's brief visit.

'Some,' he said, and I could tell by his tone that he wanted to drop the subject there.

'How many's some?' I asked, and he shrugged. His arm felt dead around my shoulders suddenly, and I could tell he was getting annoyed.

'Didn't they all count then?' I said. 'Aren't we all important? Was that why you lost count, Frank?'

'*You* count all right,' he told me, and I saw his eyes glow in the dark.

We were in the private car park, parked there in the rain. We'd gone there to have sex as usual, but I'd got my questions in before Frank could even kiss me.

'And what about Pearl?' I asked him. 'Don't she count, too?'

Frank knew me by now, he knew me too well, better possibly than anyone had before, even Billy. When he looked at me he seemed to look through me, as though reading some thoughts that I didn't even know I had.

'You're engaged to her,' I said, 'and she's my half-sister. Lily was round yesterday, Frank, and she told me. She told me what she thinks of me, too.'

Frank sighed, and ran a hand through his black hair. He leaned back in his seat and rested a foot on the dashboard, looking out of the window, a muscle working all the while in his cheek.

'Lily told me to leave you alone,' I said. 'She came round to Marge's and she told me to lay off; said you belonged to Pearl by rights.' I shrugged. 'I don't care either way, really,' I went on. 'It doesn't bother me much what happens. Perhaps you'd better get back to Pearl, Frank, Lily says she loves you.'

Frank leapt at me so suddenly that I nearly screamed. He got me by the neck, and his face was over mine in the darkness, menacingly. 'Oh, you care, right enough,' he told me hoarsely, 'you care, Ruby. You don't want me marrying Pearl any more than I want you going off and marrying that old geezer you're engaged to, that copper. You care and you know it, so don't give me that!'

I laughed straight into his face at that, although my teeth were chattering for fear that he might hit me. I trusted Frank about as much as you'd trust a wild dog.

'What makes you think that then?' I asked him. I hated the way that he'd told me I cared about him. I hated his pride and his self-importance. He assumed, just because we'd had sex, that I belonged to him for ever and I wasn't having that, I wouldn't take that from any man.

'You're just my first lover, Frank,' I said, 'that doesn't make you my last as well, you know.' The look on his face when I said this made me go cold at what I had done. I wanted to stop, but I couldn't, something was pressing me on, making me say things I would regret later, much later.

'I love you,' he said, and my body seemed to shrink inside itself.

'I can't love you back, Frank,' I told him. 'I can never love you. You've got nothing for me, but I'm going to get everything. If I stayed here with you then I'd never better myself, and that's something I'm determined to do, I told you on our first night. I can't live here all my life. If I thought this was all I could get then I'd kill myself, Frank, I swear to you I would! I want that house and I want to marry Piers to get it. I know what I want, Frank,

and you just don't come into it. I'm sorry if you thought
that you did.'

And so I was. I was sorrier than I could ever have
imagined, but sorry for what exactly I was not entirely
sure.

I let Frank think for a bit. I let him sit in silence, and I
felt the tension in his body as he stared straight ahead, out
of the window.

'We'll end up together, Ruby,' he said finally, and I
almost laughed at his words, except I'd caught the menace
in his tone. 'Whatever you do now we'll still end up
eventually, I'll make sure that we do.'

'That's daft,' I said, but he'd frightened me.

'No, it's not, Ruby, it's the truth. You want the house
and I want you. We'll see who wants what the hardest.
Don't forget, though,' he added, turning my chin to face
him with a finger, 'you're at a handicap, because I've
already had you. You haven't got a clue how to get that
house, and I'll be there before you. You call me fucking
daft, Ruby? Well, we'll see who's the daft one, won't we?
I can give you all you want, but you clear off and find it
somewhere else, if it makes you happy. Going to fucking
buy the house, are you? Or earn it with your body? Do
you know how much whores get these days, Ruby? Girls
like you get a tenner, if they're lucky. Now, how many
tenners d'you think it takes to buy a place like that? But
then you've got it into your head that brassy little scrub-
bers like you can marry into a life like that, haven't you?
Well, invite me to the wedding, Ruby, but don't expect
me to hold my breath until it happens, will you?'

I was crying by then, with anger and with shock.

'You're wrong, Ruby,' he told me, ignoring my sobbing. 'You're wrong all the way round; your mind's
wrong and your life's going wrong. One day you'll find
out, Ruby, and that's when you'll want me back. I know
I'm right, Ruby. If I'm not then I'll make myself right.
I'll make you come back to me and I'll make you love me
somehow. I'll never let you have that house, and I'll show

you you were wrong. There's no point in even trying to get it because I'll be there before you, and I'll beat you at every move. You'll love me, Ruby, and I'll marry you, and there's nothing you can do to try and stop me.'

'I'm going in,' I said, pulling at the doorhandle, and trying to get out. I was scared, but I wouldn't let it show. Frank pulled my hand away but I hit out at him, and he laughed.

'You're a two-bit crook, Frank!' I shouted. 'You'll never come to anything, the only future you'll have is in prison, like all the other blokes around here. Is that how you really see me, Frank? A handful of kids to trail up to Pentonville twice a week on visiting days? A flat in a block somewhere, bouncing prams down ten flights of stairs? 'Cos that's what you're offering me, Frank, not money, not a big house. You're common, Frank, common as muck, and you'll never be better as long as you live!'

'You'll be back to me for help, Ruby,' Frank said as I got out of the van. I slammed the door shut and put my head through the window.

'I'd rather die!' I shouted. 'I'd rather die than have to come to you for help!' And I had to lean back quickly as the van screamed away and I was left to walk home, in the darkness.

# CHAPTER 13

So I did the right thing by Frank, even if it was for all the wrong reasons, and for the next few weeks I was scratchy and irritable; irritable because Frank's parting words had left me worried, and scratchy because I missed him, at least my body did, which was as bad.

I was annoyed with myself, but took my anger out on Marge and even poor Billy, and Marge started muttering on about how I should leave now, how it was taking me too long to get out, and how I wasn't really trying to find somewhere else to live, which was true.

Mostly I wouldn't listen to her whispered complaints. After all, Billy had never said anything about it, and I didn't think he would. It was during one of Marge's sessions of muttering that I decided to go and see Lily, just out of the blue, like that. I'd done the impossible, you see, and convinced myself that I'd chucked Frank for Pearl's benefit and Pearl's benefit alone. It's wonderful how teenagers can · twist a bit of self-pity out of any situation given time.

I half-listened to Marge, her mouth full of buttered bread, going on over breakfast about how I couldn't stay after what I had seen, and Billy was in the scullery, well out of earshot, shaving his face and whistling as he did so, and I thought of Pearl, who had to be back in Frank's arms by then; and the thought brought a lump in my

throat that Marge's words had failed to do, and I decided
there and then that a little thanks might be in order for
the sacrifice I had made.

I set off to see Lily that very same day. I dressed myself
up nicely, in a way I thought she might appreciate, with
loads of black mascara on my eyes, and the latest line in
Italian stilettos on my feet. I'd kept my face quite pale
deliberately though; just a dab of powder, so that when
she saw me she'd see how stricken I was by my loss.

Lily's flat had an empty look to it, though, and I kicked
myself as I stood there, for making a wasted trip. I rang
the bell twice, and I peered through the letter-box. There
were a couple of bills on the mat in the hall, and a post-
card, so I assumed Lily was out.

I was just about to leave when I saw a figure inside,
distorted by the frosted glass, just standing by the door.

'Lily?' I shouted, relieved to find her in, and curious
to know why she wasn't opening the door. The figure
hesitated, then I heard the Yale lock snap open. 'She's
out.' It was Pearl's face, not Lily's, that peered through
the gap and I thought by her expression that she was
about as chuffed to see me as I was to see her.

Pearl had changed, I could tell that much at a glance.
She looked thinner, less lively, and she was wearing her
dressing gown, which made me think she was ill. It was
a kid's dressing gown, the sort you outgrow at around
nine or ten, and on Pearl it looked stupid, with her long
arms sticking out of the sleeves and the tasselled tie so
high up it was almost under her armpits.

'Do you want to come in?' she asked. I didn't, but I
needed to use the toilet. It had been a long trip to get
there, and I didn't fancy being uncomfortable all the way
back.

I nodded, then, and she held the door open, watching
me with wariness as I tripped along the hall.

'The lounge?' I asked politely, and she pushed the door
open to show I should enter.

It was a warm day, but the lounge had a wall of heat

of its own that rose up to greet me as I went in. There was a two-bar fire burning full volume, and a chair pulled up in front of it, as though Pearl had been warming her shins. She walked ahead of me and sat down there, her flipflops dragging on the carpet as she did so. She picked up a large jacket from the back of the chair and swung it around her shoulders, like a shawl.

So this was the act that she'd been putting on for Lily. No wonder my mother had come scampering round to Marge's house to sort me out so quickly. She must have thought Pearl was on her last legs. Pearl wasn't fooling me, though; I'd seen enough melodrama in my time to know when the lead was being well and truly swung. Besides, she had Frank back now; it was me who should have been shivering in front of that fire, not her.

'What have you got, Pearl, the flu?' I asked, sitting as far away as possible on a loose-covered armchair near the door.

Pearl shrugged. 'I'm all right,' she said.

'Well, you don't look it,' I told her, sounding sharp. 'You look like you need a tonic, or something. You ought to pull yourself together, you're putting the wind up Lily, you know.'

Pearl looked at me with bleary eyes, as though the thought of upsetting Lily had only just occurred to her. She pulled the jacket around her again so that the sleeves fell into her skinny lap, and I noticed then just how big that jacket was; miles too big for her or Lily. It was big enough for a man, and I realized with a start just who that man would be.

The jacket was a casual one in dark brown suede, with a grease mark near the pocket. The mark was out of sight, but I knew it was there because the jacket was Frank's and I knew it as well as one of my own. It was the sight of that jacket, the smell of it that set me off hating Pearl once again, no matter how pathetic she looked. We'd made love on that jacket, Frank and I, and there it was around Pearl's shoulders, and there she was wearing it as though it was her own exclusive property.

When I'm hurt I hurt back in return, and at sixteen I hurt as hard as I could, because you don't know when to stop at that age; you don't stop until you feel that you've won.

'Frank's good, isn't he?' I asked Pearl as she rocked backwards and forwards in front of the two-bar. 'The best, I should have said. He had a lot to teach me, at any rate.'

'What do you mean?' Pearl asked me. 'Good at what?' And I knew in that moment that Pearl was still a virgin, that she and Frank had never done it, or she'd have known what I meant straight away.

'Sex,' I told her, smiling. 'What did you think I meant, dressmaking?'

Some colour flamed up in Pearl's cheeks, and she looked away quickly as her eyes filled with tears. She rocked for a bit, and then she sighed.

'I ought to forgive you,' she said, piously. 'Like Mum did about Dad. She forgave him, and I ought to forgive you.'

'Lily had nothing to forgive,' I said, quick as a flash. 'You saw nothing that day, Pearl, only you made things up and went spreading them around. That was spiteful of you, and you know it. You could have broken up your parents' marriage over something you just thought that you saw. You want to be more careful, telling tales out of school.'

'I didn't tell her,' Pearl sighed. 'Dad did, not me.'

'Vic told her?' I asked. I was surprised at his stupidity. Honesty was one thing, but confessing to that sort of thing was another.

'There was nothing for him to tell,' I said, folding my arms. 'And Frank's the one you should be talking to over our affair, too. He's the one who started it, but as soon as Lily told me you two were engaged I told him to get lost. You should be thanking me, Pearl, not having a go at me. I didn't have to chuck him, you know, I only did it because of you and what Lily told me. It's because of me that you two are back together again, and I think you might look a bit more cheerful about it, if you don't mind me saying. If there's one thing I do know about Frank it's that he likes his girls to look their best, and you've let yourself go. Just look at yourself in the mirror.'

Pearl ran a hand across her face. I was keen to get away. The room was too hot and by then I felt as though I was choking. Even I was getting confused about what was the truth; all I'd wanted was to come and tell Lily I'd done what she'd told me, and to have her like me again, like she had done before. Now I had Pearl in front of me, broken down and sobbing, and I wanted her to make less fuss, so that I could just use the toilet and go.

'We could be friends, you know,' I said, to quieten her down. 'Lily says you don't have too many friends, on account of your being half-caste and everything. We are almost sisters, you know. I don't mind, if you want to be friends.'

Pearl looked up, and her face was blurred with tears.

'I do all right,' she said. 'I had trouble at school, but that's over now. It was better with Frank, he knows so many people and they liked me, when I was with him. I went out more then, but I haven't been out so much lately.'

'You'll be OK now, then,' I told her, beginning to get annoyed at all her self-pity. 'Now you've got Frank back you'll pick up with his crowd again, Pearl.'

'You really don't know Frank at all, do you, Ruby?' Pearl asked, and the pity in her voice made my spine prickle with anger.

'He wouldn't come back to me, Ruby,' she went on, 'not like that, at any rate. He's not like that, I know he isn't. He told me about you two, and he told me how hurt he was when you finished it. I told him I didn't care, I was that desperate, Ruby, I'd have had him back whatever. But he said it did matter, and that was why he'd tried to explain. He knew how hurt I was. Did you think he'd come running back to me just because you told him to?' She cried again, and let her head fall into her hands. 'His pride was hurt, Ruby,' she went on, 'and he can't stand that, I know he can't. He left, and he won't be back, not this time.'

'He'll get over it,' I said. 'He'll be back.' But Pearl just shook her head. I felt desolate enough myself at these words, and Pearl's crying was driving me mad.

I stood up to leave, and Pearl rose too, and we eyed one another, not speaking, for a moment. I needed a parting shot, something to impress Pearl – and Frank, if he ever came back.

'I'm going to emigrate,' I told her, and she looked shocked, despite her tears. I liked the sound of the words as I said them, they were dramatic and final, and I knew that was how they'd sound to Frank, too.

'I'm going to Australia,' I said, 'with Jack. He's been begging me to go, and I'll die if I stay in the market. You get money in Australia, and that's what I'm going to do.' I liked the idea more and more by the minute. I liked the effect it had on Pearl, and I could hear myself saying it to Marge and to Lily. It was proud and self-sacrificing; I could blame them for making me do it.

'I only want Frank,' Pearl said. 'I'd do anything to get him back; even the things that he did with you, if that's what he wants.'

I got angry, then. 'You couldn't, Pearl,' I told her, 'it's not like that. Some people are good at sex and some people just aren't. Some couples are made for each other, and that's how it was with me and Frank. We were good together, Pearl. He told me he'd never known any girl like me, so don't go thinking you just lie there and say yes and that's all there is to it. Frank loved me because I was special, and when Jack marries me he'll find out how lucky he is too.'

'I hate you, Ruby,' Pearl said, 'you're spiteful and you're evil and Frank's worth a hundred of you. I don't

know why he loved you, and I don't think he does, either.
I wish I'd never met you, and I'm sorry we're related.'

I smiled at Pearl once she'd finished, and she slammed
the frosted glass door in my face. I was glad Frank hadn't
gone back to her, and I was glad I'd said what I had about
Australia. Telling someone like Pearl meant my mind was
made up, and as I thought more about the idea I felt better
than I had for days. I'd marry Jack, and I'd make him a
good wife. We'd go to Australia and Frank and Marge
and Lily and Pearl could all feel guilty for making me go.
Besides, I thought, I could make money out there, money
that I had no means of earning as long as I stayed in
London. Then, when I'd finished being a good wife to
Jack, I could come home again, rich and influential by
then, the sort of girl Piers would notice, the sort of girl
he'd marry.

I was pleased I'd seen Pearl then, it had made my way
clearer. I had a plan at last, and it suited my needs in every
way possible. Once I had found my wealth, as you did
in Australia, I'd be back to claim the house, and nothing
and no one would stand in my way.

# CHAPTER 14

My life had never moved faster than it did during the months after I'd told Jack that I would be his wife. Our wedding was held the following summer, and we were to leave for Australia the very next day. I was surprised. Jack had been making plans all along. It had never occurred to him that I would not marry him.

The wedding was a big one, even by local standards, and Marge was willing to pay extra, even a nest egg that Grandad Gilbert had left her, for the privilege of seeing me off her hands for good.

I was seventeen that summer, and in my bridal dress I must have looked twenty, for I'd chosen a modern style, short and tight, with a big nylon bow on the back. My hair was piled up in a band, because I'd refused to wear a veil. I didn't want it done properly because I knew that that only happened once, and I wanted to save the proper wedding until the day that I married Piers.

They all turned out, the whole neighbourhood, although some of them looked at me sourly because they knew what I'd been up to with Frank. Even Lily came, although not with Vic, and she only waited outside the church, to pin a horseshoe on as the pictures were taken and to wish me luck with a kiss. She smelled of hair lacquer and Camay soap, and the flowers on our hairbands clashed as we kissed, which made her laugh. I looked at her laughing, and guessed that I was seeing her for the very last time in my life.

Lily may have forgiven me, but I knew that I'd destroyed something in her life, and I knew that when I came back I would have no right to visit her any more.

There was a lot of kissing on that day. Jack kissed me at the altar, and when I closed my eyes to return the kiss I saw Frank's face in my mind and opened them again in a fright. I thought that I heard Frank's bike outside in the street, during the vows, but then I decided it could have been anyone's bike and that I was being stupid and fanciful. But when the reception came, I found out that I had been right after all.

We had sherry at the reception and then we took our places in the line to welcome the guests, and as we did so Frank walked in and stood at the back of the hall. He was there just for a second – I looked away to shake hands with the vicar, and when I looked back he had gone. I felt faint, truly ill, and told Jack I was going outside for some air. Jack looked concerned, but he hadn't seen Frank, and he said he had to stay because someone had to hold the fort.

I slipped out the side door of the church hall, and saw where Frank must have gone. There was a small yard, covered by corrugated iron, and a door across the yard led to the smaller hut where the children met for Sunday school. I walked in slowly, afraid to face Frank, smelling smells that I remembered from my youth. The room was the same, a row of tiny wooden chairs, placed in order, the green-painted one at the top for the best little boy or girl of the week to sit on, and the one with the broken leg and scratched paint at the bottom, by itself, for the naughtiest child. I knew that chair well. I knew how it wobbled, and I could feel its rough wood scratching against my bare legs.

Frank stood behind that chair, a picture of Jesus in all his best forgiveness hanging on the wall behind him. Frank looked pale and hollow-eyed, and it was all I could do to stop myself rushing over and throwing my arms about him. I felt so much that I belonged to him still, despite the fact that I was, by now, married to Jack. But I had my bouquet in my hands, huge cream funeral-lilies that Billy had got me on a whim that I'd had, and my arms were full of those flowers so I kept to my place at the other side of the hall.

Frank rocked my little chair with his foot, so that the wood creaked.

'Why, Ruby?' he asked me. 'Why did you do it? Why did you have to go ahead and marry him? To prove something to me?'

'You fancy yourself, don't you?' I told him, angry that he should get so close to the truth, and angry with myself, for caring.

'You don't love him. You love me.' Frank said these words as a simple statement of fact. He lit up a cigarette and inhaled the smoke deeply, with relief.

'That room in there stinks of coppers, Ruby,' he said. 'I don't know how you can stand it.' The whole of Jack's station had turned up to give him a good send-off.

'There's nothing wrong with coppers,' I told him.

'Your Dad wouldn't agree with you,' he answered, quick as a flash.

'If you hate them that much then I don't know why you came,' I said, perching on the green-painted chair, the best little girl of the week, trying not to ladder my nylons.

'I came to see it because I couldn't believe it,' Frank said, moving up the row of chairs so that he leaned on the one next to mine. 'Pearl told me you were getting married to that copper, but I couldn't believe her. I had to come and make sure it was true. I had to see you go through with it, Ruby.'

'So you've seen Pearl again after all,' I said, fingering my flowers. 'She told me she'd seen the last of you when you went. She must be pleased as punch you're back together again. I suppose you'll be the next ones to wed.

She should've come here too, she could've caught my
bouquet. That's supposed to be lucky for the next bride,
isn't it?'

Frank gripped me round the neck, and I jumped at the
sudden movement. 'Don't play games with me, Ruby,'
he said desperately, and his face moved closer to mine, so
that I could smell him and feel him and I wanted him to
kiss me. He stood like that for a second, just long enough
for me to break apart inside, so that I would have begged
for him to kiss me, and then, when he knew that was
how I felt, that I was under his spell once again, he covered
my mouth with his own, and it was like the first sucking
gulp of air must feel to a man who has been drowning.

'You want me,' he said, his hand running down my
neck to my breasts and my waist, and I wondered how
it must feel, to make love to another man's bride on her
wedding day.

'It'll be the same with Jack,' I said, trying to push his
hand away although I wanted it to stay there with all my
heart. Frank's hands knew my body, they were familiar
with it, just as my hands were familiar with his.

'I'll feel the same,' I repeated, 'once we've done it. It's
only sex. I can't help feeling like this about you. After
tonight I'll have done the same with Jack, and my body
will belong to him instead. I'll change, Frank, though I
can't help how I feel now, you made me like this.'

Frank kissed the top of my breasts, the bits that showed
above my sweetheart neckline, and my head went back
and my spine arched a little and I grabbed at his head with
my hands, my fingers twined in his hair, clutching at him
until his scalp must have been sore.

'It will never be the same as this, Ruby,' Frank said,
sounding breathless. 'You're mine. You belong to me.'

'I belong to Jack,' I said, but my voice sounded weak.

Frank straightened up then, and his face was serious.
'You're still a kid,' he told me. 'You've got a lot to learn,
Ruby. You don't understand yet. One day you'll realize
what I'm talking about. If you go with Jack then you'll

find out too late. I might not be waiting for you, Ruby.
I love you, but I won't wait till I'm old.'

'I'm not a kid,' I said, talking childishly, 'I'm a married
woman.' And as if to prove my point, the door to the
hall fell open and Jack, my husband, walked in.

Jack looked at Frank and me, and his mind quickly
seized on the message that his eyes were sending it. Six
other coppers, mates of his from the local station, in their
smart wedding suits with carnations in their lapels, stood
behind him. A noise came from Jack's throat, a sort of
growling animal noise, and then he flew at Frank without
saying a word.

Jack moved fast but Frank was faster, and he sprang to
his feet, grabbing one of the chairs to ward Jack off.
They stood there, staring at one another, Jack weaving
backwards and forwards from one foot to the other, waiting his moment, while Frank waved the chair-legs at him
like a lion-tamer with a lion. One of his mates grabbed
me and pulled me out of the way, or I'd have joined in
with them, though God knows on whose side.

Then Jack pounced, grabbing at Frank's chair and
throwing it so hard that it shattered on the opposite wall.
He aimed a punch at Frank which hit him on the chin,
but the blow all but missed, so Frank barely tottered. Jack
came back with another punch, but missed totally this
time, which made him angrier.

'Steady, Jack!' one of the policemen called out, but Jack
was deaf to all help. He went for Frank's neck this time,
both hands raised to throttle the life out of him, and at
that Frank must have decided that he'd had enough. He
gave Jack a low and loud punch in the stomach that had
the others wincing audibly, and he followed it with
another on the side of the head that sent Jack sprawling
to the floor.

Jack went to get up, with murder in his eyes, but the
others stopped him, holding him down by his arms.

'What the hell were you doing with my wife?' Jack
shouted, still straining to break away.

Frank pulled out a handkerchief and dusted a mark from his jacket. 'Just kissing the bride,' he said coolly. Then he looked across at me. 'You'd better watch out for her,' he said, nodding in my direction. 'She's a better puncher than you are. She nearly broke a tooth trying to fight me off. You'd better get her to give you some lessons, copper.' And Frank rubbed his jaw, as though it was sore.

The relief that I felt when he said that was overwhelming, because Jack had seen nothing more than the two of us standing together, and I could see from his eyes when he looked over at me that Frank had got me off the hook.

'Are you OK, Ruby?' he asked me, looking concerned. 'Did the bastard hurt you?'

I shook my head. 'It's all right,' I said quietly. 'He was just larking about. He didn't do anything. Just a peck on the cheek.'

'You'd better clear off, son, before we book you with something,' one of Jack's friends said, tilting his head towards the door. Frank went toward the door, but he took his time because he had more to say first. He smirked at Jack, still half-kneeling on the floor, his arms still held down by his friends, and then he looked over at me and his face went serious.

'Be good, Ruby,' he said, looking deep into my eyes. 'Oh, by the way,' he added, 'I forgot to bring you a wedding present. Can it keep?' he asked.

I nodded, afraid that he'd set Jack off again.

'I'll send it on then,' Frank said. 'You'll get it when you get to Australia. Something to remind you of me.'

And Frank's words were to haunt me over the next few weeks, when they were to come true in a way that even he probably hadn't imagined.

I was up with the dawn the following day, and out by myself to say my goodbyes to the market. Jack was not there to stop me, for we'd spent the night of our wedding sleeping in separate rooms. It was Jack's mother who'd put us up, for we were short of cash once our passage was paid for, and unable to afford even the cheapest hotel. Her house was in Ludlow Street, some two miles from the reception, and Jack's mates had carried him all the way there, drunk as he was with the beer that he'd downed after the set-to with Frank. It was Jack's mother who came back in the car with me, her lips tighter than the clasp on her purse, and who pushed me rudely through the doorway, when, by rights, it should have been my new husband carrying me over the threshold.

'Save yourself,' she'd said to me when Jack stumbled into the hallway. 'I know how to deal with him. You'll sleep down here,' and she showed me the lounge, with the settee already made up with a blanket, waiting for me.

I tossed and turned all night, thinking of Jack and Frank, and at first light I was up to clear my head with a last walk round the market. I'd hoped to wake belonging to Jack, with Frank well and truly scrubbed from my mind, but it hadn't turned out like that and instead I felt lonely and still part of Frank.

'It will get better,' I told myself under my breath, 'I've just got to wait. One more night, that's all, and I'll feel married at last.' I'd love my husband, I knew I would, I just needed him to work the same magic on me that Frank had done, that was all.

I hadn't expected to be choked up by the market. It was dirty with empty crisp packets blowing about, but when I walked down the deserted street a huge lump formed in my throat, stopping me from breathing, and the only way it went away and stopped choking me was when I let the tears out at last. They ran down my face and I wiped them away with my knuckles. Places must look best when you're leaving them – I could think of no other reason why that dead-end hole should have brought out such a violent reaction in me.

I cried some more and I kicked a few stones about in the rubbish, and then for some reason I remembered Pearl's words that day in her flat. 'I'll never forgive you for all that you've done, Ruby,' she'd said, her dark eyes staring just as if she were mad. 'You tried to take Dad from us and when that didn't work you set your mind at taking Frank from me instead, you're lying when you say you didn't. I almost believed you when you said it wasn't your fault, but only for my mum's sake. You're her daughter and I thought there must be good in you somewhere, but I can tell I was wrong. You must have been born evil, Ruby, it must run in your veins along with the blood. You've taken Frank away from me just as surely as if you'd killed him, Ruby. I won't forget that, believe me, one day I'll get my revenge for that!'

I wasn't evil, though. I just knew what I wanted out of life, and there was nothing wrong with that as far as I could see. Pearl was weak, and in my book that made her stupid and her threats ineffectual. She didn't worry me, she couldn't, and the thought sort of warmed me and dried up all my tears. I was off to a faraway country and I was set to make my fortune. Pearl couldn't harm me and neither could Frank. I was married, I was a wife, and I was going to be rich.

I looked up at the sky and it reminded me of the ceiling at Rowan Hall and it was then that the tears started again because somewhere deep down inside I was frightened, frightened to be leaving Billy and frightened that now I was leaving I might never be back. I might stay in Australia and I might die there. Fear and self-pity flooded over me in terrible waves, and it was only Pearl's threat that made me snap out of it.

'I'll get my revenge, believe me,' she'd said. I picked up a stone and lobbed it through the glass of an empty shop window. It landed with a crash that made me scream.

'You won't!' I screamed. 'You bloody well won't, you stupid cow!'

And that was my farewell to the market.

# Book Two

## EMIGRATION

# CHAPTER 15

I t was grey and damp on the day that we left England,
and I was forced to wear my mac, even though I'd
promised it to Jack's mother, who'd said I wouldn't be
needing it once I got out to Australia. Only a small,
straggly group of friends turned out to see us off, as most
were hung over from the wedding, and a lot couldn't
afford the trip to the station. I stood shivering at Waterloo,
even though it wasn't that cold, and although Jack had
been frosty with me until then, for running off that morning without telling him where I was going, my obvious
misery at saying goodbye to Billy seemed to warm him
up a bit. He put his arms round my shoulders and told
me he would make it all up to me in time.

'I'll look after you now, Ruby,' Jack said, squeezing me
to his body. 'I'm your husband now and it's me you'll be
looking to for help. I'll make a go of it out there, Ruby,
I swear to you that I will. I'll make us rich, and I'll make
you really proud of me. You'll have nothing to regret,
I'll make sure of that.'

'I'm proud of you already,' I told Jack, snuffling into
his hankie as I did so, and at that moment I really did
believe I loved him, and that everything would be all
right, as he said.

Billy grabbed me just as the train got in, and he hugged
me hard. He smelled of all the good things that I was

leaving, of the fruit and the dank smells of the vegetables and of the dust in the market, and that fresh, outdoor smell of the winds that blow down there, and I cried so hard at leaving him that the others thought I would be taken ill. Marge pulled out some smelling salts that she'd bought for the wedding and held them under my nose until my eyes streamed with ammonia tears instead of the sad, salty ones I'd been crying, and then Jack pulled me away and by the time we were on the train my eyes had cleared. I saw Billy's face through the yellow, smoke-stained window, with Marge just behind him, her face wide and pink with relief, and I felt sick, really sick, so that I ran for the toilet and arrived just in time for Jack's mother's breakfast to come up part-digested.

'You all right?' Jack asked when I got back to my seat, and I nodded that I was, but I saw him frown, and when I looked at my reflection in the glass I could see that I looked really peaky.

'Don't let on you've been sick,' Jack said when the courier came round, 'or they might not let us go.' And he pinched my cheeks gently, to bring some of the colour back into them. Once the train had pulled out Jack went off to the buffet and came back with two bottles of beer and a cup of strong, bitter-tasting tea. When I'd finished the tea he tried to get me to drink some of the beer, but I'd never had a taste for alcohol and the smell of the beer only sent me rushing off back to the toilet again.

I was gone for longer this time, and when I got back to our compartment I found Jack's seat was empty. I assumed he'd returned to the buffet, but when he finally came back, weaving his way down the carriage, I saw he was empty-handed.

'Ruby,' he whispered, and his face was red with excitement, 'you'll never guess!' He was picking my mac up and getting our things together as he spoke. 'Up the train,' he said, 'in first class – my old commanding officer from the army. He's with his wife and kids and they're emigrating too. They've asked us to join them. Get yourself together.' Jack pulled me up and looked me straight in the eye. 'Mind what you say, Ruby,' he added, smelling of beer. 'They're quality people, remember. I don't want us to go making the wrong impression.'

Jack's CO was a small man, with greying hair and red, vein-mottled cheeks. He stood to shake my hand just as the train ran over the points, and he swayed and fell against me for a second, grabbing my waist as he did so. His wife looked younger and very elegant. She remained in her seat, looking away quickly as her husband lurched towards me. Her legs were slim like her face, and she wore a cream full-length coat with a small beaver collar. Her dark-reddish hair was pulled straight off her face and partly hidden by a small pillbox hat on the back of her head. She was the sort of woman that Piers might have known, and I knew how good her voice would sound before she even opened her mouth.

'My wife,' the CO said with a smile, and the woman bent her head slightly in acknowledgement.

'Philippa,' she said, as though correcting him.

'Yes,' the CO said, 'and you must call me Ralph.' He spoke to me as if addressing a ten-year-old.

'Where are your children?' I asked, looking round, and Philippa smiled.

'They're being taken care of,' she told me, mysteriously.

Jack stowed our luggage on the rack and sat down opposite Philippa, patting the seat beside him for me to sit down as well.

'But this is first class,' I whispered, shocked because I knew that we only had second-class tickets.

Jack blushed. 'I'll take care of that if and when the collector comes around,' he said, speaking through clenched teeth.

'And you a policeman,' Philippa said, uncrossing her legs and smoothing her skirt. 'Well, well!'

'Ex-copper,' Jack told her with a smile. 'I do what I

please now. Some other poor sod's wearing my uniform by now, and good luck to him.'

'No joy in civvy street then?' Ralph asked, biting on the stem of an unlit pipe. His shirt was a real one, white matt cotton, not drip-dry like Jack's. He shook his head sadly without waiting for Jack to answer. 'Common story, I'm afraid,' he said, 'lot of the chaps couldn't settle once they got back. Just taken you a little longer to find out, that's all, eh?'

Jack shrugged in agreement. 'Once you've seen a bit of the world you don't want to know London any more,' he told Ralph. 'It all looked different, anyway, by the time that I'd got back. I was just waiting for young Ruby here to make up her mind before I buggered off, that was all.'

Ralph laughed politely at Jack's joke, and Philippa allowed her gaze to wander out of the window again.

'You're off for the same reasons then, are you?' Jack asked.

'Good Lord, no,' Ralph said. 'We're not emigrating or anything as bold as that. We're just going out there for business – well, I am, anyway. Philippa has relatives in Australia, which is why we're taking the kids. Turn it into a bit of a holiday, so to speak. I have a little place in Sydney, as a matter of fact. Useful for these sort of trips.'

Jack looked surprised. He'd assumed they were going for good, like us.

'I'm from Australia,' Philippa told us. 'My family own land out there.'

'You've lost your accent then,' I said, trying to be friendly.

'We're not all diggers and okkers you know,' Philippa said, and that shut me up for the rest of the journey.

The two men shared a few beers, and Jack was so impressed to be sitting with his old CO and calling him Ralph – a man he would never dared to speak to during his time in the army – that he almost seemed to have forgotten that I was there, until two children came rushing in, closely followed by the courier who had been looking after them.

'Kids, eh?' Jack said, and he reached out a hand and ruffled the smaller one's hair.

'Just the ticket,' Ralph said with pride. The two small boys were smart, red-cheeked kids with the sort of cherry-eyed responsive faces that you only saw on children of the middle- and upper-classes.

'None of your own yet?' Ralph asked.

'No, no,' Jack said, grinning bashfully. 'We only got married yesterday. This trip is a kind of a honeymoon as well, isn't it Ruby?' And he dug me in the side with his elbow.

'A child bride?' Philippa said, eyeing me from top to toe. There was something in her gaze that made me shudder. She was perhaps the most elegant woman that I had ever seen, and I yearned to look and act like her. Her nails were long and painted blood-red, and there was a slight gap between her front teeth. Her teeth were small and curved slightly inward; they were fox's teeth, like Frank's.

I watched Philippa cross and uncross her long legs and you could hear her stockings rub together as she did so. She made the atmosphere in that rattling carriage electric with each small movement of her body. Only her husband seemed unaware of her languid sensuality. Jack and I were both transfixed and unable to speak.

I looked down at my lap and kept my own legs well out of sight under the seat. I felt fat sitting so close to that woman. My skirt was too short and if I had tried crossing my legs in the way that she did, old Ralph would have got a view of my knickers.

'Are you good with children?' Philippa asked me, sounding for all the world as though she were interviewing me for a position as a nanny. I shrugged and looked at Jack.

'She won't know yet,' Jack said quickly, angry with me for being too shy to answer. 'She hasn't come across any at home,' he added. 'There's only been her and her dad up till now.'

'A small family,' Ralph said, beaming. 'Your father must have been sorry to see you go. I know I will be the day my brood decide to fly the coop.' He patted his boys on their heads to show us who it was he was talking about.

Philippa looked surprised. 'I thought all you lot came from huge families,' she said, and by 'you lot' she could have been referring to anything.

Jack missed the slight. 'We'll make up for it though, won't we, Ruby?' he asked me, patting my knee just like Ralph had patted his kids' heads. 'Australia's the place to bring kids up from what I've heard,' he went on. 'We'll soon have a few of them on the go once we get out there, won't we, Ruby?'

I felt shocked. 'We've got to make our fortune first,' I said, and they all laughed at me, even the bigger of the boys.

'You leave that side of things to me,' Jack told me. 'You're a wife now. You'll have your hands full enough.'

'I'm going to start a business,' I insisted. I had to. It was the reason I was making the trip. Australia was a land where anything was possible. It was the place where I intended to make my fortune.

'What did you think of doing, Ruby?' Jack asked, and his face looked angry behind his smile. 'Selling fruit from a stall, like your dad?'

I stood my ground. 'A shop,' I told Jack, 'or something like that. Perhaps we could run a small café.'

Jack gripped my hand hard. 'So I'm in on this one too, am I?' he asked.

'It's been done before,' Philippa said, and we all turned to look at her. 'You should listen to your little child bride, Jack, she's talking sense. You've got to think big in a place like Australia, or you'll soon get sucked under and find yourself worse off than you were back home. A small

EMIGRATION                                    143

shop could be just the thing. Ruby could run it while you
were off at another job.'

Jack reddened and I smiled at Philippa, pleased and
grateful that she seemed to be taking my side.

'If it's capital you need there may be a few people I
could put you in touch with who might help,' Philippa
added, talking to Jack.

'Thanks,' was all that Jack could mumble in reply, and
I could tell that he was seething with rage at being shown
up.

Jack had changed in the years that I'd known him, but
I suppose I'd been too close to notice. When we'd first
met he'd been saucy and full of sap, taking any excuse to
get a feel at me, for as long as he knew that it shocked
me. Then as I'd grown, and Jack's intentions had become
more serious, he'd backed off a bit, keeping me on ice,
so to speak. I hadn't understood why at the time, it was
as though he'd been playing a game of hard-to-get, but I
was naïve then, despite my experiences with Frank. You
don't see things when you're sixteen, you just charge
headlong like a speeding train, and the rest of the world
is a blur on all sides. You only slow down when you start
needing help. Then you let the rest of the world catch up
with you, scouring its faces for one that looks friendly.
Before going to Rowan Hall that night with Frank, I'd
kidded myself that all I needed was Jack: Jack the husband,
Jack the policeman, Jack the father, who had taken over
the reins from Billy, and who would protect me for ever
as I set out into the world. All of this, and from a man I
had scarcely bothered to look at in detail.

I looked at Jack then, and wondered about his body.
Bullet-headed, with white soap trapped in the snail-like
curl of his ear, where he'd shaved in a hurry. Light eye-
lashes that seemed to blink more than most people's and
grew quicker when Jack got angry. A neck that always
wore collars, small moles trapped beneath the starch. Hair
so light on the backs of his hands that it looked like silver
fur. When we were alone that night I knew that Jack's

anger would be gone. Jack would unravel. He would overwhelm and overpower me and I would be open and ready for him. I would belong to him at last, and my thoughts of Frank would be driven from my brain.

'Are you all right, Ruby?' Jack asked, noticing me staring at him. I yawned and scrubbed at my eyes with my knuckles. For a moment I'd forgotten where I was.

'She's tired,' he told the others, and then I watched as he reddened in embarrassment as Philippa pulled a face and Ralph coughed into his hand. 'I didn't mean from last night . . .' he said, trying to cover his tracks, but he was getting in deeper and he knew it. Newly-weds are always a source of some good leg-pulls and although Ralph was too polite to joke, you could tell what he was thinking by the saucy wink he gave me. Jack should've taken it all in good part and just laughed, but my husband wasn't like that. He'd made a fool of himself in front of his CO and I could tell he thought it was my fault, for yawning.

# CHAPTER 16

The docks at Southampton were packed with emigrating families – small, tear-sodden, shocked-faced family groups, huddled together like so many islands with the great grey sea behind them. Some stood rigid, not touching, weak smiles of polite resignation cracked across their faces. Others still clung like old toffee, unable to separate until the order came to board the ship. Scattered among these sad little tableaux were the ordinary trippers, wealthy, well-heeled holiday-makers like Ralph and Philippa who wove silently and respectfully among the mourners, like ushers at a funeral.

I was glad I'd said my goodbyes back in London. With Billy clinging to my neck and the black ship bobbing gently in the waters behind us like some waiting monster, the only way they could have got me on board would have been to carry me screaming. My face felt hot and my head ached. I smelled the sea for the first time in my life and the smell made me think of black wet caves filled with green slime and seaweed, and the wind blew then, and my lips when I licked them tasted salt, so I held my hankie over my face and mouth until the smell and the tastes went away.

'Ozone!' Ralph shouted above the waves and the screeching birds. 'Good for you!' And he took in a good lungful, expanding his chest till he looked like a turkey.

'It stinks,' I said, coughing, and Philippa raised her eyes to the heavens. Their luggage all matched. It stood in a huge mountain; trunks, suitcases and soft, belted bags, waiting to be loaded, tripping people up as they made their way to the gangplank.

We had two cardboard cases and a MacFisheries carrier full of last-minute things that Marge had given me. I nursed the carrier in my arms like a baby because one of its handles had broken. In the top was a jar of Golden Shred marmalade and I could feel something broken and oozing nearer the bottom.

'You do love me, Jack?' I asked. Staring at the sea, I felt lost in the enormity of it all. That great, heaving, green-glass mass was endless and bottomless. Gulls swooped on the surface as sailors threw buckets of swill. The ship looked a monster, but it still seemed so small compared to the sea, and I was even smaller. Jack appeared not to have heard my question. I caught him looking at Philippa, who was posing for her son's photograph.

Jack turned to me then, a half-smile still on his face as though he'd been watching something that pleased him, and he realized by my expression that I'd spoken.

'You what?' he asked, cupping one hand to his ear.

'Love me, Jack?' I asked. 'I said do you love me then?' Jack laughed and rubbed my nose with his fingers, which was his way of saying that he did.

'You look like a kid in that mac,' he said, and I made him laugh by pretending to wipe my nose on my sleeve. Then he remembered Ralph and Philippa were nearby and stopped laughing quickly.

The sea smelled bad, but the ship smelled worse. There was oil and rust and a smell of diesel, like you get from taxis, and my stomach churned from the moment I stepped on board. That smell is a constant memory to me, and I can summon it up now in my mind, some twenty years later, as fresh as it was to me then.

The courier was a small woman with the sort of smile you could crack with an ice-pick, and she looked surprised when she saw we had no kids. 'Women's quarters on deck "B",' she told us, exposing her bra through her armhole as she pointed somewhere off to the right. 'Men's on deck "D", right down the bottom, I'm afraid.' Her smile grew puckered in a display of fake regret.

'You mean there's no married berths?' Ralph butted in. He and Philippa had already found their cabins. They were in a walnut-panelled suite on what I would have called the ground floor. But then they were there for the fun, not 'Ten Pound Fares' like the rest of us.

'We're on honeymoon!' I said, and Jack cut me dead with a look.

The woman looked at her list, running down it with the stub of a Lakeland pencil.

'There's no mention of that here,' she said frowning, looking concerned.

I looked at Jack.

'I never thought to say,' he said, looking at Ralph. He'd cleaned his suitcase with bootblack to try and get rid of the scuffs, and there were stains on his hands because he'd done the handles too, by mistake.

'Can't you juggle things around a bit?' Ralph asked, taking control and giving the courier a 'just-between-the-two-of-us' look, as though he were about to slip her a tenner for the trouble. The woman looked at Ralph and you could tell that she knew he was quality. Ralph's army years had given him a voice that put him light years above mere mortals like Jack and myself. The courier even stopped chewing on her Juicy Fruit as a mark of respect, although you could still smell the gum's sticky sweetness in the air between us.

'It's not as easy as that, sir,' she said, clutching her clipboard so tight to her chest that her pen leaked on to her blouse. 'There are no mixed quarters for the assisted passage passengers. We do try to make other arrangements if a couple are on honeymoon, but of course we do need telling in advance. We do try to be as accommodating as possible, but you do understand that it's not always in our power.'

She smiled a sickly chewing-gum smile at Ralph. I looked grief-stricken, but Jack had had enough public discussion of our sleeping arrangements and was off in the opposite direction.

'How bloody inconvenient for you,' Philippa said, opening up a compact and surveying her face in the mirror. There was a shred of tobacco on one of her front teeth, and she hooked it off with the tip of a nail. 'And I bet he was a victim of the old BD on his wedding night too, wasn't he, darling?'

I looked at Philippa with interest. 'BD?' I asked.

'Brewer's droop, darling,' she said without a smile. 'Most men are totally incapable of getting it up on the first night, it's a well-known fact. The trouble is, they think they're God's gift at the same time. Takes a terrible show of huffing and heaving and mutual sweat before they realize that the old John Thomas just isn't going to perform on command. I just hope you managed to keep a straight face.'

I looked at Ralph's ramrod back disappearing down the passage after Jack, and I could feel my face redden. 'We slept apart last night,' I told Philippa quietly.

'Oh, ho ho! The plot thickens!' she laughed. 'You'll be telling me next that you're a virgin too.'

I could smell her perfume as she came closer. Her breath smelled of violets and she tilted my face up to meet her own. Her eyes looked yellow, like a tiger's, but it must have been the lights on the ship.

'We can't have this, now, can we?' she asked. 'Poor old Jack will be going frantic with lust, stuck down there with all those other men like that, won't he?' and she smiled, a thin humourless kind of smile. 'And you'll be wanting to know what it's all about too, won't you?'

I nodded. I could never have told her about me and Frank, and what had gone on between us.

'Don't be in too much of a hurry though, darling,'

Philippa went on, snapping her compact shut like a trap and throwing it back into her handbag. 'There's not a lot to get excited about, you'll see. A bit of heaving and a few grunts and they're ready for a cigarette.' She grabbed my arm and walked me in the direction of the women's quarters. 'You'd never think something as crude and sweaty and boring as all that could produce the next generation now, would you?'

I shook my head. All I could see in my mind was Ralph's naked squirming body lying on top of Philippa. Cool, languid, yellow-eyed Philippa. She would be looking over Ralph's sweaty shoulder into a compact mirror.

'Your kids came out all right from it,' I said, trying to change the subject a bit.

'Oh, they're not *my* children, thank God!' Philippa told me. 'They're Ralph's. His first wife died, I think, out in Africa. Of boredom, probably,' and with a snorting laugh she threw open my cabin door.

I made my way to the deck as the ship was taking its leave of the port, and I squeezed into a little spot by the rail. It's a wonder the ship didn't list and tip us all into the water, there were so many of us hanging over the side, waving at the few people dotted about on the quayside. The sun had turned hazy by then, and there was drizzle that could have been sea-spray, wetting our tear-soggy faces. It was getting dark by the time we pulled out of port, and as the ship turned its face away from England and off in the direction of Australia, I ran round to the stern to watch until the horizon disappeared out of sight. The dockyard blurred and swam in front of my eyes and I cursed my own tears for stopping me seeing the view. I wiped my eyes with my fingers, for once untroubled by the mascara which must have run down my cheeks in ribbons. I had to look. I had to keep staring till it was gone.

Jack came and found me. 'Whatcha lost?' he asked, seeing me gazing at the land.

'Nothing,' I said. 'Just saying goodbye to England,

that's all.' But I was lying, and I knew it. I was busy
hating myself because I knew what it was that I was
looking for, and it wasn't the last view of England, not
by a long chalk. It was Frank that I was looking for; Frank
whom I had refused, and Frank whom I had not married.
I'd thought he would come. I'd expected him to be there.
I had listened for his bike and, when the ship's engines
got too loud to listen, I had squinted my eyes to see his
leather jacket in the gloom. I'd turned him down and told
myself I had no need of him and yet here I was, waiting
for him to come, and here I was, crying into the mist
because he hadn't arrived in time. I'd truly thought he'd
be there to save me.

I watched the gulls pick the last dregs from the sea and
I thought my heart would break on the waves. Hating
yourself is a terrible business, and something I was new
to in those days. I've since learned to be indulgent to my
own little inconsistencies, but the fear of not understand-
ing my own mind was fresh to me then, and all the more
sharp and painful for that.

Why did I want Frank? I knew what it was that he
stood for, and I knew that his life contained nothing that
I wanted. Frank was rubbish, nothing better, and yet here
I was wailing for him like the birds who mourned the last
crusts of bread as they sank out of reach. Thinking back,
I believe that I wanted it all, Frank and Jack and Billy and
Vic and Piers and the house, and perhaps my tears showed
I was at last learning that you have to make choices. I'd
picked Jack, and that was an end to it.

In my heart I still clung to the thought that sex was a
magical business, and that, once it was done with Jack,
Frank's spell would be over and my mind would be
cleared. Yet there on the deck of that ship I found myself
shuddering beneath Jack's friendly, protective arm, and
yearning to be touched again by Frank.

I was sick the next day, and each day after that, and Jack
told me I'd have to find my sea legs, and Philippa gave

me aspirin and some cologne to sniff from a hankie. I couldn't get the measure of Philippa, and often felt tired just trying. I found her fascinating to look at, and often watched her. Most people did, I discovered, but that never seemed to trouble Philippa, who always appeared unself-conscious and almost unaware of the effect that she had on everyone around her. Philippa was stylish in a way that I'd never seen in any woman before, and I suppose I watched her to learn how to be like her. Philippa could've handled Piers all right. She would have had him twisted round her little finger in no time. But that was just on the surface. Philippa's emotions were buried fathoms down, if, in fact, she had any. The strongest feeling I ever saw her display was a sort of mild exasperation, an expression which was never far from her features, especially when Ralph was around.

Women round our way had often joked about their husbands or called them names behind their backs, but Philippa was the first woman I'd ever met who dared to do it to his face. As the trip went on and we saw more of them I began to wonder whether Ralph actually enjoyed it, so to speak. When Ralph spoke, Philippa turned away with a bored expression. When he laughed or cracked a joke she'd inspect her fingernails in silence. When they danced in the evening she would return to the table rubbing her feet, as if he had trodden on them, although I'd found him a good dancer myself. It was Jack who was clumsy on the floor, Jack with his size twelve policeman's feet, and yet when Philippa danced with him you'd think she'd crossed pumps with Victor Sylvester himself.

I caught Jack looking at Philippa in a certain way more than once, and I remembered what she'd said about him getting into a frenzy, alone in the men's quarters at night. I even suggested Jack come into my cabin during the day, when the elderly lady I shared with would be out on a stroll round the deck.

'No,' Jack said flatly. 'It wouldn't be proper, Ruby.'

'Others do it,' I told him, although I didn't know that
for a fact. 'There's a chair we could put against the door
in case anyone came.' I knew the crew were up to all sorts
themselves anyway, so it wouldn't get us into any trouble.
There was a girl my own age in the cabin next door
who was emigrating with her family to Perth. She was
working her way through the crew on that trip, she'd
told me that much herself. She was scared there'd be no
men where she was going, so she was making up for the
shortage on the way. But Jack was not for turning.

'You deserve better, Ruby,' he said, kissing me. 'I don't
want some knee-trembler up behind a door. This has got
to be special for us, Ruby. You're my wife now, not
some two-bit scrubber I've met on the beat. You deserve
something special, that's all. Besides,' he added, looking
at my pale face, 'you're not so good at the moment. Being
afloat doesn't agree with you. Waiting till we get on dry
land won't hurt. You'll feel more up to it then.'

I'd felt 'up to it' for the past two weeks but, of course,
I couldn't tell Jack that one. Instead it was me, not him,
who lay in bed at night tormented by needs that seemed
to be splitting me apart.

About halfway into our voyage the weather started to
clear, and we began for the first time to feel that we really
were off to somewhere new. I tried to write to Billy while
I was on board the ship, I knew he would have been
chuffed to get something on the headed paper they gave
us, but each time my pen touched the paper my eyes
would mist with tears, as they had done when we'd sailed
out of harbour, and I'd get a lump the size of an egg in
my throat, and be unable to write.

Billy would have loved to have heard about all that
went on on board, of the games they organized during
the day, and different sports and competitions, just like
Butlins, and then the dinners we had at night, sitting with
the fully-paid passengers just as if we were rich and on a
cruise. I saved all the menus they gave us, but there was
never anyone to show them to. Besides, I never ate much

of the food as I was most times sick-scared that I'd make a fool of myself.

Philippa was all right. She could have peeled a grape with a butter knife if she'd needed to, but I was too busy juggling soup spoons and cake forks to get much into my mouth. Jack poured his tea into his saucer at the first breakfast we had, and he soon realized his mistake when he saw everyone staring at us. That was about the only time I saw Philippa with a genuine laugh to smother. Jack looked about, and then he quickly gave the saucer to me, as though it was me he'd been doing it for all along. I looked at him long and hard, just to show that it wasn't, and poured the tea back into his cup without even spilling so much as a drop.

The weather turned warmer still, until it was tropical, and Philippa said there'd have to be a storm to break it, or we'd all die of the heat. They let us sleep up on deck then, and it was those nights that came to be the happiest of my trip. The sky would be purple, not inky-black like in London, and you could barely see the join where the aubergine horizon met and merged with the heaving grey seas.

Most passengers just lay out on the decks and, with blankets thrown over them, got on with things they couldn't do in their single-sex cabins by night. Even the crew turned a blind eye, and you could hear the gentle moans of pleasure coming from dark nooks all over.

Jack would have none of it, though, and we slept on chairs, our heads resting on hard, sailcloth pillows, holding hands in the gentle sway and list of the ship. Then one night the peace was shattered.

I woke to find Jack's hand gone from my grasp and when I turned to find him, his chair was empty. Groggy with sleep I pulled off the blanket, wiping my face which was damp with sweat on the corner as I did so. The ship was still, even the lovers had tired at last and were sleeping. Jack had not gone far, though; I found him nearer the stern, leaning over the rail and watching the waves

break on the bows. Beside him was Philippa, and she
looked like a ghost in the moonlight. She was wearing a
white satin slip, and she must have come straight from
her bed. Jack was in his vest and pants, and his blanket
was tied about his waist. They were talking quietly and
with a sort of intensity that I had never seen them share
during the day. Philippa looked beautiful, even more
beautiful than usual. Her hair was loose and softer around
her face. Her lips looked full and wet. Her eyes caught
the moonlight as she studied Jack's full, blank-featured
face. Then she lifted a hand and touched his arm, allowing
her fingers to rest on the muscle that swells out above the
elbow. I thought that Jack would do what is proper and
pull away, but he stayed there talking as though nothing
had happened.

'Where did you go last night?' I asked him in the
morning.

Jack looked surprised. I had caught him in the middle
of folding the blankets and he stopped what he was doing
before coming up with an answer.

'What do you mean, Ruby?' he said.

'I woke up,' I told him. 'You were gone.'

'Off for a pee then, I expect,' he answered. 'Why?
Nothing wrong with that, is there?'

I couldn't stop there.

'You were with Philippa,' I said, staring at him. 'I saw
you.'

'Then you knew where I was,' Jack said, throwing the
blankets down on the chair. 'So why ask?'

'What did she want, Jack?' I asked him, and I could
hear my own voice sounding childish.

Jack looked at me and I could see that he was thinking.
'Ralph was taken ill last night,' he said finally. 'Something
he got abroad, evidently. Philippa got worried and came
to see if I could help.'

'Why didn't she see the ship's doctor then?' I said.

'She didn't want to make a fuss,' was all that Jack would

say, and then he went off with the blankets, which I took
to mean the conversation was closed.

# CHAPTER 17

Six weeks it took us to get to Australia, and by the end of that time you would have said I'd quietened a lot and lost some of my fight. Frank would barely have known me. I was thinner through seasickness and more thoughtful, thanks to Philippa. That woman had turned me inside-out. I should have hated her for making a play for my husband, and yet I felt a kind of remote detachment when I thought about Jack, while I was too much in awe of Philippa to have ever hated her as I knew that I'd hated Pearl.

Philippa didn't want Jack in the way Pearl had wanted Frank. Philippa was just playing, like a cat plays with a mouse. I watched her each and every move with fascination. I was too busy wanting to be like her to hate her.

'There it is then, Ruby,' Jack said, an arm dangling around my shoulders as we pulled into Melbourne Harbour. He'd spoken with a note of pride in his voice, but I couldn't see anything to be proud about. We'd all lined up against the rail that morning, hoping to get the first glimpse of our new and wonderful country, but what we saw turned our tongues to lead in our mouths. It was raining hard and the turn of the wind made the rain beat straight into our faces. The harbour was grey and bare, and a straggling line of wharfies awaited our approach, pale-skinned and staring as we stared back from the ship.

'Shake a leg then,' Jack said, pulling me by the arm in his impatience to be off the boat.

'I can't live here,' I told him flatly.

Jack laughed. 'She says she's changed her mind,' he called up to Ralph and Philippa, who were leaning on the deck rail above. 'She doesn't like the look of it here after all.'

Ralph laughed back. 'Too late to change your mind now, Ruby!' he called. 'They don't do round trips on this thing. You're an Australian now, you know, and this is your home.'

'Ruby can go back if she wants,' I heard Philippa say to him. 'There will be nothing to hold her out here.'

I turned quickly to look up at her, to see if I had heard her properly, but she was tying a headscarf in the wind and made no response.

We were split into three groups once we'd got off the ship; the ones who had relatives were met and taken off in cars, while the visitors like Ralph and Philippa left in the line of taxis that were waiting. Philippa pressed a large case into my arms just as her taxi was pulling out – it was stuffed full of summer dresses, and I almost cried at the indignity of receiving her charity. I needed clothes too desperately, though, to ever give them back.

That left Jack and me and a small group of passengers, waiting on the dockside like dogs waiting for an owner. Then we saw our courier waving from a bus. The bus was old and battered and painted green, like they are in the country in England.

'There's our taxi!' Jack said cheerfully, and he set off at a good pace like a kid on a school outing. He sat me near the window so I could 'get a good view of the country', and then he went to sit up front with the driver, just as though he were still in uniform. The windows were steamed with the heat and the rain, and I drew faces in the steam, like I used to do when I was a kid. My mac felt heavy and itchy and smelled musty from the rain, and the water had filled the flat sandals Jack had made me put on.

'You can't hobble around in your heels over here,
Ruby,' he'd told me that morning when he'd seen what
I was wearing. 'Australians dress for casual comfort, you
know. They won't know what to make of a young
woman in stiletto heels and a skirt that tight.' And he'd
rooted in my case till he'd come up with something he'd
considered more suitable.

So there I sat, the picture of misery, in an Aertex blouse
and cotton pleated skirt, roasting in my mac, with my
school sandals on my feet and an old scarf of Marge's on
my head. I'd wanted to take Australia by storm. I had
imagined leaving the ship like a film star, with the locals
queuing to see what real Londoners looked like, but here
I sat, huddled and miserable, looking for all the world
like some hairy great kid on her first school outing.

The bus was full of little kids, and on cue they all
seemed to start crying at once. That noise in turn was the
driver's cue to pull away. A couple of youngsters cheered
as we pulled out of the docks, but most of us had caught
the mood of gloom by then and the noise echoed hollowly
in the stuffy silence.

I've never forgotten my first view of Australia, it is as
strong now in my mind as that trip down to Surrey with
Frank. To Jack it seemed like heaven, but to me it was
the worst kind of hell. From the little I saw of the towns
we drove through, they seemed flat and dull and feature-
less after London. I'd thought to find signs of vast wealth,
but there was nothing here to envy, even when the rain
stopped. The flatness got worse once we drove into the
country, and we could see the camp we'd be housed in
coming up from miles off.

'It's a bleedin' concentration camp!' someone shouted
from the back of the bus, and the kids recommenced their
wailing. For two pins I would have been joining them.
We finally pulled up in front of a row of huts and when
we got off the bus the heat burned the air from our lungs.

'I thought they'd done away with these places,' a
woman said, trying to keep her child from running away

from her, but losing the battle because he was as slippery
as an eel from sweat and she couldn't get a grip on his
limbs.

The courier threw her a glance. 'You're lucky to get
in, as a matter of fact,' she said. 'They've all but stopped
allowing entry to Britons without accommodation.
Besides,' she added, shielding her eyes from the sun,
'you'll only be here temporarily. Your men will get jobs
and then you'll be off. This is just a halfway house, till
you find somewhere better.'

When we got to the gates we were given a knife, fork
and spoon each, and a metal mug for our tea. Then we
were led to our huts.

'There's no wardrobe,' I exclaimed.

'You had no bleedin' wardrobe at home, Ruby,' Jack
replied, and I could tell even he was getting to the end of
his tether. 'I don't feel right here,' he said, pacing the
length of our room. 'They're like the huts that we had in
the army. I feel like I'm on bleedin' parade or something.'

The hut was small, and only a cardboard partition stood
between us and the family next door. Jack put his ear to
this wall.

'You can hear them talk!' he told me. 'Every flamin'
word, Ruby!'

I could see what he was getting at. This was no place
to be thinking of deflowering his bride.

There was a gas stove and a table, and a bed that
doubled for chairs, and the flypaper that hung over the
table was thick with dead black flies. I put my mug down
on the cooker and threw Philippa's case on to the bed.

'I've got nowhere to hang this lot,' I said. I'd never had
good clothes, and now that I did I had nowhere to put
them.

'I shouldn't bother if I was you, Ruby,' Jack said, pushing at the thin walls with one hand to see if they were
firm. 'Her stuff'll never fit you anyway. You might as
well keep it all in that case.'

I pulled a dress out and held it to my chest. I'd lost

some weight on the ship, but I could see I was miles off being the same willowy shape as Philippa. I draped the dress against my body and looked in the dusty glass shaving mirror that hung over the small metal sink.

'She left me a nightie too,' I told Jack. It was the same one she'd been wearing that night on the ship. Jack stared at the crumpled satin length as I pulled it out of the case.

'That's not your type of thing, Ruby,' he said, snatching it out of my hands. It smelled of Philippa's perfume. Jack shook it as though expecting a note to fall out. 'I've had it off with your husband,' it would have read, or whatever they called that type of caper where Philippa came from.

But there was nothing, just the satin nightie and the smell of Philippa's body. Jack blushed, and threw it back into the case.

'We won't be seeing those two again, I suppose,' I said to Jack. 'They went off to Sydney, didn't they? That's miles away, isn't it, Jack?'

Jack shook his head and went back to feeling the walls. 'They're red hot in this sun,' he said. 'They should've lined them or something.' Then he looked back at me again. 'Ralph gave me their address,' he added quietly. 'They asked us to keep in touch.'

I complained nonstop during the first weeks after we arrived, and I must have driven Jack round the bend, for, surprisingly enough, he rarely complained himself. I was in the minority with my moans – Jack was excited by all that he saw, and the other wives put up with the place and made the best of it. Jack was off every day anyway, in the bus that took the men into town to look for work, though, as it seemed in Jack's case, with no success.

'It's the younger men that are getting first pickings, Ruby,' he told me one evening. 'If you're over thirty they don't want to know.'

'But you're experienced, Jack,' I said. 'You're trained for your job.'

'Yeah, as a bloody copper,' he laughed, stretching out

on the bed and kicking his boots on to the floor. 'Fat load
of bloody good that is here! Might as well be trained to
embroider chair-backs for all the good that does you out
here. Still,' he said, wiping his face on his shirtsleeve, 'at
least you've got the sun here, which is better than you
can say for North London, and you still get the feeling
that anything's on the cards. At least I'm not still pounding that bloody beat back home. I'd have gone mad there,
Ruby, I know that I would.'

I was going mad waiting for Jack. He still wouldn't
touch me, not more than putting his arm around me when
we walked, like he had done at home, or giving me a
quick peck on the cheek when I lay down to sleep. He
meant our sex to be special, he told me, and I could see
his point; at night in the camp you could hear couples at
it ten huts away. I began to marvel at Jack's willpower,
and the more that he held back the more I felt I was
missing.

At the end of a fortnight a couple of letters arrived for
us. The first was from Billy, although it was written in
Marge's loose, sprawling hand. Billy never was one for
writing, though Marge's was not much better. 'I miss
you, Ruby,' he'd dictated, 'but I seen why you got to go.
You go on out there and make a mint, and then you send
a drop back for us too, eh? I always knew you'd do
special, but the market is too quiet without you. I done
quite good at the dogs last night, so we toasted you both
in the pub. My round!' Then the letters blurred and I
cried too much to read more.

The other letter was from Ralph and Philippa. 'They've
asked us to stay!' Jack shouted. 'We can go to their place
in Sydney. We've done it, Ruby! We've cracked it at last!'

The letter was typed, and Ralph's signature sprawled
across the bottom of the page. There was more work in
Sydney, they said, Jack would get a good job. They had
plenty of spare room. Ralph would be off on business and
it would be nice for Philippa to have some company. As
Jack said, he'd cracked it at last.

# CHAPTER 18

We hitched a ride to Sydney, in the oil truck of a friend Jack had made in the town. He and Jack shared the driving, and it took twelve solid hours on the Hume Highway before we reached the outskirts of Sydney. Jack's friend was a native, and he kept up a tourist commentary for the whole of the trip, mainly for my benefit, though the sun was hot and his accent so heavy that I often found myself dozing in my seat.

The man did the trip to Sydney each weekend, he told us, to deliver to the local hardware stores, and I think he was pleased of the company just that once. Jack kept waking me to point out different features, but the landscape that I saw was bleak in its flatness, and I showed little response. I was bored with the heat and the peacock-blue sky made me restless and troubled. I longed for older buildings, even the bombed slums of London. Places with ghosts, that were cool inside, like churches. Places you didn't dare to enter and neither did the light. Houses you could stare at, like the ones we stared at as kids, where just to look into their roaring black windows would send shivers running over your body. All the buildings in Australia looked new to me, even the sandstone homes in Berrima, which Jack's friend told us were over a hundred years old. The sun had bleached them harmless and it was this harmlessness that I found irritating.

When we passed a sign pointing to a place called Gundagai Jack's friend launched into a song he told us was called
'Nine Miles from Gundagai'. He taught Jack the words
and they sang it together, but then they reached a verse
where:

'The dog shat in the tuckerbox
Nine miles from Gundagai'

and Jack fell quickly silent and nudged his friend to shut
up because the words were too strong for his wife.

'Fucking stuck-up Poms,' the man muttered, and we
rode the rest of the way in silence.

We passed a thousand low, red-roofed houses, and Jack
announced that we must have reached the suburbs of
Sydney, though the stretch of these flat houses seemed to
me to be the size of London itself. Here and there were a
few larger places, but nothing on the scale of the house
in Surrey. The money in this country seemed to be distri-
buted evenly, and though I envied the people their sapph-
ire swimming pools and gardens front and back, there
was nothing that I saw to my own taste, nothing worth
fighting for as I would fight for Rowan Hall.

I had a sudden thought that seems childish and naïve
now, but which appeared only sensible to me at the time.
It was a question that would answer all of my queries.

'Does the Queen live in Sydney, then?' I asked Jack.
His friend let out a snorting laugh and slapped his palm
on the side of the car.

'What queen?' Jack asked me.

'The Queen of Australia,' I said, and then Jack laughed
too.

'They haven't got their own queen,' Jack told me. 'They
use ours.'

So that was why they had no better houses. Billy had
once told me that the big houses back in England were
just smaller copies of the Palace where the Queen lives.
I'd never listened in geography at school, and I'd just

assumed all other countries had a similar set-up to our own.

We got to Ralph's place in the dark, but although I couldn't see much detail outside, it seemed to be in one of those tall blocks that you get a lot of at home in Holloway. The apartment was huge, though, as big as two houses, and furnished in a style that would have given Lily the vapours.

Lily could never have lived with all of that bare floor and sparse, unadorned furniture. She'd have had lace doilies all over the bare wood and the couch covered with cushions before you could have drawn breath. Philippa didn't even have curtains, just blinds, and the only ornaments that I could see were the huge leafy plants that she had in the lounge.

We were on the tenth floor, and Sydney sprawled out below us, a roll of black velvet studded with millions of twinkling jewels. We'd managed to get Ralph and Philippa out of bed and they stood there in their nightclothes, Ralph's hair on end and dishevelled, both trying to look pleased to see us as we stood, tired and dusty, in their stage set of a flat.

'I'm sorry for the trouble,' I said, and Ralph poured us strong black coffees laced with brandy.

'No bother,' Ralph said, trying to look cheery, although his eyes were bull's-eye-red and you could tell he was rattled at being seen in his pyjamas. 'I couldn't see you and your husband stuck in a place like that death camp, now could I?' he asked. 'When I got Jack's letter I told Philippa we'd have to act fast, or you'd be off home with a nasty taste in your mouths. So here you are. We were just a little surprised that it took you such a short time to get here, that's all . . .' Ralph trailed off, rubbing his eyes.

I looked over at Jack. So he'd written to them. I felt ashamed that we should have to go begging to them for help, and would have left there and then, except Philippa was running me a bath and the smell of the salts and the sound of all that hot water was too much for me to turn

down. I sipped at the coffee and the alcohol made my head
swim. My stomach growled for attention and I blushed
because the others heard it too.

Lying in that bath, with the scented bubbles under my
nose, I tried to regain a sense of my old unease about Jack
and Philippa, but the brandy had gone to my head and I
felt too good to be nervous. I sank under the foam so that
I could wash my hair too, and when I came up for air
Philippa was standing there, making me jump.

'You've got a beautiful body, you know,' she said,
smiling down at me. 'You should be more confident about
it.' I'd crossed my arms over my chest, but Philippa pulled
them away.

'Has Jack seen those yet?' she asked. I shook my head,
suddenly feeling ashamed.

Philippa put a plate of sandwiches down on the side of
the bath and bent to dip her hand into the water.

'The water's too hot,' she said, reaching for the cold
tap. 'You're turning pink, like a little lobster.' But I didn't
mind. It was the first proper bath that I'd had in my life,
the first one filled from taps rather than an old boiler. It
was better than the showers that we'd had on board ship
and I intended making the most of it, even if my skin
peeled off with the effort. Besides, I wanted to be
scrubbed and clean for Jack that night. I'd be Jack's proper
wife tonight, and then I knew he wouldn't be looking at
Philippa again, ever.

'Here,' Philippa said, wiping her hand on a towel and
smiling, 'I've left you a clean nightdress,' and she pointed
to a length of sheer emerald lace that she'd laid over a
chair by the door.

Everything in our bedroom was white; white furniture,
white walls, soft flowering white drapes, and a creamy-
white carpet that sucked at my feet, leaving bare toe-
marks in a trail behind me. There was an electric fan
gently clacking on the table beside the bed, and the sheets
were fresh white and starched icy-cold. I pulled back the
top sheet and lay naked on the bed, allowing the fan to

cool my body, eyes closed until every inch was dimpled
with gooseflesh. My head hummed with the brandy and
my pulse ran with the metallic beat of the nearby alarm
clock.

I had never felt so good in my life. I felt clean and soft
as dough and my body sang with an invisible current, like
the fan. I heard Jack talking in a room nearby, and then
Ralph's voice, deeper, thick-pile, like the carpet.

I slept for a while, and when I woke I walked across to
the chair and pulled Philippa's nightdress on over my
head. I hadn't meant to wear it, it was hers, and she was
after my husband, but I wanted to look good for Jack,
too, and my own nightie was only brushed cotton and
had creased badly in my case.

The nightdress fitted like a sheath. I pulled in my stomach so that it looked less tight there, and pulled the cups
lower on my chest so that my cleavage showed more. It
matched the colour of my eyes perfectly. Philippa could
never have looked so good in it, and I wondered why she
had lent it to me. But then, that was the thing with
Philippa; you never knew what it was she was thinking
or what she was after. Perhaps she never wanted anything
very much and maybe it was that that gave her her air of
mystery and invincibility. When you want nothing, then
nothing can hurt you.

I waited for Jack, wondering why it was that he hadn't
come sooner. Then I heard him outside the door, fumbling with the handle, and I quickly pulled the top sheet
up over my body, right up to the chin, like a kid.

Jack stood in the doorway, swaying uncertainly, his
huge body lit silver-yellow in the light of the moon and
the street-glow. I held my breath while he stared at me,
just as though he were some wild animal that might run
if I made a noise. I didn't know what he was thinking.
When you have wanted something for long enough you
begin to think that it's never going to happen, and that's
how I thought about me and Jack and sex.

Then Jack began to pull off his clothes, slowly, awkwardly, one garment at a time. I realized then that he was blind in the dark, that he hadn't seen me, that he didn't know I was watching, and the thought thrilled me even more, to be invisible, to see and not be seen, to watch his naked body that normally he would have hidden from me.

I watched Jack struggle with the buttons of his shirt and then give up with a grunt and pull the whole thing over his head, like a vest. The shirt stuck at the cuffs and another sharp grunt meant the cuff buttons were broken off. He leaned against the wall as he pulled off his pants, then peered at me again to check that I was asleep before struggling out of his underwear. I closed my eyes quickly, then, when I opened them again, he was naked.

Jack's body was surprisingly beautiful in the half-light, much finer than it looked dressed, and I felt myself go damp with longing for him. His large hands rubbed at his chest and he looked for all the world like a Greek god; silver hair close-cropped to his head, silver lashes, thick-chested and broad-thighed, like a Minotaur. I saw the fine silver hair that covered his entire body like fur, and I saw his prick for the first time, hanging there as it was between his wide thighs. There was a heaviness and a solidity about Jack's body that I would never have guessed at when it was covered by his copper's uniform, or even the lighter work clothes that he'd worn since coming to Australia. His prick was like that too, thick and heavy, bigger than Frank's, though it looked a little sadder hanging there because it was uncircumcized. I longed to touch it and be pulled into his chest, but as Jack took a step towards the bed I saw him stagger and I realized he had been sharing more than just the one brandy in the lounge with Ralph. I propped myself up on an elbow for a better look and it was then that Jack knew I was awake and watching and he covered himself with his hands and swore as his shin hit the foot of the bed.

'Ruby?' he whispered. 'You awake?'

I nodded. I couldn't speak, I didn't trust my own voice.

'I love you, Ruby,' Jack said, and crawled up the bed
to lie beside me. 'Did you hear me, Ruby?' he asked, and
he brushed the hair off my face with his finger. He kissed
my cheek and I smelled his breath, warm with the brandy.
'You're just a child, Ruby,' he whispered, 'just a small,
small girl. Don't be scared, though, you can trust me.'
He cupped my face in his hands and kissed my nose, my
mouth, my eyelids. 'I'll be gentle, little girl, trust me,
trust me, I won't do anything that hurts, trust me, trust
me . . .' It was like a mother crooning to a baby.

I tried to turn to him, but he shushed me, keeping me
on my back, the white sheet still between us.

'Wait, wait . . .' he whispered, and I felt his hand slide
down to his prick, felt it working there until it stiffened
and hardened.

Jack peeled back the topsheet and I heard a small cry
from him as he looked down at my body. Then he was
on top of me, his great bulk crushing me so that the air
rushed out of my lungs in a sigh.

'Shush, shush!' Jack stroked my hair, kissed my mouth,
smothering my sounds, for fear Philippa and Ralph might
hear. My legs were closed fast together and his prick
poked blindly at them, bending like rubber, for he'd left
me no room to move. He grunted, trying to push now
with his hand, but his weight had me pinned, growing
steadily heavier as his thrusts grew less urgent. And then,
suddenly, he was asleep.

I moved then, gasping for air, afraid that my ribs might
crack beneath his weight, and he rolled to one side, snor-
ing like a child, with one arm thrown across his face. I
lay there in the dark, my head full of anger and my
eyes swimming with tears of disappointment. I imagined
Philippa in a room nearby, laughing at me for my stupidity, and I lay for hours silently railing against her, vowing
I wouldn't be beaten.

As the crimson light of dawn oozed like blood around
the blinds I slipped out of Philippa's nightdress and threw
it into a ball on the floor. Frank had taught me things and

now I needed to use them badly. Jack was still fast asleep. I did what he had done and stripped the sheet from his body. I could hear his breathing, deep and regular. His body was warmer than mine and I chafed my hands together so that the feel of my flesh shouldn't wake him too soon.

Jack's soft stomach rose and fell as he breathed. His navel was full of the same silver-white hair that covered the rest of his body. His legs were slewed apart, and his prick half-erect on the bed of its own two cushions. I wondered for a moment whether he was dreaming of Philippa and jealousy shot through my body like the blade of a knife. Jack was mine, he belonged to me. His body was mine too, and I could do what I wished with it. I would make him belong to me.

I cupped my hands gently around his balls and his prick twitched instantly awake, although from his breathing I could tell he still slept soundly.

Bending silently I ran the tip of my tongue down its length, making wet zigzags as it came up more slowly. It reacted quickly, growing to full swollen size, nodding in expectation as I ran around its rim. It tasted of salt, like the sea-winds, and as it quivered urgently against my tongue I took the whole great head in my mouth, wetting it with my spit, sucking at it hard until I felt Jack begin to wake.

Jack groaned, but he woke too slowly and was ready to come before he'd even realized what I was up to. His head hit against my shoulder and he pushed me off him roughly, rolling on top of me in one swift movement and forcing himself inside me with a violence that made me cry out. Jack's knees ground into my shins and gripped my arms so hard that his fingers caused me to bruise. He drove into me like a machine, with long, pounding strokes, and each stroke pushed further, no matter how much I tried to resist. His face above my own broke with beads of sweat and his teeth were set in a line with the effort.

I called for my husband to stop, told him he was hurting me, pleaded with him to be more gentle, but he was mad with either anger or passion, I couldn't tell which. Then the wildness eased a little and I sighed with relief as his eyes became distant.

Jack relaxed his grip and his thrusts became less mechanical. I joined with him then, taking control the moment he weakened, moving beneath him till he carried me with him instead of fighting me. His body became spasmodic in its movements and my legs clung to his waist and as we slid together I felt the ecstasy shiver through him like electricity. Jack came and it lasted for ever and as he writhed in the pain of his pleasure I came too, laughing with the relief of the release, knowing that we were now bonded as one, that no man could rip us apart, hoping that Philippa could hear what it was I had done and be jealous of me at last.

Jack my husband, Jack my father, Jack the man who would take care of me for the rest of my life, if I wanted.

The blow hit me before I could speak, and froze an expression of pain and shock on my half-lit face. I fell back on to the pillows, tasting my own blood in my mouth, still wondering where it was the pain had come from, looking to my husband with a silent appeal for help.

Jack's hand was frozen too, frozen in mid-air, evidence of his own guilt.

Like waxworks we lay there, a tableau of crime and punishment for all the world to see and learn from. The expression on Jack's face was more terrible than the blow.

'Whore!' he screamed, and the sound must have woken Ralph and Philippa. I touched my cheek and it was hot, as though he'd burned me. 'Fuck you, Ruby!' Jack screeched. 'Fuck you!' He'd lost words, lost his mind, all he could do was curse. All I could do was freeze in terror. I'd lost the plot, I didn't know what happened next. We should have been wrapped together. He should have been telling me he loved me. I'd done my best to please him and now

I'd lost the thread. I couldn't move, I couldn't speak, I didn't know what my role was supposed to be. I could only take my lead from this madman who towered above me in the bed.

'Where did you learn it, Ruby?' the madman said. 'Where did you learn those sort of tricks?'

'Tricks?' I asked, but I don't believe the word ever came out of my mouth.

'Who taught you, Ruby?' Jack shouted. 'Who taught you all that . . . all that . . . stuff? Jesus, and I thought you were a virgin! Who did you screw before me then? How many were there? You're my wife, for God's sake, Jesus Christ, Ruby!'

He held his head in his hands and he started to cry. I wanted to hold him but was too afraid to move. I heard his words but they were meaningless in my brain.

'You fooled me, Ruby,' he said, 'you fooled me all along. Jesus, how they must've laughed at me behind my back! I should've known better – your fucking father was still fresh out of the Scrubs when we met! I should've known you'd be no better than any of the others. Jesus Christ!'

It was then that I realized; then, and only then, that Jack's jumble of words took shape in my brain and meant more than a series of curses. So it was I who had done wrong. I had pleased Jack, but in pleasing him I had forfeited his love. It was my innocence Jack had wanted as a gift, my blood on the sheet, not my talent for lovemaking. But I had been Frank's virgin, not his, and now he felt cheated. I'd learned how to give pleasure but I hadn't learned the most valuable lesson, and that was that guilt often came with the pleasure.

Jack jumped up from the bed and I cowered in case he hit me again. When I finally looked, though, he was ripping our clothes from the wardrobes and throwing them on to the floor.

'We're leaving,' he told me when he saw me looking. 'You can't stay here now, not with people like these.'

'Ralph and Philippa?' I asked, shaking my head to clear it. 'What's wrong with them?'

Jack looked at me and his eyes began to bulge. 'Not them, you stupid bitch, YOU!' he shouted, ripping the green nightdress apart at the seams. He sank down on to the bed, panting, a wodge of green lace in each hand. He stared at the fabric, and I believe he'd just remembered who it belonged to. We'd valued what possessions we had back in North London, and we didn't just go tearing up other people's property, whatever the occasion. I think that torn nightdress of Philippa's just about stopped Jack in his tracks.

'Your not fit to stay here, Ruby,' he said quietly, trying to piece the fabric together. 'They'll know, they'll find out. We've got to get out of this flat.'

I scrambled to my feet, wrapping the sheet around me like a shroud.

'And go where?' I asked Jack, less afraid of him now he was quieter. I kicked his clothes across the floor and slammed the wardrobe door hard.

'You think they're too good for me, do you?' I asked him. Jack's blow had knocked the sense right out of my head. 'Philippa?' I shouted. 'You don't think I'm good enough to hang around the likes of her? I saw you two, remember? I know what you get up to! I saw her touch you, Jack! You didn't throw her off and call her a whore! Who do you think she is, Jack? The virgin-bloody-Mary?'

Jack jumped off the bed so quickly that I had no time to duck and he held me by the arms so that the sheet fell off and I stood naked in front of him. He looked at my breasts, at my pale naked body, and I saw the madness come back into his face. He wanted me, despite all his loathing, I could tell that from the way he looked at me.

A tear fell from his face to my breast. 'I waited for you, Ruby,' he whispered. 'I wanted you so much it hurt, but I waited for you to grow up so that I could marry you and do things properly. I saved it all up for you and I wanted to give you everything, but all the while I was

waiting you must have been fucking half the bleeding
market while my back was turned. I bet you all thought
that was a right joke, eh, Ruby? You and your dad and
half the market having a right good joke at a copper's
expense? Who had you, Ruby? Who was it? Can you
remember all the names?'

I slapped his face then, not hard, but it made a loud
enough noise in those quiet surroundings.

'I never asked *you* to be a saint, Jack!' I shouted. '*You*
never made *me* any promises and you never broke any,
either. Everyone knew about you and the girls down the
Palais, and I know all about you and Philippa. I'm not
stupid, Jack, and I'm not a whore! You've no right, Jack,
no right at all!'

Jack pulled me closer to his face so that his next words
got through. 'I'm your husband, Ruby, I've got every
right,' he told me. 'And I don't want to hear you say her
name again. You're not good enough to clean Philippa's
boots and I'll give you another smacking if I hear her
name cross your lips once more, understand?' I went to
argue with Jack but he raised his hand and I closed my
mouth.

'You're a tart, Ruby,' he went on, 'a nasty scheming
little tart, but I was stupid enough to marry you, and
that's as far as it goes. I promised to take care of you and
you're still young and I'm not a bloke that goes back on
my word, though there's lots that would say I'm soft in
the head for doing so. I don't want to know what you
got up to or who with, but I do want you to remember
that Philippa's class, Ruby, and that's something that
you'll never ever be, no matter how hard you might like
to try.'

I was sick and I was angry, but mostly I was scared. I
was alone in a big unfriendly country and there was no
one else I could turn to for help. I needed Jack, I needed
him to care for me.

'You're wrong, Jack,' I told him, desperate now.
'There's been no one else, you're the first, I swear it!'

Jack stared down at me, and for a moment I thought he might kill me.

'Don't lie to me, Ruby,' he said quietly, and the chill in his voice scared me more than his yelling. 'Where d'you think you learned all those tricks then?' he asked, nodding over at the bed. 'At bleeding Sunday school? Don't lie to me, Ruby.' He gripped me by the wrist as I tried to avoid his gaze. 'I've said I'll take care of you,' he whispered, 'now don't push your luck!'

# CHAPTER 19

That night we returned to Melbourne, hitching rides from truckers on the Hume Highway and sitting straight-backed and silent in their cabins, our few belongings clutched to our chests in split paper bags. The heavens opened and it rained so hard that you could barely see the road, even with the wipers going, and when each truck dropped us off we had to walk with our clothes and hair plastered to our bodies.

We were homeless, we had no option but to return to the camp. There was no decision to be made, no plan to be discussed. Jack merely stood at the roadside with his thumb raised in the air and I sat beside him, trying to shelter our belongings with the cover of my thin cotton skirt.

All the love and tenderness that Jack had ever shown for me had now gone, just as if a great plug had been pulled in his heart and all the feelings drained out at once. His eyes were dead when he looked at me and there was no emotion in his voice, not even anger. He made me ashamed and guilty and he made me desperate.

Our hut had already been given to another couple, but Jack knocked the caretaker up and we were put in a smaller place on the east side of the camp, near the drying rails. After the comfort of Philippa's flat, and with Jack's new coldness towards me, I felt myself to be in some sort of hell.

Shocked by my own stupidity, I asked Jack repeatedly what it was I had done wrong.

'Men don't like that sort of thing,' he told me, 'not in their wives, anyway. If they want those type of tricks they can go off to a whore, that's what they're there for. With a young wife like you, I've a right to expect to be the first. That was why I loved you, Ruby, why I waited all those years. I thought you were different, I thought you had class, but I was wrong, I made a mistake. I'd had my fun with those sorts over the years, men do, they have to, but you expect to marry different. You don't want to marry someone other men have been messing with, you don't want that as the mother of your kids. But I've made a mistake and I'm stuck with you. Most men would've dumped you without question, Ruby. Now just chew on that one.'

I chewed on it all right, I chewed on it for so long that my head began to spin, but I couldn't see the logic in his argument, no matter how much I chewed it over. I had wanted Jack's experience; longed for it all those long weeks that I'd waited for our first sex together. I had yearned to learn new things, and to share all that Frank had taught me. I was proud, as well, to think of all the things I could offer to Jack. Frank had enjoyed the pleasure that I'd given him, and I'd seen Jack enjoy it too, however much he denied it. Why couldn't Jack just be honest in his enjoyment?

Each thought of Frank now cut me through like a knife. I tried hard to forget him but his face was never out of my mind. A letter arrived from Billy, and inside it was a small twist of tissue that fell out onto my lap. It was Frank's wedding gift to me, Billy wrote. He hated having to send it, he said, but Frank made him swear he'd get it to me and he didn't go back on a promise. He said he hoped I'd have the sense to throw it away.

'Don't let Jack get wind of this, Ruby,' Marge's handwriting told me. 'It's not proper for Frank to have given it, not the way things were between him and your husband. Just don't get into trouble Ruby, that's all. Jack's a good bloke for a copper and he'll see you all right if you give him the chance. Don't go stirring trouble up or you'll be out on your neck and I won't be there to look out for you.'

The twist of paper contained a ring, a gold band, as thin as wire, with a small emerald the size of a grape-pip set in its claw. I pressed the ring to my lips, then rewrapped it carefully. It was so fine that you'd have thought the paper was empty. That ring was my lifeline, a sign that someone still cared. Frank was miles away but he was still there for me, and in my eyes he was omnipotent. He'd help me if I needed it, no matter what, because he loved me.

I burned the letter and tucked Frank's ring into the lining of my shoe. Billy was right, I didn't want to go stirring things up with the ring. I'd stirred things up enough already, without any help from Frank's small gift.

Jack no longer cared about the thin walls and the presence of the neighbours. My own lack of virtue made him suddenly lax about his own morals. He rarely spoke to me or referred to me, but I was there to be taken, whenever and however he wanted. My own pleasure stood for nothing and Jack treated me as the whore that he took me to be. His lovemaking was rough and without affection and I believe that he hated himself for needing it just as much as he hated me for providing the relief.

I would show no pleasure in our sex and it was no lie, for I found no pleasure in it either. I was tired all the time with the heat, and the brilliant blue of the sky made my eyes ache for sleep. I slept during the day, while Jack was out drinking or looking for work, and I felt that I would suffocate on that narrow bed in that stifling hut.

Jack made love silently, without speaking, using words only as he came to orgasm, when he would swear angrily, shouting, hating both himself and me. At first I longed for him to touch me gently and I would cry with frustration each time that he finished and rolled off, but later I learned to join him in his roughness, to egg him on sooner so that he would finish and I would be rid of him. Strangely, the thing that he made me do most often was the thing that had made him turn away from me in the first place. Sitting naked on the bed he would force me to my knees on the floor in front of him, and then he would push my head down until I took him in my mouth, hating him all the while for his hypocrisy.

I became sick and ill with the shame of it all, and when I looked into the mirror I saw dark rings under my once-bright green eyes. Once Jack was asleep in bed at night I would feel for Frank's ring, pressing it secretly against my hot face, putting it into my mouth and rolling it around my tongue, holding it up to my eye, wet with my own spit, and peering through it, hoping that life would look different through that one, squinting eye.

I was convinced that Frank would save me. I wrote to Billy, begging him to send me Frank's address, pretending I had to thank him for the ring, as I couldn't let on how unhappy I was. I even looked for Frank each day, as though he would appear as if by a miracle, walking down the dusty track that led to our hut, come to take me back to England and the rain and the beautiful greenness and fresh air.

I woke one night from a nightmare and found myself alone in the hut, which brought on new terrors, for I could never sleep alone in the dark. I'd fallen asleep in the daylight, and must have slept for hours. I was still in my flowered cotton housecoat, the only thing cool enough for me to bear during the day, and when I looked across at the shelf by the bed, the luminous dial of Jack's watch showed twenty past three in eerie green numerals. A great flash of silver lit the hut and I screamed, although my screams were drowned by thunder that rattled the floor under my feet. I pushed myself up off the bed but then

stood clutching the table while my head swam and I
choked for air in the suffocating humidity.

'Jack?' I called out even though I could see he wasn't
there. He'd never left me alone before at night. Hysteria
rose from my stomach through my chest and I ran to the
door, my hands searching in front of me like a blind
man's.

'Jack!' I threw open the door and the first droplets of
stinging hot rain hit my face. I could see nothing in front
of me. Outside, the darkness was as thick as the air inside
my lungs.

The skin on my arms stood up in bumps and the hair
on the back of my neck bristled as another spike of lightning cut across the sky. I walked into a washing-line and
screamed as the rope grazed my face. A wind got up and
I felt dust blown like gravel into my eyes. A pain seared
through my stomach, stinging me, like the ropeline, and
I clutched at myself and fell into the wet dust. The rain
fell harder and I lay there on my side as the ground turned
to mud, panting with the pain, waiting for the wave to
subside.

It was Jack who found me there, running to where I
was curled, his face and clothes sodden with the rain, and
his eyes full of concern.

'Ruby!' he shouted, but I barely heard him above the
thunder that deafened us to all other sound.

'I thought you'd gone,' I shouted, and Jack lifted me
up as easily as if I'd been a twelve-year-old. His breath
smelled of drink, but it was not the usual beer and he was
less drunk than he often was.

'There's no need to go crawling around in the dirt,
Ruby,' he told me, but his voice was not as angry as it
might have been. He kicked the hut door open with his
foot. 'I told you I'd look after you,' he said, laying me
down on the bed.

'Where were you?' I asked, but Jack didn't answer, and
I in turn did not mention my pain. I lay flat on my back,

my eyes closed, and waited while it gradually eased and I could feel the sweet relief as it left me.

Jack took a towel from the hook on the door and wiped my face, rubbing my hair with it and then peeling off my sodden housecoat. He looked down at me for a second, as I lay shivering on the bed, and then he pulled the cotton sheet over my body, right up to my chin, like a child.

He walked across the hut and I saw him wipe his own hair with the towel, then he pulled his shirt off wearily, throwing it on to the floor before climbing out of his trousers. The storm had passed now, but a fading blue flash lit the sky like a flare, and I saw Jack's naked body as he stood beside the sink, silently staring at his own face in the mirror. The sun had browned his body and arms and made him look leaner, but his legs and buttocks were thick ghostly-white. He dried his body quickly then stood, staring ahead, running his hands over his chest and stomach, as though feeling for embraces that were not there.

There was a distant rumble, just the echo of the violence of the storm, and I watched as Jack became erect, his great prick thickening and stiffening until it stood away from his legs. He shuddered slightly, as though waking from a dream, and then he turned towards me and I saw the look on his face.

'Ruby?' he whispered, thinking I was asleep. His bare feet made slapping noises on the floor as he made his way across to the bed. I closed my eyes quickly and he stood over me for a second before reaching out to stroke my hair.

'Ruby,' he said again, and his voice sounded cracked with emotion.

Jack fell to his knees and I held my arms out to him and he clung to me. We rocked there for a moment, each gaining comfort from the other, and then Jack climbed onto the bed and lay beside me, his voice sounding strange as he went on calling my name.

There was nothing else for me but Jack, and I had scared

myself with my own blind terror when I thought that he
had left me. I needed him to be there, he was my only
means of survival, and so I clung to his neck like a child,
full of relief at having him back, determined not to mind
how he treated me in future.

Jack kissed me then, and it was the first time that he
had done so since the night at Ralph's apartment. He
groaned inside the kiss, and his body rolled against mine,
so that I could feel his prick pushing against me as I lay
beneath the sheet. Jack pulled back the sheet and his prick
pushed in between my legs and we lay there, side by side,
our bodies facing, Jack's buttocks heaving slightly as he
pushed in and out against me. The rhythm was steady
but not urgent. He pushed against me but he didn't enter
me.

'Beat me, Ruby,' he whispered, his mouth close against
my ear. 'You should beat me for what I've done to you.'
His breathing grew heavier and his eyes closed, and he
moved gently in silence. He took my hand and held it in
his own, then brought it down on to his face in a slap. He
opened my legs and his prick pushed inside me properly,
sliding deeper as he pressed up against me. I drew my
hand down to his buttock and squeezed hard, my fingers
trembling with the effort. 'Harder,' Jack whispered, drawing in breath. 'Hurt me, Ruby,' he said softly.

He kissed me full on the mouth, sucking me into himself, crushing my face and my body until I punched his
back with my fists to make him ease off.

The blows made Jack more intense. His eyes closed
tight and his mouth fell open and I rained the punches on
to him, my anger coming out in a tirade, like a storm. I
couldn't stop, and no more could he. I bit at his shoulder,
his arm, his face. My fists pummelled his back and his
buttocks. My face squeezed tight with resentment, I heard
my own panting cries of effort drowned out by Jack's
loud, quickening groans, and his rhythm increased as his
body grew wet with sweat.

'Ruby!' he cried at last and I fell back, exhausted with

the effort, and he drove on inside me, shuddering with
his own violent climax.

His back arched rigid in a spasm, and then he collapsed,
falling on to me, crushing me with the weight of his relief.
I felt his back heave beneath my fingers and I heard him
sobbing quietly, stifled by the pillow that lay beneath my
head.

'I want to, Ruby,' he said, his voice muffled and distorted. 'I want to love you like I should, but I just can't,
that's all. I can't make myself, not after what's happened.'

I felt Frank's ring then, which I prayed that Jack had
not noticed, and I cried, but not just for Frank and myself.
I cried because I recognized the perfume I had smelled on
Jack's neck as he and I had made love. The perfume was
Philippa's, I would have known it anywhere, only I'd
been too bemused by Jack's behaviour to identify its smell.
It was the smell of the nightdress she'd given me, the
smell that moved with her, following her around like a
cloud.

So Jack had spent the night with her. I wondered
whether he'd scrounged a lift again, or whether they'd
met halfway, in a motel. I couldn't see Philippa in a
shabby motel, though. Philippa would want only the best,
even in that godforsaken country. Philippa would want
cool starched sheets and fans blowing cool winds over her
and my husband as she writhed gracefully beneath his
arched body.

Was it Philippa's coolness that Jack desired so much? I
think now that perhaps it was, for Philippa professed to
having no real need for sex, except as a homage to her
great and awesome beauty. I believe that the admiration
I showed her flattered and pleased her just as much as
Jack's clumsy, roughened mating. I resented the fact that
Philippa had chosen my husband when she could have
had my own adoration and friendship. They had ganged
up against me, those two, and I felt as lonely and as
helpless as I had ever done before in my life.

I understood Jack's strange behaviour then, and the guilt

that he had needed to be beaten out of him. He'd spent the night with his CO's wife, and the only woman that I had befriended in Australia. He'd stepped down to my level, yet still he couldn't love me, still my own sin was unforgivable to him.

My mind cleared as though a mist had lifted and an idea occurred to me that must have been growing in my head all along, a fact that solidified until I was as sure of it as I was of my own name.

'You've been with Philippa,' I told Jack, and he rolled on to his back and stared silently at the ceiling as the rain drummed down. 'I can smell her on you,' I said, and still he lay there silently. 'Will you keep up with her?' I asked.

'It's none of your business, Ruby,' Jack said with no energy in his voice.

'You can't,' I told him. 'You mustn't any more. I'm your wife, Jack, I've got rights. I can divorce you for adultery.'

Jack closed his eyes as though I annoyed him. 'You can't divorce me,' he said slowly. 'You've got no one else to take care of you.'

'I could tell Ralph,' I said, and his eyes snapped open as his head came off the pillow.

'I'm your wife, Jack,' I reminded him again, 'and I need you to be here. You've got to stop seeing Philippa and you've got to get a job. You've GOT to,' I insisted before Jack could argue. 'I'll need looking after, Jack, I'm pregnant. I'm going to have your baby.'

# CHAPTER 20

As soon as I'd said the words I'd known them to be true. I was pregnant. My bleeding had stopped weeks before, but I'd put it down to the climate or the upheaval of emigrating. Then had come the sickness and now there were the pains. There was, of course, one other thing that I knew for a fact. That the baby had to be Frank's, and not Jack's.

'How long?' Jack said. 'How long have you known, Ruby?'

'Just now,' I told him, lying. 'I just realized. The periods just stopped, last time.'

Jack looked at me, and I could tell he was sizing the news up.

'It's mine, then?' he asked. I nodded.

Jack walked over to the food cupboard under the sink, and I heard him grubbing about among the cans of tinned vegetables. He came back with the Bible, the one that had been by the side of the bed when we'd arrived, and which I'd stuffed away quickly because, for some reason, the sight of it there had worried me.

Jack held the book out and put my hand upon it. 'Swear, Ruby,' he said to me, and I somehow wanted to laugh, the whole scene seemed so ridiculous. The leather Bible felt rough beneath my fingers and I wondered who had read it so much to make it get so worn.

'Swear that it's mine,' Jack insisted.

'Of course it is,' I told him, and went to pull my hand away, but Jack held it there firm, crushing my fingers on to the bound cover.

'I want to hear you swear it first,' he said, and his eyes looked wild and dangerous in the half-light.

'It's yours,' I said, looking Jack straight in the eye, and he relaxed his grip and the Bible fell to the floor.

I was amazed that Jack should have believed me then, and it still amazes me today. After all, he had been a policeman and must have seen enough criminals lying under oath. Yet a look of relief came into his eyes as he looked at me, and he got himself a job the very next day, which shows how hard he had been trying previously.

Australia seemed to suit Jack, despite the bleakness of our marriage and the conditions we had been forced to live in. It was as though he'd found his roots, had belonged there all along. He fell in with the climate and the dryness and openness of it all easily, like slipping on a glove. I believe that with the right woman as his wife he could have readily made something of his life out there, but that woman would have needed a tolerance and a certain piety that were way beyond my own capability.

I knew that Jack had loved me, and could see that he was really trying to again, in his own way. His job was outside Sydney, and it came with a rented house in a place called Jenolan, beyond the Blue Mountains. The house had room for a kiddie, Jack told me, we could make a new start. I fell in love with the name of the place, and became excited at last about our prospects.

A train took us to Jenolan, and despite my original hatred, I found some beauty in Australia from the windows of that train. The weather had cooled and the journey was comfortable. Jack had bought me a cotton smock which was too big, but which he said I'd need when the birth got closer, and which was cooler to wear than the clothes I'd brought from England.

I'd had my hair cut, too, by a woman in the camp, and

it now fell around my face in curls, rather than hanging down my back. I slept on the train, my head resting on Jack's shoulder, and when I finally awoke it was to the sight of the Blue Mountains, and the feel of Jack shaking my arm. There was a fine mist in the air, and I remember I wanted to clear the mist with my hands, like a cobweb, so that I could get a better sight of the unfolding view.

'It's the eucalyptus oil,' Jack said, nodding his head in the direction of the blue rocks. I rubbed at my eyes. Jack must have been keeping up a running commentary from one of his guidebooks, but I'd been asleep and missed the talk.

'Oil?' I asked. I'd never seen mountains before in my life and was aware of the strange pull that they had, as though drawing me towards them. Their sides were sheer drops, like cliff-faces, and I could see tall, wonderful waterfalls that ran like gushing taps down the sides.

'The blue,' Jack was telling me, 'it's from all the oil in the air. An optical illusion like rainbows. It goes when you get closer.'

And it did. The magic faded and the cliff-face turned ochre. The train pulled in at a small station and Jack lifted our cases down on to the platform. 'The gaffer said he'd send someone to meet us,' he said, and we waited.

Jack's job was with a garage, and it was a breakdown truck that finally arrived for us.

'Had some call-outs,' the driver told us, to explain why we'd waited two-and-a-half hours. He looked at our cases and he looked at his truck. 'Got no kids?' he asked eventually, as though it would provide the answer to his space problem. The platform was deserted. He could see we were by ourselves.

'None yet,' Jack told him.

'Nipper on the way though?' the man said, and he nodded in my direction.

Jack laughed, and put his hands on his hips. My stomach only had a gentle swell, which was lucky or Jack might never have believed my version of his fatherhood.

The cotton smock had a shape of its own, though, and it stuck out in front as if I was having quads.

Jack loaded up the truck, and we took off down a dirt track that would finally lead to Jenolan. The town was small, and like many others that we'd passed, and I felt a sharp dip of disappointment, because I'd thought by its name that it would be something special. In the centre of the main street stood a large verandah-ed hotel, its white paint peeling to reveal the dried tarred wood underneath. The name of the hotel was written in thin metal lettering above the façade, but the letters had grown rusty, and the Jenola Hills Hotel had obviously changed its name and trade, as 'Danny's Bar' was painted on the newer sign that hung above the door.

There was also a foodstore with trolleys outside and a wide spread of low houses, and we drove straight through the deserted main street and out the other side. The land was flat again here, and the mountains just a shadow that loomed in the distance.

We passed through forests of eucalyptus trees, their bare creamy-white trunks branching out way above our heads into a crown of spotted leaves that bent under their own weight in the still, humid air. I heard bird wings beating, but was always too slow to see the flight, although I could hear the birds cry from the branches above my head. The air began to burn again as I breathed it in through my mouth. The truck in the sun grew too hot to touch, so that we moved very little in our seats, for fear of leaning on metal.

'Got you a great place,' our driver told us. 'Just north of the Turnout. Used to be Joe Mac's place, before he died.'

The Turnout was the name of the garage, Jack told me. The Turnout West, named because it stood on the turning that pointed towards the western side of the country. Jack had grown quieter, and I thought that maybe he was disappointed by what we'd seen too.

The garage stood on the edge of the highway, and a

mile up the road was the house where we were to live.
There were eight houses in all, scattered untidily over a
half-mile of track, and around the brick-and-wood houses
lay a handful or so of stocky old chrome caravans.

One house alone stood out from all the others, and that
only because it had a tended garden and a swimming pool
round the back. I prayed and prayed for the place to be
ours, but our driver told us it belonged to the boss, but
that his wife lived there alone most times, because of his
business in town. He winked at Jack as he said this, and
I assumed the boss's wife was the sort of woman the
workers would discuss over beers.

Joey Mac's place, where we were to live, was a large
brick shed, nothing more, with rambling wood outhouses
built on as an afterthought, and a rusting corrugated roof
that steamed hot in the sun. Out the back was a glass
lean-to filled with old shelves and boxes, and a cat lay
pressed against the glass, its tabby fur parting to show
white underneath. The cat may have been sleeping or
dead, I couldn't tell, but the place made me shudder, even
in that dry heat.

There was a dusty yard the size of the front lawn,
and beyond that a garden, which was surprisingly well-
tended. At the end of the bushes I saw a caravan, run-
down and painted brick red, raised on to blocks where
the wheels should have been.

'That's old Shirley's place,' the driver said, pointing to
the caravan, and then he told us that Shirley was dead
too, along with Joe Mac. 'Just her kids live there now,' he
said, 'along with a few animals. Refused to be rehoused.
Stubborn lot, the Abos.'

I looked around to see what he meant, but he had turned
back to Jack and they were walking inside. The door of
the caravan was open and I fancied I could feel eyes
watching me from the gloom. I shielded my eyes from
the sun, but my head felt swimmy with the heat and I
turned to follow the others indoors.

The house was better inside than I'd expected, but not

good, for all that. The kitchen was large, and appeared to have been modernized some time in the early fifties, judging by the Formica surfaces and the enamel gas oven. There were packets of stuff still on the shelves, vast dust-covered cardboard boxes containing cornflour and oatmeal and welded, aged jelly crystals. I rolled up the window-blind and became lost in a cloud of grey dust. A fridge in the corner stood taller than my own height, and I opened the door slowly, afraid of what I might find inside. It was empty, but I staggered back nevertheless, caught by a wave of trapped and stale air.

'Bit of bicarb do that all right,' a voice said behind me, and I jumped.

A girl stood between the netting door screen and the open door. She was smaller than me but stocky. I noticed her sandals before the rest of her. They were brown stitched leather with holes cut out in front, the type the kids wore back in England. Her dress was old, too, and tied at the waist with a leather belt, but it was her face that truly fascinated me. Her skin was brown, the colour of dark caramel, and her face was freckled. She had deep-set troubled eyes and a nose that was screwed up, as though she were laughing. Her hands fiddled with her belt and she swayed slightly as she stared at me, as a child would do.

''lo Abbey,' the driver said, coming into the kitchen, his hands stuck deep into the pocket of his shorts. 'What you up to here, love?'

'Come to see if there's work,' the girl said, looking at the floor as she spoke.

'Our Abigail here does some helping for the Missus up the road, don't you, girl?' the driver said. 'She'd do odd jobs for old Joey too, at times, although chances are there was more to it than that. Old Joey and your mum were real close friends now, weren't they, Abbey?' he added, and the girl looked away, rubbing the side of her sandal in the dust.

'Real good friends, eh?' the man laughed. 'Specially

about – oh, how long back would it be now? Fifteen,
sixteen years?' The girl walked out and the man laughed
after her.

'Don't mind her, Missus,' he said, picking at his teeth
with a matchstick. 'Her and her brother won't get under
your feet too much, she's just nosey to see her new neighbours, that's all. Abigail's all right, but her brother's not
the full quid. She'll yabber on when the mood takes her,
but he's quiet enough most times. You ever come across
an Abo before?'

I shook my head.

'There's a few round here,' he said. 'Them two's
humpy's down the end there. Rumour has it they were
old Joey's kids, though no one could ever prove it, of
course. Not as black as the usual Abo, though, not the
boy, at any rate!'

I saw Abigail's brother the next day, in the garden. He
was digging at some weeds with a hoe and he stared at
me silently when he saw I was watching. I smiled, but
his face was expressionless. We looked at one another for
a minute and then he went back to his weeding.

Jack was kind to me the night that we arrived in Jenolan.
He sat me down on the low bed and he pulled off my
shoes and placed them in the narrow wooden wardrobe.

'Somewhere to hang the clothes, then?' he said, peering
in through the door as though into a vast cupboard. There
was a short rail inside and two broken wood hangers. The
wardrobe smelled of mothballs, but I had no clothes to
hang there anyway. Jack had made me leave all of Philippa's stuff in the case back in Melbourne.

Jack lifted my legs and made me lie down, and then he
chafed my hands in his own and ran a hankie under the
tap, to lay on my forehead. Tears squeezed out from
under my lids at his kindness.

'I'll get us some more stuff,' Jack said, 'furniture and
what like. There's a place in town. We passed it in the
van. There's enough rooms, anyway,' he went on. 'The

scullery's quite big, and there's a spare room I can do up for the kiddie. You seen the pool up the road?'

I lay still, too choked with my own tears to answer.

'Perhaps she'll let us use it,' Jack said. I knew then that he would write home and say we lived next door to a house with a swimming pool. Jack always did that, he could make anything sound good if he tried. His mother must have thought we were living in Hollywood Boulevard from the way he wrote to her. I had a different way of hiding the truth. My letters home just stopped altogether.

I could never have told Billy what it was I was going through. Pride would never have let me, and I know that the knowledge of how I was living would have cut him to the quick. Poor Billy had made every sacrifice to see that I was well spoilt in my childhood, and I didn't want him knowing how that spoiling had finally turned out.

Jack tried to be kind for a few weeks or so but, as I said, Australia suited him. It soaked him up slowly and greedily and then his kindness was lost to me for ever.

# CHAPTER 21

It was Australia that took Jack away from me more effectively than either Philippa or my affair with Frank. I knew it then and I am just as sure now; my views about him have not changed over the years, as they have on so many other subjects.

It was the Australian outlook that suited Jack so well, if not in the cities then certainly in that outback hole we lived in. He complained daily about his job, but he'd been given the manager's post, and enjoyed the small amount of power that it carried. He got on with the men too, became one of them in fact, which was something that he'd never been able to do back home in London.

The other men took to Jack at once, which was unusual in those days, when the British emigrants were still known as Whingeing Poms, on account of their capacity for complaining about everything and everyone. It was as though the Australian manhood had been waiting to welcome Jack with open arms. He even looked like them once his face had browned and his sleeves were rolled up, he worked as hard as they did, which was unusual for Poms in those days, he drank as hard too, and his attitude to his wife was one that they could sympathize with. The only thing Jack lacked in their eyes was the quick verbal humour which was an Australian characteristic, and which was the only thing I could see to appreciate in them.

The bars still closed early in those days, and the six o'clock swill down at Danny's Bar was legendary for miles around. Jack was sold on the custom within days, and his behaviour towards me turned quickly to the way it had been when he'd lived in the camp in Melbourne. Every evening he was drunk, and soon it was regular for him to be carried from the truck into the house by one or two of his mates. They had a sort of secret society against all the wives, and you could lie in your bed and hear them shushing and giggling like kids as they planned how to get indoors without too much trouble from the missus. Most of their plans were in vain. The effort was wasted, another part of the legend, because the wives that I met never stood up to their husbands anyway. I was no exception. The pregnancy tired me and I had no fight left. I thought of the women I knew at home, women like Lily who breathed real lethal fire, and I wished she were there to help me, for my own fire had gone out long ago.

When Jack helped carry another mate home then I knew he would be sober enough to try and make love, and I would undress ready for him, or he'd tear my clothes with his clumsiness. There was no pleasure in this coupling. I would lie back, subservient, and Jack would take me in the only way that occurred to him, and it would be over quickly, which became the only blessing.

I think that Jack wanted me even less than I wanted him, but the mating was part of the rituals of manhood, and he was determined to claim his rights whenever he was capable.

When he came home too drunk for sex I would watch him turn maudlin, and I think of the two outcomes of the drinking I would have chosen sex, as remote and cold as it had become, every time. Jack cried when he became very drunk. I would listen to his sobs in the darkness of the bedroom, and I would hear him slobber over Philippa, mumbling her name as best as he could pronounce it in his state, and once I found him dribbling over her satin nightgown, which I thought had been left back in Melbourne.

I wonder what she would have thought of him at those times, if she could have seen him crying to the point of retching, pawing over her old nightie as though her body were still inside it. I believe that Philippa would have laughed at him, or been disgusted, as I was. Sometimes I felt angry enough to beat him with my hands, but I was frightened he might find pleasure in the beating, as he had on the night of the storm.

My loneliness became a gaping void that grew deeper and more painful by the day. I carried Frank's baby inside me, though, and it was only the baby's company that I believed at the time kept me sane.

My stomach had swollen, and when I was alone I would talk to the swelling, telling it about its father, and of the times that we'd had in London. I thought of Surrey and the cool, elegant house that I'd thought once to own. I remembered the roses and the soft dank earth that the roses grew in, and which gave off its own perfume. My unborn child was a boy, I was sure of that, and would look like Frank, which pleased me, despite my fear of Jack.

I wore Frank's ring all the time during the day, only taking it off at night, when I knew Jack would be home. Then Jack stopped coming home at weekends, and I knew that he was with Philippa. The crying at night stopped too, for which I was grateful. Then the sex stopped as well, and Jack and I moved in different orbits.

I thought of my plans, of the business I had hoped to run, and I was too tired to feel any regret that they had come to nothing, or that the house had gone, and Piers with it. The only thing I had to hold on to was Frank's child, which I knew to be truly mine.

The local women tried to be friendly. The boss's wife came first, tapping at the door screen some two days after we arrived. Her name was Mrs Haast, which she spelt out for me, but told me at the same time that I was to

call her Nadia, a familiarity which I believe she regretted
by the end of our meeting. Her legs were fat and she wore
a scarf tied in a knot around her neck. She had talcum
caked under her armpits, but I could see what the local
men saw in her. There was a sort of fullness about Nadia
that none of the other local women had. Yet she carried
her overblown figure with an air of gentility that was rare
around those parts.

Nadia was careful with her English too, picking her
way through our language with the same dainty tread as
she had picked her way up our dusty front yard to the
house. It was *my* accent that caused the trouble when we
spoke. Her eyebrows would meet with the hint of a wince
as she tried to decipher my cockney. I didn't cause her
too much trouble though, because on the whole I kept
my trap shut and let her do the talking.

'Going to do this place up then?' she asked, staring
round the scullery as I was too impolite to sit her in
the front room, which was where a local of her station
obviously expected to be taken. She'd brought some cakes
in a round tin and some wine which she said was home-
made. The tin lid stuck when I went to open it and a
couple of her buns rolled out on to the floor. When it
finally fell open I caught her look of horror as I placed
them back in amongst the others.

'You're expecting then?' she asked once the tea was
poured and the incident with the cakes forgotten. I
nodded.

'Lovely,' she said, without enthusiasm. She had no kids
of her own, I found out, though her old man was
rumoured to have sired a few in the town in his time. I
never saw her husband, and I don't think Nadia did either,
but she cashed up the till at the garage at the end of every
week and banked his money for him anyway, taking just
enough to live on herself, plus a few quid more for what
she called 'luxuries'. I had seen Nadia's luxuries on the
first visit she paid me. It was a wonder she could move
with the gold that was hanging off her wrists and ears

and around her throat. She caught me eyeing it all and
fingered a heavy pendant between her plump fingers with
an expression on her face that was almost coy.

'I have to wear it all,' she said, smiling at me. 'It's never
safe to leave it lying around in the house. You don't know
who might walk in and take it.'

'I thought you knew everyone around here,' I said. Her
bird's-cry of a voice was beginning to grate on my nerves.

'I do,' she told me, looking at me knowingly. 'That's
why I keep it on. You should be careful when you go
out, too.' She looked in vain for some jewellery to compare with her own. My wedding ring didn't count, I could
tell the way her eyes skimmed over it, and her lips pursed
with pity when she got as far as Frank's skinny gold ring.

I'd disappointed her, I could tell. Nadia was obviously
bored and lonely out there and I think she was almost
hoping for a bit of female competition to challenge her
authority as queen of Jenolan. Lily would have done for
her, or maybe even Philippa, although I was sure Philippa
would never have set foot in such a backwater in her
life. I'd shortchanged poor Nadia, with my drabness and
poorness and unwillingness to talk. I did not even allow
her the pleasure of appearing impressed by all her wealth
and social standing.

Nadia downed her tea and decided to give me one last
chance before departing.

'It's those two you should watch,' she told me, nodding
her head in the direction of the back door. 'Those two at
the end of your land. Joey Mac let them live there but
then I suppose he had no choice. Keep your eye on them,
though. They'll understand if you show them you're
watching.'

'Abigail?' I asked her. 'I thought she worked for you,
Mrs Haast?'

Nadia sucked in her lips till her mouth was just a slit
in her face. 'She helps out now and again,' she said, rising
from her chair and looking at her watch, 'but I only allow
her in when I'm there. You never know, that's all.' She

looked out of the door and in the direction of Abigail's caravan. 'Heaven knows what goes on in there,' she said, and looked back at me, waiting for me to take up the cue and ask. I picked up a tray and started stacking the tea things.

'It's not right,' she went on, annoyed at my indifference but determined to tell me what she knew all the same. 'That great strapping lad living squashed in that small van with his sister like that, it's not natural. Heaven alone knows what goes on in there, heaven alone.'

'You mean you think that they fuck?' I asked her, pouring the tea dregs into the sink.

Nadia's face drained of colour and her eyes rounded till I could see the blue veins at the sides. Her mouth opened and closed like a fish's and she pulled her gloves on while she thought what to say.

'Thank you for the tea,' she said finally, and she swept out, leaving the screen door banging in her wake.

The other wives took their turns at visiting me through that week, but I could tell Nadia had spoken to them, warned them about me, because they brought their cake tins and left quickly, without staying for tea. I didn't care. If they were all like pale shadows of Nadia then I decided I was better off feeling lonely.

I began to do crazy things alone in the house, the sort of things truly lonely people do, like crying hysterically and talking to themselves. Then I got ill, and Jack decided to take things in hand, for a change.

At times when he'd been sober he had complained about the state of the house. He'd supposed I'd have scrubbed it from top to bottom by then, like I knew Nadia and her cronies were dying to do, from the looks they'd given it when they visited. I should have been throwing things out and painting the shelves, but firstly I was too tired and secondly I didn't know that I wanted to, I quite liked leaving things as they were, being surrounded by things that had belonged to old Joey Mac, who had died there. It was almost like having company, as though the house were expecting him back any minute, and I knew if I painted things and claimed the house as my own then I'd be admitting I lived there, and expecting to stay for ever.

So I'd lived with the jelly crystals and packets of bicarb, but Jack finally blew up and chucked the lot out. I went down with some sort of fever so I heard rather than saw him jettisoning all Joey's stuff, but when I finally got up out of bed I found Abigail standing in the kitchen, preparing a meal.

'Hello, missus,' she said, and smiled. Her teeth were wide and white against her dark skin.

'Don't call me missus,' I said, steadying myself against a chair.

Abigail shrugged and went back to stirring the gravy. I sat down on the kitchen chair and the unvarnished wood scraped at the backs of my legs.

'What are you doing?' I asked.

'Breakfast,' she told me, and giggled. When she laughed like that she covered her mouth with her hand, as though ashamed of her huge teeth. I think that was the first time I realized that Abigail suffered painfully from shyness.

'He asked me to help out,' she said when she saw me watching her.

'Who? My husband?' I asked and she nodded, giggling again into her hand.

'Did he say that he'd pay you?' I was worried that Jack might have taken advantage of her, but Abigail nodded yes.

'*Some* money,' she told me. 'Not much, but he said I can sleep in the house. Said you didn't like being alone at night. That you get ill. Our van's too small for the two of us. Can't get far enough away from Henry for my own liking.'

'Henry?' I asked.

'That's my brother,' Abigail told me. 'He does the garden down there. Big boy. Always whistling. Drives me mad, too.'

I thought of Nadia's accusations and looked down at my hands.

'I'll be glad to stay here,' Abigail said, smiling, 'if you'll have me.'

'Not if I have to eat gravy for breakfast,' I said, and Abigail laughed, doubled up, as though I'd said something funny and that set me off, so that I laughed too.

It was Abigail who became my only friend in Jenolan, and it was Abigail who first taught me to find the beauty in the Australian countryside. She cleaned the house, tutting all the while at my neglect of the place, and she cooked good meals for me until I found my strength again and was able to take some exercise, which she told me would be good for the baby.

We walked each day, short distances at first, but as the weather cooled and I felt myself getting stronger, the walks became longer, each day in a new direction.

Henry would watch us from the steps of the van, but he never came with us and he never returned my wave of greeting. I remembered what the driver had said about him not being the full quid.

'He's handsome, your brother,' I told Abigail one day.

'Who, Henry?' she said, and her face split into a grin.

'Doesn't he ever go out?' I asked her. 'Only I've never seen him far from the van.'

'Nowhere to go much,' Abigail said. 'Most men go to the bars in town but they made it pretty plain they didn't want Henry and the others in there.'

'Because he's simple?' I asked, and Abigail sucked at her bottom lip.

'Henry's not simple,' she said, kicking at the ground with her sandals. 'He's pretty smart. It's Aborigines they don't want in there. Don't like to be reminded that it was us got here first, I suppose.' Abigail fell quiet then and we walked on in silence. I thought of Vic and Pearl and the similar way that they lived back home.

'It's your country,' I said to Abigail. 'Why d'you let

them do it?' But Abigail just laughed as though I had said
something stupid. Her laughter echoed in the high trees
and set the birds off with its noise.

'There's only a few of us in the town,' she said later.
'Most are a way out and don't come in too often. They've
got their own land and they keep to themselves, unless
the tourists come. I'll take you one day if you want.
Introduce you.' But I didn't want to be a tourist myself
so I kept quiet and hoped she wouldn't ask again.

'I could show you the caves too, if you like,' Abigail
said. 'And the rocks. You'll like the rocks. Bring you
some peace.' The thought of rocks and black wet caves
made me shiver in the hot sun.

I liked having Abigail in the house. I would sit at the
kitchen table and watch her work, not for one moment
caring how lazy I must seem to her, because my
depression had brought on a kind of lethargy that was
impossible to shake off, even if I'd wanted to, which I
didn't. I was happy being miserable and just sitting there,
day after day, listening to her chatter, which became endless once she knew me and the shyness had worn off. I
think Abigail needed someone to talk to just as badly as
I needed someone to watch. Watching her work brought
me a strange kind of peace, as though I were a child
watching my own mother in the kitchen. Abigail nagged
me like a mother, too, constantly and loudly.

'You should go out,' she would tell me. 'Get into town
or something. Sitting here you'll grow old, like the
others.'

'The others?' I asked, dipping wafer biscuits into the
milky coffee she had made for me and which I had let
stand for so long that a skin had formed on top.

'The other wives around here,' she told me, waddling
around the table with the old-woman walk that she had.

'How do I get there?' I asked her. 'I've got no transport,
and Jack would go mad if I hitched.' I felt a prisoner of
the area I lived in. Jack used a van from the garage to get

about, but I had only been in it once, when he'd driven
me to the clinic for a check-up.

'You could walk,' Abigail said, and with her back
turned to me I couldn't tell if she was joking.

'The town's miles away,' I said, but she just shrugged
and I guessed that she would have walked it, pregnant or
not.

The other women in the area ignored Abigail as often
as they could, and Jack made a point of not talking to her
when he was home, as though she were invisible in the
house.

'You shouldn't get so friendly with her,' he told me
one night as we lay in our bed. 'Stan from work said his
wife'd seen you walking with her towards the Westway.
You want to be careful, Ruby. You know what people
think of their sort around here. It's the other wives you
should be palling up with, not the local Abos. How d'you
think it looks, Ruby? You're rude to the other wives when
they come round to welcome you and then you go off
with some black who lives in one of them run-down vans.
I'm manager down at that garage, Ruby, I've got to mix
with the others and I've got to get their respect. You go
on acting like that and we'll find no one'll be speaking to
us around here before long.'

Jack rolled on to his side then, but he had one last thing
left to say. 'And don't encourage that Abo boy, either,'
he said in the darkness. 'There's something not right about
him. I've caught him looking at you a few times. You
don't know what's in their heads. If I find him near the
house I'll knock his teeth down his throat and yours, too,
if I find you were encouraging him.'

I can't stand this life, Jack, I thought to myself, although
they were words that I did not dare to say out loud. I
can't stand this place and I can't stand this poverty. My
spirit was dying there, I could feel that. Soon I would be
like the other wives, moulded into a kind of permanence,
happy to live my life out the best that I could. Getting
by, like the wives I had seen at home in the market. I

couldn't leave. I had no money of my own, and no means of even getting to the nearest town. The only thing that I did have was the baby. My baby. Frank's baby; the only thing that I owned that Jack could not control. I clung to that unborn baby as a reason for continuing with my life just as fiercely as it must have needed me as a means to begin its own.

Then a telegram arrived from London and I thought that our troubles were over.

# CHAPTER 22

'**M**e mum's dead,' was all that Jack said, and then he crumpled the telegram into a ball and threw it angrily at the wall where it rolled to the floor by the back of the easy chair. He went off to work, slamming the door hard behind him.

I fished for the telegram, smoothing it out on the wooden floor. 'Regret Mrs Stanley passed away Heath St. Nursing home,' it read, and then 'Letter to follow'. I wondered who had sent the telegram as Jack's mother was his only relative. He'd talked about sending for her once he'd made some money. I recrumpled the telegram and replaced it exactly where he'd thrown it.

I didn't see Jack for five days after the telegram arrived and by the time that he did come back a letter was waiting for him. It wasn't difficult to guess where he'd been. Philippa's apartment was the only place he knew in Australia, apart from Jenolan. His eyes were bloodshot when he came into the kitchen, but he seemed to be sober despite that. I watched him from my chair, but he couldn't meet my gaze. Then he saw Abigail and shouted at her to get out.

Jack took the letter down from the rack and read it quickly before sliding it across the table towards me. It was handwritten and headed with the printed address of the nursing home. They'd cared for Jack's mother and

seen to the funeral arrangements for him. They said there
was just the sale of the house to arrange. They hinted that
they would have liked a small donation to the nursing
home from the proceeds of the sale.

I looked across at Jack. 'She owned her house?' I asked.
Jack nodded. He looked confused in his tiredness. I
watched him get a beer from the fridge and drink it down
straight, belching and wiping his mouth afterwards. 'She's
dead,' he said, and there were tears in his eyes.

'We'll get this money,' I told him, tapping my finger
on the letter. 'It's all we need, Jack! It'll start us off, like
you always wanted! It must be a few hundred at least!
You can start up in business, we can get out of here at
last!'

Jack looked at me, and his eyes seemed to grow dark.
'What the fuck's this "we"?' he asked, so angry that I
leaned back quickly in my seat. 'That's *my* money,' he
told me, '*my* mother's money. Money she left *me*, not us!
She didn't work all her fucking life to keep the likes of
you, Ruby! You weren't fit to kiss her feet! If I'd ever
told her all about you . . .'

'I'm your wife!' I shouted. 'This money's for both of
us! We can go somewhere better, bring the baby up somewhere proper! She'd've wanted that!'

Jack sank into a chair and hid his face in his hands. 'It's
not enough for you and Philippa,' I said, 'but it'll keep us
two OK. Get us out of this hole we're living in. We can
do it now, Jack. Things will go right for us at last. All
those things you said we'd do out here . . .'

'Shut up!' Jack shouted so loud that my hands went up
to my ears.

'Leave it!' he screamed. 'She's still warm yet! Forget
the fucking money! Drop it, Ruby, for Christ's sake!'

But I couldn't drop it, for it was my only way out of
Jenolan. I watched him get drunk, sitting there at the
kitchen table. Perhaps I should have sympathized, like
Philippa obviously had, but I was too desperate for that,
the money was too important to me. It wasn't much, but

it was all that we would ever have been able to expect and I needed to know that Jack would use it towards our release from poverty.

I watched his head droop towards his arms and then I stood up and approached him quietly.

'Let me get you to bed, Jack,' I said gently. He shook his head as though trying to clear it. I stroked his hair with my hand and he started to sob again. I pulled him to his feet and he stood there swaying, his eyes unfocused with tears and the beer that he'd drunk.

I pulled his arm around my shoulders and struggled with him to the bed. He fell heavily once we were there and lay spread-eagled on the blanket. 'Philippa?' he asked, blearily trying to raise his head off the pillow, but I shushed him and pushed him gently back. I undressed Jack slowly. The job took an age and when I'd finished I fell back, exhausted with the effort.

'Jack?' I said, shaking him so that his head lolled.

'What about the money, Jack?'

He opened his eyes. 'What money?' he said.

'The money for the house,' I told him, 'your mother's place. We've got to work out what to do with it. You've got to talk to me, Jack. We've got to make plans.'

Jack looked up at me, and his eyes tried to focus. 'Ruby?' he asked, as though surprised to find it was me there, stroking his face and kissing him on the cheek. I could tell I'd waited too long, though. Jack's eyes closed and his head fell back on to the pillow. He was dead drunk, and I knew I'd get no more out of him that night.

Jack disappeared for days on end after that, and each time I was terrified that he'd taken the money and left me for ever. Losing Jack would not have worried me, but I was frightened of being left alone and unable to support myself. I wrote to Frank, out of sheer desperation. He was the only person who I could ever expect to help me, if he still cared for me, that was, and I prayed that he did.

'Dear Frank,' I wrote, 'I made the worst mistake when I married Jack and came to Australia. If you could see how I live now you would pity me and want to help me, and there is no one else that I can ask for help except you. It would kill Billy if he found out and anyway he has no money to help me. It is killing me living out here. Jack is away all the time and when he is home he is drunk. We live miles from anywhere and I have no friends. You have to help me, Frank. I am desperate. Please send me some money so that I can get back home before I go mad. You said you loved me. If you do you have to help me. Love, Ruby.'

I wrote the letter hurriedly, without thinking what it was I was writing. I was too proud to tell Frank that I was carrying his child, and frightened that the thought of it might put him off helping me. I couldn't see Frank as a father, and I was scared the news might make him bolt. When I think about that letter now I can see how callous it must have sounded. At the time, though, I merely thought it truthful and to the point, and Frank's reply, when it came, was like a hard slap around the face.

'Dear Ruby,' he wrote back, 'I believe that luck is something that we bring on ourselves and so, in a way, you've got all that you asked for. You never loved Jack yet you married him and took him for all that he'd got. Poor sod, no wonder he's on the booze now. You're a grown woman now, Ruby, and you made your own trouble. I tried to warn you, but you wouldn't hear of it and now this is what you got for your pains. We all have to learn, and you're learning the hard way. I'm sure you are enough of a fighter to look out for yourself. You married the man, Ruby, and now you have to make the most of it. I know that I loved you so don't go throwing it back in my face. It was Jack that you chose, and it was Jack that you married. He's your husband now, and I'm afraid that it's not my place to help you. Frank.'

I wept when I read his letter. The only ray of hope was in the address at the top. It was the address of a club in London, where I assumed that Frank had to be working now. I'd had to send his letter in an envelope addressed to Billy, with strict instructions for Billy to pass it on to him. I knew Billy hated dealing with Frank and at least I had an address now where I could contact him direct.

I had no other hope of getting help. Abigail listened to my problems but her attitude seemed similar to Frank's.

'Why d'you marry him?' she asked me. 'All wallopers are the same. You picked trouble. Mind you,' she added, chopping at some vegetables, 'he's still better than most around here. He's a good-sized man, and at least he doesn't beat you when he gets mad.'

'Is that what the other men do?' I wanted to know.

Abigail nodded. 'Lots anyway,' she told me. 'It's the native sport around here, wife-bruising. Specially on a Saturday when they've all been into town.'

I looked at Abigail, but I couldn't tell if she were lying.

'How would you know?' I asked, getting annoyed with her. Abigail smiled and shook her head as though I had a lot to learn, which made me angrier.

Weeks went by, and Jack said nothing about the money, even though I knew that he had it, and that it was in the bank. His trips to Sydney became regular, as did my questioning of him once he was back.

'We could move,' I told him, but he always seemed not to listen. 'We could buy somewhere in town, somewhere newer, maybe with a pool,' I suggested. 'At least some new furniture, or a car I could drive. I can't stand it here like this, Jack. I see no one and I talk to no one. If we had a car I could get around a bit. I'll need it when the baby's born. We need a nursery. We could buy a TV.'

In the end Jack broke. 'There is no money!' he shouted, turning on me.

I stared at him, my mouth open in mid-sentence. 'No money?' I asked. The room seemed to spin around my head.

Jack stood over me. I clung on to consciousness, afraid to pass out in case he hit me as Abigail said the other men hit their wives.

'It's gone,' Jack said, and his face was red with anger and shame.

'You spent it?' It was as though my last lifeline had just been severed. I felt the baby move inside me and I thought for a moment that I would be sick.

'It's not spent,' Jack said, and his voice was quieter. 'It's invested.'

'Invested?' I could do little but repeat his words. 'You don't know anything about investments, Jack!' I said. 'How could you . . .'

'Ralph did it for me,' Jack said, and his face suddenly looked drained. 'He wanted some capital for something. It sounded good. He told me all about it. He said we'd be partners, that we'd make big profits.'

'You just gave him our money?' I asked.

'No, of course I didn't just give it to him!' Jack said, looking away. 'I'm not a fool, Ruby! I saw enough of jokers like that while I was in the police. Ralph's no con man. It was a good business investment. I knew what risks I was taking. Ralph was in the same boat. He put money up too. If it lost, we both lost.'

'So what happened, Jack?' I asked. 'Did it lose? Did you lose all our money, all our future? Has it all gone?'

But Jack wouldn't answer me and I wondered if he was lying. He stood up from the table and walked slowly to the door. I let out a wail that they must have heard two houses away. The noise set the dogs off at the end of the property. I heard the door screen bang and then the slamming of the main door. I threw my head on to my arms and cried tears of self-pity until I slept with the exhaustion of it.

# CHAPTER 23

I wrote to Frank again. God help me, I didn't know when to stop. But as I've said, I was desperate, and I was sure Frank would find me a way out if I begged him hard enough and often enough. All I knew was that I had to get out of Jenolan, and that Frank seemed to be my only hope.

This time I told him about the baby.

I don't know how I told him or which words I used, for the events that followed have wiped the exact wording from my mind. I wasn't scared by what the letter might have triggered off, but I was terrified of living my life out in Jenolan, and I prayed that Frank might have a change of heart if he knew I was carrying his child.

I was big with the baby by then. I'd gone a full seven months, but for Jack's sake had had to make it seem five, and each day that I looked in the mirror and stared at the size of my swollen belly I became more and more alarmed that he would notice and guess the truth.

I received no reply to my letter. I waited each morning by the mailbox at the end of the front path, and most times the postman just walked by with a smile and a nod of the head. Only twice did we have a letter, but each time it was for Jack, and only some stuff about his tax.

Henry was often around at that time of the morning. I caught him watching me several times, probably wonder-

ing what I was doing there in my flowered housecoat,
waiting by the gate as though looking for Jack to come
home. I tried to ignore him, as Jack had told me to, but
I found him fascinating and so often stared back.

Henry was quite young, no more than nineteen Abigail
had told me, a year older than me and two years older
than his sister. Abigail looked no more than a kid until
you saw her walk, and then her strange, old-lady's shuffle
made her look older than her years. It was being short
and squat that made Abigail walk that way, plus I guessed
it was something that she'd copied from her mother,
who'd been quite old when she'd had her children.

Henry looked as though he came from another litter
altogether. He was tall, about six feet four, and as broad
and muscled as Abigail was short and plump. His face
always held a scowl, though that may have been his features rather than his expression, and he kept his black
curly hair tied back with string when he worked.

I'd heard him whistling, but he'd always stopped once
he saw me, and worked in silence, his knife scything
through the overgrown weeds or his spade slicing through
the dry dusty earth. I wondered what Abigail had told
him about me. I wondered whether they talked at all now,
since she'd moved up to the house. She seemed to ignore
him, and I thought again about Mrs Haast's accusation
that maybe they had sex together. I couldn't imagine it
somehow, and yet since I'd caught Marge with our Billy
I knew that anything was possible.

If Jack ever wondered where it was that I went to each
morning, he never asked. After a few weeks I gave up
looking altogether, which was the biggest mistake I made
and I have never forgiven myself. It was Jack who met
the postman the day that Frank's reply to my second letter
came, only it wasn't really a reply, as I was to find out
later. I was in the kitchen with Abigail, spooning some
flour into a dish, letting it drop like sand in an hourglass,
thinking that I would die if my life in Jenolan had to go
on much longer.

I thought at first that Jack had forgotten something and I didn't bother looking up, I was concentrating too much on spooning my flour. Then I noticed that Abigail had stopped working and was drying her hands on her apron, and I looked over and saw Jack's face.

He was looking at Abigail, not at me. I wondered what she could have done wrong.

'You won't be staying here tonight,' Jack told her and his voice sounded calm despite the redness of his face. 'You stay down in your humpy out the back.'

Abigail started to say something, but obviously thought better of it.

'Understand?'

Abigail nodded, and went silently back to her washing.

Jack looked at me then, quickly, just a glance, but even in that brief moment I saw something in his eyes that I'd never seen there before, not even on the night at Philippa's. Yet still I wasn't worried, though Abigail seemed uneasy.

'What's up with the boss?' she asked me once he'd gone.

'Don't call him boss,' I told her, spooning my flour. 'Just call him Jack. He's not your boss, like I'm not the missus.'

'He pays me,' Abigail argued.

'Not enough,' I told her.

'He looked really mad,' she said, scrubbing the sink down with scouring powder so vigorously that her whole wide behind wobbled.

'Maybe it's something to do with Henry,' I said. 'Maybe he caught him looking again.'

'At him?'

'No, at me, stupid. I told you Henry watches me. You know what Jack thinks. Henry had just better be careful, that's all. What's he looking at me for anyway, Abigail? He just stares. I can't tell what he's thinking.'

Abigail shook her head slowly. 'Can't see why the boss would send me out of the house for that,' she said, ignoring my question. 'Must be something up bigger than that.'

There was something bigger, but I wasn't to find out what it was until after dark, when Abigail had gone. She left reluctantly, whether because of the narrow put-you-up that she was leaving behind, or from some sort of second sight, I never knew.

'You OK?' she asked as she trailed her case out of the door.

I nodded. The lights had gone off in one of the power faults we were always getting and the kitchen was lit by candles. It gave the room a sort of golden flickering rich-ness that would never have been there if the electricity were on. All the junk in the room was concealed by shadows. There was a smell of hot cakes and Abigail had left me with a mug of milky coffee that was cupped warm and steaming in my hands. The steam smelled of the cinnamon that she'd grated to dust on to the froth on top. There was a wind blowing up outside and I heard the loose window in the larder rattling with each new gust. I should have got up and fixed it, because of the dust, but I felt too lazy and so sipped at my coffee instead.

I heard Jack's steps on the dirt and gravel path and quickly wiped my milk moustache off with the back of my sleeve. I hadn't heard the van and I couldn't hear his mates and I wondered whether he'd been down at the humpy chewing Henry's ears off. The thought of Jack actually hitting Henry seemed ridiculous, as Henry was so much bigger and Jack was an old man by comparison, but I didn't doubt that he'd try it, given the provocation, and I guessed that Henry was enough afraid of Jack to have taken a considerable beating without fighting back.

Jack looked cheerful enough when he came in. He was even whistling, which reminded me again of Henry. He was sober too, though there was beer on his breath when he kissed me on the cheek, then he went over to the sink and rolled up his sleeves for a wash, something that he used to do at our flat in London when he'd come round straight after a shift, but which he'd never done since, all the time that we'd been married.

He lathered soap up his arms to his elbows, rubbing at his forearms and knuckles as though dealing with ingrained dirt. Then he took the bristle scrubbing brush down from the shelf and set about his nails until he'd brushed so hard that I thought they would bleed. He ran his hands and arms under the cold running water and then pushed the tap off with his elbow, like a surgeon preparing to operate.

I pulled some withered potatoes out of the string bag on the back porch and started preparing a meal. It felt odd because I hadn't cooked since Abigail arrived, but I didn't know what else to do. Jack just took a seat at the table and started watching me and inspecting his clean hands. I put some water on to boil and stood over it, feeling uneasy for the first time. A sudden draught blew one of the candles out, but Jack made no move to relight it. He just sat there at the table watching me, and when I looked at him he was smiling, which started my hands shaking a bit because he rarely smiled, and never for no reason.

The water steamed up and boiled and I turned to get the potatoes from the table, but Jack was there behind me, he'd got up without my hearing him. I froze, like animals do when they're scared, and we stood like that for some minutes, the water bubbling in front of me, waiting for its potatoes, and Jack standing right behind me, not touching, but so close that I could hear him breathing.

'You bitch,' he whispered, and he spoke so softly that for a second I thought his voice sounded kind. It was his tone that scared me more than anything else. There was no anger in it, only in his words. We looked for all the world like any loving couple, with him whispering endearments into his pregnant wife's ear.

'You whoring scheming fucking little bitch.'

A chill shot over my body, so sharp in the warm kitchen that the gooseflesh stood up on my arms.

'I shall kill you.'

The tone was the same, soft, almost loving, so that my ears strained with the effort of thinking they must have heard wrong.

'You missed the post today, you cow.'

His hand came round in front of me, holding an open envelope up to my face, too close to my eyes for me to be able to read it. I pulled my head back. The envelope was addressed to Jack. It was handwritten in neat printed letters and the postmark was blurred but I could see it was from England.

'Take it out,' Jack said, and his words sounded distorted, as though his face were pulled about with anger. I didn't move. I couldn't.

'Take the letter out!' he repeated and this time his voice was loud enough to make me move out of fear. My shaking fingers found the corner of the letter inside and I pulled it out, but only halfway. I didn't need to pull it any further, because I recognized it already. It was *my* letter, the last one that I'd written to Frank, the one where I'd told him that the baby was his, and that I had to get out of Australia.

Jack brought his hand down, the one holding the letter, so suddenly that what happened next seemed like an accident. His wrist hit the saucepan handle and I tried to jump, to move out of the way, but Jack was there behind me and I was trapped. I held my arms out to shield the baby and boiling water poured over my hands and my forearms and my legs and at first there was no pain, but then the skin blistered as I watched it, and then my mouth opened and I turned to look at Jack, my eyes wide with shock, no words able to form on my lips.

Jack grabbed me by the hair and dragged me over to the sink. The water was there, the sink was full of it, the soapy water that he'd not let drain after washing his hands for so long. Jack pushed my head down into the sink and my mouth filled with the suds and I felt my face going under so that suddenly I could hear nothing, only the watery sounds in my ears and the sound of my own pulse as I tried not to swallow down the water that was in my mouth.

'Bitch!' Then I heard Jack's voice screaming in my ears and I knew that I was out of the water.

He ducked me under four times, and each time I thought that I would die. I tasted the soap in my mouth and it stung my eyes so that I was blinded. I wanted to plead with him, to beg him to stop, but my mouth was too busy gulping down air for me to be able to say anything coherent.

My blistered arms waved in the air grabbing at anything, my fingers scrabbling blindly over packets and plates, pulling things down, breaking things that I could half-hear falling before my next plunge under the suds.

Jack tired of trying to drown me and I felt the pressure of his hands ease from the back of my head, and I fell out of the water and slid to the floor, choking and retching. My letter was there beside me, fallen into a puddle of water, my words just swimming blue ink, all disintegrating in front of my eyes.

I felt Jack's hand on my hair again and my head snapped back, so that I caught a look at his face. I didn't see his arm swinging back above me, but I felt the blow, and the second one, as my face hit the door of the sink cabinet and the skin on my cheek split apart like ripe fruit. I could hear Jack screaming, long jumbled streams of senseless abuse, and I scuttled like an animal across the kitchen floor, trying to get to the door, or to some furniture to hide behind. One of my eyes had closed. I could feel blood running from my nose, warmer than the water that ran down my face. There was no pain yet, only a wild desperation to survive and stay alive. I crouched down behind a chair and covered my belly with my arms, curling into a foetal ball, just as the baby must have been inside me.

'The baby . . .' I managed to say. 'Please, Jack, the baby . . .'

'YOUR fucking baby!' Jack screamed. 'FRANK's fucking baby! Not mine, Ruby, no, never that! HIS! HIS bloody kid!' I felt the blows on my body, a torrent, like rain, and then Jack kicked me, and then I felt the pain for the very first time. It shot through my body, on the inside, not out, tearing at me like a hot knife, so that the kicks and the punches didn't matter any more. I saw bright burning red in front of my eyes, and then I saw the blackness that meant oblivion, coming at me like a stormcloud, and I breathed with relief because I knew that the pain would soon be ending.

Someone was wetting my face and I put my arm up to defend myself because I thought it was Jack, and that he was attacking me again, but I felt my arm pulled down gently and I heard someone shushing me and soothing me, and I knew the voice was Abigail's, and I tried to tell her what Jack had done. My voice made no sense, though. I could hear it in my own ears, thick and unintelligible. Then the pain came over me again, in a wave, and the words were driven out of my mouth for me.

'Oh God, Abbey!' I felt a release, as though something inside had just washed away with the pain, and there was a warm wetness between my legs, and I heard a scream that was Abigail's, not mine.

Then the blackness came to collect me again, to save me from all that I suffered, and I embraced it like a long-lost friend because I knew that it was the only friend that I had, and the only release I could hope for.

'A shock like that can often bring on premature labour.' I heard a voice that I didn't recognize, talking as though down a long tunnel, coming at my ears in waves, like the pain, but the pain had gone and only a numbness remained in its place.

'What was she doing up there in the first place?' the

voice said. 'A woman in her condition. Not a thought for the baby, of course.' There was a hand on my forehead, a man's hand, rough and dry and elderly.

'I'll leave her these for the pain.' I heard the rattle of tablets being placed on the bedside table.

'Hospital.' It was all that I could say. My mouth felt strange and shapeless.

'Do you know how far the nearest hospital is?' the voice asked. 'Anyway, there's a power cut. The storm's brought down some trees. You're safer in here than travelling. I've stitched up the cuts and there's nothing been broken. You've your husband and young Abbey to take care of you.'

'He tried to kill me.' I spoke to the voice though I had no idea who it belonged to. The words were unclear. I heard a strange, embarrassed laugh.

'You nearly did for *yourself*, young lady,' it corrected me. Then I heard a door close and felt that I was alone.

I woke the next morning to the sun burning my face. The blinds had been left open and there were flies buzzing lazily in the heat. I tried to sit up but my bandaged hands had no strength to support me, and I fell back on to the pillow.

They say that you forget pain, but I can feel that agony now, and the mental pain that I had to endure when Abigail told me that my baby had been born dead. I wanted to die too. I wished that Jack had killed me then, as he'd threatened to. I didn't want to live.

# CHAPTER 24

The hatred grew inside me, in the space that the baby had left. Unlike my child, though, it needed nothing from me to exist. It grew independently, suffocating me with its strength and its size, taking over my entire body, giving me no time to mourn my loss, or to feel the pain of my own injuries.

When I woke in the morning it was there, welling up with my consciousness. First I would feel for my child and find it gone. A wave of pain would rise up in me, but the anger was there with it and hate rode on its crest. All that I had had been taken from me. I was too sore to move, and my face too swollen to talk. So it was hatred that kept me alive, made me eat the soups and baby slops that Abigail fed me through straws. It must have worked my lungs when I had no desire to breathe, and it healed my outer body without my consent. I would gladly have died. I had nothing else to live for.

The sense of loneliness that I felt was unbearable. My child had been my only friend and my only possession. I even turned against Abigail, hating her for being a part of the country that had killed my child.

My husband was a thief – he had stolen from me every-thing that had ever mattered. He had taken my willpower and my freedom and even my desire to live. He had taken me from my father and from my home, which I had thought that I hated, but for which I felt a longing that could bring tears to my eyes in a moment. He had taken my beauty too. I could feel how badly my face was ruined, although Abigail refused me a mirror. At night I felt the surface of my skin with my fingertips and my body was an unfamiliar shape. My mind had changed and become deformed by Jack's beating; I found it only natural at the time that my body should have followed suit. So much hatred could never have lived inside the beautiful face that I had once had. Jack would see my outside and know what he had done to my inside too.

I could feel that my eyes were swollen to slits. They must have looked sly and scheming, which was right. I could not close my mouth. I felt that I looked like a monster. Abigail tried not to look at me when she talked to me. I frightened her with my looks. I would do the same to Jack.

They let me hold my baby, I think, though I may have been dreaming. It had black hair, like Frank, but it was wrapped so tight that I couldn't see its face. It was so small that I begged them to let me keep it but they took it away and I had no strength when I tried to cling on. I was frightened of hurting it too, if I clung on too hard, which was stupid because it was dead, and I knew that at the time.

'You're young, you've plenty of time to have another,' I heard someone say, and I wanted to laugh because monsters don't have perfect children, as this one had been perfect.

Jack came in to see me plenty of times, and it was as though nothing had happened. He looked the same. He talked the same. He showed no guilt or pity at what he had done. He showed nothing at all, if anything he seemed perkier, as though he'd shrugged off a burden that had troubled him for a while. His new occupation of murderer obviously suited him well. Perhaps he thought he had taught me a lesson at last. Perhaps my beating had finally earned him full acceptance with all the other men in his

circle of mates. Perhaps it was his last initiation ceremony
into the manhood of Jenolan.

It was as though the baby had never been, and to Jack
I suppose that it hadn't. The baby was Frank's, and he
had killed it. It had given Jack the chance to even an old
score. Now they were quits, perhaps, in Jack's mind.
He'd told the doctor that I'd been climbing to change a
light bulb and felt faint and fallen, but the doctor must
have known, which was why I wasn't sent to the hospital.
They liked life to be easy in our area. They thought that
you only found snakes if you went around poking at
things with a stick and our doctor wasn't one to want to
go looking for snake bites.

The doctor stood by Jack's version of the story and he
went about his work as usual and I said nothing because
I knew that was the way it should be. It wasn't the way
I wanted it and it wasn't the way my baby wanted it,
either. Nothing that anyone could have done would ever
have been equal to the crime that Jack had committed
against us. They gave me tablets for the pain and tablets
to make me sleep, but I fought against the sleep because
the pain of renewed remembrance that I woke with each
morning was more than I felt I could bear.

When I was finally able to speak, when my mouth
shrunk to size and my lips found some feeling, then my
anger spilt out like bile, without purpose or true targets,
and most times it was aimed at poor Abigail, for no other
reason than that she always was there. I feel shame now
to think of the words that I spoke to her, while she was
guilty of nothing more than being the only person who
was trying to help me.

She bathed my face and I swore at her. She changed
my nightclothes and bedding and lifted my head off the
pillow to feed me from straws, and yet I looked at her
with such hatred in my eyes that I often saw her flinch at
my gaze. I don't know now why she stayed. We were
friends, yet not in such a way that I would ever have felt
obliged to nurse her through the night if she had been ill

and on her sickbed. My baby was the only living creature that I had ever felt such selfless love for in my life, and once it was killed I failed to either recognize or understand that emotion in other people.

Yet still Abigail stayed, and I am now eternally grateful for her care, for I think that I would have died without her, either from neglect, or by taking my own life. She told me stories like a mother tells a child, long, far-reaching stories that at first I was too numbed to listen to, and which later I screamed at her to stop because each word brought pain to my head.

Gradually the stories registered in my mind, though, and I found them first soothing, then stimulating. She told them rhythmically, reciting, not pausing to think, and I realized with time that they were legends, not stories, and that she was telling me of the race that she came from.

The stories were simple – I could listen as I wanted, though the characters were numerous and I lost track of the names and various relationships. There were terms that I did not understand. There was no time-scheme in Abigail's tales. I tried to ask her to explain, but she told me that all time was now to the Aborigine, and that was how it felt in my head, with the pills and the pain, so I stopped asking questions and just listened instead.

'There is no death,' she told me, and I started to cry, for my baby had died and I knew that to be a fact.

'He didn't die,' Abigail said one day, and she held my hand in a shy gesture of comfort.

'He's dead,' I sobbed, my control falling completely to pieces with those two simple words.

'He's alive,' Abigail insisted, but in a whisper that I barely heard above my own crying. She had tears on her cheeks as well and in my fuddled state I hated her for daring to cry for my baby. She had no right to. He was mine. He belonged only to me.

'His spirit will never die, missus.'

I let off a stream of language at this that makes me blush to think of it now.

'What good's his spirit to me?' I shouted. 'It's him I want, not his spirit! I want my baby back, Abigail! I want my baby!' And I tailed off into the kind of wailing that Abigail had to subdue forcefully for fear that Jack would come in and lose his temper all over again.

But Abigail was persistent.

'His spirit's alive,' she said a few days later. 'He's free. You'll see, missus.'

I looked at her with my monster face and my slitted eyes must have drained her of all courage, but still she continued, until I was too weak to argue.

As my mind cleared, little by little, newer terrors would occur to me.

'Where is he?' I screamed out one night, grabbing Abigail so hard by the forearm that she jumped up in her chair with a cry. She must have been sleeping, her eyes were red and bleary in the flame of the nightlight, and she had taken the crochet bedcover from the end of the bed and laid it over her body, like a blanket.

'Who?' she whispered, her hand clasped to her throat in shock.

'My baby?' I asked, and my voice broke as always on the words. 'Where is he? What did they do with him?'

'He's in the graveyard in the town,' Abigail told me. 'He had a proper burial. They said he was old enough.'

My head sank back on to the pillows with relief at this, although I don't know where I found the comfort in Abigail's words, as I held no strong hopes of religion. Perhaps I had been scared that Jack had just thrown him into a hole in the garden, like a dead animal.

Then my thoughts centred on Frank.

Jack had murdered our child but it was Frank, the baby's own father, who had returned my letter and therefore brought about his death. Frank had addressed the letter to Jack, not to me, and it must have been in his

mind to wreak some terrible revenge on me by doing so.
I felt myself slipping, losing all my footholds on life. In
my loathing for my husband I had told myself that I loved
Frank. I had his ring. It was the only thing I owned that
I treasured. Yet it was Frank who had betrayed me to
Jack, a man who he hated. I felt myself falling, yet it was
hate that dragged me up yet again. I was buoyed up by
it, it supported me. It gave me a reason for living and a
reason for regaining my strength. I had something to do.
I had to get revenge for my baby. An eye for an eye,
that's how we did it in London. I had no one to turn to.
I would have to get that revenge by myself.

'You can't live here,' Abigail told me as she held my arm
on my first walk round the back yard since the night that
Jack had beaten me. The air smelled sweet and seemed
full of noise. Sickrooms are quiet as the grave and I
enjoyed the sounds and the warm sun on my back. I
looked round towards the sun and my head spun with the
birds that circled the blue sky. My body ached, but I'd
long since learned not to bother with the pain. My face
felt flatter, the swellings had gone down. I was less of a
monster, though when I saw Henry watching me, I wondered what thoughts went through his head. I walked like
an old woman, with his sister's support. My stomach was
flat, I no longer carried a child, yet my face was bruised
and cut.

'You have to go now,' Abigail whispered, 'you can't
live with him after all this.'

'All the men beat their wives,' I reminded her in a flat,
tired voice that sounded nothing like my own. 'I'll learn
to live with it if the others can.'

Abigail turned to face me, and her mouth was round
with shock. 'He nearly killed you,' she said. 'He'll kill
you proper if you stay. He's a bad man, missus.' Her face
looked dark, as though she knew more than she was
prepared to tell me.

'You don't know what *I* did to *him*,' I said. 'He found

out that my child wasn't his. That's why he did what he did. It was my fault, Abigail. I don't want you thinking bad of my husband.'

Abigail dropped my arm as though it had burned her, and I staggered, losing my balance.

'You're lying!' she told me. 'You don't think that at all! You hate him, I know you do!'

I caught at a fence and held on till the world stopped spinning and I could catch my breath again.

'Don't tell me what I think,' I said. 'Don't dare to tell me that I'm lying. You don't know, Abigail. You don't know anything. You live in that van at the end of our yard and God knows but you're screwing your own brother. You clean other people's houses and they lock up their valuables in case you take them, and you've got the nerve to tell *me* what to do!'

I saw the pain in Abigail's face, but I couldn't stop, I swear that I couldn't. It came out as it had been coming out for weeks, pouring from my mouth in a stream, my voice rising as it did so. I saw Henry stop work and throw down his spade and come running towards us.

'I'll tell you what I can't do, Abigail!' I screamed. 'What I can't do is to leave. That's what I can't do, if you're interested, because where would I go? I've no money, I've no home but the one Jack provides for me, there's the baby to think of, oh God . . .' I sank to my knees as a new wave struck me. I knew, but I'd forgotten and it came back with the force of a mallet blow. There was no baby any more. Hands caught me and I felt myself being pulled to my feet, though I was still screaming somewhere in my head, and my ears were ringing with the sound of those screams.

Henry lifted me and he carried me towards the house, but then I saw Abigail's arm on his elbow, and I saw she was shaking her head.

'You're not allowed in there, Henry, you know you're not,' she said.

I saw a cloud of anger cross the boy's face, and he

looked at the house as though he hated the place as much as I did.

'Better come indoors then,' he said, and he carried me across the yard to their caravan.

I welcomed the shade as we walked inside, and he laid me on the bed gently, as though he was handling a child. I looked around the small room and wondered that he could stand upright, he looked so tall in there. Abigail followed him, her face wrinkled with concern.

'I'll clear off,' Henry said. 'You stay till you're cooled down.'

Abigail held a piece of rag under the tap and laid it across my forehead till I could think.

'I'm sorry,' I said, and I started crying again. 'I've got no strength any more. I don't mean to fight with you, Abigail, it's just that I can't stand the thoughts that are in my head right now. You don't know how I feel – you can't. Don't ask me to discuss Jack or the baby because if I do I'll frighten you, that's all. You don't want to know what I'm thinking and you don't want to know how I feel. You just treat Jack the same, as though nothing's happened. Be like him, and forget it, Abigail. Then if anything happens you can say you knew nothing about it, like the doctor and the others in this place. You don't want to go poking into other people's business, Abigail. Just treat Jack with some respect and stay out of his way. Keep your nose out of things, that's best.'

Abigail's mouth shut like a trap and she stared at me, lying there on her brother's narrow bed.

'He'll kill you some day,' she said.

'Forget it,' I told her, and turned my head into the pillow.

'You can't stand for it, I know you won't.'

'Shut up.'

'When you're strong again you'll leave.'

I sat up, exasperated by her persistence.

'And just where could I go?' I asked her. 'I don't have a car and there's no public transport takes you anywhere round here. Do I just hitch into town and book the best room in the hotel? I told you, Abbey, I've no money and I've got no friends to help me. Do I just stroll off into the outback like you Abos are supposed to do? How long d'you think it would be before Jack came and found me wherever I went? I'd be dead for sure then.'

'You'll have to kill him then,' Abigail said, at least I thought that's what she said, but she spoke so quietly that I may have been mistaken. I looked quickly at her face, but it was expressionless, as though she had never spoken. She just stared at me. Had she really spoken my own thoughts out loud, or had my imagination just put them on to her lips? For I had decided days ago, long before I heard Abigail say it, that I would have to murder my husband.

It was three weeks before I was strong enough to leave the house on my own. My wounds were healing. I had found a mirror and my reflection scared me less than I had thought it would. My face had lost its prettiness, though, it was leaner, hollowed at the cheeks. My eyes looked larger and empty of everything but the liquid. They swam like round green lakes, without fire or life, ready to spill over if my control faltered for a second. But there was fire still in my face, vivid red-heat fire in the shape of the scar that ran from my cheekbone to my mouth, etched across the white flesh like a slow and very deliberate symbol of all that I'd been through.

I licked the tip of my finger and ran it down the line in my skin. It had no feeling. It could have been painted on. My face fascinated me now. I could not get enough of looking at it. Before it had been like a pretty mask, saying nothing, covering my feelings, but now it told stories, like an elaborate tapestry. If I ever forgot what Jack had done to me I had only to look in the mirror for the story of that night to come to life.

My eyes had hollows that were grey shadows around the water-green irises. My skin was whiter, transparent, so that I could see the network of cotton-thin veins that ran beneath the surface. There was an explosion of yellow and blue below my chin, where a bruise was fading like rotten fruit. My lashes looked black and wet, stuck together with tears.

'I'm going out to the rocks,' I told Abigail when she saw me dressed and alone in the kitchen. She knew where I meant. There were rocks a few miles off that she said held the spirits of her ancestors. She'd told me stories of them while I'd lain in my bed recovering. She'd told me they held magic powers, but I doubted whether even she believed that. Aborigines used to meet at the rocks to pray. It was quiet there, and beautiful, and I needed some peace.

Abigail ran round the kitchen like a headless chicken, her feet dragging the floor in her too-big sandals.

'I'll come too,' she said, pushing her arms into the sleeves of her cardigan. 'It's a long way. You won't make it by yourself. You'll need company. There's wild animals and things out there.'

'I don't want you there,' I said, stopping her. 'I want to be by myself for a bit. That's why I'm going.'

'You don't know the way.' Abigail was not about to give up.

'You said it was in a straight line,' I told her. 'You told me you could point to it and get there by walking in that direction. There's no wild animals out there, Abbey, you told me that yourself.'

In the end we agreed that she would come part of the way, just to make sure I was on the right track, but I made her promise not to come further with me.

I walked slowly, which I could tell annoyed Abigail, whose movements became lithe and more graceful when she walked in the open. I had noticed that before, the way her heavy, old-lady's walk would be shrugged off once her feet were bare and walking on flat dry dirt once again. She strode ahead of me, her long arms swinging and her head constantly turning, as though she expected someone to be following us.

I felt my head clear as we put some space between ourselves and the house. I kicked my shoes off as Abigail had done, and tied the laces and hung them round my neck, but my feet were sore by the time the laces were knotted, and we had to stop so that I could put them back on again.

'Can you hear the noise of the land?' Abigail asked, and as I listened I believed that I could. There was a kind of low humming that seemed to come from the earth beneath our feet. It was all around us, but if you listened too hard it stopped.

'It's my ears,' I told her. 'It's just the heat buzzing in my ears.' But Abigail shook her head and grinned, as though to say that there was a lot that I still had to learn.

I would have kept to the road, for I still liked the closeness of passing cars and trucks, but Abigail walked us across country while I followed, out of breath and panting in the heat. As the sun rose higher I began to sweat, and pulled off my cotton shirt to wrap around my head, like a scarf. I saw Abigail look sideways at me then, and I laughed because she looked prim at finding me walking in my bra and shorts, yet there was no one around us for miles.

'Something up?' I called to her, laughing.

'Someone might see,' she muttered, rushing on.

'Who, Abbey?' I asked. 'Some of those wild animals that you were on about? Or do we come across a few large cities in a minute? There's no one about, Abbey, you can see that for yourself.' But I saw Abigail glance over her shoulder as though still thinking that we might be followed.

We walked into a cathedral cover of high eucalyptus trees and I dragged at Abigail to make her stop, so that I could lie in the cool perfumed air until my blood stopped racing in my veins.

'I'm exhausted,' I told her, lying back on a bed of moss.

'I told you not to come,' she said, chewing at some grass.

'You're an old woman,' I said. 'You fuss like some old granny.'

Abigail smiled and showed her huge white teeth. 'I'm younger than you, missus,' she said, grinning.

'It's up here,' I said, tapping my forehead. 'You've the mind of a three-hundred-year-old witch. All the stories you told me, all those legends and religious stuff. You must've been old when you were born.'

'You believed some of it, else why are you here?' Abigail said simply.

'I told you,' I said, 'I just wanted to be on my own for a bit. Now I've got you lumbering along with me for company. You drive me mad, you know, Abigail.'

'You've come here to find the spirit of your baby, that's why you've come here,' Abigail said, and she'd stopped smiling.

'I don't believe all that crap,' I told her.

'You're alone in the house all day,' she said. 'There's no need for you to walk all these miles just to be alone. You could have sat indoors to do that. You've come here for the same reason that all my people came here, to pray for their dead and to ask the rocks to show them where their spirits have gone to. Once you know that, you can be at peace.'

'Don't talk stupid, Abbey,' I said angrily. 'You don't believe all that rubbish either. You were born in the town, not in some Aborigine camp in the outback. Why, your dad wasn't even black – you're half white, your dad used to live in the house, everyone knows that.'

'Henry's dad,' Abigail said quietly. 'Mine was full Aborigine.'

'Well, that doesn't make you some kind of seer for the whole tribe,' I said, struggling to get to my feet.

'Your baby's soul is out there,' Abigail said, walking off ahead again. 'If you don't pray for it, it will never find its home.'

I left Abigail a few yards further on, when we could see the rocks in the distance.

'Buzz off,' I told her.

'I'll wait,' she said. 'You won't find your way back otherwise.' I knew she was right, but I was annoyed just the same.

The rocks were disappointing when I reached them, just a few bald stumps standing out in an area of flat red dust, like a desert. The air was cooler, and I unrolled the blanket I'd brought with me and stretched out on it.

'If there's any magic in you you'd better do your best,' I whispered, staring up till the sun burned spots in front of my eyes. My head ached with the heat and the effort of getting to the rocks. I sat up as the pain grew sharper, crossing my legs in front of me and rocking to and fro on my buttocks as I groaned out loud with the relief of being left alone at last to mourn.

A shadow crossed the sun and the air grew silent and I licked at my dry lips and sipped some water from my flask. The place was empty. Abigail's gods were not there for me, there was no magic, just a feeling of isolation alongside the deep well of gratitude I felt at being truly alone.

The rocks stood tall in front of me.

'I could die here,' I said, letting my head tilt backward so that the sun beat down on my closed eyelids. I had spoken aloud, and it was as though my words had started a chain reaction, for the dying sun threw out spears of ochre flame as it sank finally behind the stones, and from the core of the flame came a noise that startled me to my knees.

There was a heavy beating, whirring sound in the air and shadow-patterns formed over the sun. A large wild bird, as red as the sun's rays, had unfurled its wings and prepared for flight from the rock. I watched open-mouthed and frozen in sudden shock. The bird soared into the darkening sky as though shot from a gun, its

wings beating heavily and furiously, its long beak pointing towards the heavens.

'Your baby's soul is out there,' I heard Abigail's voice
say in my head. 'If you don't pray for it it will never find
a home.'

I prayed for it then. I prayed so hard that my knuckles
turned white from the effort.

'Let the bird take my baby's soul,' I prayed. 'Let it be
free to go with it!' And I let my head fall into my lap as
I cried tears of pure relief.

I heard a noise behind me but I didn't jump or move
because I had lost all of my fear, and because I had known
all along who it was that Abigail had been looking for as
we'd walked together through the bush.

Henry stood there, silently watching, as he'd watched
me so many times from the garden, his face impassive,
just watching and waiting.

'Henry?' I asked quietly. Perhaps he was the god. He
looked grey and solid in the darkness, as though he had
been hewn out of the rocks themselves.

'Abigail told me . . .' he began.

'She told you to keep an eye on me,' I finished for him.
My voice sounded strange, sort of deeper and cracked.

'Are you mad?' Henry asked.

I shook my head slowly, rubbing life into my bloodless
legs as I did so. 'No,' I whispered, 'I'm not mad.'

'Did you see it?' he asked, stepping nearer until I could
hear his breathing and it became one with the sounds of
the land and the night. 'Did you see the bird?'

I nodded again and tears began to roll out of my eyes.

'Abigail told you,' he said. 'It's good, your baby has
found a home.'

'That's crap, Henry,' I tried to say, but the words
wouldn't come because I didn't believe them. Instead I
made a noise of choking in my throat and then I broke
down completely and I was glad that Abigail had sent
Henry to keep an eye on me because all my remaining
strength had left me, and it was Henry who carried me

home and Abigail who tucked me like a child into my
bed.

# CHAPTER 25

I was with Jack for three years after the death of my baby. I stayed because I knew that I had to, because there was no other option open to me. The waiting was a discipline. The strength that I needed to get through each day gave my hatred a fine point, so that it was sharp and well-turned, like a superbly-honed sword.

We lived surprisingly normally. Jack stayed out most nights at first and would spend most weekends away, I guessed, in Sydney. He never mentioned the baby, not once, and he never once harmed me again either, although he would have done on more than one occasion had I not carried a knife when he was drunk and made sure that he knew it. Our marriage seemed normal to the outside world, and I took care that it did. I even went into town with him several times and sat with the other wives in the outer bar while the men drank beer in the next room. We sat placidly, most times silently, and some women even knitted, while their husbands laughed nearby. I told those who asked that I'd miscarried, and that we were trying for another baby, and I would take Jack's arm as we walked to the van to drive home.

I even asked Jack to take me to church one Sunday, but it was then that he turned on me and I could see that I'd gone too far.

'They'd never let you past the fuckin' door, Ruby!' he

shouted, and his anger was so sudden that it took me off-balance.

He pushed his chair back from the table and ran for the drawer and I said a quick prayer and crossed myself because I thought he'd beaten me to the knife at last, and that he'd kill me for sure. I only wanted to see where my baby had been buried there and to pray for it, but I couldn't tell Jack that for fear he'd go wild.

It was the Bible that he pulled out, though, not a knife. 'This used to mean something to me, Ruby,' he said, lifting the book level with his face and stabbing its cover with his finger. 'You swore on this, remember?' He grabbed me by the arm, but I pulled away.

'You swore in front of God, Ruby, but you told the biggest lie of your life, didn't you? You swore to God that that child was mine. And you want to turn up in church just as though nothing had happened. You'd get a fuckin' lightning bolt strike you down before you got one foot inside the door if there was any justice in this world. You're a barefaced heathen of a liar! You're evil, Ruby, that's what you are! As evil as they come, and if you think I'm taking you to church then you must think that I'm fuckin' mad.'

Jack calmed down after this and continued his dinner, the Bible near at hand on the table, as though to remind me of the lie that I had told. I walked slowly to the sink, clutching at furniture as I went. Jack's shaving mirror hung there from some string, and I looked at my face in it. I was white. My eyes bulged with fear. The scar stood out livid against the whiteness. The other signs of Jack's beating had gone, but the scar would never heal. All time is now. The scar was my past and my present and it would be there for all my future. Perhaps it had always been there and I'd just never noticed it. What else was there, just waiting to come out?

Henry continued to ignore me, as before. He just stared, as though waiting for me to do something, to make the move that we all knew would come. Perhaps he wondered why I took so long about it. Abigail wondered too, I could tell from the way that she watched me.

The letter from Marge arrived during the second year of this period of waiting, and for a time I thought that the end had come. Billy had cancer, Marge wrote, and did not have long to live. It was in his lungs, she said, they'd found it at a mass X-ray unit that had come to the market. Her huge sprawled writing had swum in front of my eyes and only one thought had been in my mind; that I had to be with him, that I couldn't let him die so far away from me, that it was right that I should be there, that without me there would only have been Marge.

I went straight to Jack, to the garage where he worked, Marge's letter still in my hand. I believe the news had no effect on him, for his expression barely changed and he carried on with his work.

'I've got to go back,' I told him. I was prepared to beg and plead if that was what Jack wanted.

'What for?' Jack said. There was a customer in the shop, and I think he was embarrassed. The man stood there in the corner, spinning a carousel of postcards of the Jenolan caves, while a bluebottle climbed the window beside his face. He showed no sign of leaving.

'I've got to be with him,' I said, dropping my voice a bit. 'He's my father, Jack, he'll need me.'

Jack turned to look at me. 'There's nothing you can do,' he said. 'They won't expect it of you. Your home's here now. You can't keep popping back for everything.'

'But he's dying, Jack!' I said.

'My mum died,' Jack said, and he turned back to his papers. '*I* wasn't there. It can't be helped. These things happen. You'll make him worse if you turn up; then he'll know he's on the way out. Chances are he doesn't even know it's serious yet. How d'you think it'll look to him if you go rushing to his bedside? Better to leave him in the dark, give him a few happy weeks, anyway.'

At last the doorbell pinged as the customer left the shop and I let my voice rise as we no longer had an audience.

'I've got to go!' I shouted. 'You can't stop me, Jack! It wasn't the same with your mother, she was old and she went unexpected. Billy's still young and I've got time to get there. I've got to go!'

'And where do you suppose the money's coming from for the trip?' Jack asked. 'We're skint, Ruby. I couldn't afford to send you to the next town, let alone to England. I'm sorry about Billy but you'll just have to accept it. If they want you there so badly then they'll have to send the air fare. I can't stump up for it, I couldn't even start to.'

I grabbed at Jack's arm and he looked about quickly, hoping that no one was watching.

'There's that money of your mum's,' I said, 'from the sale of her house. I know you invested it but surely Ralph'll let you have some back on tick? I'll pay you back, I'll do anything!'

Jack went red and I thought he was angry, but instead he looked away and I saw him choosing his words.

'I can't get at that money,' he said slowly.

'Ask Ralph,' I said. 'I'm sure he'd understand. Please try, Jack! It's your money, he's got to let you have it.'

'Ralph's not here,' Jack told me. 'He's back in London.'

'Write to him then!' I begged. 'Phone him – you must have kept in touch! You're business partners, aren't you?'

'I haven't seen him for months,' Jack said. 'I don't know about the business, he hasn't been in touch to tell me.'

'You've lost the money!' I said, stepping back from Jack's desk. 'It's not invested, is it? It's gone. Ralph's lost it.'

Jack looked up then, and his face had turned nasty. 'He invested it,' he said. 'I don't know where he is, but the money's ticking over, it's OK. It's just not anywhere where you can get your dirty little hands on it, that's all.'

I sank into a chair and covered my face with my hands. 'Oh God, it's all gone, isn't it?' I said. 'He's got the lot, hasn't he, and now he's gone and lost it? The only money we were ever likely to get, and you've blown the lot, haven't you, Jack? What happened? Did he find out you were screwing his wife?' It was lucky the man came back for the postcards then, or I think Jack would have punched me hard enough to knock out some teeth. Instead he gave me a terrible look, which told me that most of what I had guessed was right.

I still held on, though. I bided my time, because I knew I had to wait if I was ever to be free of Jack. Billy died, and I thought my heart would break again. Two deaths of people I had cared about, and I could attend the funeral of neither. Apart from the fact that I missed his letters, even though it was Marge who'd written them for him, Billy could still have been alive. For a while I thought he'd gone to prison again and that Marge was too ashamed to tell me.

The time to leave came later, a whole year later, and it wasn't my baby or Billy that decided me. Something else pushed me over the edge and made me know that I'd waited long enough.

It was winter in Australia but that didn't seem to make any difference to the weather for it was hotter than it had been some summers in London, and it was cloudy at the same time so we suffocated in the stiflingly humid heat. It was as though you had to pull the air into your lungs, as though the heat had thickened it, like pea soup, and some afternoons I just lay on the bed, exhausted with the effort of trying to breathe. My thin cotton housecoat stuck to my body as though it were painted there, and my hair was plastered to the back of my neck.

Jack had been home more often lately and his presence there annoyed me. Both our tempers were short in the heat and I was scared something terrible might happen. He'd started coming home at weekends now, so I guessed he was no longer seeing Philippa. He'd turned to me again for sex, something he'd avoided doing for months. The sex no longer appalled or disgusted me, for I no longer had cherished memories of those times with Frank to compare it with. I just ignored it, rode above it, as I had

learned to do with the pain when I had been lying in bed
after my child had died. It would end. I had plans. My
life there would not go on for ever and was therefore
bearable. My one fear was that Jack would make me
pregnant, and I scrubbed my body clean at the sink after
he had finished, as though washing away his sweat would
somehow clean me of any chance of conceiving.

The beer had made Jack fatter. He was a dead weight
as he lay on top of me. I could barely draw breath and
yet when I did breathe it was to inhale the smell of his
warm, earthy body. I hardly moved when he took me,
just lay there on my back on the bed and parted my legs
so that he had no need to hurt me. Jack was neither brutal
nor gentle and my silent passivity seemed to egg him on,
rather than put him off. He needed no arousing, he would
just turn to me and enter me, and be finished in a moment.
Once he tried to kiss me, but I turned my head away
and he never tried again. I wondered whether he missed
Philippa, and whether their sex together had been similar.
Somehow I could never imagine it being any different.

I was twenty-one years old. My birthday had been a
week earlier and Abigail had baked me a small cake. My
childhood and my youth were over. I was a woman, and
looked it. There was no innocence in my face and no
hope, either, yet I felt that the time to leave was close,
and a flame had burned up in my eyes again.

As I lay on my bed I watched Abigail through the half-
open door. I was drowsy and drugged with the heat, but
Abigail worked, it seemed to me, happily. Her back was
turned and bent over the sink. Her elbows were wet and
there were suds on her face and her hair. She looked
orange in the low light from the bulb by the stove.

Henry had bought Abigail a transistor radio for her
birthday and she played it around the house when Jack
wasn't there. She liked old dance music, like waltzes and
foxtrots, and there was a waltz on when Jack walked in,
which was why she didn't hear him. I knew Jack was
drunk because this was always the time of night for him

to be drunk, though he'd come home by himself and was
therefore able to stand.

Jack watched Abigail from the doorway, his eyes taking
in every movement as she bobbed about by the sink in
time to 'The Blue Danube'. I thought how happy the
three of us would have looked if that moment had been
caught in a picture. There would have been the small,
safe, low-lit kitchen, its yellow light bathing everything
in a comfortable glow, like a dying fire; there was Abbey,
working contentedly at the sink, and Jack's tall shape
leaning in the doorway. His arms were folded and he
almost seemed to be smiling. There was the half-open
door to the bedroom where I lay in the darkness, but I
was resting on my elbows by then, and alert to any sound
or movement.

Jack crept up behind Abigail and he was light on his
feet for a drunk. She didn't hear him until he was just
behind her and then she whipped round, spilling suds and
hot water in her wake.

Jack just grinned down at her. He looked massive beside
her and I saw real fear on her face.

'I'll turn it off,' Abigail said, and she reached for the
radio, though Jack stopped her.

'Let it play,' he said. 'It's good music. I thought you
Abos were only into war dances round the old camp fire,'
and he laughed at his own joke. 'D'you know how to
waltz, Abigail?' Jack asked, and Abbey shook her head so
that her hair fell over her face. Jack put his hands out like
some Edwardian dandy and cocked his head to one side,
waiting. Abigail's hand went to her mouth and she sucked
at her fingers.

'Don't want to dance, boss,' she said quietly. 'Don't
know how to.'

'I'll show you,' Jack said, and his voice sounded kind,
though his smile was growing darker.

Abigail shook her head a little, and that was when Jack
grabbed her.

'I'll show you,' he repeated, and his arm went round

her waist while he held her right hand out to the side. He pulled Abigail around the kitchen table in a stiff, ragged waltz and the scene would have been funny had the skin on my arms not been standing up in bumps, and my mouth not been dry with fear at what might happen next.

'One-two-three, one-two-three,' Jack shouted out as they circled the room, and the nylon ribbon bow came loose from Abigail's hair and fell to the floor, where Jack trampled it next time round. I felt, rather than saw, the tears of fear well up in Abigail's eyes. I knew that she wanted to struggle, to pull away, but Jack held her trapped like a mesmerized rabbit.

'Leave her!' I said. I'd got as far as the doorway but Jack hadn't noticed. His head snapped back with the shock of hearing my voice, though God knows where else he'd expected me to be, he must have been more drunk than he looked. He stopped whirling round suddenly, and Abigail fell against the table.

'*I'll* dance, if you want,' I told him, and he looked at Abigail and then he looked across at me and for once I think he was stuck for words. '*I'll dance with you!*' I shouted, and even Abigail looked scared.

Jack wiped his hand across his mouth as though I'd caught him kissing her and I believe he swore, though he spoke so softly that I couldn't catch his words. He left the house and I heard him go off down the path to the road, and I stood over Abigail as she sobbed, leaning on the table.

'Did he ever touch you before?' I asked her and she shook her head, though she didn't turn to face me.

'Did he, Abbey?' I had my hands on my hips. She was still then, and when her face came round it was streaked with dirt and tears.

'Not much,' she said. 'Nothing much. Or I'd've told Henry.'

'And just what would Henry have done?' I asked her. 'He's about as afraid of Jack as you are.'

'He wouldn't have to fight,' Abigail mumbled. I pulled her hand away from her mouth.

'What then?' I asked. 'What else?'

'There's ways,' she said, and her ambiguity made me mad enough to hit her.

'What ways?' I asked, pulling at her arms to make her talk to me. 'What do you know? How would Henry get his own back on the boss? Tell me, or it'll be me that's hitting you, not Jack!' But it was Jack who scared her, not me, I could tell that from the look on her face.

'Is it the curses?' I asked her.

'What curses?' she said.

'You told me, Abbey,' I said, shaking her, 'you told me when I was sick. You said your people put curses on their enemies, and that those people always died soon after. Does Henry know how to curse people, Abbey? Could he kill Jack for me?'

Abigail's eyes opened to the size of pickled onions and she looked almost comic standing there, with me shaking at her arms.

'They're just stories, they're not true,' she gibbered. 'I just told you those things while you were getting well. You couldn't think straight, I just talked about anything. I made them up, that's all!'

'Pointing the bone, that's what you call it, isn't it?' I told her. 'Can Henry do that? Can he point the bone, Abigail?'

Abigail shook her head. 'Henry can't do anything,' she said. 'He's not even full Aborigine. No one does that thing any more. It's just tales the Abos put out to scare people.'

'You're lying,' I told her. 'You believed it when you told me, I could tell you did, just like I can tell that you're lying to me now.'

Abigail started to shake, and I tried to talk to her calmly, because I could see she was getting hysterical.

'Abigail,' I said quietly, 'I can't stand it any more. If I live with Jack for one more year then either he'll kill me

or I'll go mad anyway. He killed my baby. He nearly
killed me. He lost all our money so that I couldn't be
with my father when he died. Now he's starting on you.
I could see the way he looked at you, Abbey. How long
before he starts to treat you like he's been treating me?
He's like a dog with a rat to worry, Abbey. He could tell
you were scared and that makes him worse. I've got to
get rid of him, Abbey, I can't live like this any more!'

Abigail sank down into the chair, her head shaking
slowly from side to side. 'I'm sorry for you, missus,' she
said, 'but there's nothing I can do. I can't help you. If you
get found out you'll get arrested. I can't see you go to
jail. I don't mind about the boss, he won't touch me
again, he was just drunk. I'll get Henry to keep an eye
out for me, that's all. It'll soon stop.'

'It'll stop when he's dead, Abigail,' I told her, and I
shouted despite myself, 'not before!'

Abigail looked me in the eye then, and I could tell that
she agreed even though she kept shaking her head. She
would help me too, I could see that. So my period of
waiting was over. The time had come, as I knew it would.
Seeing Jack pawing Abigail had been the sign that I'd been
looking for. All time was now. This was when it should
happen, I could feel it as strongly as you feel a storm
coming on a clear summer's day. Jack had to die, he
deserved to die. It was justice, the way Abigail's people
did it, and the way my people did it. An eye for an eye,
and Jack was marked out for revenge, just like Frank.

# CHAPTER 26

I believe I should have felt some horror at my own actions at that time, but in truth I can say that I felt none at all, only a kind of elation at the thought that soon I would be free of the fear and of the debt that I owed my baby. I cannot remember having any doubts about what I planned to do, or any feelings of remorse either.

Jack could have felt no sense of foreboding at what was to come, for he continued in his fatal ways; with his threatened abuse, his drinking, and the enforced sex that I endured every night. I watched him court Abigail with a drunkard's charm, touching her when she worked, watching her as he ate his supper, and laughing at the fear that she showed when he stood too close and worried her.

I watched Abigail too, and she knew what I was waiting for. I believed in her stories, and I knew that she had the means, somehow, to help me. A week passed, then a fortnight, and I became scared when nothing happened. Then, in the end, she came to me after all.

'The curses don't work,' she said, standing before me wringing her hands. 'It's all just superstition, something crazy to scare the enemy.'

'You did it, didn't you?' I asked her, and she looked down at her feet. 'Abigail?'

'I saw an old man,' she said, quietly. 'He scared hell out of me, but he said he'd do it. I think he was just mad though, missus.' She tapped the side of her forehead. 'I think maybe he could scare someone to death all right,' she went on, 'but I don't think he's got any real powers. They're all just stories, I told you. You shouldn't hope for too much.'

'How long, Abbey?' I asked, grabbing her shoulders. 'How long before it works?'

Abigail shrugged. 'A few weeks, maybe. I don't know,' she said, so offhand with fear that I wanted to shake her harder.

'Didn't you have to pay him?' I asked. 'Didn't he want money?'

Abigail nodded and looked suddenly embarrassed. 'He told me that the first time I went there,' she said. 'He wanted a lot of money when he found out who it was I wanted the bone pointed at. He said white men were dearer, and men with power like the boss would be even more. I did a deal, though, knocked him down a bit.'

'How much?' I asked, suddenly afraid. I had no money and nothing to sell. The thought of having to pay the old man had only just occurred to me.

'It's OK,' Abigail said. 'He's been paid. It's all done.'

'How?' I asked her. 'Where did you get the money, Abbey?'

Abigail grinned then, and I saw those great white teeth for the first time in ages.

'She always accused me of stealing from her,' she said. 'I did nothing more than what I'd already been blamed for.'

'Who?' I asked. 'Mrs Haast?'

Abigail nodded.

'You stole from Mrs Haast?' I could see that woman in my mind, white-faced with anger, and I smiled because Abigail looked so proud of herself.

'But she wears all her jewellery,' I said. 'She told me that when she came here!'

'Not all the time she doesn't,' Abigail told me. 'Not

when she's down at the van with Henry, anyway. Then she takes it off.'

'Henry?'

Abigail nodded, watching my expression change.

'But she spoke about Henry as though . . . she told me you and Henry . . .'

I could finish neither sentence. Abigail did the job for me.

'And that's why she won't be asking for the ring back,' she said. 'Or calling out the wallopers, for that matter.'

I was amazed at Abigail's deviousness, and shocked to think of Henry and Mrs Haast together in that dingy caravan he lived in. Abigail got up to leave, but then she stopped in the doorway.

'There was something else,' she said, and I could tell from her voice that she was debating whether or not to tell me. She fished in the pocket of her apron and came out with a small folded paper bag.

'The old man told me to tell you,' she said. 'If what he's done doesn't work properly then you're to give the boss this.' She pushed the bag into my hands and ran off down the path. I unfolded the paper carefully and looked inside. There was some powder there, rough, dirty-looking stuff, like tea-leaves mixed with dust. I held it to my nose but surprisingly it had no smell. I stuffed it into my pocket and turned the sound on Abigail's small radio up full, as though frightened the neighbours might hear my thoughts.

I waited for three weeks, watching Jack each day for a sign that the curse might be working. If he coughed in his sleep I was awake at once. If he groaned when he was drunk I would feel my stomach turn. Even the sweat on his brow after a day in the sun took on a sinister aspect. He was sick once, and that was all, and I suspected the drink rather than any curse.

I took my disappointment out on Abigail, questioning

her all the time, demanding to know how long I should wait, though I realized she knew no more than I did.

'It was no good,' she would say. 'I told you, missus, the old man has no power. I told you all along. Use the powder, that might work.'

'I can't,' I told her. 'The stuff must be poison. Jack might taste it – he'd kill me then if he thought anything.'

But I tried a bit on him, just a few grains in his coffee, because I was desperate, and because I no longer cared about myself, and because my depression had made me reckless, so that I was no longer bothered whether I went to prison or not. There was nothing else waiting for me, even with Jack dead. I just needed the relief of knowing that he was gone for good.

Jack fell ill straight away, and the speed of the poison jolted me out of my stupor so that I shook with fear at the thought of what I had done. I felt no guilt for Jack's suffering, but I was worried for Abigail and, at last, a little, for myself.

Jack took to his bed with what he described as a weakness, and he felt no pain, for which I was pleased, or he might have been suspicious. I sat by his side on a small bentwood chair like the dutiful wife I had to pretend to be, and when the fever came on him I mopped his brow with a wet cloth, as Abigail had mine when I was recovering from his beating.

He talked a lot in his sleep, and called Philippa's name several times, which made me whisper silently to him to die, because I hated him all the more. As I watched him lying there in the bed I wondered over and again how this man could have been the same man that I'd trusted to care for me when I'd married him in London. We'd both been liars, of course, I know that now. Jack had lied about his character, which was miles away from the dependable copper that he'd pretended to be, while I'd lied unwittingly about my innocence, and then about the baby when I'd said it was his. The lies stacked up on both sides, but I could see Jack's crimes as the greater.

I went for the doctor the following day and my hands shook as he made his examination, so that I could not pour the tea that I had made for him through worrying about his diagnosis. How I stood there silently watching as he tapped Jack's chest and took his pulse I shall never know, but I found the courage to do it, for if I hadn't called the doctor then I'd have been a suspect for sure.

Abigail stood wide-eyed in the kitchen and I took her hand once and squeezed it to show that I had the strength for both of us.

'You doing this for me, missus?' she asked in a child's voice.

'For you?' I was surprised. 'Why?'

Abigail swallowed as though her throat were blocked. 'Because he started touching me,' she said. 'Because you were scared for me.'

'I did it for myself,' I told her. 'What I saw him doing to you was just a sign to tell me to get on with it, that's all.'

'Thank you, missus,' she said, anyway, and smiled as I patted her arm.

'It's a fever,' the doctor said when he'd packed his case away. 'But then you knew that already, didn't you?' He frowned at me and I nodded my head, trying to look concerned.

'What caused it?' I asked, and he looked annoyed.

'It's a virus,' he told me. 'Half the town are down with it, surely you knew? Watch it, it goes to the lungs if you're not careful. Ring me if he starts having trouble breathing and we'll have to get him off to hospital to drain them. Look after yourself too, if you don't mind. Get young Abigail to share some of the nursing. If you get down you may catch it too.' And with that he left, leaving the door screen banging in his wake.

Jack began coughing that night and it was dawn before he slept, exhausted with the effort. I slept at last too, my head resting against the tallboy, and when I awoke it was to see Jack lying there, staring up at me with a terrible

look on his face, just as though he'd read my thoughts
while I'd been sleeping.

'Ruby?' he asked, and I jumped up, clutching my
throat. His voice was hoarse and his skin looked grey. 'I
need some water,' he said, and I relaxed a little and went
about filling the jug in the kitchen. When I got back he
was dead, it was as simple as that. No sound, no screaming, no accusations, Jack just died while I stood by the
sink. I closed his eyes with my fingers so that he should
not stare at me any more and I crossed myself because it
seemed the right thing to do.


'His heart gave out,' the doctor said and I watched, not
daring to breathe, as he signed the certificate. 'I'm sorry,
missus. He was a strong enough man but the booze
must've weakened him. Small children around here have
lived through this fever but the beer must've weakened
his heart already. I warned him what it can do to a man,
drinking as hard as he did, but he wouldn't listen, none
of them ever will. Shame, though, to see a man cut down
in his prime like your husband. He was a good man,
there's lots around here that will miss him, and you can't
say that for many of the Poms you meet.'

When he'd gone I found Abigail standing by the bed,
staring down at Jack's body.

'The doctor said he was a good man,' I said, and I felt
Abigail shudder slightly beside me.

I went in again later. Jack looked as though he were
asleep, but his face looked younger, like it had back in
London, before all the troubles. The doctor must have
crossed his arms over his chest. There was a candle by
the bed that Abigail had put there, as though Jack would
be afraid of the dark, as I was. You could see the veins
on his eyelids. I pushed his hair back off his forehead, as
you would with a child. His nails had dirt under them
but I knew I could never bring myself to clean them.
There was a nurse coming in the morning and I thought

she would do it. They laid people out. I wondered what it was that they did.

Jack's hands interested me. They lay so still, crossed together. They had been all over my body, inside my body, and they had been used as fists to punch my body. Yet they lay there so quietly. All time is now. I waited for his eyes to open again and for him to accuse me, but accuse me of what? I'd tried to kill him, but the doctor had said it was his heart and the fever and the drink. Would his eyes open as they had done before? His lids looked like moth-wings and I couldn't believe they would remain so still. Any minute they would flutter and I'd scream. His eyes would be red in the candlelight and he'd call out my name but instead of asking for water he'd tell me that I'd killed him. All time is now. Jack the policeman Jack the husband Jack the father Jack the childkiller Jack the corpse. Jack be nimble Jack be quick Jack jumped over the candlestick. The candle guttered in the breeze and I pressed my hands over my eyes.

'I wouldn't have done it, Jack,' I whispered. 'I never meant to. You made me do it, Jack. You made me hate you and I couldn't live with you. One of us had to die and you deserved it more than me.

'You're a stupid sod, Jack," I said finally, and I left the room, blowing the candle out before I did so.

# CHAPTER 27

I left without telling Abigail and the thought broke my
heart as I sat on the train to Sydney. One small cardboard case, that's all I had to take with me, and in it two
frocks, Frank's ring, my spare shoes and my letters from
Billy that Marge had written. I'd waited for the few quid
of insurance to come through from the garage and that
had covered my fare and an occasional meal on the way,
plus the dress that I was wearing which was from a cata-
logue of Mrs Haast's, and which hadn't fitted me once it
had arrived.

The rest paid off loans for Jack's funeral. It's strange,
not knowing whether you murdered your husband or
not. At that time I hardly cared, I was just thankful he
was dead. When I think of him now I forget all the bad
things he did but then his scar reminds me and I'm glad
that it's there on my face or I might forget all the pain I
suffered at his hands and start to feel guilty instead.

I stood at his graveside and I stared down into the hole
they had dug for him and I remembered how he had told
me I was evil. He was wrong because I finally got into
that wood-and-corrugated-iron hut of a church and I sang
the hymns and no one stopped me. I sat at the front with
Abigail and it was worth it for the dirty looks we got
because she wasn't family and she wasn't even white and

therefore should have been at the back by the door, not near the altar and the cross where Jesus could see her.

When I thought of Abigail I cried. She couldn't come away with me, though, for she knew about Jack and the powder I'd given him. You can't have people around you that know things about you because people like that have power over you and are dangerous, a fact that Philippa was about to find out.

Philippa answered the door herself and I could tell she was surprised to see me because her eyebrows went up in a curve. She held the door partly closed and stood blocking the gap as though barring my way into the flat.

'Jack's dead,' I said, and this time her face didn't move at all, so that I wondered at first whether she already knew, but she couldn't have, which meant instead that she didn't care at all. All Jack's crying over her and drinking because of her and cursing me for mentioning her name and all the time she hadn't been bothered whether he was alive or dead. I wanted to laugh, knowing that. It was the best revenge on Jack, better even than my own had been. I felt at that moment as though Philippa had reached out and touched me, and as though we were the same after all, kindred spirits who had somehow conspired to bring about my husband's downfall.

'What are you doing here?' Philippa asked. I could smell her breath, it smelled of violet cachoux. Then she saw my suitcase and she looked quickly back at my face.

'I've come to get Jack's money,' I said. '*My* money now – the stuff that he had invested with Ralph.'

A small spot of bright pink appeared on Philippa's cheeks, but her face never changed. I could have been the milkman asking for his order for all the interest she showed in my words.

Philippa hesitated for a moment and I could see she was making up her mind about whether to let me in or not, but I stood my ground as I would have waited there all day if necessary. I had nowhere else to go and nothing else in the world to do.

She stood back then, and extended one arm, like a
butler. She looked over my shoulder as I walked in, as
though she'd been expecting me to be with someone else.
When she saw the passage was clear she shut the door
with a sigh of tired relief.

'Ralph's in England,' she told me, 'I'm here alone.' Jack
would have loved that, it was a missed opportunity for
him.

I walked into her lounge and sat straight down on her
long beige settee. Philippa stood watching me from the
white marble fireplace. Her dress was white too. It was
short and her legs were covered by cream-coloured tights.
She was wearing her hair long and straight and she pushed
it back off her face as though it annoyed her.

'How do you know there *is* any money?' she asked,
and in saying that she told me that there was. I felt a
heave of relief in my stomach. If there had been no money
I would have been penniless and destitute.

Philippa reached for an ivory box on the mantelpiece
and pulled out a cigarette, tapping it first on the box
before putting it into her mouth and lighting it.

'Jack told me,' I said. 'Jack told me everything. Ralph
invested it for him. They formed a company together and
got other backing. I want it back, Philippa. It's mine, I
have a right to it.'

'And if I say no?' Philippa asked, but she wasn't being
vindictive, I could tell from her tone that she wasn't even
that interested. She was just testing the water a bit, trying
to see exactly how much I did know.

'If you don't, then I will tell Ralph about you and Jack,'
I said.

Philippa nodded. 'Strange thing,' she said, 'I don't even
know if I care whether he does find out. You might be
doing me a favour, Ruby. Ralph's going down, you
know, they've caught up with him in London. He may
get ten years if they find him guilty, which they undoubt-
edly will. He's fiddled half the City, you know. He fiddled
Jack too, though your Jack was far too much in awe of

my husband to ever dream there was anything going on.
Ralph used to type him out phoney half-term reports. A
child could have seen they were made up but Jack never
suspected a thing. Now I'm here holed up with Ralph's
kids and anything he could manage to salt away before
the courts came down on him. Do you want to see a copy
of the last statement Ralph sent to your husband?' Philippa
asked. I nodded.

She left the room and came back a few moments later
clutching two sheets of paper. The smaller one she pushed
under my nose while the larger one was folded and placed
beside her on the mantelpiece.

I inspected the sheet she had given me. There were two
short lists of figures on it, and above them the words:
'Melbourne Mining Corp.' and a list of shareholders'
names, among them my husband's.

The total at the end of the list of figures had been typed
in red ink. It came to $300,000. I looked at Philippa.

'The fact that the figure is in red means that the company was in debt to that amount,' she explained.

'But you said there was some money . . .' I began.

'Did I?' Philippa smiled. She took the other sheet from
the mantelpiece. 'I also said those were the figures that
Ralph showed to Jack,' she told me. 'Would you like to
see the real figures now?'

She placed the larger sheet in my hands and I laid it out
flat. It was covered with figures, proper-looking, complicated ones typed in small neat type.

Philippa saved me looking for the total. 'A quarter of
a million,' she said.

'In red?' I asked. She laughed.

'No, darling,' she said, 'in black, very very much in
black. Your Jack was worth a fortune yet he never even
knew it, now don't you find that amusing? Ralph did:
very amusing. Now you may as well have it. I'd love to
see Ralph's face when he finds out I've given it to Jack's
poor widow and child – where is the child, by the way?'

I folded the paper and clutched it to my chest as though

afraid ever to let it go from my grasp. Philippa's words
came to me from a long distance and my eyes blurred
with tears. I realized she was waiting for an answer.

'My child?' I asked, and my voice sounded thin with
relief about the money. 'The baby died, Jack must have
told you that.'

For a moment I saw genuine concern cross Philippa's
face, and she looked away quickly. 'No,' she said. 'Jack
didn't tell me that. I thought it was alive. He even told
me its name and how it was getting along.'

'Then he wouldn't have told you the rest then,' I
answered. 'Jack killed the baby. He beat me when I was
pregnant and the baby was born dead. It had no name
and if he told you it did, then he was lying to you.'

I saw Philippa wince as though I'd hit her, and her
hands began to shake. 'You'll have to go now,' she said.
'Really. I'll get the money for you, cash if you want, only
please, you must go, Ruby. You can stay in town if you
like, I'll pay for the hotel.'

I didn't move. 'Where did it all come from?' I asked
her. 'You don't invest a few hundred and come up with
all that lot, let alone start offering it in cash.'

Philippa grinned, though she still looked nervous and
keen to be rid of me. 'Ralph had some of the biggest
scams going over in England,' she said, proudly. 'He'd
ripped off half the City, as I said, which was why he kept
this bolt hole over here, just in case. Half the money just
got lost in these little accounts. Your little nest egg is just
the result of a few months' hard work for my husband.
The companies he fleeced it from will hardly notice it's
missing.'

'Why give it all to me then?' I asked.

'*All*, darling?' Philippa smiled. 'Did I say that was all
the money? I'm not a fool, Ruby. Ralph has mounds of
the stuff salted away over here, and most of it in my
name, too.'

We stared at one another, Philippa and I, and then she

gestured towards the door but I shook my head to show her I wasn't leaving.

'I want to stay here, please,' I told her.

She closed her eyes in a sigh and sank down into the nearest armchair. 'I thought you might,' she said slowly.

'I need your help, Philippa,' I said.

'I told you the money was yours,' she said, rubbing her fingertips across her brow. 'You don't need help now, Ruby, not with a fortune like that. You can buy yourself anything, go home if you want to. I can't bear having you here though, you make me feel guilty.'

'I will go home,' I told her, 'but not yet. I've got plans, Philippa, plans for when I go back. There's a house that I want to own, a house that I've wanted since I was a kid.'

'Buy it then,' Philippa interrupted.

'It's not as easy as that,' I told her. 'It's a family home, a very upper-class family home. To own it I'd have to marry into the family. I need you to help me with that.'

Philippa snorted, and I could tell that she thought I was either stupid or just plain mad. I went on though, telling her the whole story, about how I'd met Piers and my plans for the house, and after a while she stopped laughing at me and I could see I had her full attention at last.

'I want you to teach me,' I said finally. 'I want you to show me how to spend my money correctly. I want to learn to talk like them, like you, Philippa. I want to dress right, I want you to teach me how to be the sort of woman that Piers would marry.'

'Pygmalion!' Philippa said, throwing her arms in the air. I watched her in silence because I didn't know the word then and was embarrassed by my own ignorance. I thought that class could be learned. Philippa knew otherwise, of course, but at least she was intrigued by the idea, and bored enough to take an interest. She laughed for a while and then she agreed.

'It will take some time,' she said. 'You talk like a waitress.'

'I've got time,' I told her, 'and I talk worse than a waitress.' I remembered the way Jack and I had laughed at what we'd thought to be the posh accents of the nippies in Lyons the time that he took me for tea there when we were dating.

Philippa had been educated in England, and it was England that she used as the grounding for all my tuition. There was no class in Australia, she told me, just the rich, the less rich, and the poor. Money had nothing to do with class, she said. Some of her boarding-school friends had come from titled families without a penny to their names.

We spent money like water, though, in the days that followed, touring the few British design salons in Sydney and stocking up on clothes that I found ridiculously plain and depressing.

I was fed on a diet of imported *Tatler, Harper's* and *Country Life* and in the end I felt I knew the faces on those gossip and society pages as well as I knew my own. The exploits of the upper class in Britain were like Arthurian legends. Over endless pots of tea, I learned about the marriages, the scandals, the lineage and the possessions, debs and May balls and shooting seasons and horses, but for every one thing that Philippa told me I learned a hundred others just by being around her and copying the way that she was. Philippa was a walking education in how to be aristocratic. I copied her movements and her walk and when she laughed I copied the sound. I thought her accent was impossible but after a few weeks I could hear myself sounding like her. I believe it unnerved her, seeing her own shadow following her around, but I was desperate to be like her and impervious to her obvious discomfort.

I didn't need to be taught, all I had to do was copy. Philippa was the type of woman that Piers would fall for, I was sure of it. I had a foot on the path at last. I had found my way back to Rowan Hall.

# Book Three

LONDON

# CHAPTER 28

When the wheels of the aeroplane hit the tarmac with a screech I peeled off my sleepmask and looked out at the country that I called home. There was a greyness and a drabness about England that was as familiar to me as the colour of my own eyes. When you live here and you love it, you know the drabness is a façade; it's just that England doesn't like to show its hand straight away like other countries do, it's a secret you can only share if you were born here. In Australia it's all clear blue skies and space, and that is what you will be getting for the next hundred years, but England reveals its beauty sparingly, bit by bit, a little at a time. Go out and look for it and you'll be lucky if you find any, but shut your eyes and keep your head down and it'll be there to surprise you when you least expect it. Anyway I found beauty even in the familiar dusty streets and black dirt-covered brick buildings and my memories of Australia blurred a little as I gazed out at it all.

I had been in Australia for five years, yet I had changed so much in that time that I would have been surprised if anyone had recognized me. The ripeness of my youth had been worn right away to be replaced by a leaner, more knowing person who had no desire to communicate with strangers. Men no longer whistled at me. If they admired my body in its close-fitting Paris-designed suit then their eyes took on a look of shock when their glance reached my face and its scar. Philippa said I should have it dealt with by surgery, but I preferred to keep it because with the shock came a look of respect and that was a reaction I cherished.

My cardboard suitcase had gone – now I had a studded bound trunk and six brown leather cases. My hair was straight and sleek and coiled up under a soft suede hat that matched the coat I was wearing. I wore gold and diamond-stud earrings and a plain gold band on my wedding finger – not the ring that Jack had given me when we married but a wedding ring nevertheless – one I had bought myself, for I was a widow now and it was right that I should wear the correct trappings.

'The Dorchester,' I told the taxi-driver, and I smiled inwardly as his eyes made the usual journey around my body, taking in the coat, the cases, the diamond earrings, and then the scar . . . He nodded quickly and looked away.

'Your scar is beautiful,' Philippa had told me, 'but it is shocking. People will be lost for words when they see it. It is so obvious – they will want to ask how you got it but etiquette will stop them, and that will make them uneasy.' She was right – my pea-green eyes seemed to have darkened to deep emerald and I would hold men with my gaze and dare them to stare or ask questions, enjoying their discomfort.

My voice had changed and I loved the sound of it now – it was only when I became tired or excited that I slipped back into quick-running cockney. I spoke slowly and carefully; I had learned new ways of expressing myself. My voice was an imitation of Philippa's – clear-cut, like glass, with the same rounded vowels. I would sigh like Philippa, rather than throwing my head back in a laugh, and I had learned to move with the same feline grace. I even smoked just like she did.

I was twenty-two years old and I was rich, and I felt that I could do anything. I could have bought Rowan Hall

outright, but I knew that family homes like that did not
come on to the market unless the owner died without an
heir. The place belonged to Piers, and I was determined
to marry him to get it. I loved him, and I always had. He
remained beautiful and perfect in my mind; the slim, pale-
haired boy who leaned against the bannister at Rowan
Hall. He was untouched by time. Unlike my other memories, Piers stood out in sharp, clean, undefiled relief. I
clung to this image of him as the basis of my very exist-
ence. It was fated to be so, I told myself. My life had
become entwined with Rowan Hall and with Piers since
the long-ago day of the children's party and I refused to
see it as leading in any other direction.

The taxi swerved to avoid a bike and the driver swore
and then apologized. I grabbed at the handstrap by the
window. I felt vulnerable without Philippa there to correct
me. We had become friends in Australia, and I missed
her. I missed Abigail, too, but the thought of her great
friendly brown face scared me because she reminded me
of a nightmare that I preferred to leave a thousand miles
behind me in my past. There had been several occasions
when I had nearly told Philippa that I might have murdered my husband, but thank God I kept my secret to
myself as I have since learned that there is no one you can
trust. Yet I think that Philippa would have enjoyed my
story all the same.

Philippa never once showed shame over her affair with
Jack but then she had never cared for him and I think she
assumed the same about me. When I asked her why she
had slept with him she told me it was because he was
handsome and rough and built like a bull, while Ralph
was polite in bed, and constantly apologizing. She always
chose rough men like Jack, she told me, and I realized
then that affairs were her hobby. She had no conscience,
it was not in her breeding, and that was how she had
managed to pack Ralph's kids away to a boarding school
on the south coast of Australia so easily.

Ralph would write to her from prison at least once a

week and she would read his letters aloud to me, laughing
all the while at their pitiful tone and at the fact that he
begged her to tell him she loved him. They all said that,
she told me, and by 'all' I assumed that she meant my
husband too. She wrote back to Ralph twice, and her
letters were long and steamy and passionate, full of fabri-
cated emotion that she was never capable of feeling.

I think Philippa saw me as some sort of kindred spirit
rather than as a friend, but while I admired her and copied
her every gesture, I knew that I had loved and would love
again, and that I had hated enough to kill, which was
something she would never be capable of. Philippa loved
only herself, though I believe that she did become fond
of me, in her way. I told her about Frank, and my motives
of revenge, but I could see that she didn't understand. I
had described Frank in detail and she saw him only as
another rough desirable hero, not a villain, like my husband.

'He loved you,' she told me.

'He betrayed us,' I said, 'both me and our baby.'

'Love makes men do crazy things,' Philippa said. 'He
didn't know what Jack would do to you. He would probably kill himself if he knew.'

'He knew all right,' I replied. 'He knew Jack and he
knew what he was like better than I did.'

'*He* knew, darling,' Philippa said, 'you almost lost that
letter "h".'

I asked Philippa to come back to London with me, but
I think she was too afraid of being arrested like Ralph;
her name was on too many documents she said. I sensed
that she was genuinely homesick for London and the
society that she'd left behind there. I could tell how strongly she missed it when she told me where to go in London
and who to visit. She described Ascot and Henley with
what looked almost like tears in her eyes, and her stories
of Fortnum's and Simpson's left her sitting quietly for
hours afterwards, reflecting.

'Send me back some preserves, darling,' she said and,

after a while, 'Oh, and some rum truffles. You won't forget, will you?' I promised, but she made me write the brand names down at least ten times.

'You know I hate Ralph for taking me away from all that,' she told me, and that was as near as I got to finding a motive for the terrible way in which she appeared to treat him.

By the time I left for London I fancied I knew all that there was to know about life among the upper classes, but the lobby of the Dorchester Hotel, with all its ancient grandeur, soon had me trembling in fear that I'd be found out.

I had forgotten how much the English set store by first impressions – the receptionist had only to glance at my clothes and my monogrammed luggage and my room key was handed to me before I needed to speak a word. I gave the porter a small tip once my bags were in my rooms and he thanked me in a voice that reminded me of home.

I pulled the long net curtains to one side and threw the large windows open to look down on Park Lane below. A breeze hit my face, sending the nets billowing out behind me like a bridal veil. I closed my eyes, inhaling the smells of a thousand trees and a thousand cars and a thousand years. I was home at last, and that thought gave me all the confidence I needed.

Stepping back, I shut the windows again and smoothed my hair into its bun. I looked at the telephone, but resisted the impulse to ring Philippa straight away.

'You have to have the confidence,' I told myself in the new strange voice, 'Elizabeth Gordon-Edwards.' I moved to the mirror. The name fitted the woman I saw there. Using my middle name and the hyphen had been Philippa's idea. You didn't get Rubies in the upper classes, she'd told me, only on tiaras and brooches, anyway, which I thought was a shame. Elizabeth was all right though. It was good enough for the Queen.

My eyes felt tired and there was a pulse throbbing in my temple. I looked at my watch, the one Philippa had told me to buy, the one she had described as 'the best', like everything else that we'd bought for me to wear. Like my clothes and my jewellery, the watch was horrible; subtle and boring, yet horrendously expensive. I'd gone for the flashier stuff that Billy would have liked, but Philippa had steered me away and back to the 'best'.

'You don't go around showing your money, darling,' she'd told me, 'you just smell of it, very, very faintly. That will be enough for the right sort of people, you'll see. You're not trying to impress your market pals, remember, you're after the real blue-bloods. If you go around shrieking "I'm rich!" they'll run a mile, I promise you.'

I looked around at my suite of rooms, with its heavy drape curtains and antique furniture that stood on legs that looked too frail to hold its weight. I imagined Marge on one of the gilt chairs, her weight overflowing as the slender legs bowed beneath her. There was a basket of fruit on one of the tables and I tore off the cellophane, sticking my nose into the mound of oranges, apples and grapes beneath, and breathing in deeply, and for a moment I was back in the market again. I thought of Billy and retracted my head quickly before I began crying. I picked up the internal phone and a voice answered promptly.

'Take the fruit out of my room,' I said, and there was a brief silence at the other end before the voice replied curtly, 'Certainly, madam.'

When the boy arrived I rewarded him with a big tip and then winced once he had gone. 'People only give big tips to cover their embarrassment and ignorance,' Philippa had told me. 'Give the correct amount only, never more and never less. If you are displeased with the service, then give nothing at all.'

I wandered into the third room of the suite. The bed had been removed, as I had ordered, and replaced by a desk, partially concealed by a huge arrangement of flowers. I lifted the vase to a side table and sat down at the desk, running a hand over my tired eyes. I kicked off my shoes and pulled the phone book out of the drawer. I was jetlagged and the bed looked inviting, but I had work to do. There were people I had to trace and facts I had to find out, and the sooner that I did both the better, or my long journey back to England would have been wasted.

I would have to wait at least a week for the results of my inquiries, and I used the time to try out Philippa's training. At first I thought that she had been wrong, that she'd lost touch with the look in London, because everyone appeared scruffy to me, with long hair and casual-looking clothes. But then I found them, Piers's people, and I realized that nothing much changed for them and that the look I had been taught was right.

I spent the first days alone, taking tea at the Ritz, walking down Bond Street and shopping in Asprey's. I had my hair cut at Sassoon's and I bought clothes from the Cardin boutique. I had a manicure and a facial at Elizabeth Arden's and then I walked across to Fortnum's to eat cream teas in the Fountain Room. People watched me and I saw them discussing me but I believed Philippa's words when she said it would be my beauty they'd be discussing, and my scar, rather than any suspicions that I didn't somehow fit in.

One day a rose was brought to my table and the waiter pointed out the man who had sent it and I nodded to him and he smiled and I went back to my meal. So I *was* beautiful. I felt it, and I saw it when I looked in the mirror. The pain was there, it would never fade, but my suffering had lent to my face a dignity that had been lacking in the prettier days of my youth. I was thinner and I carried myself elegantly, as Philippa had done. It would be enough, I thought. I knew that Piers would love me.

I looked up some friends of Philippa's and showed them the note of introduction she had written for me. It was lies, the lot of it, but it seemed to do the trick. They believed I was a school chum that she'd met again in Australia and if my act wasn't perfectly up to scratch, they must have put any failings down to the fact that I'd lived abroad. Australia was my safety net. If I used the wrong knife or accidentally ordered a dish from the wrong course I merely put it down to the fact that 'That's the way they do it over there, bad habits learned quickly, I'm afraid!' and they would laugh and forget the incident. We went racing and we went to Henley and all the time I was looking for Piers, or waiting to read word of him in the papers.

When the letters came I rushed with them up to my rooms, my hands shaking so much that I could barely rip open the envelopes. There were three or four sheets of paper inside each and I smoothed them out on the desk to read them. They were both from the same source – a private detective that I had hired on my first day in London.

Piers's name was on the top of the first sheet and I read the information underneath hungrily, devouring each sheet before racing on to the next.

He was alive. He still had Rowan Hall. He wasn't married. I clasped the sheets of paper to my chest just as I had Ralph's business figures when I'd found out that I owned a fortune. The rest of the information was relatively unimportant, yet I read each page several times until I'd committed each word to memory. His mother had had a stroke and was looked after by a nurse, spending half the year in a home for the elderly. Piers had become engaged in 1964, to a Lady Jennifer FitzAllen, but the engagement had been called off some six months later and no reason ever given for the cancellation. The lady in question had married the Hon. James Carrington, a member of Piers's circle of friends, the following spring and now had two children and a home somewhere in Scotland.

Piers had recently taken a job with a firm of stockbrokers, but had left the company soon afterwards amid some acrimony and threats of court action. Now he was

back living off his inheritance again, and was personally
in debt. His London address was in Belgravia.

I picked up the other sheets and read Frank's name
across the top. I flicked through the papers quickly, reading very little that I did not already know. The only thing
that surprised me was that he had somehow kept out of
prison. The detective had obviously found him a more
difficult subject and the typed facts in front of me were
scant to say the least. Frank had done well, by his own
terms. He owned two casinos, one in Soho and the other
in Mayfair. There were details of the clubs, but these did
not interest me. He was married, but had no children.
His wife was not named, and his home address was only
given as 'Central London area'. No tips for the detective
for this report then. Still, it was enough.

I looked at the two reports lying side by side on the
desk. Revenge first, I thought, and then pleasure, yet I
knew that there would be pleasure in the revenge, too.
When that was achieved I would feel complete again, and
my child could rest in peace at last. I had killed Jack for
murdering my baby but I knew in my heart that its real
father had been equally responsible for its death. I had
written to Frank twice for help yet he had returned my
second letter and addressed it to Jack. He must have
known what Jack would do, how violently he would
react, he'd seen evidence of his temper in the Sunday
school on the day of my wedding. He was as guilty as
Jack and my revenge would be as sweet.

I went to the wardrobe and pulled out the dress that I
had been saving for this purpose. It was different from
the stuffier things that Philippa had made me buy. This
was one garment that I had chosen myself and it was
exquisite in a way that Philippa would never have
approved. It was a long, ankle-length tube of the finest,
deepest red satin velvet. Ruby red, the colour of my real
name. It was backless and sleeveless, held up purely by
two thin straps of imitation ruby stones that glittered like
the real things in the lights of my room. I pulled the

dress on and admired my reflection in the gilt-framed full-length mirror. The fabric fitted like a sheath and its rich redness was like vivid blood against my pale biscuit-coloured skin.

There was a box on my dressing table and I opened it carefully. Inside was a necklace – huge paste diamonds with a large fake ruby set in their centre. I held it up to my bare neck and laughed at the result. Tiny pinpoints of reflected light covered my chin and my hair. I looked terrific – 'a million dollars', as Frank would have said. I pulled out the combs and let my hair fall out over my shoulders.

'Philippa would never have approved,' I told my reflection, but I knew that Frank would, and that was the whole point of buying it.

# CHAPTER 29

The roulette wheel spun and the small silver ball buried itself in a red-painted niche, and when the wheel finally slowed the croupier sang its number out in French. It was not the number I had chosen. The last of my pile of chips was dragged away from the table and the croupier watched me, expecting me to move from my seat. I stayed there, though, smiling. He rolled the wheel and the other punters placed their bets. As the ball was about to be flicked into the wheel I unclipped my paste necklace and slid it across the table to the number ten Red. The croupier shook his head and made to push it back to me.

'No cash, no valuables,' he said, 'only chips, madam.' I leaned across and pushed it back firmly.

'It's all I have,' I said. 'You must give me a chance to recoup my losses.'

The croupier must have pressed a security button underneath the table because a bouncer in a monkey-suit appeared out of nowhere and, grabbing the necklace, steered me away from the table.

'I think you've gambled enough, madam,' he said reasonably. 'Don't want you goin' home without the Crown Jewels now, do we?' He tried to give me the necklace, but I forced it back into his hands.

'I want to see the owner,' I told him. 'You can't refuse

me a bet. You've stolen all of my money and now you won't give me a chance to get it back.'

The bouncer looked down at the necklace. 'This stuff isn't even real,' he said.

'You've got a nerve!' I shouted. The other punters were beginning to watch by now and I could tell my bouncer was getting edgy. He wanted to drag me out of the club there and then, but I could tell that he thought I was hysterical, and might scream the place down, which would be bad for business. He looked at the scar on my face and ran a finger down his own cheek, as though imagining the pain it must have produced.

A door behind him opened and a man stood in the doorway. The bouncer suddenly looked worried.

'Problem?' the man asked and the bouncer nodded.

'She's been trying to bet with these . . .' he said, showing my necklace to the other man. 'I told her she couldn't, but she's getting a bit . . .'

'Perhaps you'd like to settle the matter in my office,' the man said, and when I heard his voice the second time I knew that I'd found Frank.

I walked in front of him into the office and I could hear the bouncer breathe with relief that I'd gone quietly and without making a fuss. The casino was a classy one – I'd needed one of Philippa's friends to book me in there that evening, and their clients would obviously not enjoy the sort of scene that I was intent on creating.

We went through the outer office and up a small flight of twisting stairs to a larger room with a desk in one corner. The room was lit like the casino downstairs, a gloomy green half-light from the Tiffany lamps on the tables. Frank was too busy admiring my body to care to look up at my face, though.

'Can I get you a drink?' he asked.

I shook my head and smiled. 'No – thank you.' It was Philippa's voice at its best, pure golden honey poured over sharp, clear, crackling ice. I smoothed the velvet dress over my hips carefully.

'Your tables really have taken all that I possess, you know,' I lied to Frank.

Frank waved me to a seat across the desk opposite him and threw my necklace towards me.

'Well, that won't get you much,' he said.

I looked surprised. 'My husband gave it to me!' I told him.

'Sorry,' he said. 'It's fake.'

'A little like me then,' I said, and turned the beam of the desk lamp upwards, so that it hit my face.

Frank stared at me for a moment, and he looked at the scar, and then he looked at my eyes and I saw at last a movement in his own, as though the pupils had contracted. His face became paler in an instant, as though the blood had drained from it, and he stood up, nearly knocking the chair over as he did so.

I stood too, and stepped towards him, smiling. 'Frank,' I said.

He had changed in six years, but not as much as I had expected. He looked broader in his black evening suit with its square-cut shoulders and his dark hair was longer, not greased back in the way that it had been when I'd known him, but falling in thick black curls around his face and down his neck. He wore no tie and his white shirt was open at the neck. His skin was tanned and he smelled of expensive cologne. There was a thick gold rope chain around his neck and a heavy gold ring set with diamonds on the little finger of his left hand. He raised that hand to his face and ran the fingers over his lips as though trying to keep back words that threatened to emerge. He was the market boy made good, the perfect image of all a barrow boy would dream of. Oh God, Billy should have seen him then! How he would have admired the Italian suit and the patent leather shoes, and the cologne that smelled of at least twenty quid a bottle and the diamonds that were real, and the cocktail cabinet that stood behind him, which was in fact a whole wall because it was so huge. How Lily would have loved the

vast white leather couches that stretched across the wall
behind me, beneath a smoked-glass window that looked
down on to the punters below. She would have coveted
the coloured glass Tiffany lamps, their multi-coloured
glass throwing muted rainbows about the room, and the
white fur rugs on the floor, and the redundant chandeliers
on the ceiling above. There were paintings of women on
the walls and a wide varnished open fireplace with an
imitation fire flickering inside.

The room was wanton and erotic in its tastelessness. I
looked at Frank and he was master in his own kingdom,
filling its spaciousness with his presence, just as Billy had
been king of the market. There was a certain powerfulness
in Frank, a certain rightness in him, in the way that he
was matched by his surroundings. It came from his confidence and arrogance, his certainty that somehow he
could get anything he wanted, and I could tell from the
way he looked at me that my presence in that plush office
had just confirmed his own little theory. I had come back
– he was omnipotent after all.

Frank was still handsome – more handsome even than
I remembered; handsome in a way that somehow twisted
my insides as I stood and looked at him, so that I nearly
forgot all the wrong that he had done to me, and remembered only the lust that we had shared back then, before
I'd married and left for Australia.

I longed for him even as I stood there, knowing all that
I did about him, remembering all the hate that I had so
neatly stored up inside for him; he was still everything
that my body wanted and I knew it then and he knew it
as well.

All the years fell away from me and my body's response
to his presence was instant. I was ashamed of my own
reaction, of the dryness in my throat and of the greediness
in my body.

'You never forget your first man,' Frank had told me,
and he was right. Like an obedient dog I was trained and
conditioned and no amount of bitterness could have wiped

that training away. We were the same, Frank and I, the same deep down, each hating the other in a way that could not be forgotten, and both aware that our bodies harboured no grudge and needed the other with a strength that was terrifying.

'I came back, Frank,' I said. 'I got here, I did it. And now I'm broke. You really took all I had left tonight. You have to help me, Frank, you owe me that much at least. I have nowhere else to go, I had to come to you.'

The speech sounded pitiful, but I smiled as I spoke, as though it was nothing serious that I was telling him. I wanted to match Frank's confidence, although it took all of my strength to do so.

'Ruby,' Frank said, as though only just confirming my identity, and his voice saying my name was the sharpest memory, which cut me through like a knife. There was a seriousness in Frank's face that I had never seen there before. He was still Jack-the-Lad, the chancer from the funfair, but there was something else, too, that had grown up inside him, as though it were he who had been through all that I'd suffered in Australia, and a chill went through me because his seriousness frightened me. I tried to think of us as I had thought of us before, as a bit of fun, as a stage in my growing-up, but events change you, my motives had become darker, and 'fun' now seemed as foreign to me as it must have seemed to Marge in our market days.

'What happened to your copper?' Frank asked. 'The bloke you married?'

'Jack?' I said, looking casual. 'I left him, Frank, I couldn't stand it any more. We're divorced. He did this, you know,' and I pointed to my scar.

'You should never have married him, Ruby,' Frank said, and I marvelled at his conceit, which could make him so blind to his own guilt. Frank never once asked about his child, and that surprised me, for I should have thought that he would have been curious.

'My baby died,' I told him, annoyed by his callousness.

I hadn't wanted to tell him, I'd planned to lie as I had about Jack, but I couldn't, I had to hurt him somehow.

'Oh,' Frank said, 'I didn't know about that. I'm sorry, it must have upset you.' He could have been speaking about a stranger's baby instead of his own.

'Your baby!' I wanted to scream at him. 'Yours and mine, Frank! Jack killed it, and you did too! You sealed its fate and mine when you sent back that letter addressed to Jack!' But I sat quietly in my chair, never moving, waiting my time as I had waited with Jack. The right time would come, I knew it, and the thought was all that calmed me.

'You've done all right for yourself then,' I said, looking down through the smoked-glass window at the casino.

Frank shrugged, to signal modesty. 'I do all right,' he said. 'I've got plans to expand.' His eyes never left my face as he spoke to me, as though he were searching for something, waiting for something, as though our words meant nothing and the true words lay somewhere beneath, somewhere he could see if he looked hard enough.

'Why did you come back?' he asked.

'Oh, I don't know,' I replied. 'What else could I do? No husband, no money, no job. I missed England, too,' I added. 'I missed it from the first day I got out there.'

'And you were always going to do so well,' Frank said, and I could hear the bitterness in his voice. He still hated me for not marrying him, even though he'd taken his revenge long ago.

'I made a mistake,' I said, and I looked him straight in the eye, returning his stare.

'What about your lord and his manor?' Frank asked. 'Was that a mistake too, Ruby? Or have you come back to trace him now that you've learned to talk "proper" English?'

I shrugged. 'You get funny ideas when you're a kid,' I said, 'then you learn to grow up, Frank.'

Frank swallowed. 'You weren't such a kid then, as I

remember,' he said, and his voice had grown thicker and quieter. 'You knew enough, in those days.'

'Things that you taught me,' I said, and I watched his hands clasp at the edge of the desk, and I ran a finger over the bodice of my dress, where it met my breasts, and I saw Frank's eyes, and I smiled because I knew then that I still had some power over him and the thought pleased me, because with that power I would get all the revenge that I wanted.

It was as though someone else knew what was happening between Frank and me in that room at that moment, because as I watched his eyes linger over the curve of my breasts I heard footsteps, frantic footsteps, dashing from the casino through Frank's outer office and up the stairs to the room that we were in. Someone outside was doing more than just hurrying, they were running towards Frank's room as though their very life depended on it. They were desperate, clattering footsteps, the sort a woman would make if she were being chased and running for her life. They stopped, though, when they reached Frank's door, as if whoever it was was more scared of what she might find inside the room. The pause was only momentary, then the door burst open and a woman stood there, out of breath and panting, a hand clasped over her chest, her face wild and distorted with fear.

'They told me . . .' she panted, gasping for air. 'They told me you were here . . . I knew . . . I knew from the description . . .'

I rose to my feet, now it was my turn to be confused. The woman was tall once she got back her breath and straightened, and expensively, tastefully dressed. Her hair was pulled high off her face, giving her eyes a slanting, almost cat-like appearance. She was slim, like a fashion model, though her breasts were fuller and there was a slight swelling around the waist that she had tried to hide with the high-waisted evening dress that she wore. I should never have recognized her at all, had it not been for the high, almost childish voice that she spoke in, which was so out of keeping with the way that she looked.

'Pearl?' I asked. I saw the same sheeny dark skin, now filmed with sweat from the exertion of her run. Her wild animal eyes looked across to Frank but he kept his eyes away from her, on the table, on his hands, and a look of desperation came on to her face, as though he'd given her the answer she expected. I thought for a moment that she would crumple, but she didn't. She stood there for a second in the doorway, swaying, unsure of herself, and then suddenly she seemed to become composed. She pulled up to full height, which was some three or four inches taller than my own, and pushed a hand through her hair, as though tidying away loose ends. She took a breath and tried to smile and then, strangest of all, she extended her hand.

'Ruby,' she said, walking across to me. 'How are you?'

It was as though she'd been studying with Philippa, as I had. My own reaction was less friendly. I was annoyed that she was there, and that she had interrupted us, and her obvious struggle with her emotions had been embarrassing to watch, because I had not understood the cause behind it. She was standing now like some figure in a tragedy, her eyes flashing pitifully from Frank to me, and her hand extended limply by her side.

Pearl wanted help from Frank, I could see that much at the time, but it was also obvious to all of us that no help would be forthcoming. Frank stepped backward and his face disappeared into the shadows.

'Ruby's broke, Pearl,' he said. 'She wants to know if she can have a job.'

Pearl clutched at her stomach, and I recognized the gesture at once – it was one I had had a habit of doing myself a few years before, when I had been pregnant with Frank's child.

'You want to work here?' Pearl asked.

'That's not exactly what I asked for,' I said, annoyed with Frank for twisting my words, and for telling Pearl

about our conversation, too. 'I'm broke, that's all,' I told
her. 'I thought that Frank might be able to help. You
needn't worry, it's nothing to do with you.'

Pearl looked across at Frank again, and there was pleading in her eyes.

'It's Pearl's decision as well now,' he said, in a carefully
measured voice. 'She's my wife now, Ruby, she has a
say.'

I can't remember precisely my reaction at this piece of
news. I should have guessed, of course, but then a lot of
people have a certain slow-wittedness about them when
it comes to the major turning-points in their lives, and I
just happen to be one of them. I know that I wanted to
laugh, and I would have done if Frank had not been
watching me.

I looked at Pearl, and I remember thinking how unremittingly cruel Fate was to her. I'd taken Frank from her
once, years before, and now here I was back again to do
the very same thing. Different circumstances, different
reasons, but the same result nevertheless. She knew it too,
I could tell from the hopelessness in her great dark eyes.
That was why she'd been running; she'd known what I'd
come back for the minute she'd found out I was there.
There was only one thing different this time, as far as I
could see, and that was that we were all playing for much
higher stakes. Pearl was married to Frank now, and carrying his baby, and Frank knew that he stood to lose both
if he gave way to the desire I could see he still felt for me.

Frank's baby. I looked at Pearl's gently swelling stomach and at the protective hand that she had placed across
it, as though I were a witch and had the power to shrivel
it in the womb. An emptier aching began in my own body
that turned to blood-red anger once my brain registered its
cause.

I stood there and I smiled. 'Lily must be ecstatic,' I said,
'she always wanted Frank as a son-in-law.' I walked over
to Pearl and kissed her on the cheek, ignoring the way
she pulled her face away from me.

'A baby too,' I added. 'Congratulations! I never imagined I'd come back to find I'd been made an aunty. How's Lily taking the idea of becoming a grandmother?'

Pearl didn't answer, so I pointed towards the cocktail cabinet. 'Don't you have any champagne in there, Frank?' I asked. 'It's not every day you get to celebrate this type of family reunion.'

I smiled as Frank walked like a robot to the drinks cabinet and I watched his face all the while as he opened the bottle of champagne.

'To the baby!' I said once our glasses were full, but a knock on the door interrupted us before we could drink the toast.

It was the bouncer, the same monkey that had tried to get me jumped for betting with my necklace. He eyed me as I stood there, a glass of his boss's champagne in my hand, then he handed Frank a note and waited for a reply.

'He's causing trouble again,' he whispered to Frank, 'he's after credit again. I told him no way, but he's getting a bit loud and annoying the other punters.' He looked across at me as he said this, as though to remind me of our first meeting. 'I thought I'd check with you first that he's who he says he is,' he added.

Frank read the name on the paper and his expression changed suddenly. He glanced across at me and I was unable to interpret the strange look of satisfaction in his eyes.

'Give him all the credit he wants,' he said suddenly to the bouncer, and the man looked up in surprise.

'But you never . . .' he began, but Frank cut him off.

'I make exceptions sometimes, Charlie, you know that,' he said. 'Give him whatever he asks for but don't let the other punters get wind of it or they'll all be after credit. We like to keep our better customers happy, you know.' He screwed the paper into a tight ball and the bouncer left the room quietly. I looked down through the smoked-glass window and saw the bouncer moving through the crowded casino, walking quickly, until he reached a figure waiting by the door. The two men exchanged words and then the slimmer one threw off his overcoat and tossed it towards the bouncer, clapping him on the back gratefully and making his way into the club. I saw him sit at one of the tables and then I looked back at Frank. He had emerged from the shadows where he had been watching me closely. There was a smile back on his face again, and I shuddered to think what had put it there.

# CHAPTER 30

My life moved like smoke, curling then unfurling, as
if it had winding trails of its own to make. For a
while it hung, weightless, in the air, although its path was
inevitably upwards.

I hired a car and chauffeur and drove down to Surrey
and I stood on the hill and looked down on the house. I
saw it with new eyes, for I was its equal at last. I fooled
myself that money was class, and believed that my wealth
had somehow put Rowan Hall and the life it contained
within my grasp; that I could walk in through the door
and talk to its inhabitants and eat with them at table and
that they would believe me to be, so I thought, one of
themselves.

The house still had me under its spell – it was all that
I wanted and it was home to me, I felt that strongly. I
knew it was not for sale, my detective having made dis-
creet inquiries, and I knew there was only one path to its
ownership, and that was through marriage to Piers. I
never once thought this idea to be a fanciful one; it was
fact and it was right. I had sworn as much on the day of
the coronation party, and without the house my life would
have been wasted, as wasted as Marge's or Billy's.

I loved Piers still, although the boy from my memory
was dead, and a man had grown in his place. I was determined to go on loving him, and the only obstacle to that

love was the longing that I still felt for Frank. At the same time I hated Frank, and my need for him only led to my hating myself.

When I got back to London I packed a small case with some cheap dresses I had bought from Australia and I booked out of my rooms at the Dorchester, arranging for my trunks to be placed in store. It was hard, packing away all my newly found wealth, but I was depending on Frank's pity to get me nearer to my revenge. I felt the need to move quickly, for I knew I could not begin to live properly until my child's death had been paid for.

My cash and jewellery were stashed away in a strong-box in a Mayfair bank, and I moved into the room Frank had found for me with as few worldly goods as when I had arrived at Philippa's.

Pearl's attitude towards me was pitiful. She had bought flowers for my room, a small, miserable-looking place over a betting shop Frank owned, just off Beak Street. Pearl's bright orange chrysanthemums looked out of place against the lime-coloured walls and the grubby mauve settee with its pull-down bed and its satin frill-edged sheets. The place had been lived in by a prostitute before me, and I still got men ringing the downstairs bell in the middle of the night, even though I had ripped her name down from the doorplate.

I think Pearl was embarrassed by the place – I was her half-sister after all and should by rights have been offered a bed in her home. However, we all knew that I couldn't stay with her and Frank, not after what we'd been through. She didn't know why I had come back from Australia, but she could guess that I was after her husband and, soft though she was, she wasn't giving him to me on a plate. The flowers, then, were by way of apology for the state of the room, as was the offer of new clothes.

'I don't fit many of mine any more,' she told me, cradling her small bump with her hands.

I opened the wardrobe and hung what I had on the wire

hangers inside. 'I've got that red dress I arrived in and a
couple of frocks,' I said.

I closed the doors and our faces stared back at us from
the mirrors on the outside. Pearl smiled as soon as she
saw me looking at her, but the smile came too late for I
had already caught the look of fear that it covered up.

Pearl was scared of me, scared to death, and not just
because she feared for her marriage. She seemed physically
frightened of me, as though I were a wild animal that
might suddenly turn on her and attack her, yet she still
needed to be around me, as though following me closely
was the only way to reassure herself that she was safe.

I felt no pity for her really, she was just a bit-part in
the drama that was unfolding between me and Frank and
Piers. I was so involved in it that I hardly noticed her,
except to be annoyed at the way that she followed me
around. Seeing her made me think of her baby, and thinking of Frank's child made me yearn for my own. I became
angry then, angry that her baby was alive while mine was
dead, and I didn't have enough room in my head for that
sort of anger, it was too full of revenge and plans for my
future.

'How long are you staying for?' Pearl asked, and there
was pleading in her eyes. 'Please, please go away,' she
had wanted to say, and I smiled and shrugged because I
thought she was spineless in not coming straight out with
it.

'Don't know,' I said, 'I've got nowhere else to go really.
Billy's dead and I know Lily won't want to see me. I've
got no one else, you know, and Frank did offer me a job.
I wouldn't want to let him down now, would I?'

Just for a second a flash of the old hatred came into
Pearl's eyes, but it died as soon as it appeared, and the
cold fear returned in its place.

'Where are you working?' she asked.

I smiled. 'Didn't Frank tell you?' I said. 'He's got me a
place in The Horseshoe, across the road.'

The Horseshoe was Frank's other club, not as classy as

the one in Mayfair, but I'd had a look around and it was plush enough, nicer than I'd expected for that part of London. I was to learn to work the tables as a croupier and the idea amused me, I was almost looking forward to it. I was not a gambler, despite my little show for Frank's benefit in his Mayfair casino, and I intended to enjoy watching people losing money over nothing for a while.

'Why are you here?' Pearl asked in a whisper. 'Why did you come back, Ruby?'

I didn't answer her, I just carried on unpacking my case. When I turned to face her I was smiling, and my arms were full of underwear and spongebags. 'When that baby's born I'll be its aunty,' I finally said to Pearl, pushing past her to get to the bathroom. 'Won't that be nice?' My voice echoed down the hallway, but I heard no answer from Pearl to echo in return.


It was ridiculously easy to get my chance for revenge on Frank, even easier than I had hoped, though I'd guessed that his arrogance might have left him wide open to a quick stab in the back. I learned my job quickly so that I could keep my eyes open to the comings and goings at the club and the betting shop. Unlike Billy, Frank had never been in prison, but I knew he could never keep on the right side of the law. Jack had been after him till the moment he'd left for Australia and I knew that, with time, I could discover a few of his little tricks.

I had been working at the club four months when Piers walked in, and I nearly dropped the deck of cards I was dealing when I saw him in a party by the door. He was drunk, they all were, about half-a-dozen or so of them, all crowding together and making so much noise that the bouncers looked edgy and fingered their knuckles as though expecting to have to use them.

I looked around to leave. I did not want Piers to see me, but as I froze where I stood I saw the faces of the punters in front of me, waiting for their cards to be dealt, and annoyed at the break in the game.

Piers and his friends staggered to seats at the next table and I carried on dealing, though my hands were shaking and my throat had gone dry. I could have been mistaken, yet I knew that I was not, for Piers looked the same as he had done years ago, only taller and a little older. Apart from that, his features had barely changed at all. I found him as beautiful as I had done as a child. His beauty was extraordinary, like a statue or fine art painting, and I couldn't understand how other people could ignore him, why they didn't just stand staring at him, as I was longing to do.

I fingered my scar, and suddenly wanted to hide it. The dress that I was wearing felt cheap. I thought of all the good clothes that I had, stored away until my first meeting with Piers, and now there I was in the black velvet evening dress they supplied at the club, sleeveless and laced at the front, the neck plunging low and my breasts pressed high so that the punters should become distracted and hardly feel the pain of the money they were losing.

A cheer went up from Piers's table and some money was pushed across to his side. Frank was in the club that night, and I looked across at his office, and saw him watching me from the doorway. He looked at Piers and then he looked across at me, and I blushed. I think that look told him all that he had been needing to know, because he stepped back into the shadows of his office again and quickly shut the door.

One by one Piers's friends seemed to get bored with the game or run out of money and leave the casino, until only Piers and one other man remained. They seemed to have sobered up slightly by then, or at any rate the game had quietened them, for they sat silently at the table, smoking cigarettes and staring thoughtfully at their cards.

Some time after midnight the friend finally threw his cards down on to the table and sat back in his chair, laughing, but Piers seemed hardly to have heard him. I

could tell he was losing, and there were beads of nervous
perspiration on his forehead. He lost the next game, then
put his money down for another. The croupier looked
across to Frank's office for approval, and I turned quickly
to see Frank nod curtly once, from behind his window,
and the croupier took Piers's bet.

Piers obviously won the next game, and the one after
that, and I saw him relax a little and order more drinks.
It was his friend, though, who approached me, just as the
casino was closing, touching my bare arm and making
me jump.

'Drink?' he asked. He was shorter than Piers, and a few
years older. His hair was short and combed straight back
from his face. It was a handsome face, but the cheeks
were scarred with pockmarks.

'No,' I said, packing away my table, 'no, thank you.'

The man walked around in front of me. 'Just a quickie,'
he said.

I shook my head. 'Against the company rules, I'm
afraid,' I told him. 'We're not allowed to socialize with
clients.'

The man smiled and shrugged. 'Pity,' he said, and
walked back to his table.

I turned to go to the cloakroom but a figure was blocking my way. 'Missing out on an opportunity?'

I looked up at Frank's face, set hard with anger in the
half-light. 'That's the best offer you'll get from that sort,
Ruby, you should have jumped at it.'

Now I was mad. I went to walk past him but he
grabbed at my wrists. 'Let go of me, Frank,' I whispered,
but the harder I struggled the harder he held me. He
pulled me back around the corner, out of sight of the rest
of the casino, and pinned me against the wall.

'Why, Ruby?' he asked. 'Why them? We're scum to
them, you know we are. How do you think you look to
that sort? Just another tart that works the tables, that's all;
the type you try it on with for the price of a drink; the
type you don't even have to try remembering fucking

names of, for Christ's sake! Do you still think you can
marry him, Ruby? Dressed up like you are, sounding like
you do? What is it with you? Why do you have to ruin
lives like you do?'

I wanted to speak, to hit him, to move away, but I
couldn't, it was as if his torrent of words had frozen me
to the wall.

'Why did you turn me down, Ruby?' he asked. 'Why
did you go and marry that middle-aged bastard and run
off with him to Australia? What were you trying to prove?
That you're better than the rest of us? Is this what you
want, the sort of leering groping that you got tonight?
How do you think you looked, standing there staring at
him all night like some dozy cow? You're stupid, Ruby,
blind and fucking stupid! You don't need them and you
don't need their bloody stately homes! They're nothing
now, Ruby, things have changed. Their sort don't run
the country any more and they don't own the money,
either. They're powerless brainless twerps who go around
spending what they never had. They're dead meat, Ruby,
a slice of this country's history that's dead but won't lie
down. They owe it all to us lot now, Ruby, *we're* the ones
with the brass and the power. They're nothing, Ruby,
nothing!'

I looked up at Frank's face and that was my first mistake. Frank's face was so handsome it hurt. It had a mag-
netic effect on me. I forgot all that had happened since
that night in Rowan Hall, the first time he had made love
to me, and I just wanted to kiss him. I saw my childhood
in Frank's face. I saw his eyes that dipped right down into
my soul, so that he knew me better than any other person
alive.

'Christ, I loved you, Ruby,' Frank whispered, and he
kissed me with such tenderness that I felt the tears spring
up in my eyes. I wanted to lean against him, to be pulled
against his chest, and to tell him the things that had happened to me, to forget he was ever involved.

'You loved me too,' he said, his mouth pressed up to my ear. 'Why did you behave like you did?'

My pride came back then, a great shaft of it, so that my back straightened and I pulled my face away. 'Leave me alone, Frank,' I said. 'You've no right to expect anything from me, just leave me alone.'

'I can't, Ruby,' he shouted. 'Don't you see that? Can't you tell how I feel? Do you think I want this, that I'm proud of behaving this way when I've got a wife like Pearl and a baby on the way? It's you, Ruby. It's you who came back, you who turned on the torture again. I hate you for what you did, Ruby, for what you're still doing, even now, but I want you and I *can't* leave you alone.'

Frank went to kiss me again then, and I raised my hand to ward him off, but he grabbed at the hand and by the look on his face you'd have thought he'd discovered the Holy Grail.

How he'd spotted it twinkling in the darkness I'll never know, but his ring was there on my wedding finger, I'd forgotten to take it off, and from the way that he pressed it to his lips I could tell that he saw it as a token of my love for him, no matter how hard I'd protested otherwise.

'What do you want, Ruby?' he asked me again, but I couldn't answer him.

'I'll never beg you, Ruby,' he said, still holding my hand to his face. 'I won't be pathetic like that copper you married or the poor sod you've got your eye on now. It's you who'll have to bloody beg, I've done as much grovelling as I'm going to.'

'You're a coward then, Frank!' I said, pulling my hand away. 'You call Jack pathetic but you weren't too proud to let him do your dirty work for you, were you?' I was screaming now, my temper finally gone, and Frank pulled me further up the empty corridor, out of earshot of the punters.

'I'm surprised you didn't drop Jack a few quid, too, for beating me up the way he did!' I shouted. I hadn't meant

to say any of that but I was out of control and my screaming went on.

'*Your* kid, Frank!' I yelled. 'Your kid, and you let Jack
kill it, like he nearly killed me!' It was as if a dam had
burst, the words came tumbling out and I could do
nothing to stop them.

'How could you, Frank?' I shouted. 'How could you
bloody well do that and still tell me you loved me?'

Frank's eyes were wild and staring and he stepped back
as though afraid of me. 'You're mad, Ruby!' he said, but
his voice sounded uncertain. 'I don't know what you're
on about.' I think I hated him more then than I ever had
before in my life.

'You sent Jack my letter back,' I told him. 'What did
you think he'd do when he found out my baby was your
bastard? Tell me he still cared? Offer to bring it up as his
own? That wasn't Jack's style, Frank, and you knew it!
He hated you, Frank, more than anyone he knew, apart
from me, that is. How did you think he'd react when he
read a letter like that? I had to kill him just to get away
from him, Frank. Just because he hated you and me so
much that he would have killed me first if I'd have stayed
there. That's the situation you left me in, Frank, but then
you told me it served me right for going off with Jack in
the first place. Was that my punishment for not choosing
you? Did you do all that out of love for me, Frank? Was
that what was in your stupid fucking head at the time?
Was it?'

Frank looked dazed and just stood there shaking his
head. 'I don't know what you're talking about,' he
repeated.

'Don't lie to me, Frank!' I screamed and grabbed at
Frank's jacket, but he had heard enough already and he
ripped it out of my grasp and turned to walk away. I saw
his back disappearing through the doorway and I carried
on screaming long after he had gone.

'Frank!' I screamed over and over again. 'You bastard!'

# CHAPTER 31

I waited. I waited six weeks, then another two, because I still wasn't certain I'd shown my cards too early, and now I wasn't even sure how to play the hand that I had.

I waited until the casino was quiet and I knew Frank was in his office and it was then that I went up there, and he seemed to know that it was me because he didn't look surprised and he locked the door behind us as if it were the most natural thing in the world.

'I want you,' I said to him, leaning against the door. 'I'm begging.'

Frank came at me like a wave, crashing against me, flattening me to the door, crushing my body till I could neither breathe nor think. He ripped my dress in two, it fell apart, useless on the floor, and then he picked me up, lifted me under the arms and held me up against the wall until our faces were level, and he kissed me, bruising my mouth, biting my lip; he kissed my eyelids when my eyes closed with the sweetness of the pain, and then his tongue ran down my cheeks as though hungry for the salt my tears had left there.

There was nothing I could do, I was too slow, I moved in a different time. I reached for Frank's buttons when he cried out to me to take off his clothes so that he too could be naked, but my hands were clumsy and useless. I had lost my strength and it was Frank's hands that tore at his

shirt and undid his belt and pulled at his trousers so that
they joined my dress, at our feet.

I merely marvelled at him, I gazed at his face and
smiled. I looked at his eyes, with their darkness and their
longing, at the long black lashes that swept traces of
shadows across his cheeks. His eyebrows, that were in a
constant frown, and the tanned softness of his skin, and
the mouth that reached for my own, and for my neck,
my breasts and my belly. His mouth devoured me, but
all in a second, because Frank had no time, he had waited
too long for me already.

His body was tense with the waiting, and with the
holding back. He told me a million times that he loved
me, and it was like a chant that was the music to our lust,
a never-ending whisper that could have been his voice or
my own.

Frank lifted me again, my back still pressed to the wall,
and when he lowered me gently I found his prick waiting.
I parted my legs and it was inside me, impaling me. My
muscles contracted around it, taking it greedily, and
before we could move Frank came, and I came too, only
some seconds later so that he was holding me as I finished
and clutching me to him, whispering in my ear and comforting me as though he would never let me go.

The tension and the strength now gone from us, we
sank on to our knees on the floor, Frank still holding me
in his arms, still kissing my head and soothing me as
though comforting a frightened child.

'I thought I'd lost you,' he whispered, 'I thought that
you'd never come to me. I kept thinking about what you
said the other day and none of it made sense. I thought
you'd lost your mind, Ruby. I was so frightened I'd lost
you for good.'

Frank lay back on the floor, his arms out to either side
and his chest and ribcage heaving. He closed his eyes and
I placed my hands, palms down, on his chest. He smiled,
and I ran my hands over his chest, his shoulders, his neck.
I placed my fingers around his throat and they didn't

reach, only the thumbs touched at the front. I bent and pressed my lips against his own and he didn't move, but his breathing grew harder. With the tip of my tongue I drew a line, from his forehead to his nose, along his chin, down his chest, and then, stopping at his stomach, I paused and pulled away. Frank's hand moved to the back of my head and he pushed my head down on to his stomach and I felt his hand run over my shoulder and my back. A light went out somewhere on the floor of the casino and the office became darker and the silence between us grew electric.

I cupped Frank's balls in my hand and squeezed gently until the stiffness returned to his prick. I heard him groan and I leaned my head forward and touched his prick with my tongue until it bounced slightly with pleasure. We made love slowly this time, lying on the floor. Frank rolled on top of me and his movements were rhythmical and sweetly slow and controlled, and he watched me all the while, as though savouring the fact that I was there beneath him and calling for him, begging for him as he had wanted, as he had thought to beg for me.

I cried out with the pleasure and I clung to his body as I came. It was just like the first time, as if no time had passed and I had never been married and I had not left Frank for a life in Australia. Then the moment was gone, and we lay side by side on the floor, panting.

I pulled my clothes together, holding my torn dress about my body. Frank put his jacket around my shoulders and kissed me on the neck, so that I shuddered.

'Where are you going?' he asked.

'Home,' I told him.

'Don't leave,' he said, and he grabbed my shoulders and tried to turn me around.

'Why?' I asked him, looking him straight in the face. 'What else would you have me do?'

He winced slightly at my accent, as he always did when I spoke as Philippa had taught me. 'You love me,' he said, and he said it as much to convince himself as me.

'Do I?' I asked, and the look of pain on his face was to haunt me for many years to come.

'No, Ruby,' he said quietly, 'not again.'

I rose to my feet, afraid for a moment that he might try to kill me. 'What else did you expect?' I asked. 'Did you want me to stay and marry you this time, Frank? I thought you'd already got a wife. Besides,' I added, pulling his jacket round my shoulders, 'I've got other plans, you know that, I always have had. Did you really think I could love you after all that you've done to me? You're common, Frank, a common little crook with no taste and a massive ego. You don't deserve me, Frank, you don't even deserve Pearl. You're a coward and a liar and a murderer – you didn't even have as much backbone as Jack, and that's saying something!'

Frank came towards me, but I was too quick for him. I turned the key in the lock and ran from the room down to the casino. Pearl was sitting there at a table in the darkness, exactly as she had been sitting there when I'd walked past her on my way to Frank's office. I smiled at her but she didn't see me. She was looking at the office, and at the window, with its venetian blind. The blind was down, of course, but she didn't need that to tell her what had just gone on in there between Frank and me. Her face was ashen and her hands were clutched to her stomach, as though she were in pain.

'He didn't send that letter back, you know,' she said, just as I had walked past her. I froze. The words made inroads into my spine before they'd even reached my ears. We stood back to back, only a few yards of darkness separating us. Her voice sounded confident, but dead of all tone.

'You came back for revenge, didn't you?' she asked. 'I thought you'd come back to get Frank, but it wasn't that, was it? You don't want him at all, do you? You just wanted to get your own back for that letter, didn't you?'

I felt a movement behind me. When I looked round I saw that her face had fallen into her hands.

'What do you know about that letter?' I asked Pearl, and my voice sounded funny.

'Everything,' she said. 'I opened it, I read it, and I sent it back, Ruby. I thought you would have guessed that. I've been waiting, Ruby, waiting for you to tell me that you knew. Frank never saw your letter. He knew nothing about your baby being his. We're married, Ruby. Did you think I'd let him read about that? I told you I'd get my revenge and you gave me the perfect opportunity. The point is that it didn't work. Frank still loves you, even after all this time. He can't stop himself, you see. He's tried to love me but he can't while you're still alive. You spoil everything, Ruby, every time.'

I walked round to her, stood in front of her, and I still couldn't believe what it was that she was saying to me.

'Jack killed my baby,' I told her, my heart pounding. 'He read that letter and then he killed my baby.'

Pearl looked up at me, and I saw the last bit of life die in her eyes. She looked grey and like a zombie in the half-light. Her eyes were wide open but they were dead. They moved slowly down my clothes, down the ripped dress that I held together with my hands, and across the shoulders of her husband's evening jacket that was draped around me. My face was swollen and bruised and my hair was damp with sweat.

'Frank was all I ever wanted,' she said.

'And yet I got him,' I answered, and I walked quickly out of the casino.

They arrested Frank the next day. Someone had phoned the police and spilt the beans on all his little rackets. They got him for involvement with the local gang, too, but I knew that one charge was trumped-up because I'd been looking into it myself and drawn a blank. Frank would have no truck with the local villains, and it had got him into trouble when they had tried to coerce him into their little protection rackets.

The irony of the situation was blinding. I had been

working for Frank while I'd tried to find out enough
about him to get him picked up by the police, and then
I'd changed my mind and backed down, and now somebody else had done the job anyway. I knew who that
somebody was, too.

'You stupid cow,' I told Pearl over the phone.

'It doesn't matter,' was all that she said, and then she
hung up. Her voice sounded empty, just as her face had
looked the previous night in the casino.

The door to their flat was open when I got there, and I
heard music playing somewhere in the distance. I couldn't
see Pearl living in a place like that. I could only see Pearl
in Lily's flat, with its fairy lights and scatter cushions. The
place where Pearl and Frank lived was elegant and tasteful,
almost like Philippa's. The door opened as I knocked on
it, which made me shudder because that happens in
movies, when someone's been murdered.

I stepped inside, calling Pearl's name, but no one
answered. The only sound was Nat King Cole wailing
somewhere in the background, in a room far off down
the hall. I hated looking at the place where Frank lived
with Pearl. There were photographs on the wall, large
framed shots of Pearl and then Frank, and then of Frank
and Pearl together. Pearl's shots were professional, and I
guessed she must have done some modelling in the years
that I'd been in Australia. There was a framed magazine
cover, with her face looking out like the face of a beautiful,
confused child. There was a shot of her on a catwalk, and
a half-naked shot, warm and amber-toned, with Pearl's
long slender body just wrapped in a sheet. The photograph next to it was of her and Frank, kissing on their
wedding day, and beside that was a gap, where a photo
had been removed.

The hallway led into a vast room. The music stopped
and I held my breath, but then there was a click and it
started again, the same song. There were huge windows
down one side of the room, and half of them had been

left open, so that the wind had sucked the curtains outside
where they waved like arms calling for help. There was
a grand piano in front of the windows, and rain was
blowing against the black varnished mahogany.

I looked at the paintings on the walls – the place was
like an art gallery. They were abstracts, wild splashes of
primary colours that swept you up like the eye of a hurri-
cane. A small Burmese cat appeared from behind a cane
chair, rubbing around my legs and mewing. I picked it
up and it purred as I tickled its head. I followed the music
and found the bedroom. The room looked crazy after the
empty order of the lounge. Wardrobe doors were hanging
open and clothes had been ripped off the rails. Cupboard
drawers were on the floor, and jumpers and shirts were
strewn in a trail around the bed. On the bed itself were
two leather suitcases, gaping open, both half-filled with
clothes. I'd found what I'd come for.

'She's left him,' I breathed, and the kitten nuzzled my
chin.

There was an envelope on the bedside table, and Frank's
name was scrawled across the front. Pearl had opened my
letter to Frank and now I had no qualms about reading
hers. I ripped the envelope open and pulled out the sheet
of paper inside. Pearl wrote like a child. The handwriting
was unformed and shaky and there were a lot of furious
crossings-out.

'Dear Frank,' she wrote, 'I shopped you, but I expect
you guessed. I also did another terrible thing, years ago,
something I never told you about, though she knows
now, and I'm sorry. She told me her child died because
of it, and that child was yours, she wrote that in the letter.
Frank, I can't bear to see you two together. I know you
love her, whatever you tell me, and I know that you've
always loved her, from the day that you first met. I was
there, remember? I think I knew before you did. We
should never have married. Remember, Frank, that she
doesn't love you, though, and that I loved you more than

I could ever tell you in a letter. That was why I did what I did, I couldn't bear it, that's all. I love you. I love you.'

I went to screw the letter up, but on second thoughts placed it back in its envelope and returned it to the table. I didn't care that anyone could see that it had been read. The letter was a mess, just like Pearl. She'd just walked out on it all, pregnant as she was, and by the look of the room she'd left without clothes or belongings. In her position I would have stayed, it was her home and it was beautiful. The child was Frank's, he owed her a home. I was sick of the music and I was sick of the room that had been torn apart by Pearl's anger.

'She's gone,' I said again, but I was wrong. The door to the bathroom was ajar, and I pushed it wide open with my foot. Pearl lay in the bath, and she was dead. She hadn't gone, she'd changed her mind. She'd stayed in the beautiful home, and she'd stayed for ever. Her lips were blue. She was dead. Thick red blood ran from her arm down on to the floor. Her hand held the photo, the one missing from the wall. The glass was broken and I couldn't see the picture because it was drenched in blood, but I guessed it was another one taken at Frank and Pearl's wedding.

I stared at the scene in front of me and felt my stomach risé into my mouth. I couldn't be sick there, though, not in Pearl's luxurious bathroom. The kitten smelled the blood suddenly and fought to escape from my arms. I held it tighter and it scratched my arm. I looked at the thin red line there and then back to Pearl in the bath. I didn't know that blood smelled. The white tiles were streaked with it and the water she lay in looked like all the blood from her body. I thought of the blood that I had spat on to the earth outside Rowan Hall on Coronation Day, the blood from Piers's kiss, the blood that had signed my pact. There was no need for Pearl to have used this much. It was too much, it was everywhere.

I saw a white face reflected in the mirror over Pearl's body and realized it was my own, stretched gaunt at the horror of the scene. My face was frozen with the pain of it, while Pearl's head lolled back comfortably, a half-smile on her lips.

'The baby,' I thought suddenly, and it was then that my legs gave and I sank slowly to my knees. 'Oh, God, Pearl, the baby!' The baby would be dead too. She had killed Frank's first child and now she had murdered his second. It would be dead inside her, and all because she loved Frank as she had always loved him. I grew angry with her, lying there smiling, her head thrown back as though proud of her terrible revenge, and then I felt pity, because her lips were blue and because I felt she had known no better. I felt tears on my cheeks and I spoke to her softly.

'You stupid cow, Pearl,' I told my sister over and over again. 'You stupid stupid soft cow.'

# CHAPTER 32

Frank got five years. I visited him in prison but it was too soon after Pearl's death and he could hardly bear to look at me. I took him Pearl's letter and he read it, and I told him what she had meant by the references to my letter and my baby and I think he understood, but I couldn't be sure. There was a hardness about him; an anger that I'd never seen before. It was as though he didn't care, not about any of it. He screwed the letter up, as I had been wanting to do, but I noticed that he didn't throw it away, he stuffed it into his pocket instead.

I had an excuse for my guilt, but he had none, apart from his feelings for me. I wanted to touch him, to make it all right by loving him, but I couldn't. There were two barriers between us: the prison wire mesh, and the invisible barrier in Frank's brain.

'You don't hate me now, then?' was all that Frank had to say to me, and it was strange that I didn't. I had no need to any more, not now I knew it was Pearl who had betrayed me. I was amazed at Frank's strength. I'd expected to find him a broken man, full of remorse and tears, but he was as solid as a house. I almost felt that he pitied me, which was wrong, from where I was sitting.

The Nat King Cole song had been going through my head. I didn't know the words, but the tune haunted me nevertheless. Whenever I heard it I saw Pearl, and that was a sight I could have done without. The sight is still with me, more vivid even than it was then. I felt no guilt at the time, I saw her death as her own fault, but now I know to share the blame, and it fills me with a horror that I can barely describe. It was an eye for an eye then, though. Pearl had killed my baby and it was only right that she should be dead herself. I didn't go to the funeral because, even then, I knew enough to realize that I should never have been able to face Lily over Pearl's grave.

With the hatred gone, my need for Frank was strengthened, but I still had other plans. I'd worked all my life for the ownership of Rowan Hall and now the stage was set, so to speak. The minor characters were out of the way, for that was still how I saw Frank and Pearl in my life. I was a widow, and I was wealthy. Philippa had taught me how to act like one of Piers's own class. I washed my mind of Frank; he was an episode, nothing more. He would have dragged me back to my past, while I had miles to cover in my future. I left the prison and returned to my room and I took off my clothes and threw them into the bin. I would have burned them, it would have been more apt, but you don't start fires in seedy rooms above betting shops.

It took me a week to find the sort of flat I was looking for, a top floor apartment in the most exclusive part of Belgravia. I paid six months' rent in advance. The agent had looked shocked when I'd suggested it, but it made me feel positive and gave me a base I felt sure of. The flat was furnished and, to my eyes, had the look of a place that the Queen would have felt proud to live in. It was old and it was grand and as full of antiques as Rowan Hall itself.

There were bell-pulls and tasselled curtains, with nothing matching in the way of patterns, which, I'd learned, was tasteful, although at first my eye had been offended by the casual hotchpotch of fabrics and colours. There were two heavy settees facing a low antique table, and an oak-framed fireplace with a huge gilt mirror above it. There were colours and there were no colours, but the general tone of the place was beige and dull green; the colour scheme reminded me of dead cabbage leaves but there was an opulence about the general décor I knew Philippa would approve of.

I stocked the cabinet with bottles of good-quality alcohol, though I barely drank myself, and hung a few expensive outfits in the wardrobes. 'Old money,' Philippa had said, 'nothing flashy or showy. A few well-chosen things that are expensive but worn.' The idea annoyed me, I yearned to dress in Yves St Laurent and Cardin, but instead I had chosen subtly. A tweed skirt. A camel cashmere coat. Scarves by Hermès. Gucci shoes. A Burberry raincoat. My only indulgences were the few Chanel suits that I had bought for town wear, and the half-dozen ballgowns and evening dresses that I had ordered from Hartnell. Of my old clothes I had saved only the red velvet dress, the one that I had worn on my first visit to the casino, and that was pushed away to the back of the wardrobe in an old Harrods carrier. It was a tart's dress, compared to the new clothes that I had collected.

I had my hair restyled and conditioned, and a toner put over the blond so that the lighter shades were darkened a little. I had my nails manicured and my eyebrows plucked into two neat arches. I spent a fortnight in Cannes and came back lightly burnished by the sun. The change in my appearance was subtle but at the same time drastic. I looked the part. I fitted my surroundings. Looking at my reflection in the mirror in the flat, sitting on the settee, I fitted so much that I frightened myself.

'The quick brown fox . . .' I said, and the accent was accurate, I knew Philippa had taught me well. I had read aloud from the *Tatler*, hour upon hour, until the words turned around and made sense in Philippa's ears. So now I was ready. I phoned Philippa's friends, explaining my absence by a visit to a sick aunt in the country. The aunt had died, I said, and left me a little something in her will. I saw the greedy acceptance in their eyes. They were dispossessed, this class, they shunned the sight of money, yet they needed it like the blood in their veins. Frank was right, their lifestyles ate away at the stuff with a voracious appetite yet they had no means of acquiring more except through inheritance.

The fifteenth of July, 1972. It was the date of the Grosvenor Square Ball, and the night that I met Piers again. It was the night that I had waited nearly twenty years for, the night that my life was to begin.

There was a band and a merry-go-round with painted horses and stalls with hoop-la and shooting, and the summer night was the sort that you only get in your past, with the last crimson rays of the dying sun turning the sky to indigo velvet before your eyes. It had rained, and the air smelled wet and fresh, and we picked our way across the wooden planks that had been put down to stop us treading in the mud. The night was spinning with the rich braying sound of the shrieks and laughter of the rich and titled and comfortably-off. I linked arms with my escort, a banker called Giles, a man wealthy enough to impress Piers, but ugly enough to make him think that he was in with a chance if he wanted me. I wore a tight strapless ballgown in pink chiffon, printed with deep pink and green roses. The skirt was full from the hips, and my hair was pinned up with two matching pink flowers.

Piers was there, as I had known he would be, and he was there with a girl, the daughter of an MP. I felt powerful that evening, and knew that nothing would stand in my way. It was the meeting that I felt I had been working towards for the whole of my life; I knew that it had to work. It was a moment that was predestined. Nothing could go wrong because it was written in our fate.

The music was loud, too loud to speak without shouting. Giles handed me a Buck's Fizz and we watched the dancers before moving towards the sideshows. The coloured lights and the music reminded me of the funfair, so many years ago, where I had met Frank and seen Pearl for the first time, but the voices around me were different and the air smelled of Joy and Rive Gauche instead of fried onions and sweat.

I knew in a moment that Piers had seen me. I felt it in my spine, in the ghostly fingers that coldly counted each vertebrae until they reached my neck. I turned slowly and he was there, standing behind me, watching me in that heavy-lidded way that he had watched me at the children's party at Rowan Hall. He leaned against a tree and he seemed to be smiling, but I saw his face only intermittently in the flashing lights of the roundabout and I could not be sure, not even of the fact that he was watching me. He held a drink in his hand and he raised the glass, and now I could see that he was smiling, but not at me. I turned towards the merry-go-round and the MP's daughter was there, riding one of the painted horses, her face as gaudy as the horse itself, flashing round, waving to Piers, her mouth split open in a grin of exhilaration.

The merry-go-round slowed and her waving became more furious.

'Want a ride?' Giles asked, and I shook my head.

He laughed loudly, as though I'd said something extremely funny, a habit he had when he was stumped for words. 'Did I tell you how adorable you look tonight, Lizzie?' he asked, placing his arm about my waist.

'Elizabeth,' I corrected him, 'and you're crushing my dress, Giles.'

He laughed again. 'You're so awfully cruel to me, Lizzie,' he said in a baby voice, 'and I'm only trying to be the perfect gentleman.' He pressed his nose into the nape of my neck and inhaled noisily. 'You look adorable and you smell adorable,' he said. 'Doesn't she, Joffy?' He turned to another woman from our party, a small blonde who had arrived with her brother.

'Doesn't she what?' Joffy asked, yawning.

'Smell divine,' Giles said, patting my hand.

'Oh, I should think so,' the girl answered. 'I haven't got close enough to tell. You carry on though, Giles,' she added, pushing past us, 'don't let my opinions bother you. By the way, Giles,' she added in a loud voice, 'you do know you're pissed, don't you?'

Giles gurgled with delight. 'Have it your own way,' he said good-humouredly and slugged back the last of his drink.

'Do you know that chap?' I asked, inclining my head towards Piers and his partner.

'Who?' Giles was peering fuzzily in their direction. 'Bicester? Of course, everyone here knows the Honourable Piers, I should think. That's why we're all over this side while he's standing right over there.'

'Is he unpopular then?' I asked.

'Oh he's popular enough,' Giles told me. 'Just can't afford to get too pally with him, that's all. Can get your fingers singed – the Hon. Piers has been known to touch a bloke for a couple of thou. on a good night, and you can kiss that off as a tax loss, unless you're prepared to wait the odd decade or two, that is. Great chap with a gun, though. And quite handy at the odd chukka, when he's sober enough to stay on the horse, of course. Showed himself up in front of the P. of W. just the other weekend, in fact. Rolled right off his mount and lay there laughing in the middle of the ground. Got kicked out of the Guards' Club for that sort of behaviour. Face of a choirboy, though. Never think of it to look at him. Same when we were at school. Never got caned, always blamed it on some other poor oik.'

I clutched Giles's arm before his reminiscences dragged on any longer. 'Introduce me,' I said.

Giles's eyebrows raised a shade. 'Particular reason?' he asked.

'None to interest you,' I answered, smiling.

Giles shrugged. 'On your own head be it,' he said, leading me by the elbow, 'but don't say that you weren't loudly warned. And watch out for the squid that he's with. Josie Penduggan can be a cow when she's sober but when she's pissed she's poison!'

There was no flicker of recognition in Piers's eyes as

we were introduced. He held out his hand and I took it and Josie sniggered, though I didn't know why. She held her hand over her mouth and her drink spilt as her breasts jiggled.

'Piers had just spotted you,' she said to Giles. 'Asked what an oily City toad like you was doing at a do like this.'

Giles threw back his head and laughed as though he'd just received a compliment. 'At least I manage to *keep* my oily little seat in the City,' he said pleasantly, and a flicker of anger crossed Piers's face.

'How is the Square Mile these days?' he asked Giles.

Giles pulled a face. 'Dead as a dodo really,' he said. 'Not really recovered from last spring, but surely you should know? Don't tell me you've dropped out altogether?'

Piers ignored the question. 'Any red-hot tips, Giles?' he asked. 'Anything you'd like to tell me now that you're here being boring?'

'Insider trading, Piers?' Giles asked, and he laughed so much that his drink sprayed out of his mouth.

'You know I'm not an insider, you stupid sod,' Piers said calmly. 'Just thought I might ask, that's all. You never know.'

'It's the delicious Lizzie here you ought to be asking then,' Giles said, pulling me closer. 'I've probably got more invested on her behalf than you'll see in a year, you arrogant bastard!'

Piers looked at me then, and I believe that he really saw me for the first time in my life.

'Trust this idiot with your life-savings then, do you?' he asked, and his eyes never left my face.

'I believe the risk has paid off already,' I told him steadily and I felt his eyes move down my body. He was drinking me in, soaking me up. My scar fascinated him, I saw his eyes return there and my skin burnt again under his gaze. There was an awkward silence and it was Josie who finally broke it.

'Win the pools then, did you?' she asked, and the question broke her up into a fit of loud giggles.

'Why don't you go and play with the gee-gees again, darling?' Piers asked her, politely but pointedly. The glare that she gave him in return would have cut through ice.

'I want to dance,' she said loudly.

'Well I'm sure young Giles here will be only too pleased to oblige,' Piers said, pushing Giles towards Josie, so suddenly that he lost his balance and staggered up against her.

'He's pissed!' Josie complained.

'Well, you should make a good pair then,' Piers told her. 'Mind how you go, now!'

We stood in silence once the other two were gone, Piers surveying me over the top of his drink like a racehorse owner sizing up a thoroughbred.

'I should apologize for my date,' he said finally.

'Don't bother,' I told him.

'Why not?' he asked.

'Because she's unimportant.'

Piers smiled at this. 'Why haven't we met before?' he asked.

'We have,' I told him. He looked faintly surprised. 'You just don't remember, that's all.'

'Not possible,' Piers said, and he laid a hand on my arm, just lightly, but I felt the blood run from my feet right up to my head, and I knew I was blushing, as I had as a child.

'We were children,' I told him, 'and we were never properly introduced.'

'A little chum of my sister's?' Piers asked.

'Something like that,' I told him.

He watched me for a while, and I returned his stare. I could tell that he was intrigued.

'D'you work then?' he said eventually.

'God, no!' I exclaimed. 'Well, not since my marriage, anyway.' A shutter came over Piers's eyes.

'A happy marriage?' he asked, his voice grown quiet. I

nodded. 'So what's a happily married lady doing out on the town with an old lech like Giles?'

'It *was* a happy marriage,' I told him. 'My husband died a few years ago, in Australia.'

'I'm sorry,' Piers said, but his expression had relaxed again.

I shrugged and sighed a little. 'It was on the cards,' I said. 'He was considerably older than me. A wonderful man, a friend of my father's.'

'And your father?' Piers asked.

'Dead too,' I said, looking sad. 'A few months before my husband. It hit me very hard, I'm afraid. Being an only child I was forced to come back to England to take care of all the arrangements. The legal side of the estate was torture, even though I was the sole heir. I'd intended to go back to Australia, but you know how it goes and somehow I'm still here.'

'I'm glad,' Piers said, 'very glad that you decided to stay.'

Was it then that he decided to marry me? I believe that it could have been, for he led me on to the dance floor without asking and pulled me tight against him as the band played slow songs for the lovers and the drunks amongst the crowd. I knew that the bait was my money, but the trap was intentional, for I also knew that I could make him love me, too. If it was the money that he needed, then it was his house that was my goal, and I admired his single-mindedness for it was a quality that I had in abundance. Let greed be our cement then. But let love also grow out of that. How could I not love Piers? He was the key for me to Rowan Hall. And how could he have failed to fall in love with me, too, when I held what he most wanted, most needed, to survive?

We were beautiful, a golden couple, no longer children, but matured to handsome adults. I was twenty-six on the night of the ball, and Piers was some five years older. We danced together, turning with the magical colour of the lights that spun overhead, and our eyes became fused, each upon the other's, until there was no crowd of braying hounds around us, only Piers and I, and his beauty was just as I had remembered it to be; he didn't become lesser in the flesh.

His lips pressed my ear when he spoke. I felt his nose in my hair and his breath against my neck. I felt his suit beneath my fingers, and his hand pressed hard into the small of my back. The band struck up a faster beat but we ignored it, merely moving to the edge of the floor. 'Piers!' A figure pushed between us, prising us apart, clutching at Piers's arm, pushing him away with a laugh that made me wince.

'*Harper's* are here and I promised them a shot,' Josie said, and I turned quickly and walked away without once looking back.

'You're so damned rude, you know!' I heard Piers say to Josie.

'Well, if you think I'm going to stand around while you go groping that piece of brass, then you've another bloody think coming, darling,' I heard Josie say, but the last words faded as I moved towards the exit.

'Leaving without me?' Giles asked, out of breath from chasing me through the crowd.

'No,' I said, pulling my wrap around my shoulders. 'You can drive me, if you want.'

Giles looked pleased at this, and I took his arm as we walked to the car where the chauffeur was waiting to open the doors.


I took no phone calls for the following four days, and then I phoned Giles.

'Seen your friend Piers again?' I asked, after a few minutes' chat. There was a pause.

'Oddly enough, yes,' Giles told me. 'He asked me to lunch today out of the blue, as a matter of fact. What made you ask?'

'Just curious,' I said. 'He's a bit of a strange one, that's all. I got the feeling he was trying to check me out the other night, financially, I mean.'

Giles laughed. 'Oh, that would be our Piers, all right,' he said. 'Straight to the point; has to be, with the upkeep of his place hanging over his head. Sword of Damocles, you know, typical of the British aristo. Don't let him tap you, though, unless you've got money to burn.'

'Look, Giles,' I said, 'I got the distinct impression that he thought you were joking when you mentioned my investments. Just something he said, but it was a bit of a put-down, nevertheless. I think he may need cutting down to size, you know. What do you think?'

'Piers does have a way of putting most women down,' Giles agreed.

'Well, look,' I said, 'if he does happen to mention me over lunch, and ask you anything about my circumstances, could you just play them up a bit? I mean, let him know that I'm more than just some spotty little kid that his sister used to play with? I know one shouldn't flaunt one's status, but I really couldn't stand his arrogant attitude, you know. If he tries to tap me for some of it, then we'll both have the last laugh, won't we?'

Giles was delighted, and agreed at once. 'Don't worry, Lizzie,' he said. 'By the time I've finished with Piers he'll believe he was dancing with Jackie Onassis herself!'

The phone rang the following day, at four. Piers tried to sound casual, but there was an eagerness in his voice.

'Just bumped into old Giles,' he said. 'Gave me your phone number, I hope you don't mind? Cost me lunch, so I hope it was worth it.'

'Worth it in what way?' I asked. There was a pause.

'Well, I hope that you'll agree to see me again, for one,' Piers said. 'The rest we can work out as we go along. Do you eat lobster? Of course you do. I'll pick you up at nine. Giles gave me your address.'

Piers was fifteen minutes late, and when he arrived he was slightly drunk. He looked around my flat, and I could tell that he approved of all that he saw, especially the well-stocked drinks cabinet.

'Well, you know your vintages,' he said, holding a glass of malt whisky up to the light for inspection.

'It was my husband's line of business,' I told him. 'Didn't I tell you?'


We drove to Piers's town house, a small, fashionable place just off Flood Street, in Chelsea. The house was on three floors, white-painted and flat-fronted, and scruffily neglected inside, although the old masters on the walls appeared to be genuine, and the collection of guns that he showed me proudly in the cellar seemed to have been oiled and polished with elaborate care.

He poured me champagne, and a scotch for himself, and sank down into a wide armchair, with one leg hanging over the arm.

'Take a seat,' he said, smiling.

I fingered my glass. 'I thought we were eating,' I replied. 'You said something about a lobster.'

'That's all in hand,' he said, patting the chair beside him. 'Now, sit down and relax. You look like a scared young virgin.' I smiled, and took the seat.

Dinner was served an hour later, by which time Piers was drunk and my champagne had turned warm in my hands. It was served by the cook, on a small round Chippendale in the back room; Lobster Thermidor with iceberg lettuce, and small bowls of chocolate mousse, decorated with crystallized violets, to follow.

I blanched at the weapons needed to tackle the lobster. Philippa had covered them verbally, but I was unsure how to attack it in reality. I needn't have worried, though. Piers tussled with his for a while, but he was far too drunk to handle them. I followed suit, and we laughed at our efforts together.

'Some music,' he said, as we walked back into the lounge. He put a record on the player and Frank Sinatra's smooth brandy voice soon came spilling out of the speakers.

Piers walked unsteadily towards me, putting my glass down on the table and pulling me gently nearer. He looked into my eyes for a moment, his hand cupping my face, and then he kissed me, prising my lips apart with his own, pushing his tongue between my teeth, and inhaling deeply as he did so. I stood immobile, not moving, not protesting.

Piers took this as submission. His hands ran down from my shoulders to my wrists. His kiss became more urgent, yet still I didn't move. He grabbed at my breasts, massaging them through my dress with the palms of his hands, and I felt his erection through his trousers, pressing into my stomach.

My dress was buttoned down the front. Piers fumbled with each button and I waited until he was finished, until he saw my pale pink cotton bra and the white petticoat that I wore over it. I waited for the last button to be undone, till the dress hung open at the front, and then I pushed him away and pulled the dress together, a look of shocked horror on my face.

'Piers!' I whispered. 'For God's sake!'

He smoothed his hair back with his fingers and shook his head a little, to clear it. I could see that I'd surprised him, but he smiled and moved towards me again.

'No!' I said, and he stopped.

'What's wrong?' he asked. 'I thought . . .'

'You thought I was easy,' I said, open-mouthed with surprise. 'You spoke to Giles and he told you a pack of lies! What did he tell you, Piers? That he'd had me too? Are you supposed to compare notes over lunch tomorrow? You must think that I'm cheap, Piers, like that dreadful, common girl you took to the ball.'

'I thought you wanted me,' Piers began, 'I thought that I'd read you right . . . at the ball . . .'

I snatched my bag from the hall table and ran down towards the front door.

'I'll get a cab,' I said, opening it. 'I expect an apology.'
'Go to hell!' Piers shouted, and I slammed the door on
his words.

# CHAPTER 33

I was seen in all the right places after that, and I knew that Piers saw me there, too. My private detective knew his every move socially. I paid him more, and he found out other things about Piers's private life; things that I knew I would use if I had to. There was nothing now that would stop me from owning Rowan Hall, even Piers himself, though I was still determined to love him.

Piers was easy to find, you just followed royalty. There were the 'royal' events that dotted the year like social confetti. Each year was the same, the royals did their rounds, and the English socialites orbited in their wake. I saw the same faces, heard the same laughter, the same conversations repeated a thousand times. I no longer feared discovery; Philippa's name cut through social barriers like a knife. Ralph's imprisonment for fraud was never mentioned, except in the vaguest of terms. Philippa was a blue-blood who had married beneath her. She had made a mistake with her marriage, it was easily done. She was still of 'them' despite this, and I was accepted easily into the fold.

I had a few regular escorts – Giles was just one of them. When I next met Piers I was with Guy, a property dealer. Guy was older than Piers, and owned more than double the land. I took Guy's arm as a friend introduced us to Piers and his partner, a white-faced blonde I saw him tak no apparent interest in, and looked quickly away from Piers, as though bored by the meeting.

'We've met,' Piers said, rather rudely, as my name was mentioned. Guy looked at him sharply, but Piers ignored the stare.

'I didn't realize you two knew one another,' our host said, smiling.

'Oh, only in the strictest non-biblical sense,' Piers said, and the smiles around us froze with shock. The blonde girl holding Piers's arm dropped her hand away slowly and coloured to a shade of deepest beetroot.

Someone laughed and the others joined in, pleased for an opportunity to break the tension that was obviously building.

'You still have something of mine,' I told Piers, and this time our voices were drowned a little by the resumed chatter that was going on around us.

'What's that?' he asked, leaning forward to catch my words.

'My apology,' I whispered. 'I'm still waiting, Piers. I'd like it before next month. That's when Guy and I announce our engagement, you know.'

Piers looked at me, and his face had turned to stone so that I could not tell what he was thinking. He looked over at Guy, who nodded slightly and threw back his drink.

'No congratulations then?' Guy asked, good-humouredly, and Piers's face darkened.

'I'll wait until it's official, if you don't mind,' Piers told him, and pulled his partner off to queue at the buffet.

Once they were out of earshot Guy grabbed my hand and kissed it. 'Rather sudden, wasn't it?' he asked, smiling at me. 'Didn't even have a chance to get to Asprey's for the ring, let alone tell the old man!'

I stood on tiptoe to kiss him on the cheek. 'You don't mind, do you, Guy?' I asked.

He patted my arm. 'Bloody flattered,' he said, coughing over his cigar. 'Haven't been any beautiful women in my family since before the Great War. May I take it you're

up to something?' I nodded. 'And the announcement in
*The Times* can wait?' he asked.

'For the time being, at any rate,' I laughed. Guy looked
pleased. 'If you're stitching up young Bicester then you
have my full backing,' he said. 'He needs taking down a
peg or two. And I can't say that I mind if my name is
linked to the most beautiful woman in London. D'you
intend marrying him, then?'

'Perhaps,' I said, sipping my orange juice.

'Could be in with a chance there,' Guy told me.
'Haven't seen his feathers so ruffled by a woman before.
Looks like you might just get him by the short and curlies,
my dear.'

I smiled. 'That's exactly what I had intended,' I said,
and we burst out laughing together.

The flowers arrived the following morning, a dozen
yellow rosebuds with a note attached, from Piers.

'Will this do?' the note read.

'No,' I said to myself quietly, 'but you're learning,
Piers, you're learning.'

The phone rang a few hours later. 'Lunch at Blakes?'
Piers's voice asked on the other end.

I paused, and I could hear him breathing in the silence.
'I can't,' I said.

Piers sighed. 'Tomorrow then,' he said, finally.

'If you like,' I replied, and he hung up.

He was angry when he arrived the following day, I
could hear it in the way that he drove his car, its wheels
squealing as they crushed against the pavement when he
parked. His eyes skimmed the flat quickly for his roses,
but I'd thrown them away. He was off-balance. I wore
the lightest pale silk dress that clung innocently to my
body, accentuating each curve, but I made him wait by
the door while I threw my raincoat over my shoulders
and left the flat fully covered. We walked apart. Piers
touched my arm but I pulled away quickly.

'You're not really going to marry that old fart Guy, are

you?' Piers asked once we were in his car, and I shrugged, which annoyed him more.

'Why not?' I asked, and he shook his head.

We ate oysters and grilled trout and Piers drank a bottle of chilled Chablis.

'Why did you turn me down?' he asked, as the dessert was placed in front of us. 'Nursery food,' he added, pointing his spoon in the direction of the two vast mountains of treacle pudding, running with slopes of yellow custard, that we had been served. I pushed my plate away, while Piers dug into his own with undisguised relish.

'Do all women say yes to you, then?' I asked, calling the waiter over and ordering a black coffee.

'Of course not,' Piers said sharply. 'But I can read the signs as well as the next man. You gave me the come-on all night at the ball, then you turned tail and fled the moment I touched you. What else was I supposed to do?'

I smiled. 'Perhaps that's what we ought to find out,' I said.

Piers's glance took in my hair and my dress and my mouth as I sipped my coffee. The silkiness returned to his voice and his hand reached for mine across the table. 'And what about old Guy?' he asked, his eyes narrowing.

'Oh, I should think he'll survive,' I said, and Piers laughed, reassured again of my interest in him. I leaned across the table and I kissed him lightly on the lips, and his crystal glass fell over, spilling Chablis on to the white linen.

I saw Piers three times over the following ten weeks, and each time it was for lunch, and each time when I left him it was with a chaste kiss on the cheek. Then the last ball of the season came, and Piers asked me if I would go with him. Josie was in France, competing in a three-day event, and I had known Piers would be without a partner.

When the ball was over a crowd of Piers's friends climbed into his Rolls and we drove off through London as the sun rose out of the mist.

'Where are we going?' I asked, but Piers merely laughed.

'You'll see,' he said, tapping the side of his nose.

'Slumming it!' one of his friends suddenly shouted, and the others burst out laughing, as though the idea genuinely amused them.

We drove through the West End, and then down narrow cobbled streets to the centre of Covent Garden, where the vans were just due to load up. Piers pulled in at the kerb and a lorry tooted behind him, and when the engine was switched off I closed my eyes, afraid of the sights and the smells that I knew were there to greet me. The car emptied and the morning air felt fresh against my face. I tried to hold my breath, but I couldn't, and back came my childhood in a rush. I smelled the fruit and the flowers and the exhaust from the vans. I could separate each smell, take each aroma, layer by layer, and identify it without even trying. There was the exotic fruit and the peaty brown vegetables. There were the soiled cabbage leaves squashed underfoot from the day before. I could smell the oranges and the new white wood from the crates they were packed in. I smelled the oil from the tarpaulins that covered the stalls and the dank creamy scent of half-opened mushrooms. I saw Billy in my mind, as vividly as if he were standing there, and I watched him prune the leaves off a cauliflower as he held it in one hand, and I wondered why his fingers didn't come off the way he sliced with that knife. Marge was watching from behind her own stall, the sleeves of her old brown coat pulled over fingers to ward off the cold, looking the way Billy might if the knife happened to slip . . . I heard the voices and they were the same. I felt relief at tones that were so familiar to me. A rush of homesickness hit me that was stronger even than any I'd experienced in Australia, and it was all the more painful to me because I had no home to go to now. Billy was dead and I lived somewhere else . . . I *was* someone else. I screwed my eyes up tight

to stop the tears and I dug my fingernails into my palm
to try and stop myself thinking and feeling such hurt.

'Come on!' A friend of Piers's tugged at my arm and I
stepped out of the Rolls to face the stares of the market
porters. I knew what they were thinking, I would have
been thinking the same. There was a café nearby. I followed Piers's friends inside.

'Breakfast!' they all shouted, like a pack of baying
hounds.

There was the sound of chair-legs scraping back as they
took seats around the Formica-covered tables. The tables
felt greasy through a coating of oil and gritty sugar. Necks
craned to stare at the menu, chalked up behind the
counter.

'Bacon.'

'Bagels, too, I believe,' someone called out. 'They're
baked fresh somewhere in the East End. Fucking amazing,
if I remember right.'

A girl from our party staggered up to the counter,
clutching a crochet shawl around her bare shoulders. 'The
loo!' she shouted to the woman behind the till. The
woman's face remained impassive. She looked Italian, but
she could have been from Albania for the little she
appeared to understand of the question. 'Oh Christ,
Duncan, come and help,' the girl called out. 'I'm busting
for a pee!'

We had bagels and coffee and soft-scrambled eggs, and
two of the men did a duel with the plastic tomato sauce
bottles while another threw slices of bread on to the floor
to prove they always fell butter-side down. A schoolfriend
of Piers's grabbed my arm and tried to get me to dance.
His eyes rolled unsteadily and he slurred his words when
he spoke.

'Fuck off!' I whispered, grabbing my wrist from his
wet palm. I pushed my chair back and made my way
towards the door.

'I say, everybody!' I heard him call behind me. 'Old
Lizzie here's just done a marvellous impression of the

colloquial cockney, bloody amazing! Told me to fuck off
in the best cockney tones! Do it again, Liz, let's hear some
more!'

But I'd made it as far as the door and did not turn
around. Piers was standing there, arms folded, leaning
against the door-frame, a cigarette in his slim fingers. 'I'm
going outside,' I told him. 'I feel sick.'

I ran out of the café and along the cobbled streets. I
turned into a narrow lane beside the docking yard and I
leaned up against the wet grey wall, gasping for breath
and sick with my own anger. There are times when your
own body beats you and gives up, and this was one of
them. It was all within my grasp, but suddenly I didn't
want any of it. I wanted to go home. I needed to be back
where I belonged. I'd lost my bottle, but I was too proud
to admit it. 'You *didn't* belong there,' I reminded myself
angrily, thinking of the market, with all its casual warmth
and security. You forget the boredom. You forget the
frustration. Nostalgia is a lethal sentiment and it was
attacking me with full force. I looked across at the café
that I'd left in such a hurry. You could still hear their
voices, their full-volume laughter. For a moment I was
disgusted by them. I saw them through my father's eyes.
The magic was gone, and I wanted it back.

I closed my eyes and tried to think of the house. It was
all that I wanted. It was mine, it had been since the day
of the party. I had spat into the dirt outside the door and
sworn to have it and if I couldn't get the one thing I had
lived my life for, then I might as well not have lived it at
all. The others in the café were just a means to an end,
that was all. It was there, within reach, it had been easy,
it had taken less than I'd been prepared to give. I would
have been prepared to kill anyone who stood between me
and Rowan Hall, it was as simple as that. The thought
frightened me. Had I killed my own husband? I'd nearly
told myself that I hadn't, that his death had been a coincidence, that the doctor had been right. I saw Pearl's arm
hanging over the side of the bath, its trailing snake of

blood like a ribbon winding down to the floor, taking the
colour from her skin. Her eyes had been open, but there
were no pupils, just the whites. Too much had happened
now. I had to go on with my greed. I had to be right,
just as Frank had to be wrong.

'Bad vintage?'

I jumped. I thought it was Frank, but he was in prison;
it was Piers who stood there watching me, smiling.

'Sorry?' I asked. My face must have looked white, like
a ghost's.

'Bad vintage,' Piers repeated, 'the champagne you
drank. Makes you queasy. Brought it up yet?' I shook
my head. 'Should do, you know – clears the head and all
that.'

'I'm all right,' I told him.

'You look it.'

I looked across and his eyes gleamed in the shadows of
the narrow alleyway. He came closer and I thought that
he might kiss me. He reached out a hand and wove his
fingers into my hair.

'Lizzie,' he said, and I stopped breathing, afraid that he
might know me now, afraid he might remember the child
I had been. That first meeting had meant so much to me,
I couldn't believe it wasn't etched on to his memory too.
But he didn't, mine was just a name to him, nothing
more.

Piers licked his tongue lazily across my top lip, and his
hands grew tighter in my hair. He pulled my head back
and he sucked at my neck, and each kiss was a question:
'Can I? Will you?' I told him yes with my mouth, my
body loosened against him. The questions stopped, he
had his answer, he knew in the way that I kissed him
back. We were in the same game at last, after the same
thing.

'Oh Christ, Lizzie,' he breathed into my neck. 'I can't
wait. It has to be here.' He pulled me further into the
shadows until they were like a blanket to us, and we were
hidden from the road. 'There's no one here, they can't see

us, it has to be here, Lizzie. I want you, Christ, I want you.' His words came out like unravelled string, they went on and on, spoken into my face and my neck and the swell of my breast. He talked to my body, not to me, and my body answered him in its own language, egging him on, saying yes even when the questions had finished.

I felt his fingers work up my skirt and it was then that I pushed him away. He looked startled in the shadows, there was a half-smile of surprise on his face. Perhaps he thought I had pushed him off so that I could finish undressing. Maybe he thought he was being too slow, that I was more impatient than him. I hit him then, hard about the face, enough to wipe the smile off, but not to make him stumble.

There was no mistaking that signal. Piers wiped his hand across his cheek and the anger in his eyes was like the flare of a match in the darkness. 'You bitch!' he said. 'You stupid frigid fucking little bitch!' There was blood on his lip and he pulled out his hankie to dab it off.

I smiled. I was pleased, sure again of myself as I had been before the trip to the market. I'd seen what I'd wanted to see: the look in Piers's eyes before the anger had knocked it away. 'Cat and mouse,' Philippa had said to me, and once again I knew she was right. I felt a surge of excitement run through my body as I watched Piers standing in front of me, his face as white with anger as mine had been with fear and uncertainty just a few moments before. I had all but won. The thought rang through my head till it drowned out all other sounds. I wanted Philippa to be there, to show her how right she had been, but she had known all along, she was part of the same breed. She knew what the men wanted, how their minds worked, better than they knew themselves.

Piers turned and walked away and I watched his back with the first electric hum of victory singing in my veins.

'Just one more round to play, Piers,' I whispered in the darkness. I had strength again, I knew what I wanted and I knew that I was right in wanting it. Piers had shown his weaknesses to me and I was prepared to be his provider, if his house became mine in return. I would take it in marriage, as I had always meant to take it. I had lured Piers with my money, and now I knew that I could make him need me in other ways too. I had seen it there in his eyes when I'd hit him, that split-second flash that had confirmed that Philippa had been right.

I phoned Piers the following day, and he said nothing when he heard my voice, but he listened, which was all that I wanted.

'Five minutes before midnight,' I told him. There was silence, and then the phone went dead in my hand and I was left with the dialling tone buzzing like a wasp in my ear. I smiled and placed the receiver in its cradle. I knew then that he would come, that he would be drawn towards me via the baited trail that I had left for him, like an animal drawn into a trap, even when the scent of the bait is almost erased by the smell of its own fear.

Piers would not believe that I could turn him down so violently and so consistently. He would need to prove to himself that I had been wanting him all along or, just as happily, that I was frigid. Nothing less could do for him, to soothe his ego and play suitor to his pride. Besides, he had seen something else there, just a glimpse, but the scent had been strong enough and I knew that he would come.

My flat was in darkness when I pulled open the door. Piers peered into the gloom, I believe he had thought that I was out. The clock was chiming – he had rung the bell on the first chime of twelve.

'You're late,' I said. I wore an ankle-length ruby suede coat with tight black leather gloves and black stiletto shoes. My hair was pinned loosely into a pleat – I looked as though Piers had just caught me going out for the night.

Piers looked for a second unsure of himself, and it was the first time that I had seen that expression on his face.

He was dressed formally and he looked clean, like a child that is straight from the bath and still smelling of soapsuds. His hair was combed back off his face. I wanted to press my own face into it and smell the shampoo and the sweetness of the hair before the sticky smells of sex took over, like heavy, heady perfumes.

Oh God, Piers, you were within reach then, you were so close that I could have leaned across and touched you and the uncertainty would have lifted from your face like a bride's veil and you would have taken me there and then in my flat, most probably on the floor, on the rug that lay over the parquet, but I knew that I couldn't do that, for we were locked in a game then, you and I, and I had sworn to be the winner, for all that it meant I should sacrifice.

You'd shaved closely, so closely that your palely-tanned skin looked blush pink along the cheeks. There had been hot towels wrapped around your face, and creamy soap and fine cologne. I thought of my father and could smell the Imperial Leather that he always used, poured into his cupped hands and then slapped on lightly, to avoid too much stinging. Your suit was pressed and looked like card, and your white shirt collar looked like cake icing in the light from the hall. I watched your mouth with its thin smile, your eyes were like angels' eyes, so blue and large, and there were shadows from the lashes on your cheeks. I wanted you to kiss me every bit as badly as I'd wanted you to kiss me in the rose garden, but the memory of that kiss and the aftershave sting of shame it had left behind made me refrain from touching you, or from showing you how much I cared.

'It's cold,' Piers said, and I stared at him silently. He swallowed, I saw his Adam's apple bob above his tie-knot. 'You were on your way out?' he asked.

I shook my head. 'No.'

'Your coat,' Piers explained.

I looked down at it, fingering the buttons. 'I can take it off,' I said.

Piers stepped forward. 'Let me take it for you,' he began.

I stepped back. 'No!' I shouted, and he stopped, frozen in his movement to reach for the buttons. '*I* can take it off,' I said, and I did, and Piers swallowed again, for I was naked underneath. The coat fell on to the floor with a light sound, like silk. Piers stared at my body, and my gloves and my shoes, and his hands fell to his sides and his face became like marble.

'Don't you want me, Piers?' I asked him, and my hair fell loose as I shook it out of its comb.

'What the hell are you playing at?' Piers asked. He wiped the back of his hand over his mouth. His hands were beautiful, perfectly manicured, slim, long-fingered, piano-player's hands, the sort you would want on your body. I thought of Jack's rough stubby fingers and I shuddered. It's strange how the dead will come back and haunt you like that, unwanted and unannounced, butting in with their smells and their memories in a way that you would never have allowed when they were alive. I pushed Jack out from between us.

'Don't you want me?' I asked Piers again, my voice softer this time, more serious.

There was a long pause. Piers's eyes never left my body. They swept over me like fingertips, going back to the same spots. I imagined his eye-lashes brushing over me like bird feathers.

'You know that I do,' he said at last, his voice husky and broken and coming from a long way off. He was in my flat now, in the darkness there with me. Our eyes shone like silver stones in the thin dagger of light from the street outside. I took another step backwards.

'Beg for it then,' I told him.

Piers's head jerked upwards, his eyes now on my face. 'What?' His mouth had fallen open, a faint trace of a smile at its corners. I was joking, I had to be joking. Grown men don't beg. Grown men have too much pride.

'I want to hear you beg for it, Piers,' I told him. 'I want

to *hear* you beg and I want to *see* you beg. I want you on your knees, that's all.'

The smile-traces vanished in one and the match of anger flared up in an instant. 'You must think I'm bloody mad!' Piers said. His tongue licked his lips like a snake. I shook my head slowly. He lunged at me suddenly but I kicked at his shin with the pointed toe of my shoe and he stopped to bend and rub it, his hair now dishevelled, falling over his face.

'I told you, Piers,' I said patiently. 'If you want me you will have to tell me, and when you tell me you will have to beg.'

Piers remained frozen, caught in the street lights.

'Is this a joke?' he asked, but I didn't answer.

'Beg, Piers,' I told him, and the anger suddenly seemed to drain out of him.

He looked around the room, as though worried that he might be watched, and then his face became a mask and his knees crumpled and he slid to the floor.

'Please,' he said, in a voice that was barely audible. 'Please, Lizzie.' He knelt in front of me, his elbows pulled into his ribs, head bowed, rocking slightly backwards and forwards. 'Please,' he repeated, no tone left in his voice. He looked up at my face and he looked worried, as though truly scared I might refuse him. There was wrinkled skin on his forehead and his hands were clasped as though he had a pain in his stomach.

'Take off your jacket,' I said, and he pulled it off slowly, carefully, like a child undressing for its mother, folding the jacket in two and laying it out on the floor. I stood on it, my heels making dents in the fabric.

'Now your shirt,' I ordered. His hands were shaking, which was why he was so slow with the buttons. We were like children who discover a fantasy that they can both believe in and play along with. His shirt came off over his head, like a vest. The tie lay on the floor, still knotted, like a noose.

I kicked the shirt and tie to one side and nodded towards his trousers. 'Now those,' I said.

Piers looked up at me, then slowly unbuttoned his flies, pulling his trousers down to his ankles and kicking them off, then his socks. He looked at me again and I nodded. He paused for a second, staring at the floor, then quickly slid out of his underpants, kneeling in front of me naked, his body pale and surprisingly slender, his long delicate fingers hiding his erection from me in a gesture that was almost feminine in its coyness. I pushed his hands away with my foot and his penis bounced a little with the pleasure of freedom. His arms dropped to his sides. I raised my shoe to his chest and ran it in a line down to his groin, tapping his penis lightly with my heel as I did so. I watched it grow until its head was pink and swollen, and Piers's eyes closed and his hands curled into fists.

I pushed his head down with my hands, pressing them into his clean shiny hair, and making him stand on all fours, like a dog. 'Follow me,' I told him, and I walked slowly into the bedroom, Piers crawling closely behind, his erection swaying like a tail between his legs.

When we reached the bedroom I pulled him up to stand beside me and it was then that I kissed him, reaching on tiptoe to do so, cupping his face with one hand, and cupping his balls with the other, squeezing them gently until he groaned with pleasure and tried to reach out for me, to pull me to him, but instead I pushed him away, pushed him on to the bed, and watched him as he lay there, spread-eagled on the cold satin counterpane.

'Tie him, darling,' Philippa had told me. 'It's what they all love, what he'll be expecting,' but I couldn't do it, not then. I reached out my nails like cat claws instead and ran them, all five, from his chest to his stomach. They left red trails behind. Piers waited, shuddering, in the darkness.

'Don't try to touch me,' I ordered, and his hands relaxed immediately. He was like a carved crucifix, his pale slim body stretched and twisted with longing and pleasure, his head tilted back on the pillow, his chin and neck exposed and vulnerable, as Pearl's had been when I found her in the bath. Another ghost. I pushed Pearl out of the way.

I straddled Piers's legs and took his penis in my hands, rubbing its tip with my thumbs till the first bead of juice appeared, running my fingers down the long swollen vein, working its length gently until his back began to arch and he cried out with the agony of holding back.

I released him quickly then, reaching towards the bed-side table and scooping an ice-cube from the champagne bucket beside the bed. I pushed the cube into my mouth, running it round with my tongue until the corners had melted, and then I took his penis into my mouth too, pressing the cube against it, touching it with my tongue until Piers let out a breath of surprise and his body relaxed, though his eyes remained closed. Then I took a handful of the ice, crushed, diamond-like fragments this time, and pressed them against his balls, so that he shouted out loudly and sat up, but I pushed him back on to the pillows and began the whole routine again. We made love like this for two hours, each time with me bringing him to the brink of orgasm, and then each time cooling him down with the ice, then at last, when the ice was gone, I opened the half-bottle of champagne that was left and let it foam over Piers's body, as achingly, sweetly cold as the ice had been, but with its sharp needles of fizz making him groan out loud yet again.

Then I slid on top of him, with the champagne still foaming, and his back still arched in painful ecstasy. Piers came almost immediately, clutching at my hips, pulling me further on to him, pushing deeper inside me, brutal for a moment after so much inactivity, his fingers digging deep into my legs as he grabbed at me blindly. I was all he wanted in the world at that moment. His hands ran to my waist and he sat up, reaching for my breasts hungrily with his mouth. He pulled me back with him, so that we lay stretched out on the bed, and then he came in a spasm that jerked us both together and then he clung to me like

a child, and we fell apart, the alcohol evaporating on our
bodies, cooling us, as Piers fought for breath at my side.
I reached across and held him until he quietened and
his breathing became slower and deeper, and he slept.
Then I said my silent thanks, to Philippa, for being so
right about everything, and to my detective, who had
somehow discovered Piers's exact tastes in sex, something
that most of his previous girlfriends had obviously overlooked. Prostitutes must have been bribed to give the
information . . . I shuddered, but it didn't matter. I was
neither shocked nor disgusted. I had discovered the keys
to Piers's soul, and they were all that mattered: money
and sex. They gave me the power over Piers that I needed.
I remembered the little girl with her underwear stitched
to her skirt, but I no longer felt the pain of her embarrassment, because that pain had gone, had been exorcized as
we had made love. I had enjoyed it too, that was what
had surprised me, had liked seeing Piers on all fours,
begging me to allow him to make love to me, had enjoyed
the pain and the pleasure that I had measured out in equal
portions. There was more to come, too, for I had discovered ways of pleasing Piers that even he would have
never thought possible. The money could wait now, I was
too clever to give him any until after we were married. He
was mine now anyway, though, of that much I was sure.
Piers was mine, the house was mine. I pushed Piers, still
asleep, away from me, and clutched my legs to my chest,
rocking myself with pleasure at the thought that I had
them both at last.

# CHAPTER 34

I stood in the grounds of Rowan Hall and gulped down the damp mossy air like a man who has just been saved from drowning. Perhaps I had been drowning in London. It had rained all night, and the rain had heightened the smell of the earth and the grass and the trees that were all around me, their leaves whispering together in the wind, their wet bark humming with sodden life.

I was full of it, filled to the brim, overflowing with my own cleverness. I was to marry Piers, eleventh Earl of Bicester. It had all been worth it; the deaths, the deceit, the suffering had all added up – I was to own Rowan Hall, and that was all that had ever mattered.

I no longer had doubts about my past. That life had gone, was dead for ever. I had been born in the wrong place, that was all, I had never belonged there, and now I was home at last. Twenty-two years it had taken me, twenty-two years ago I had stood on that spot outside the front door, with the sound of the Queen's coronation buzzing in my ears, and I had made a promise to the house and to myself, and now I had come back to claim it, to make good the pact that I had made as a child.

I was nearly thirty. No one who had known me then in the market would ever have recognized me now. The bubbling child, full of fair beauty and confidence, had gone. I was leaner and more elegant, as I am still today.

I had copied Philippa and I had become her. I was as much a part of the house and its class as I had been a part of the market and its people.

My hair was darker, a deeper ashen blond, not the riot of sun-ripened curls that I had had at seven years. My skin was tanned, only my eyes held the same colour, the green merely deepening like leaves as summer passes. My clothes were still hand-made, but by couturiers, not Aunty Marge, and I wore real jewels now – I looked at the ring on my finger, the only one that I wore. It had been placed there by Piers that morning, a family ring, not mine, but his, to be passed on through the generations, like the house. Its metal had become thin with age, but the fine mounts still clung fiercely to the emeralds and white diamonds that were set in their claws.

'The stones match your eyes, Elizabeth,' Piers had told me, and they did. I had held them next to my face and looked at them in a mirror.

'Green is unlucky,' I'd said.

'Not in this family,' Piers had told me, and he'd kissed the back of my neck. I'd pulled away from him, it was a habit that I had.

'We make good marriages in this family,' he'd said, and I'd thought of his mother, with her mad soldier husband, though she'd claimed to have loved him until the moment that he'd died. His mother had hated me, of course, when he had taken me to visit her, had seen things in me that Piers could never have seen, but then she was just old, and when he'd taken her aside and, as I guessed, told her of my money, she'd come back with the veiled-eyed politeness that I'd received from the other members of his family.

Rowan Hall had been opened for our engagement. No one lived in the house now, just a skeleton staff: a housekeeper, cook, and a maid once a week, in case Piers or his sister should visit. I was never told why Piers's mother lived mostly in a retirement home for officers' wives. Piers merely said that the house was too big for her alone,

but I think the move had just happened and that they had
forgotten most of the reasons for it.

There was no gardener, no handyman, and the neglect
was like a disease that had penetrated the entire building,
everywhere that you looked there were symptoms of
ruined old age. I had cried when Piers first took me there,
I'd cried as you cry when someone you love is dying. I
cried for its lost beauty and grandeur and grace. I knew
then why my money had come to me, not merely to act
as a bait to lure Piers, but to restore the house, to give it
life.

I had shaken with excitement as we'd first driven to
Rowan Hall. Piers had been so offhand, had joked about
it. 'An old tart in need of a facelift,' he'd called the place,
and I'd had to laugh with him, to pretend his comment
was funny, even when I'd seen the house again and had
felt the tears in my eyes. I'd almost hated Piers then, for
allowing the neglect, for not bothering. He'd been busy
lifting our bags from the car, the car keys dangling from
between his teeth, for all the world like Grandad Gilbert
as he'd lifted us kids from the back of the Humber.

'A money-drain,' Piers had said with his back to me,
so he hadn't seen the look on my face. 'A murdering old
whore, she's killed off half my family and now she's intent
on rubbing me out too. She eats money, Liz, just lies
back there eating the stuff.'

I looked out at the hill that cupped the house in its giant
hand, and I thought of the night when I'd stood up there
with Frank, too scared to come closer until he'd forced
me. I thought of how we'd made love there, in the hall,
and of how it had been my first time, and how Frank had
said that was special. The hill was livid green, like the
emeralds, like my eyes. I could feel its grass beneath my
bare feet, the wet spongy moss as I ran towards the gardens, shouting in the darkness to Frank to be careful, that
somebody might see us.

The house was rotting, its bloody flesh showed through
its skin. It had peeled away, flaked in the rain. Stones had

crumbled like teeth, and there were aching hollows in the
brickwork. The windows no longer gleamed; one was
cracked, a dark line running like the scar that ran in a line
across my own cheek. The name carved above the main
doorway was no longer visible, long overrun with thick
black ivy. Rowan Hall was like a tomb in a churchyard,
black birds circled the chimneys like ravens.

It began to rain. The front door opened, a black hole.
'Get inside,' Piers shouted from the car, 'before you get
wet.'

'You should have taken these off,' he told the housekeeper as we stood inside the hall. He kicked at one of
the dustsheets with his foot. 'You knew we were coming
down, I told you to expect us.' The woman shrugged.
Piers was the petulant boy again. His face in the pale light
of the hall was a mere fourteen years old. His jacket was
a school blazer. I looked up, over my head. The beautiful
sky had gone from the ceiling. The clouds had yellowed,
the blue faded with age. It had corroded, been eaten away.

'Damp,' Piers said, watching the direction of my gaze.
'Pity,' he added, 'I used to like all that when I was a
young sprog, used to lie on my back on the floor and
pretend I was dead and gone to heaven. Gave the staff an
awful fright, finding me there in the darkness. Some mad
relation painted it up there, I believe, after reading a book
on da Vinci. Bloody bad taste, really, having one's hall
done out like the Sistine Chapel. A spot of eggshell emul-
sion would look a lot better, really.'

'I love it,' I said, turning slow circles on the spot.

'Do you?' Piers seemed truly amazed.

My tour of the house was brief and perfunctory. Doors
were opened and slammed shut before I had time to look
inside the rooms, and the only place that we stopped in
was the kitchen, where Piers seemed happy to relax on a
wooden chair and ruminate in the warmth of the oven.
The elderly cook seemed impatient to have us leave. We
were in her way, she was trying to prepare lunch, but her

tuts and banging of pots only seemed to amuse Piers, and he lit a cigarette and leaned back in his chair.

'The smells,' he said, breathing in deeply. 'Takes you back, doesn't it, Lizzie? Baking, fresh bread, roasting meat? I lived in this room as a child, you know. It was the only warm place in the whole house. The rest of it used to scare me rather, all dark shadows and creaking boards. Full of ghosts, I should imagine, all one's bloody ancestors breathing down one's neck all the time. I used to curl up in here when I was home. No one ever used to miss me.'

He rummaged in a cupboard over the large sink and pulled out a bottle of brandy and two dusty glasses. 'A toast, I think,' he said, pouring generous measures into each glass. 'To the crumbling pile!'

I smiled and raised my glass, but no liquid passed my lips. I wouldn't drink to that toast, I had another of my own. 'To Rowan Hall,' I said inside my head, 'to its restoration and to its new owner,' and then I sipped, and the liquid burned my throat. Piers could keep to his kitchen then, the rest of the place would be mine.

I had the front of the house stripped of ivy and the crumbling stucco replastered, and I paid an artist from London to reconstruct the ceiling in the hall. Piers was right – the cost of those two jobs alone made a large dent in my resources. The rest of the repairs I would leave until after we were married. My money was still a bait, I had no intention of spending it all on the house until after I'd walked up the aisle.

I believe Piers was amused rather than concerned by my interest in the house. I toned my excitement down for him, told him that I was merely renovating it for the engagement party that we would be holding there.

'If you like,' he told me, but he stayed in London while the work was being done.

I watched the scaffolding go up inside the hall and outside, on the walls; a thin silver skein stretched out

across the façade. I stood outside, in my woollen skirt and
cardigan, my hair whipping around my face, and I
watched as paint was peeled back, layer by layer as it
seemed, the old whiteness chipped away, and new plaster
moulded in its place. The hall ceiling flaked when the
artist prepared it for repainting. I picked up small curls of
brittle paint from the floor, sniffing at them like an animal,
trying to preserve it as it crumbled between my clumsy
fingers. Whole chunks had to be pulled away, but the
artist preserved what he could, although he said that it
made his job more difficult.

I found myself staring, my fingers in my mouth,
watching each new stroke of his brush, unable to relax
until I had seen that his work was good enough. It was
the same. I breathed again with relief. It was going to be
an impressive copy. The mad relation could have been up
there, guiding his hand as he painted. The artist was mad
too, he spoke to himself as he painted. I took him tea and
he would take his brush and paint warpaint on his face to
make me laugh.

He must have felt at home then, for I was mad as well.
I toured the empty rooms like a ghost each day, never
tiring of seeing them, never able to get enough of the
house. He would see me descending the main staircase,
stopping to press my nose against the varnished wood of
the bannister, inhaling the smell of the polish and the
varnish. I opened all of the windows fully, throughout
the entire house, even though it was autumn and the
housekeeper complained of the chill. The air was like life
coming back into the rooms. I watched it billow the
curtains, saw the dust rise and fall in smoke-like clouds.
I watched the mists from the hill as they fell on to the
gardens, and I smelled the real smoke from the fires of
leaves in the grounds. The dampness wouldn't go though.
It came from the hill and from the overgrown gardens. It
was as though the house were half-buried already and the
foliage was only waiting to claim the rest of it; the dark
ivy whose tendrils crept over the walls, the mosses that

covered the roof, were like fingers of a hand that would
never release its grip.

Most of the furniture was gone, sold by his mother,
according to Piers, but I liked the rooms empty, so the
fact never bothered me. The autumn sun grew pale in the
sky, and by winter it was quicksilver, rising like the moon
over a carpet of white frost. Still I walked about those
empty rooms, wrapped in sheepskin, the breath forming
white clouds as it left my mouth. We lit a fire in the hall
and I sat in the high-backed chairs, warming my hands
by the flames, while the smell of paint filled my nostrils
and the quiet sound of the artist's brushes, working white
clouds on to my ceiling, filled my ears.

The painting outside looked beautiful. I knew it was
like fresh icing on a cake that had long gone green with
mould inside, but I didn't care. The place was like me
now, it looked the part, though inside it held its own
secrets. I'd patched up the scars, that was all, but the
cosmetics were confirmation of my intent. They sealed
the pact for me, bonded us together for ever. Besides, the
work gave me an excuse to be alone in the house, to be
absorbed by it and to absorb it.

As I gazed at my white palace I believe that I was
happier than I had ever been before in my life. This is
how it would be once I was married. I would live in the
house, and Piers would live in London. He phoned me
daily, begging me to go back there, but I knew that the
phone calls would stop once we were wed, once he had
learned to make do, and to find his way back to his
prostitutes. I would be left alone here then, and the house
would be mine, truly mine.

Piers would come down at weekends and we would
make love in the four-poster, and I would yearn for his
visits, yet be glad again once he was gone, and I was
alone. I would work on the house, room by room, until
it was a palace inside once again, better than before, and
when my money ran out, as I feared that it soon would,
I would find more from somewhere, I didn't care how

Piers could borrow from friends, or I could ask Philippa. My thoughts were vague, hazy like the mists, but I believed that it was my fate to finish the job and therefore I felt safe in fate's hands.

'You have to come back, Lizzie,' Piers had insisted at last, and I agreed. Winter was upon us, the ceiling was finished. The artist had signed his work, and we'd opened champagne to celebrate, drinking it from the mugs that I had been using for our tea. 'There are plans to be made,' Piers had said, and I told him I would be back in London within the fortnight.

He was waiting in my flat, a paisley silk dressing gown tied loosely around his waist, an open bottle of champagne and two glasses on the floor at the side of his chair.

'Christ, Lizzie,' he said, 'you can't know how much I've missed you. What did you do down there all that time? Were you having it off quietly with that extraordinary painter chap? He looked like a bloody moron. Did you let him have you on the top of his scaffolding, in the hall? Tell me what you did.' He gripped my wrists tightly, and his eyes narrowed with pleasure. It was the story that I knew Piers wanted to hear, the truth would only have bored him. 'Did you?' he asked again, tightening his grip. 'Tell me!'

'Of course I did,' I lied, and I let my hair fall loose from beneath my hat.

Piers's grip on my wrist relaxed, and his eyes half-closed as he listened. His hand reached up inside my jumper and he began to fondle my breasts, almost absent-mindedly. 'What did you do?' he asked, and his breathing grew louder in the quiet, darkened room.

'He went down on me, of course,' I told him. 'I made him lick me until I came. We did it up there, like you said, on top of the scaffold. I felt it rocking beneath us, it could have fallen at any time. We could both have been killed.'

'Did anyone see you do it?' Piers asked. His dressing gown had parted at the front and he held his erection in his hand, massaging it gently, his eyes now fully closed, his neck arching back over the chair-back.

'I think so,' I told him. 'The staff, I expect, and then there were the men outside, painting the front. I believe they could have seen us through the windows.'

'What did you do for him?' Piers asked. 'Did you beat him first? Did he enjoy it? Did he beg you as I did?'

'Of course.' I pulled off my clothes and let them fall in a pile on to the floor.

'Show me,' Piers said. 'Show me how you did it.'

I slapped him hard about the face, three times, and he fell on to the floor and lay curled at my feet.

'Like that,' I said calmly, and I prodded him lightly with my toe, enough to make him roll over on to his knees. I kicked his exposed buttocks hard with my shoe and he rocked slightly, backwards and forwards, on the floor. The opened champagne bottle lay there beside him and, as I picked it up and licked the rim, he quivered. I knew just where to insert the neck, just how far to push it.

'And then I did this,' I said, and Piers screamed with pleasure. Our lovemaking had begun.

And now I was finally there, we were engaged. Our guests had witnessed the occasion, and they were toasting our luck at a party. My emerald silk ballgown fluttered in the breeze about my legs. I could hear them in the distance, at the other side of the house, the music from the band that played in the marquee, the voices rising in alcoholic excitement. I fingered my ring. It was vicious, it scratched at my finger and snagged in my dress. The smell of wet roses caught at my nose. I followed the narrow path around to the back of the house and let myself into the rose garden. The lock had rusted stiff now, I had to turn the key several times before it gave and the door fell back on its hinges with a creak that echoed into the high black hill.

I had let the roses grow as wild as I had found them.

They were top-heavy and overgrown. Dead, brown-paper heads hung there alongside the newer blooms. Weeds had grown up and obscured their roots and stems. Yet still they grew there, soaking the goodness out of the full earth, sharing every drop with the tangled weeds and ivy, determined to live there no matter what. Their colours were bleached to grey in the moonlight, but their scent was still as rich, it choked you if you came unprepared, but I had sought it out, and I drank in every drop.

The path was overgrown, just a thin white ribbon that trailed around the bushes. I walked along it carefully, like a tightrope-walker, balancing with each step, touching the largest flowers, feeling the velvet of their skin. I lost my balance then, stumbled a little, and when I reached out to steady myself a large thorn tore against my palm so that I jumped back with a cry. I swore quietly and sucked the blood from the wound.

'Still got the turn of phrase of a fishwife, then?' a voice said, and I all but screamed again, except that my hand was in my mouth and so I bit at my palm instead.

'Frank?' I whispered. I took a step, but I had lost the path now and stumbled again. Strong hands caught my arm. Frank pulled me up and in a movement his arms were about me.

'Pleased to see me, darling?' he asked, and he tried to kiss me on the mouth.

I pushed him away, and he laughed. 'Missed me that much, eh?' he asked.

'What the hell are you doing here?' I asked him. 'You're in prison!'

This made him laugh again. 'I behaved myself,' he said, 'they let me out – sorry about that, Ruby, you're obviously disappointed. I thought you'd be pleased to bump into an old friend at a boring bash like this. Help liven things up a little, I'd have thought.'

I looked at his jeans and his casual jacket. 'How did you get in here?' I asked.

Frank grinned. 'That's more like it, Ruby!' he said.

'Thought the old accent had slipped for a bit back there. Now you're back at your haughty best again. I like to hear you talking like that, it makes me laugh. You sound like the Royal Family, only they don't swear like that when they cut themselves.' He took my hand and wiped the blood away with his hankie. 'I got in like all the others, Ruby,' he told me, 'through the front door, how else?'

I looked up at his face. His black hair was cut shorter, and looked less wild, but there was a dark look in his eyes that made me stop struggling. I was afraid then, afraid of Frank, and of what he could do to me. He scared me physically, he had grown stronger and harder in prison, his grip on my arm was as firm as a vice. But what scared me more were the things that he knew about me, the things that he could have told Piers, that he knew about my upbringing.

Frank's eyes stared into mine – I refused to look away, to be the first one to back down. I stared back, defiantly, despite the dryness in my mouth and tightness in my stomach.

'Did you get all that you wanted then?' Frank asked. 'Did you cop the lot then, Ruby?'

'It's Elizabeth now, Frank,' I told him. 'I dropped Ruby, it didn't fit!' He held me tighter.

'Let me go,' I said, but I couldn't struggle. Frank smiled, and his smile frightened me more than the ice in his eyes.

'I want to know, Ruby,' he insisted. 'Did you get exactly what you wanted, was it all worth it? Tell me, Ruby, yes or no?'

'I'm happy,' I told him, and he laughed again. I wanted to make him quiet, I was frightened that someone might hear us.

'Don't tell me you're in love with him,' Frank said.

'Of course I am,' I said, 'we're getting married.'

'He's marrying you because he loves you?' Frank said. 'And you're marrying him because you love him? That's very sweet, Ruby. Allow me to congratulate the two of you together. Where is your fiancé, the lucky man? I really do need to talk to him.'

I pulled my arm free at last and grabbed Frank's lapels as he started to walk away. 'Don't you dare talk to Piers!' I said.

Frank looked surprised. 'Why not?' he asked. 'We should raise our glasses. We've so much in common, Ruby – I used to love you too, once, remember?'

'I'll kill you if you let on all about me!' I whispered, desperately dragging at his coat.

'Like you killed your first husband?' Frank asked, and his smile was so wide that his teeth stood out white in the moonlight. My arms dropped to my sides like lead. I felt a coldness creep over me like the mist from the hills, permeating my body, its fingers digging into my heart.

'Remember how we broke into this place, and what we did on the rug in front of the fire?' Frank asked, turning towards the house. 'You wanted this place even then, Ruby, as I remember, it was something of an obsession with you. I thought you were out of your mind at the time, but you've done it, you got here. You must be proud, you've sacrificed a lot for all of this.' He turned again to face me and a cloud slipped over the face of the moon, turning Frank's head into a dark silhouette.

'What do you want, Frank?' I asked him. 'Is it money you're after? You can have whatever I've got if you leave me alone.'

'Why don't you just get me thrown out, Ruby?' Frank asked, and his voice was thick with anger. 'There must be a couple of monkeys around here just itching to scrape their knuckles on the likes of me. Why don't you call for them, watch them eject the riffraff?'

'Please, Frank,' I begged, 'don't spoil it for me now. This place means everything to me, just leave me alone.'

'So it *is* the house that you're after,' Frank said, and the smile returned to his face. 'Quite a stroke of luck, then, that you should fall so much in love with the guy who owns it, as well. You did say you loved him, didn't you, Ruby? You're not just marrying him to get your beautiful grasping little fingers on the house or anything, are you? This is the sort of love affair that films are made of, isn't it? I'd hate to think you were compromising yourself for the sake of a few bricks and a bit of furniture, Ruby. Tell me you love him, just the once? Help keep me happy, let me hear it from your own lips, eh?'

I tried to push past him, but he stopped me. 'You're mad, Frank!' I said. 'You're scaring me!'

'Get on all right with his relations, do you?' Frank asked. 'Not seen through the accent yet? That sort can usually spot a phoney a mile off. You must have done your homework if you pulled the wool over their eyes.'

I pushed again, but he pulled me to him. 'And what about your love-life, Ruby?' he asked, in a quieter voice. 'Up to scratch, is it? I'd always thought there was something a little bit odd about these public-school types, myself, but then there's no accounting for taste, is there? As long as it's between consenting adults, that is. You *are* a consenting adult I take it, Ruby? Everything OK on that side, is it?'

The strength had left my body. I felt my legs sag as Frank pulled me tighter to him. 'How do you know about that?' I asked in a whisper.

'There's not much I don't know about you now, Ruby, Frank told me. '*You* pay a private detective and *I* pay him more, that's all. You see? It wasn't difficult. We're alike, remember? We think alike, we act alike. Once you remember that, the rest is easy to work out.'

'Why?' I asked. 'Why did you do it?'

Frank buried his face in my hair, and I felt him breathe in, as I had breathed in the scent of the roses some moments before. His mouth stayed pressed against my ear. 'One day you'll realize why, Ruby,' he said softly, 'and I won't need to tell you.' He paused, stood silently against me. I felt his heart beating through his jacket.

'You had my baby,' he said, and he spoke so gently

that the tears sprang to my eyes. 'I didn't believe it, Ruby,'
he said, 'I swear I didn't believe it until you showed me
Pearl's letter. Jack nearly killed you, he killed our child,
and you thought it was my fault.'

I was sobbing then, I'd been broken. He'd brought it
all back with his voice and his gentleness, everything that
I'd thought was buried so far away.

'I didn't help you, Ruby,' he said, stroking my hair. 'I
wasn't there for you.'

'It didn't matter,' I sobbed, 'I didn't need you. *I* did it,
Frank, I did it myself. I had my revenge, I got it for our
child, so that its soul could get peace.'

Frank waited till my sobs had subsided, and then he
lifted my chin and kissed me so sweetly on the lips that
I could almost have cried again, had my eyes not run dry
years before.

'And you'll live this lie, and you'll live this life, just to
get your hands on this house, Ruby?' he asked. I couldn't
answer him.

'What is it?' he asked. 'Tell me what it's got that's so
special? Why is it so important to you, Ruby? There are
other places you could buy. Why this one?' He slid his
arms around my waist as I turned to face the house.

'It belongs to me, Frank,' I said. 'It has done since I
first saw it. I couldn't take it then, because I was poor
and I was little, and I didn't know how to speak or act.
I learned to be ashamed of myself here, Frank, right here
in this garden. I saw all of this beauty, and yet there I was
in an ugly dress, with a dirty face, and when I left home
that morning I thought I was it, only I wasn't, Frank, I
wasn't anything. I was nothing at all. I just decided, that
was all. I'd come back properly. I'd take the house as I
knew I should take it, only I'd be right for it, I'd have it
all next time.'

'And now you're something,' Frank said.

'Yes, Frank,' I told him, 'I know how to talk as well
as them, and I've got more money. I've got the confidence, Frank, I did it all, and I made Piers love me, too.'

Frank looked sad. 'You don't get there with money and the right clothes, Ruby,' he said. 'You don't even want to get there at all. They've got nothing you didn't have already. Money doesn't do it, Ruby, because they don't have any. You're making a mistake. You'll clap your hands and it will all be gone one day, like a dream.'

I straightened, wiping tears off my face with the back of my hand. 'You don't understand, Frank,' I said, 'I've already got it, I'm there.'

'You'll be married to a sexual pervert and you'll have nothing between you,' Frank said, his face a mass of dark shadows.

'He's class, Frank!' I shouted, and I sounded like Jack when he spoke about Philippa. 'Piers has taste and he knows how to do things. He comes from a class that will always have everything that you can't and you're jealous because I've found a way to reach it all!'

Frank went to speak but seemed to think better of it and instead lifted my hand and fingered my engagement ring. 'Is this what he gave you?' he asked, and I nodded. 'Bit bigger than my tiddler, isn't it?' he asked quietly, then he raised my hand to the light and looked more closely.

'It's fake, Ruby,' he told me, 'no better than that cheap necklace you came into my place wearing. Phoney and cheap, like the bloke who gave it to you.'

'Don't talk rubbish,' I said, grabbing my hand back. 'It's the family ring, it's been passed down for generations. It's worth a fortune.'

'It's worthless, Ruby, look!' Frank said, and he walked me to the back of the house and slid the stones hard down a pane of glass. 'No mark,' he said, running his finger down the window. 'Diamonds cut glass, Ruby. What you've got here's a fake, like I said. They probably pawned the real thing years ago and had this one made to keep appearances up. That's what they're like, Ruby, you're marrying into an image, not reality. The one bought you may have been small but at least it was real

He lifted my other hand and smiled with satisfaction as he saw his ring there.

'I'll get you a better one, if you'll let me,' he said, fingering it. 'Ten times the size, if that's what you want.'

I took Frank's ring from my finger and threw it out into the rose garden and it was so light that we didn't even hear it land.

'That's what I want, Frank,' I said, and we stared at one another in silence, me wanting to cry for what I'd just done, and Frank wearing an expression that even I couldn't interpret.

'Introduce me to your fiancé then,' he said quietly, 'let me see what he's got for myself.'

'No, Frank!' I begged. 'Don't! Don't let me down! Please!' But he pulled me away from the garden and led me towards the front of the house.

'You'll get bounced, Frank!' I called. 'It's a private party. They're all there in dinner jackets.'

The guests were dancing in the overheated ballroom but they parted like the Red Sea when Frank dragged me inside. I saw Piers in the distance, talking to a group of his friends, and I saw one of them nudge him as they saw us approaching.

Piers looked confused when we first stood in front of him; me with my streaked make-up and dishevelled hair and Frank in his casual clothes, looking for all the world like a gipsy among the other well-heeled guests.

'What the hell . . .' Piers began, looking first at me and then down at Frank's outfit. Piers looked small and slight beside Frank, and for his part Frank looked like a thug compared to Piers's slim casual elegance.

'I'd like some champagne, old chap,' Frank said sarcastically, 'to toast the engagement.'

There was a pause, and I thought I should die in the heavy silence around us as the other guests stopped talking to listen. I looked at Frank pleadingly, but he didn't see me, he was staring at Piers, challenging him with his eyes.

Piers blinked once and then, to my amazement, a polite

half-smile slid across his face. 'Well, of course, Frank,' he said quietly, snapping his fingers at the waiter, 'but I had no idea you two had already met. What's happened to your hair, darling?' he added, looking slightly embarrassed as he aimed this question at me. 'You look like you've been pulled through the proverbial hedge backwards! I know this impossibly handsome great brute here has the worst reputation with women in the whole of Mayfair, but, really, you two can't even have been introduced yet! What is this, Frank, *droit de seigneur* or something? What have you two been getting up to?'

Piers smiled at his cleverness and his friends laughed at his joke, but Frank looked annoyed, and his clasp tightened on my arm.

'Don't be such a stupid bastard, Piers,' he said, and I looked up at him, shocked, as the smile died from Piers's face.

'Oh, don't worry, Liz,' Frank whispered, pronouncing my name carefully, 'Piers and I are old friends, aren't we, Piers? Your beautiful fiancée here was about to get me frogmarched off the premises for being improperly attired, weren't you, Lizzie? I told her we went way back and that you didn't give a sod what I turned up in, but I'm afraid that she didn't believe me, and I'm afraid that I may have upset her trying to convince her.' Frank turned to me and kissed my hand. 'My apologies,' he said. 'Now where's that bloody champagne, Piers, I want to toast you two properly.'

The rest of the engagement party went by in a bloodless rush. I did the rounds, heard myself say the right things, but all the time my eyes were on Frank, wondering how he knew Piers, my ears aching to hear what he might say about me. I waited until all the guests were gone, until the music had finally ended, and I found Piers in the library, sleeping drunkenly in one of the great leather chairs.

I shook him awake. 'Piers, how do you know that man?' I asked.

He looked confused. 'Which man?' he asked. 'There were several at the party.'

'That Frank What's-his-name?' I asked. 'Why did you invite him?'

Piers just looked vague. 'Oh, known him from way back,' he said, and closed his eyes again.

'But the man's a lout,' I said. 'Why was he here? Who invited him? Did you? He wasn't even wearing black tie.'

Piers smiled. 'No,' he said, 'he wouldn't. Not his style.'

'So why did you invite him?' I asked. 'He was rude to you in front of the guests, yet you smiled at him.'

Piers's smile was even more enigmatic. 'Be nice to him when you see him, Lizzie,' he said, curling back into the chair. 'He's a powerful man, is our Frank. Better not to cross him, that's all.' And he went back to sleep, still clutching a decanter full of brandy to his chest.

I walked across to the window and pulled back the heavy curtains to look at the gardens in the inky-black darkness. My ring snagged in the heavy brocade and I untangled it carefully, making sure none of the stones loosened. I looked at the ring, at the stones glinting in the light of the study lamp, and I thought of what Frank had said, how he'd shown me it was fake. I looked back at Piers, now sleeping soundly, and I could feel a blinding anger building up inside me; anger at Frank, at Piers, at anyone.

I slashed my ring down the glass of the window in a sudden, stabbing gesture, then I looked at the results. The glass was like my face, scarred in a curve that made my breath catch in my throat. The bastard had tricked me like a magician; the window was scratched, nearly cracked right in two. I put my finger into my mouth and sucked at the ring, running the tip of my tongue around the stones.

'Go away, Frank,' I said to myself. 'Go out of my life, don't ruin things now.' And I slammed the window shut, locking it fast as though keeping out evil spirits.

# CHAPTER 35

I'd expected our wedding to be at Rowan Hall, but Piers had refused, and there was no budging him. He mumbled something about a family tradition and when I grew angry with him he grew angrier, so I dropped the subject and we spent the spring in London instead, visiting friends, meeting distant members of Piers's enormous family, and planning the wedding, right down to the smallest detail.

Piers had insisted on paying for the whole affair, and I was surprised again at his stubbornness in refusing to discuss the matter. The wedding was going to be expensive, yet he faced up to the huge bills we were running up without a single word of misgiving.

I had never questioned Piers on the matter of finances, but I had Giles's tales of his debts to his friends still in my head. Piers's friends and family lived with a strange disregard for day-to-day debts. They lived to a standard that their class had accustomed them to believe was their right, and they hid their vast debts behind all the extravagance, knowing that someone would bale them out when the time came.

I imagined that Piers had relatives with more solid resources, someone to fund him when the family name was at stake. Then there was my own money, which knew he had his eye on, but none of that explained why he was waving off the wedding bills with such casual abandon. I waited for him to arrive at my flat any day, cap in hand, and beg me to lend him some money, but he didn't. Perhaps it was then that I found a new respect for him, that he took care of all the finances so generously and so totally, and in a way that was so unexpected.

We were to be married at the Savoy Chapel, and the reception was to be held in the River Room. I was delighted with the place, we took tea there, and I gazed out on to the grey Thames beyond the Embankment Gardens, and Piers held my hand across the round gilt table, and told me that he loved me and was proud to have me as his bride. Our faces were in the newspapers, my wedding dress was to be copied by a fashion house the day that I was to wear it.

I had picked a new designer to make it for me, a young Polish girl straight out of St Martin's School of Art, whose sketches had been the most beautiful of any that I had been shown. It was a dress for a princess, and young Ruby would have loved it. It was extravagant but elegant, like the floor-length bouquet of hybrid red roses that I would be carrying, and the diamonds that I intended to wear around my neck.

I had so few guests of my own, just a handful of friends of Philippa's that I had used to get my foothold when I'd arrived back in London, but I needn't have worried, for Piers's relations more than filled the list. He showed me his guests' names, neatly typed for the invitations, and when I saw Frank's name halfway down I froze, the list still in my hand.

'Why does he have to be invited?' I asked, and Piers laughed.

'Frank?' he asked. 'Oh, he's all right. You just saw him on a bad night, that was all.'

'He's common and he has no manners,' I said. 'I don't want him at our wedding, Piers.'

Piers shook his head. 'No can do,' he told me, 'he's down there, so he has to come. I told you, Lizzie, he's a

powerful man. I like to keep him sweet, that's all, we can
shove him up the back or something, you won't even
have to know that he's there. Anyway,' he told me, play-
fully hitting me on the head with the rolled list, 'don't be
such a frightful snob. You don't use words like
"common" these days, it's considered offensive.'

I smiled back at Piers, but I was frightened. I thought
of my first wedding, of how Frank had fought with Jack.
I didn't want him there, I didn't want him watching me.
Frank liked his drama, he could have been waiting until
the wedding to tell all the assembled guests about my
past. I shuddered, and rubbed at my arms. I couldn't let
Frank be there, I couldn't take the risk.

I phoned Frank the next morning, and it took all the
courage that I had to dial his number. He sounded sleepy,
as though I'd woken him.

'Piers has invited you to the wedding,' I told him.

'Great,' he said, yawning, 'I'll go out and hire a top
hat. That's what your sort wear to do's like that, isn't it?
Or would you rather I wore a flat cap and went round
insulting the guests?'

'I don't want you there, Frank,' I said.

'You surprise me, Ruby,' Frank said. 'I thought you'd
have been pleased of a bit of back-up from the old days.
Can't be too many you asked from the market, can there?
Is old Lily still alive? Perhaps she'll turn up with Vic, I
haven't seen him for years. And what about Marge, Ruby?
She must be chuffed to bits, seeing you do as well as you
have. What's she wearing to the wedding? That old brown
coat she used to wear on the stall, or did you buy her
something new for the occasion?'

'Shut up!' I shouted. 'Shut up, Frank! You're not going,
that's all. I don't want you there, I don't want you turning
up!'

'The accent's slipping, Ruby,' Frank laughed. 'You
want to watch it. You don't want to go letting yourself
down on your big day in front of all those aristos you're
marrying into, now do you?'

I put the phone down, and I was trembling with anger. It was another week before Frank's letter arrived, and I had to wait until Piers had read it before I could see what he had said.

'He can't make it,' Piers told me before I had time to take in the contents. 'You should be happy, Lizzie, you got your wish.' Piers looked worried, concerned, but I was too relieved to take any notice. My toes curled with pleasure, I could have kissed Frank's letter as I held it in my hand. He wasn't going to be there – he was going to leave me alone. The relief was so great that it surprised even me. I felt something snap inside me and I sank down into a chair, huge curling tears that came with the release of tension rolling slowly down my cheeks.

'Are you ill?' Piers asked, taking my hand.

I shook my head, I felt stupid but I couldn't speak.

'It's just the wedding,' I said eventually. 'I suppose things just get on top of you, comes out all in a rush, sort of thing.' Piers smiled and patted my hand, reassured by my quick explanation.

'Too much too soon,' he said. 'Take it easy for a bit, leave the rest of the arrangements to me, eh?' I had no idea what he intended, but Frank wasn't coming, that was all that mattered, and I was happy to nod my agreement, and only too happy to oblige.

I stood in my wedding dress on the morning of my wedding, and I looked at my own image in the mirror. I ran the tip of my index finger along the scar on my face, and I smiled. I had everything that I wanted. My skin glowed pale caramel against the creamy whiteness of my dress. My hair was pinned up and there was a crown of roses around my head, their smell so close to my face that it reminded me of the gardens of Rowan Hall. I would have children that would run in those gardens. I would create new life there, renovate, redecorate, restore each single sacred solitary feature of the place with all the breathless awe of a devoted lover.

Piers would become impatient with me, would summon me back to London to be with him, but I wouldn't leave a second time, he couldn't make me go. I loved Piers, I told myself that as I looked in the mirror. I loved him for his beauty and for his class, which was why I loved the house itself. I would make him join me there, show him what I had done to the place, and how much he belonged there. We were sewn into the tapestry of the house now, Piers and I, its fate was our fate, its history had been passed into our hands.

There was a light laugh behind me, and I turned to see Philippa, arms outstretched, watching me from the bedroom doorway. I was thrilled to see her, no longer threatened by the secrets about me that she knew. She would never have told, she was as much a part of the deception as I was. I had used her name as a reference to get into her society, and she loved the joke, the excitement of the lie, almost as much as I did myself.

I did not move to embrace her, despite her open arms. They were a gesture, nothing more. 'Look at you,' she was saying as she stood there, 'look at what I have created!'

I winked at her instead, and she let out another laugh, a low, throaty one this time, and she clapped her hands together, as though applauding my performance.

'Bravo, Ruby,' she said, smiling at me, 'bloody bravo, old girl!'

She had come to London just for my wedding; done deals with the fraud squad so that she could be there. In return for a few extra pieces of information on her husband they had dropped investigations against her altogether, and she was free again to live wherever she chose.

'I'm not on the run any more, Ruby,' she'd told me over the phone some three weeks before.

'You sound like some terrible desperado!' I'd replied, and she'd laughed.

'That's exactly what I've bloody well felt like these past few years!' she'd said, with more laughter. Philippa laughed a lot in London, it was her home, and she came alive there. I loved watching her, she was so confident, so in control. She told me that I looked the same now, but I had trouble believing her.

'I feel as though I'm looking at myself, Ruby – sorry, Elizabeth!' she told me, lighting up a Gauloise and sinking down into a chair. 'It's a lot like looking into a mirror, you've picked up so many of my expressions. I suppose I feel almost maternal. Money and breeding obviously suit you, Ruby, you look so bloody young. I'll strangle anyone that takes me for your mother as you go floating up the aisle! God, it feels strange,' she added, fluffing up my sleeves and giving my skirt a pull as I passed her, 'I feel a sort of cross between Old Mother Riley and the Baron Frankenstein! I almost wish I hadn't come, Ruby, I don't think I can cope, after all!'

She drew on her cigarette and I laughed and bent to kiss her lightly on the cheek.

'You look younger than I do, and you know it!' I told her.

'And here endeth a rather sickening bout of female arse-licking!' Philippa laughed. 'We both look bloody terrific and well-preserved and all that, and we know it, and so, I assume, does the groom-to-be, and all his assembled guests.'

I had introduced Philippa to Piers a few days before the wedding, soon after she'd arrived in England. We'd all had dinner at the Connaught, and I'd watched as Philippa sized Piers up in her lugubrious, cat-like, crafty way.

'He's a bastard, darling,' she'd told me afterwards, 'just like the rest of his type, a thorough bastard.' But I could tell that she'd approved, by the tone in her voice and the look in her eyes. 'You do realize that he believes that the sun rises and sets entirely for his own benefit, don't you?' she had asked.

I laughed. 'Piers isn't like that,' I'd told her.

'They're *all* like that,' she'd said, and meant it.

'Ralph wasn't like that,' I answered. 'You could twist Ralph around your little finger.'

'Ralph was different,' Philippa had said, sipping the peppermint tea that I'd bought because I'd remembered she liked it. 'Ralph was pompous and arrogant, but underneath it all he was insecure because he knew that he wasn't really top-drawer, while I was. Besides which, he was older and impotent most of the time by the time I married him, and then there were the children from the first marriage. He had a lot to be grateful for, Ruby, as I was constantly reminding him.'

'Then why did you marry him?' I asked. Philippa's marriage had been a constant source of mystery to me. She was beautiful and wealthy and she could have had her pick of London society, but instead she had chosen Ralph, who was neither handsome nor dashing.

Philippa shrugged. 'I didn't want to be in love,' she told me, 'I disliked the way that it made one behave. It was easy not to love Ralph, and easy being treated well by him. He was harmless and he loved me, and he turned a blind eye to the little affairs that I was prone to. I could never have married someone young and beautiful and unremittingly selfish, like your Piers. I'm too selfish myself, I could never have stood it. I need to *be* loved, not to give love, you see. When you love someone like Piers you allow them to walk over you, to trample you underfoot until you're too weak to cry for help. There's a certain amount of masochism involved in being in love with somebody like him, and I'm afraid that's not my scene, I prefer it the other way around. Take Ralph, for instance, he's still writing me potty love notes from prison, even though he knows that I've made it worse for him in there by adding to his sentence, and even though he must know that I won't be around by the time that he gets out. That's the sort of adoration that I need, Ruby, not some semi-narcissistic obsession.'

'Piers loves me,' I told her, and she snorted.

'You think so?' she asked. 'You look alike, did you

ever see that, Ruby? Take away the scar and the two of
you could be twins. In his own image, that's what you
are, and that's what he loves you for, apart from your
money. He sees himself making love to himself when you
two have sex. You're both as beautiful as one another,
and in the same slim pale sort of way. That's why he
loves to hear about your fantasy lovers, Ruby. He can
imagine himself in your shoes, making love to all those
men.'

'You're too cynical,' I said.'You see things in the worst
way.'

'You think so?' she asked. 'I believe I just see the truth,
darling, crystal-clear, not smeared over by some murky
dark emotions.'

'You should meet Frank,' I said, 'you two have a lot in
common when it comes to your opinions of Piers.'

'Your childhood sweetheart?' Philippa asked, raising
one eyebrow in an arch. 'I'd love to, darling, if all you've
told me about him is true. I love a little rough trade.' And
she shuddered with pleasure at the thought of it.

'Well, you're out of luck today, I'm afraid,' I told her,
laughing. 'Frank is not going to be numbered among the
guests.'

Philippa rose from her chair and dusted imaginary
crumbs off her suit. 'I'm surprised,' she said. 'From the
stories you tell of him I thought he'd have been right up
there in the front pew, waiting to bust Piers's nose the
minute he married you. Not even a little chain-rattling at
the front gates, darling? The man's losing his touch –
either that or he's fallen out of love with you at last. I
was just dying to see all those bulging muscles and flared
nostrils breathing fire and brimstone as he lost his love to
yet another man. Weddings can be so boring without that
kind of scene to liven them up. I love that bit when the
vicar asks if any man knows why the couple should not
be married, there's that wonderful dramatic pause – I'm
sure Frank could have come up with a few good reasons
why the marriage should be null and void.'

'I asked him not to come,' I said.

'And he agreed?' I nodded, and Philippa looked surprised and disappointed. 'Not the man you described to me then,' she said as she pulled on her gloves. She looked at her watch and suddenly leaned across to kiss me on the cheek, kissing air, rather than flesh, which was normal with her. 'We're late,' she said. 'Your beautiful groom will get twitchy if we keep him waiting too long.' She started towards the door, but I held back.

I pulled myself up to full height and I took one last look at my reflection in the mirror. It was Ruby the child that was looking back at me, her face drained of blood and her eyes grown big as saucers. She looked frightened and lost, not proud and happy, as she should have done. The mirror was so old that the glass looked dusty; my child-image was fading in front of my eyes. 'I did it, Ruby,' I whispered, 'I got there, I got it all,' but the face just stared, though the pink mouth formed shapes around my words. The hand moved up to the cheek, its finger moving down the scar. It was my hand, it wore the same pale oyster satin glove. I looked down at my own finger and I felt a strangely calm sense of fear.

'You can handle Piers, darling,' Philippa said behind me. 'It's OK, I've seen you with him, you control him perfectly.'

I turned then, and smiled, and grasped Philippa's hand. We left the flat quickly, hurrying down the stairs, Philippa holding on to me for all the world as though she was expecting me to turn tail and run at any minute, but I didn't. It had taken my whole life to come to this point. I was to be the owner of Rowan Hall, and no ghosts of my childhood would be there to put me off.

So it was done, I was married. I took my vows, spoken in the hearing of God himself, and I became Piers's wife, for better, for worse, for richer, for poorer. I clutched my glass of champagne and listened as our luck together was toasted, and I gazed out over the Thames, over the grey river whose waters plaited in their rush to reach the sea, and I saw my own reflection in the windows of the ball-room, a woman now, in an expensive dress. I plunged my nose into the roses of my bouquet, and I was happy at last, my promise was kept.

We led the dancing, as was our job by tradition, and the other guests applauded before joining us on the floor. Piers spun me around and the guests began to laugh as the spinning grew faster and I called to him to stop, I was becoming dizzy. The yellow chandeliers revolved overhead, and then Piers slowed and kissed me, before I had my breath back.

'Should you beat me tonight?' Piers asked. 'My wife, my little lovely wife?' I looked at all his guests as we danced and I wondered whether they had something rotten at their core too, like Piers, like my husband.

They had secrets, this class, the class that I had married into, the class that I thought I had become. They flaunted signs of poverty like my class flaunted sought-after afflu-ence. Their suits were fraying, decaying, smelling of cam-phor. The old ones were powdered like dandies and their teeth were rotten. Where I came from you had your teeth out by fifty and a brand-new set put in, but these old people hung on to their teeth, and they were as yellow and as worn with age as the jewellery that they sported.

The young ones were no better, though they tried. The girls were as lumpy as Marge must have been at their age, and had long tousled-ratty hair that fell over their faces. They had thick eyebrows and thick hairy legs and the boys down the market would have given them short shrift for not being got up properly and not making the most of themselves.

Lily would have been horrified at all that mousy. undyed hair, and at the way that they used no make-up. All those flat, breastless chests, and not a piece of padding or uplift in sight. She'd have approved of Philippa, though. I caught Philippa's eye across the varnished floor and she winked at me slyly to let me know I was doing

OK. Philippa had natural assets. She had class *and* beauty, and that made her something special.

The candles were lit at the tables and the air filled with the smell of wax and candle-smoke as the wedding breakfast was laid. There were plates edged with gold and napkins starched like paper, and I watched Piers's shining face in the flickering light, and he looked golden and beautiful, an excited, spoilt child. Piers could do anything, get anything, have anything that he wanted. He had no shyness, no fear of being watched. Confidence was his privilege, granted at birth. In return he had forsworn some of the deeper emotions. I watched other women at the wedding watching him, and I knew I had stolen him from them. He was beautiful, he was charming, he was touched by the angels, and I had taken him, gorged myself on his beauty. His old girlfriends would go away like the retreating sea and they would wait and return like the tide. One day I wouldn't be good-looking, I'd be pregnant and undemanding, and they'd try again. I'd be in Surrey and Piers would be up in London, and it would be all right because that's how things are done and you don't make a fuss once you're married.

I swallowed champagne and I laughed out loud, and Piers asked me why I was laughing.

'Those women,' I told him, 'they can't wait to get their claws into you again. They hate me for stealing you right from under their noses.'

Piers laughed, and kissed me on the cheek. His lips felt cold, he was getting drunk. 'How did you steal me?' he asked. 'What was it that you did?' He forked some pink ham into his open mouth, a flat handkerchief-sized slice that folded and was gone.

'I'm a witch,' I told him, 'I cast a spell, didn't you know? I made you love me, you had no choice in it.'

Piers grabbed my thigh and squeezed it. 'Some bloody good spell!' he said, and he pulled at my skirt until my leg was bare, and a roar went up from the younger men at the wedding, which caused me to blush crimson. Piers

fell to his knees in front of my chair and the roar grew
louder and lewder. He pushed my legs apart and gripped
the garter I wore between his teeth, tearing at it like a
dog until it broke, and then showing it to the crowd like
a trophy.

The gesture signalled the end of the formal side of the
wedding. Chairs were pushed back and bread rolls began
to be thrown at Piers as he climbed on to the table and
stood, arms akimbo, my garter still in his mouth. Older
guests melted away and the crowd became louder, the
sound of exploding champagne corks more frequent. The
best man told rude jokes in a monologue style and three
girls debagged him when his jokes became boring. The
band started up playing fifties' stuff, jives and rock-and-
roll, and men took off their ties and undid their collars in
their eagerness to get at the girls.

Piers pulled me up, but he was unsteady on his feet.
'My beautiful, beautiful wife,' he said, and he pushed me
out on to the dance floor amid a volley of dried peas and
bread pellets.

'I want you, Lizzie,' he whispered in my ear as we
danced, 'I want you right here, do you think we can find
somewhere? I want to claim my marital rights.'

Someone screamed behind us, the voice barely reaching
out above the music, and we turned to see a girl rise high
above the crowded floor, her face red with excitement
and her Laura Ashley ballgown ripped under each armpit.
She fell in time with the music, then rose again, her
partner's hands around her waist. Suddenly other couples
followed suit, and the room erupted into a riot of jive
dancing that reminded me of the Palais when Frank and
I had been kids.

Piers bent to kiss my neck but I pulled away. 'We can't
leave, they'll miss us and come looking,' I said.

'So what?' Piers whispered. 'Let them find us. I don't
care who sees, serve them right for not minding their
own business. I'm your husband now, Lizzie, remember?
I've got rights in the eyes of the law. You promised to

obey me, and I'm ordering you to do your duty by me.
I want to fuck you, and I want to do it now.'

He was joking and he was drunk, but there was a
kind of childish petulance in Piers's voice that made me
shudder. It frightened me how quickly and easily he could
turn me into a child again, an overwhelmed, embarrassed,
poor little thing to be bullied by the rich boy because she
knew no better.

'We'll wait,' I told Piers loudly, pushing his hand off
my arm. 'We'll wait till tonight, till we get down to
Surrey.'

Piers drank his glass of champagne in one gulp, bending
his head back to do so, so that I could see his Adam's
apple bobbing as he swallowed. Then he shook his head
slowly, rocking slightly on his heels with the effort of
doing so. 'Not Surrey,' he said, putting a finger to his
lips as though trying to quieten me. 'Surprise!' he added.
I turned to look at him.

'We're going straight home after this,' I told him, 'it's
all been arranged. We're spending the wedding night at
the house, we don't fly to Kenya until Tuesday.'

Piers shook his head again with a grin so stupid that I
suddenly wanted to slap him. 'Not the house,' he kept
repeating.

'But I sent my things down there!' I shouted, trying to
be heard above the music.

Piers grinned. 'They're all here now,' he told me, pointing at the floor. 'We're staying here,' he added. 'Honeymoon suite, the best in London. Champagne, soft beds,
room service . . .' He lunged at me again, but I pushed
him away and walked off, exasperated.

I'd wanted to spend the first two nights of our marriage
at Rowan Hall. I hadn't been there for months and Piers
had only managed to keep me in London by telling me
that we would go down there as soon as the wedding was
over. Even the honeymoon had been delayed so that we
could begin our married life in the house. I grabbed
another drink from a passing waiter and did as Piers had

done and gulped it down in one. The alcohol hit my empty stomach and then flew up to my head like a 'try your strength' machine. I closed my eyes to let the effects settle, but the room was still spinning when I opened them again.

The crowd of guests were a fused blob of colour that heaved and swayed like the surface of the sea. Their voices became an angry buzz in my ear, and the music grew more raucous, like the music at a fairground. I took another glass of champagne and swallowed half of its contents, cradling the two glasses to my chest as I wove between the dancers. The crowd parted to let me through, I was the bride after all, though someone still managed to tread on my train, which wrenched my veil painfully from my head.

'Are you all right, Ruby?' Philippa had me by the arm. I stared at her and tried to talk.

'Piers has only bloody well gone and changed our wedding night without so much as bloody well telling me,' I told her. Philippa smiled broadly and then suddenly we were moving out of the room, walking too quickly so that I stumbled over my dress.

'Hold on!' I shouted, but Philippa still kept up the pace, appearing not to have heard me.

'You're drunk, Ruby,' she whispered when we got outside. 'Listen to yourself, your accent's slipping.' My hands flew to my mouth and I giggled. 'No more drink!' Philippa told me, and I could tell she was serious. I sank down on to the marble steps and hung my head between my knees until the hotel lounge stopped moving around me. Philippa ordered two strong black coffees and we sat side by side, sipping them.

'I wanted to go down to Rowan Hall,' I told her when my head had cleared a little. 'I wanted us to spend our wedding night there, it was important to me, Philippa.'

'You'll have plenty of time to screw yourselves silly down there, darling,' Philippa said, patting my arm. 'A couple of extra nights aren't going to make any difference.

What I really want to know, though,' she added, sidling a little closer and pointing my chin back in the direction of the ballroom, 'is who that gorilla in a dress suit is who's been handing Piers vast wads of cash all evening? Is he some sort of walking wallet or something? Every time Piers needs any money for tips or anything he keeps having to get it from that chap, and I think it's all rather mysterious! Who is he, Ruby? I'm suffering agonies of curiosity, do put me out of my misery and tell me!'

'Where?' I asked. I forced myself to concentrate on what she was telling me, and as my mind cleared, and I realized who she was talking about, I felt a sickness deep in my stomach that sprang up every bit as quickly and forcefully as the drunkenness had. I looked around for the toilet. Philippa saw my face and dragged me off towards the cloakrooms, waiting by the cubicle as I threw up noisily and exhaustingly inside.

My skin was chalky as I emerged and I bent over the sink, swallowing handfuls of cold water and splashing it over my face. Philippa silently handed me a towel as I straightened. I was sucking in air, feeling better now, my head completely cleared.

'You do know him then?' Philippa asked.

I nodded. 'He works for Frank,' I told her, 'he's the bouncer at one of his clubs. He tried to throw me out the first night that I went there. God alone knows what he's doing here, or why he should be giving Piers money. If anything, it must be Piers who owes Frank, I think he's run up a few debts in his casinos in the past.' It was as though I had been shown a huge riddle, while my brain was too fogged to get a grasp at the answer. I looked at Philippa, hoping she might help me, but she merely shrugged.

'Curiouser and curiouser,' she said, lighting a cigarette and perching her bottom on the washbasin.

'Why is he here?' I asked again, shaking my head, trying to make sense of what Philippa had seen.

'Would Frank be lending Piers money?' Philippa asked

exhaling smoke rings that circled my head like cumulus clouds.

'Why should he?' I asked. 'He hates Piers. Why should he lend him money, and at our wedding too? He didn't even want me to marry him. Why lend money to a man that you hate, and who already owes you? It doesn't make sense, Philippa.'

Philippa picked up her handbag and snapped it shut. 'Ask Piers,' she said, decisively. 'You're his wife now, and his money is yours as well. Ask him, Ruby, it's the only way you'll ever find out.'


Piers was playing spin-the-bottle with some friends when I found him. He winked at the men as I pulled him away, and they let out the same lurid jeer that I had been hearing all afternoon. We found a quiet spot in the corridor outside, and I propped Piers up against a wall and asked him about Frank's henchman.

'Philippa says she's seen him give you money, Piers,' I said.

'Philippa should mind her own bloody business then!' Piers shouted. 'I know she's your friend, Liz, but she's a shrew and a bitch and I don't want you keeping in with her. She virtually seduced Darius Folton-Brown over the dinner table last week, right under poor Suzie's nose! By the way, darling, Pamela Waterhouse says that she doesn't remember you from schooldays after all, do you think you could go and put her right or something? She's got an awfully loud voice . . .'

'Piers!' I shouted. 'What's going on? If you don't tell me I'll go up and ask the man himself, in front of everybody!'

Piers seemed to crumple in front of me, and for a moment I thought he might slide down the wall. I put my hands under his armpits and he leaned his weight against me.

'Our man Frank just owes me, that's all,' he said, and his eyes closed.

'Why?' I asked. 'Owes you what, Piers? I thought you owed him?'

Piers nodded slowly. 'I did,' he said, 'but I don't any more.'

'You paid him off?' I asked, shaking him. 'What did you do, Piers? I don't understand? Where did you get the money, did you borrow it from someone? How did you pay him off? Who do you owe now, Piers? Why didn't you wait till after the wedding? I would have given you the money then.'

Piers smiled at me and kissed my cheek. 'Even you wouldn't have had enough, my darling,' he said. He leaned his head back against the wall and sighed. 'Couldn't wait,' he mumbled.

'What couldn't wait, Piers?' I asked, waving the waiter to fetch us some coffee.

'Frank,' he said, 'the debt. Bastard called it in a week before the wedding. Sorry, Lizzie. Mucked up the honeymoon.'

'The trip to Kenya?' I asked. 'That doesn't matter, Piers. You've spent enough on the wedding already. I'll never know how you found the money to pay for all of this.'

'Didn't,' Piers said. 'Frank paid.'

'For the wedding?' I asked. A hollow had opened in the pit of my stomach, and I thought for a minute that I might be sick again. 'Why? Why should he?' The riddle was getting more tangled with every word Piers spoke. I knew that I'd find some sense in it somewhere, if only I could see it more clearly, but it kept escaping my view each time that Piers opened his mouth. Then he began to tell me the truth and I wished that I had never tried to work my way to the heart of it at all.

'He said he wanted to,' Piers began, 'that he owed me now, that he thought we made a lovely couple and he wanted to see us get off to a good start. You know what those types are like, Liz – kick you in the teeth and then get all sentimental and pay for your bridgework after wards. They cling to their twisted little moral codes lik misers, Lizzie, and they think it absolves them from all blame. You get real hoods in those parts of London, the sort that would shoot you as soon as look at you, but then they go and buy their mothers flowers on Mothering Sunday and they think that means they've got the moral fibre of a saint. Even Hitler loved animals, Liz, but that didn't make him all right when it came to slaughtering Jews. God, I hate his sort, with their sharp suits and their hairy chests . . .'

I shook Piers again and he looked back at me, startled. 'I owed Frank too much, Liz,' he told me. 'I told him you were loaded and that I'd see him all right, but he said that wasn't good enough and he called in the collateral. Then he went and insisted on paying for the wedding, as though that made it all right somehow. We're OK though, Lizzie, we're clear of the debt and he's said he'll reimburse you for the work that you had done.'

'What work?' I asked. 'What collateral, Piers? What are you talking about?'

But I knew. I knew before the words had even left his mouth. I knew that Frank owned the house now: the riddle untangled for me suddenly and there its core lay in front of me, as clear as day, a golden grain of truth unveiled at last before my eyes.

The truth stung me like a whip. I pulled away from Piers, reeling with the pain of the blow. There was no confusion this time, no cherished few seconds to act as a buffer before the truth finally sank in. I knew it immediately, the pain was instantaneous. It was almost as though I had known it all along, that I had only goaded the information out of Piers as some sort of formality before I could react publicly.

'You gave him the house,' I said, and my voice sounded flat and distorted, as though it had come through deep water.

'I know you were fond of the place, Lizzie,' Piers wheedled, 'but we could never have honestly afforded it. I know you tried with those little repairs, but look how much they cost alone. The place is a virtual ruin, it would have got through your money like water and come out the other side looking for more. We've still got the places in London, darling, perhaps you can spend some time doing those up, if that's what you like . . .'

I cut him short. '*Why didn't you tell me?*' I screamed, and my voice was so loud that people emerged from the ballroom to listen. '*Why didn't you tell me before the wedding?*'

I began punching Piers and there were a few sniggers behind us. God knows what those guests thought we were arguing about, some sexual inadequacy that Piers had only just revealed to me, no doubt. Someone grabbed my wrists and I turned to face him, panting.

'Hold on there!' a stranger said, some friend of Piers's, and I pulled my arm away.

I looked at Piers, propped against the wall, his eye closed against my barrage, a glass still clutched in his hand. '*You bastard!*' I screamed. '*You filthy stinking stupi rotten bastard!*'

It was my old voice, the old Ruby. All the niceties ha gone, stripped away by Piers's words. I looked at hir there and I hated him more at that moment than I'd eve hated Jack, who I'd killed; because I'd been weak whe I'd hated my first husband, but now I was stronger an my hatred had some fire to it. If I'd had a knife I woul have run him through there and then, but I didn't, so ran away instead.

The crowd parted for real this time, afraid of me they were, because they thought that I'd gone mad. didn't know where I was running until I found him, a I knew Frank's great monkey was expecting me from t' size of the grin on his face.

'*Where is he?*' I shouted.

'The boss?' the gorilla asked, and his obvious enjoyme of the scene made me angrier still. 'In his new house should imagine,' he said, and he slowly sipped more the lager he was nursing. 'Did you want to see him the he asked. 'He might be busy, you ought to make an appointment. I think he's got the decorators in,' and his shoulders shook at the cleverness of his own joke.

'Piers could never have owed him that much,' I said, trembling uncontrollably. 'He could never have been allowed to run up those debts in your club. Frank doesn't allow that sort of credit. He's stolen my house, I want it back.'

The bouncer smiled. 'Our Frank's always had a soft spot for a title,' he told me. 'Doesn't like to refuse the aristocracy, especially when they insist. Your husband was very insistent in his demands for credit at our club. He even touched Frank for several sizeable loans of cash too, I believe, on the side. You want to watch your husband, madam,' he said, his voice lowering confidentially, 'he's a bit apt to go off the rails, if you know what I mean. A bit loose with the old purse strings according to some of our staff. It was as well Frank decided to help him out when he did, or you'd never have been sent off in this sort of fashion, I can tell you.'

I stared at the man for a second, taking in his words, his nerve and his stupid arrogance, then I ran out of the room, through the hallway, out into the driveway that faced on to the Thames. I needed the fresh air. I needed time to think.

Our wedding car was still there, parked outside, the chauffeur sitting with his hat off, biting into a slice of our cake. I clambered into the back, pulling my skirt in behind me, and as I did so he quickly threw his slice of wedding cake out of the window where it was swiftly swooped on by London pigeons and sparrows.

'Drive me down to Surrey,' I said, and I gave him directions to Rowan Hall.

He looked at me nervously in the mirror all the way down, and I suppose I must have looked a curious sight, still in my wedding dress, my face full of anger and my hair tumbling in rats' tails down my shoulders. I forget my true thoughts on that fateful drive, I just know that

at some point during the journey Piers moved out of my
sights and the fight stood between Frank and myself once
again. I hated to be beaten, yet he'd stolen the house from
me, the one thing that I desired in life, and then paid for
my wedding to make me look a fool into the bargain. I
had no idea in my confused state of mind as to why he
had done it; my brain was bursting in my skull. I remember the impatience I felt at the slowness of the car, though
it must have been doing over sixty, for I kept telling the
driver to hurry.

We pulled into the drive around dusk. There was a
sweetness of perfumed flowers in the air, but I had no
time to appreciate it. There were lights on in the house
and I ran up to the door, pounding on it with my fists,
yelling and demanding to be let in.

The door fell back with a speed that left me dumb.
Frank stood there in the hallway – my hallway – and on
his face was a grin that I would have washed off with acid
if I could have done.

'Ruby!' he said, smiling. 'What a surprise!' His eyes
scanned my body in a glance. 'I was just having supper,'
he said. 'You're welcome to join me, though I must admit
you're a bit overdressed.'

He was massive in the doorway, his figure nearly blocking the golden light from the hall. He was wearing black,
a black roll-neck sweater and black trousers, and his hair
hung in dark curls around his face and down his neck. A
dog trotted up and settled at his heels. It looked like Lady
but I couldn't be sure. It sat there panting, its long pink
tongue lolling over its chops, its great dark eyes watching
me with all the amused interest that I saw in Frank's eyes.

I walked up to Frank to strike him, but the dog growled
and leapt at me, and it was Frank who pulled it off.

'Why, Frank?' I shouted. 'Why did you do it? Did you
hate me that much? Did you have to take everything?'

Frank's smile died and the look that rose in his eye
froze the words that I had for him in my throat.

'You'd better get back to your wedding, Ruby,' he said threateningly. 'Your groom will be missing you.'

'Don't make fun of me, Frank,' I said. 'You can see what I've done.'

Frank lifted some lace from my dress with one finger. The fabric was torn, a ribbon came away in his hand. 'You blew it, Ruby,' he said, quietly, 'that's what you've done.'

'You stole my house!' My voice rose, and I could hear it waver. 'You took it from me, Frank, and then you paid for my bleeding wedding! God, you're a cold-faced bastard! Why didn't you just show up yourself and smash Piers to a pulp, like you tried to with Jack? I was expecting you to, you know!'

Frank smiled. 'But I've got power now, Ruby, real power; a man of means and a man of property. Men like me don't do things like that any more. I don't fight with my fists now, Ruby, I fight with my head. There's more than one way of flexing a muscle, you know. Your husband owed me money, Ruby – lots of it. What I did I had a right to do. I paid for your wedding because if I hadn't he'd never have been able to have afforded to marry you.'

'But you didn't *want* me to marry him!' I shouted. 'Why did you let it go ahead?'

Frank's face was a mask. 'Because it was what *you* wanted, Ruby. You told me you loved him, remember?'

I was confused, afraid to speak because Frank was tying my words and thoughts into knots. Frank watched me for a moment, standing there silent in the half-light, and then he stepped back and motioned me inside.

'You'd better come in, Ruby,' he said, quietly. 'Perhaps it's time you looked around my new home.'

# CHAPTER 36

I stepped inside the hallway and the dog padded on ahead of me, crossing straight to the fire that was crackling in the fireplace and throwing herself down full-length on the rug in front of it.

I tried to speak, but my thoughts had gone. Everything was as I remembered it, the furniture, the carpets, the paint on the walls, all restored to how it had been when I'd first visited the place as a child. I could hear the wireless in the next room, not giving news of the coronation this time, but playing music, soft, sentimental stuff that must have been around when Frank and I were dating. The place smelled of polish again, and candlewax and coal and I felt a rush of nostalgia that was like a wave inside my body.

'It's the same,' I said, and moved towards the sitting room.

Frank pulled me back gently, holding on to my shoulders. 'Don't go in there, Ruby,' he said softly. 'It's not finished yet. I only had a few days, remember?'

I stopped. 'The furniture, everything, you bought it all back, it's all the same.' I couldn't believe it, it was like a scene from a pantomime, the moment when the fairy waves her wand and everything you wish for comes true.

'I bought it as they sold it,' Frank told me. 'Most of

went in auction, the rest I picked up from dealers. It helps
to have friends in the business.'

I turned to face Frank, and I knew then that I loved
him, that I had always loved him, *would* always love him.
My life fitted into place as I stood there, as though Frank
was the last missing piece of the puzzle, and only now
did the whole mess make sense. It was like those games
that you get for Christmas as a kid, when you fiddle
around with them for ages, and then they fall into place
as you're about to give up.

Frank pulled me towards him and I stared into his eyes,
trying to find some mirror there of my own, violent
emotions. His eyes, that close, looked like wet black paint.
I saw images in the blackness, but they were shapes that
I didn't recognize and I looked away, once again unable
to interpret Frank's thoughts.

I felt his breath, I felt his skin against mine. I smelled
the smells of the house, felt its presence all around me,
and I knew then that I had everything in the world that
I wanted. I'd come home at last, and I was there with the
man that I loved.

When Frank's lips came to my mouth I felt a release of
tension that had been inside me for ever. I felt myself
drawn up into Frank, into his kiss, at the mercy of his
tongue and his teeth, and he could have swallowed me
whole, I felt so small and so pliant and so willing to be
taken. I felt him pull Piers's ring off my finger and when
I looked again he had replaced it with his ring, the one
he had sent me in Australia, the one I had thrown into
the rose garden.

I looked up in surprise, and Frank was smiling. 'Don't
ask,' he said, 'but it took me all day.' I smiled and kissed
him. 'Do you love me now, Ruby?' he whispered. I
nodded.

'Say it then,' he said, 'let me hear you say it at last.'

'I love you, Frank,' I said, and I meant it.

'Like you loved Piers and Jack?'

I felt the first cold sting of fear then, a wafer-thin current that ran straight through my veins.

'I've always loved you,' I told him, 'all along. You told me I did, Frank, but I never believed you. Now I know you were right, only I was just too stupid and too proud to ever admit it before. I love you, Frank, and I love you properly, with all of my heart and with all of my body.' I was desperate for Frank to believe me this time. I looked at his eyes and something in them seemed to relax, and then I relaxed as he kissed me, and I knew my future was secured, for I knew that Frank trusted me.

'Prove it, Ruby,' Frank said. 'Prove that you love me, show me how much.'

'How?' I whispered, but I knew what he wanted before he'd asked.

'Make love to me,' he said gently, 'Here, in your wedding dress, where we did it before, the first time. Show me, Ruby. Don't just tell me, show me.'

I wound my fingers into Frank's hair and I pulled his face towards me and when I kissed Frank this time it was the gentlest, tenderest kiss that I'd ever given in my life. We fell on to the floor beneath my precious ceiling of painted clouds, and it was there that we made love. It was slow and it was careful and I found myself crying at the beauty of it all.

When we were finished, and the fire had died, Frank lifted me into his strong arms and carried me up the wide staircase to the bedroom that he'd prepared for us. As he laid me on the high, ancient bed he kissed me again and then we slept, exhausted; our bodies entwined in a way that Fate must have meant them to be all along.

# CHAPTER 37

When I awoke it was morning. I felt the tattered
ribbons of my dress, the stale taste of the champagne in my mouth, and for a moment I thought I was
with Piers, in our room at the Savoy. Then the golden
light of the sun fell on to my face, blinding me, and I
rolled over in the bed and remembered at last.

It was Frank that I could taste in my mouth now. I
clawed damp strands of hair from my face and sucked at
my fingertips to taste the last of the salt. My body ached
with what we had done. I felt Frank's hands and his mouth
and his strong gentle body on my own. He loved me now
as he had always loved me. The house was mine at last,
despite the strange turnaround of events. I had all that I
wanted, more even than I had dreamed of. Piers was like
a pale memory in my past. I couldn't believe that I had
married him, that the wedding dress I had put on so
proudly just hours before lay a torn and crumpled mess
on the floor beside Frank's bed. I would get a divorce.
Frank would help me, Frank knew everyone. Then I
would be free to marry him and my house would become
our home.

I turned towards the light, expecting to find Frank
beside me in the bed. I was alone. I tried to move, to sit
up, but the hangover hit me like a bag of wet cement and
I fell back on to the pillows with a groan. It felt good just

to lie there, like being sick and off school as a child. I could lie there and forget all my problems. Frank would solve them now. Frank would take care of me as Billy had taken care of me as a child. I didn't need to worry, I had everything that I wanted.

I turned the story around in my mind, my eyes closed and a half-smile on my lips. I thought of the way Frank had schemed to get me, the way he had fought for so long to bring me here again. He had lured Piers by his weakness for gambling, just as I had lured him by his weakness for sex. Frank had used Piers without mercy and I admired him. He had beaten me to the one thing he knew that I wanted, and now, by getting the house, he had got me as well. It was my trap he had set and I loved getting ensnared in it.

I stretched, and felt the warm blood coursing slowly through my body. I had thought Frank's motive was revenge, but it had been love all along. He had wanted me every bit as badly as I had wanted the house and he had been prepared to do anything to get me.

I looked at my wedding dress. Why had Frank paid for my wedding? Why hadn't he just taken the house from Piers and then told me that he owned it? Why had he complicated things by allowing my wedding to go ahead? Now I had to get a divorce, and it would be ages before I could marry him. Did it confirm the strength of my love for Frank to know that I had left my groom still drinking champagne at our reception to run off into his arms? Or did he just hate Piers and want one last thrust of the knife before he took me for good?

I thought of how Frank had restored the house for me, how hard he'd worked to replace each piece of furniture and I became dizzy at the thought of how much he must love me. The bed had become cold without him there. Moving slowly, I pulled myself up and wrapped myself in Frank's huge bathrobe. I saw my reflection in the mirror at the end of the bed. My face was pale with two living pink spots on my cheeks. My eyes were bright and burn ing again with fire. My hair was a mess, a tangle of matted strands that fell over my face. I tried to pull my fingers through it but it was no good, I had to leave it as it was. I walked unsteadily to the washstand and felt the pain in my head recede to a dull ache as I splashed water over my face and neck.

I threw open the window and a rush of cool air invaded the room. I leaned right out, drinking in the air, the smells, the sun, the noises of the house. 'I'm here,' I whispered to it. 'I kept my promise, I've come at last.'

The hill was there to protect us, rising up in front of me like the vast wave of longing and nostalgia that the mere sight of it produced. The scent of the roses was more unbearable nostalgia – with it came memories that assaulted me without mercy. I saw my precious roses, their heads nodding to show their approval. There were the green lawns surrounding the rose garden, stretched out like felt, where the other children had eaten their tea as Piers and I had kissed on Coronation Day. I felt the plasterwork beneath my fingertips. It was too much all at once. I closed my eyes and let my face bake in the morning sun. The house was mine. It had always been mine.

A noise startled me and I looked down, hoping to see Frank. Instead I saw a workman on the path below, laying out ladders, whistling as he did so. I let my chin rest on my hands and watched him for a while but then he must have felt my eyes on him, because he looked up suddenly and gave me a little salute.

'Morning, ma'am,' he called, and I nodded back in reply. So Frank was still working on the place, restoring it totally, I hoped. His money had to be endless, then. It didn't matter if it wasn't, I would have enough to finish the work off. I smiled at the sudden thought of all my money. Did Frank know how much I still had left? I tugged his bathrobe around me, thinking of his reaction when I told him that I was rich too. Maybe he did know, he seemed to know everything else about me since I had arrived back in England.

'What are you restoring?' I shouted to the workman, and my voice sounded right in that clear air, like Philippa's voice; like Piers's mother's.

The man unfolded some sort of plan on the ground and was studying it with a frown, a pencil tucked behind one ear. 'Not restoration,' he called, shaking his head and smiling up at me, 'not on this bit, anyway.' He looked back down at his plans. 'Rear extension, according to this,' he said.

I grabbed at the window-ledge to steady myself. 'There?' I asked, and he nodded.

'Seems so,' he answered.

'What sort of extension?' I shouted, leaning dangerously out of the window.

'Conservatory,' the man called up. 'Bloody great big one, too, if you'll pardon my French.'

'You'd better check,' I told him, 'there must be some mistake. There was never a conservatory there! There's not even enough room! You'd have to knock the rose garden down to get a thing that size in here!'

I was obviously sounding stupid and the man merely shrugged, choosing now to ignore me as he turned his attention back to his plan. I ran across the bedroom and pulled the door wide open. 'Frank?' I called, but there was no reply, the house was silent. I rushed to the stairs. There was a smell of fresh coffee coming from the direction of the kitchens and the sound of movement and voices from the lounge. I ran down the stairs, almost stumbling in my rush, and I pulled the lounge door open, calling out to Frank as I did so.

'Frank, there's some idiot out the back who seems to think he's got to knock my rose garden down to make way for some sort of . . .' I began, but then the words cut off in my throat. The lounge had been gutted, but not restored in any way that was familiar to me. The wood panelling had gone. The heavy, dust-coloured chandelier had gone. The parquet had been ripped up, and none of it had been replaced authentically. The room was now office – Frank's office, from the way that he stood behind a massive black teak desk that dominated the far end of the room. His hands were resting on that desk, astride more sets of plans, and his face looked surprised and irritated, as though I'd interrupted something important.

I looked from Frank's face back to the room. The new furniture was modern and bare and minimal, like the stuff in Philippa's flat in Sydney. The walls were imitation grey marble and there was a fitted carpet on the floor. The ceiling was hung with chrome-backed spotlights and the only chair, a black leather armchair in front of Frank's desk, was filled with a short, middle-aged man dressed in the sort of sharp suit you only saw back in London. The man had swivelled the chair round to see me and now he looked embarrassed as he half-rose to greet me. I stopped talking immediately, aware of how I must look, in Frank's bathrobe, with my hair falling over my face.

'Elizabeth!' he said, and to hear him use my second name, that one that I'd used just for Piers and his cronies, made my flesh crawl with sudden fear.

'Frank,' I whispered, 'what have you done to the lounge?'

'Office, Elizabeth,' Frank corrected me. 'It's my office now, and I'd prefer you to give me some warning before you come barging in next time.'

I walked further into the room, unconcerned now at the other man's embarrassment. 'There's a man round the back about to knock down the rose garden,' I told Frank. 'You'll have to stop him, he's made some terrible mistake with his plans.'

'Mistake?' Frank asked, and there was a muscle working way in his cheek as he stared at me. 'I don't think there's any mistake, not at this stage, anyway. Perhaps you'd like word with the designer and architect if you're not happy with any of the plans.' He held a hand out to the man sitting opposite. 'Derek,' he said, 'meet Elizabeth, the Earl of Bicester's beautiful new bride.'

The man rose to his feet and nervously extended his

hand but I ignored it, I couldn't tear my eyes away from Frank's face. He was still playing a game with me, he had to be, and I wanted to see his expression change when he first dropped his front and started to laugh.

'The Earl was the previous owner of this place, as you'll no doubt remember me telling you,' Frank went on, addressing his remarks to the architect. 'His bride here has even broken into her honeymoon to see how the work's going on, haven't you, Elizabeth? You'll have read about the wedding, of course, Derek – it was in all the gossip columns. Or maybe that's not quite up your street when it comes to reading matter? I always was more of a *Sporting Life* man, myself, wasn't I, Ruby?' He smiled a smile that chilled the blood in my veins. 'This lady and I go back a long way, Derek,' he said, still smiling at me as he spoke. 'I call her by her childhood name, don't I, Ruby?'

'I don't understand, Frank,' I said in a low voice. Frank stopped acting then, I could tell the way his face changed.

'A moment, Derek, if you don't mind,' he said, and the man nodded and walked out of the room. I barely moved to let him pass.

The door clicked shut behind him and Frank sat down at his desk. 'Sleep all right, Ruby?' he asked.

I stared at him but I couldn't move. I wanted to sit down but my legs would never have got me as far as the chair.

'Frank?' My voice was weak, full of shock. 'What are you up to here, Frank?' I asked.

'Up to?' He tried to look surprised but the look wasn't convincing.

'Frank, why are you doing this to me?' I asked. I didn't cry. I didn't shout. My brain was too numb, too deep in shock. It would thaw, I thought, given time. Things would become clearer if I could only have a minute to think. 'You're ruining my house,' I said.

'*Your* house?' Frank asked, and this time there was

phoney surprise on his face, just a level stare on his face
as he watched me across the plans.

'*Our* house,' I said, willing to concede the point if it
meant that he would only stop the man working in the
gardens. I moved across to the desk, tried to spin the plans
around to see if Frank was serious. The action knocked a
lamp on to the floor but Frank made no move to retrieve
it; it just lay there rocking, its light swinging wildly about
the room.

'Don't,' I said to Frank. 'Don't ruin it.'

'Ruin it, Ruby?' Frank asked. 'Now that's a matter of
opinion. Some people would say it was your husband
who'd ruined it; some would say it was ruined when I
got it. It was Derek's opinion that I'd been had by your
husband when I took it in return for the sort of money
he owed me, Ruby. It took a few thousand just to sort
out little problems like the damp and the dry rot. I don't
believe there would have been a house standing here much
longer if I hadn't bought it, Ruby, so don't go telling me
I've ruined it.'

'I thought . . .' I began.

'You thought what?' Frank asked, leaning over his desk
so suddenly that I found myself backing away.

'I thought you were renovating the house,' I said, with
less strength than I wanted in my voice. 'I thought you
were restoring it to how it used to be, Frank.'

'And so I will, in parts,' he told me, watching my face
all the while. 'We've got to tart it up a bit here and there
though, we want our punters to be comfortable, don't
we, Ruby?'

'Punters?' The word had a shock value all of its own.
It rang in my ears like the tolling of some terrible warning
bell. A dull pain started in the back of my head and I
rubbed at my eyes, trying hard to see some sense in
Frank's words.

'Punters?' I asked. I spat the word out. I didn't even
like the feel of it in my mouth. 'What punters, Frank?
What are you talking about?'

'Gamblers, Ruby,' Frank told me, and he relaxed and stepped back from the desk. 'My life's blood – and yours too, if you decide you want a cut in the business. I'm turning the house into one of the classiest clubs in the country, Ruby. What else did you think I'd be wanting it for?'

My head filled with black fog, so that I thought I might faint. 'You're joking, Frank,' I whispered, 'you have to be.'

Frank shrugged. 'Look at the plans if you don't believe me,' he said, turning the papers round so that I had a clearer view of them.

I tried to look but I didn't need to. I could hear the truth in his voice.

'You bastard,' I said. 'You can't!'

'Can't?' Frank asked, and his voice began to sound angry. 'Can't, Ruby? Who are you to tell me what I can and can't do? The place belongs to me now, I can do what I bloody well like with it!'

'But we were going to live here, Frank!' I pleaded. 'Last night, I came back to you. You told me you loved me. I thought this was for us, to live in alone!'

'Is that what you thought, Ruby?' Frank asked. 'Is that why you came down here?'

I held my head. The pain was getting worse.

'Why are you doing this to me?' I asked him. 'You told me you loved me!' I was repeating myself but I didn't care. I could find no other words in my head.

'No,' Frank shouted suddenly, so loud that I put my hands over my ears. 'Last night *you* told me you loved *me*, Ruby, remember?'

'But I thought . . .' I began.

'You think too much, Ruby,' Frank cut in, 'that always was your problem. I've warned you about it before. Let me finish your sentence for you. You thought you could manipulate me, that's right, isn't it? You thought I'd done all this for you and that I'd be sitting here waiting the moment you decided to come running at last. Am I right

Don't shake your head, Ruby, tell the truth for once in your life. Tell me how much you really hate me but how much you're willing to crawl to me on your belly if it means you get the only thing you've ever wanted in this life! Tell me!'

Some sense fell into my head then. I began to see what Frank had done. The trap he had set had not been to catch me but to test me, and I had fallen straight into the middle. He had been trying to see how far I would go, how low I would crawl to get ownership of the house. That was why he had fleeced Piers and why he had paid for our wedding. He had wanted to see if I would go through with it, whether I'd marry Piers just to get my hands on the house. Then he'd set the bait again, let me know of my mistake, just to see if I would run out on the man that I'd told him I loved, and into his arms with what he thought were more of my lies. I saw it all clearly for one blinding instant and I wanted to tell him he was wrong but I couldn't, the lies wouldn't come any more.

I sank down into the chair and held my head in my hands until the room stopped spinning.

'What do you expect me to do now?' I asked, more to myself than to Frank.

'You're a married woman, Ruby,' Frank answered, and his words sounded as hard as the expression on his face. 'I expect you to go back to your husband. He must be wondering where you've got to.'

'But I don't love Piers, Frank!' I cried. 'I love you!'

Frank sprang around the desk and gripped me by the shoulders. 'But you loved Piers when he had the house, didn't you, Ruby?' he asked.

I tried to turn away from his words but he wouldn't let me.

'You told me so yourself, Ruby,' he said, 'you told me that you loved him, that I wasn't good enough for you, that Piers was class, while I was just dirt!'

'I was wrong . . .' I began.

'But now I've got the house and – guess what? Suddenly

you love me and you were wrong about Piers all along!
How does that sound to you, Ruby? True love or true
greed? I'm too stupid to know the difference, aren't I? I'm
supposed to confuse the first with the last!' He let me go
and I fell back into the chair. 'What a coincidence, eh,
Ruby?' he said, 'that you should change your mind about
me the very minute you hear I own this place and come
flying away from your wedding just to fall into my arms.
I've been here all along, Ruby. Why did you choose yesterday to finally decide that you loved me?'

'I came here to blame you for robbing my husband,' I
whispered.

'Like the loyal little wife that you are!' Frank shouted.
'And then somewhere on the journey the truth hit you
and in a blinding flash you realized you loved me, is that
it? That's really touching, Ruby, a truly touching, sordid,
grubby little story. Even you can do better than that.'

'I love you, Frank,' I said, and he laughed. 'I kept your
ring,' I added, and I held my hand out towards him. 'All
those months in Australia, even after all I thought you'd
done to me, even when I thought you were guilty of
killing our child, I still kept your ring, Frank. Jack
would've killed me too, if he'd ever found me wearing
it.'

A look of pain shot across Frank's face at the mention
of our baby. 'Don't, Ruby,' he said, and his voice sounded
softer, though his face was still like cold hard rock.

'Don't what, Frank?' I asked him. 'Don't remind you
of what I went through? Do you know how much I hated
you then? I killed my husband for what he did then, but
I hated you more for I thought that you'd caused it. I
loved our baby, Frank, more than anything on earth.
When it died I thought I'd died too. But you don't want
to hear about that, do you, Frank? That's not playing by
the rules now, is it?'

Frank turned his back on me and I heard him groan.

'Last night, Frank,' I whispered, 'last night I know you
loved me.'

'I have loved you, Ruby,' he told me, 'more than you'll ever know or begin to understand because you're not capable of that sort of love yourself, I've realized that now. I've loved you since the moment I first saw you, though God knows why, when it's brought us to this. I've loved you and I've ached for you but I'm not like you in one thing, Ruby: I'm too proud to settle for second best. I knew I could have you the minute I took over this place and I knew you'd make a show of loving me once you knew I'd got it, like you did last night. But I don't want your lies, Ruby. I'm smarter than Jack and I'm craftier than Piers and I want more than either of them ever got. I want you to love me, Ruby, as completely and absolutely as I once loved you.'

'I do love you, Frank,' I said and he swung around with an anger that frightened me.

'Don't give me that crap!' he shouted.

I sat up in my chair. 'Sell it to me then,' I said.

'What?' Even Frank looked confused.

'Sell me the house, Frank,' I said. 'Then you'll know. Then you'll be sure. You'll never believe me as long as you own it. If I have it, you'll know, though. You'll believe me then when I tell you I love you.'

I was excited suddenly, the pulse was beating fast in my veins. Frank looked at my face and I thought he was weighing the idea up in his head. He liked a gamble and I hoped the odds appealed to him.

'You've put us at stalemate, Frank,' I said. 'As long as your name is on the deeds here you'll never know whether to trust me or not. Let me buy it from you, Frank. I'll pay a good enough price. Then you'll see that I want you as well. Then you'll find out I was telling the truth last night. You knew, Frank, you must have known when we made love. I might lie to some men but I can't lie to you. It was never like that between Piers and me.'

Frank stared at me a while and I held my breath, praying for him to agree and sell me the house. Then he grinned, slowly and almost casually, and I froze as I watched that smile because it signalled to me that I had lost.

'You must think I'm fucking stupid,' Frank said.

I jumped up from the chair, wild with anger because he thought that he'd beaten me, because I thought that I had lost.

'Yes I do, Frank!' I screamed. 'I do think you're stupid! More stupid than Jack and more stupid even than Piers! I don't want you,' I said, panting, 'I never have done. You sicken me, you always did! I let you make love to me to get back at Pearl and after I thought you'd killed my child I let you again to get my revenge. Do you think I'd've let you touch me otherwise? You're right, Frank, I'd do anything to get this house and only you will know just how low I was prepared to stoop to get it. As low as you, Frank! That's how far I was prepared to crawl!'

I thought he would hit me then; the smile just froze on his face at my words.

'You do love me, Ruby,' he said quietly.

'You're wrong,' I said, shaking my head.

We stared at one another for a moment, and it was as though a wall had sprung up between us.

'It's my house, Frank,' I said, 'mine by rights, no matter whose name is on the deeds. I won't beg from you and I won't lie to you any more. Do what you want with it, turn it into your precious casino if you like, only you won't keep it because it belongs to me and I'll get it back one day. It's me you stole it from, Frank, not Piers. He never cared for it and neither do you. I'll always belong here and it's here that I'll end up. You can't stop me Frank, nobody can!'

I ran from the room at that, there was nothing more to say. Frank went to stop me but I reached the door before him.

The car was waiting in the driveway, the chauffeur at the wheel, and I wondered whether Frank had planned this as he had planned everything else. 'Take me to London,' said, and the car purred into life. I was still in Frank' dressing gown but no expression of surprise or shock crossed the man's face.

As we pulled across the drive I saw Frank watching from the open doorway.

'Wait,' I said, and the car pulled up beside him.

Frank and I stared at one another through the glass of the car window and I could tell from our faces that we realized neither of us had won. I looked at him from the rear window as the car finally drove away and I saw him grow smaller in the distance until the car turned a bend and he was gone.

In my mind he was still laughing at me, the bastard, I could still see the grin on his face.

I curled into the car seat and the tears started to run down my face.

The chauffeur studied me through his mirror for a second as I wiped my face with the sleeve of Frank's robe.

'Would you like me to return to the house, madam?' he asked quietly.

'Did Frank tell you to say that?' I asked him.

'No, madam,' he told me, 'I just thought . . .'

'Take me to London,' I said coldly. 'I'm never going back.'

# CHAPTER 38

But I did go back to the house, of course I did, for how could I have kept away, knowing it belonged to me and knowing what Frank planned to do to it?

I caused a scandal when I returned to London, and the papers were full of my marriage of four hours. My name was like dirt in London society and even the friends who had claimed to dislike Piers all shunned me in turn in disgust at what I had done. Only Philippa remained, and I felt her loyalty waning as my isolation became more obvious. Each day came calls from Piers's solicitors and now he is divorcing me, which I want, and threatening to take me through the courts for my money, which I will never allow.

I need my money for Rowan Hall. I have never given up on it and I never will. It will be mine, I am sure of it now. I only have to wait, and I am good at waiting, I have waited over twenty years already.

'It's Frank you love, darling,' Philippa tells me with monotonous regularity, 'I always knew it, only you were too blind or too stubborn to see.'

Philippa has said this so often now that I begin to wonder whether she is also in cahoots with Frank. Nothing would surprise me any more, though I think that may be paranoia. Of course I agree with her but I would never admit it, my pride is too fierce to allow it. I wa

blind, I was stupid, I was everything else that Frank called
me and worse, I suppose, besides. Frank is all that I have
left now, and he has all that I want.

I went to the house, I had to see it, I had to find out
what he'd done. It was there, of course, though it could
have been bulldozed. I would have done that from spite,
had our roles been reversed. But then I would have never
come back, and I know Frank is waiting for me. He
wouldn't flatten property just to make a point like that.

I stood on the brow of the hill, as I had done on our
first date, and I saw the house and I saw the rose garden,
and I knew then that my future was safe. The ladders had
gone, a gardener worked there alone and quietly, pulling
weeds out from around the flowers. Frank was bluffing
then, the game between us goes on. He has dealt his cards
and now it is my turn to show my hand. He still loves
me, I know this now for sure. The house glowed in
the morning sunshine. It needed me still but there was
contentment now in its waiting. It is being cared for at
last by someone who loves it. It is a palace again, Frank
has restored it to its full glory.

If I were to run down that hill and race in through the
door there would be a fire burning in the hallway and a
dog asleep on the rug. The office would be gone now and
the panelled wood back in its place. I know that, though
I cannot see it. I know it as surely as if I am there. Frank
has done all he can, it is my turn to make the next move.
It will take time, but as I said, I can be patient. No lies
this time, I have to convince him of the truth. I have told
him that I love him and now all I have to do is convince
him. I know I can do this, I am certain it is possible.
Without ever realizing it Frank dealt me the trump card.
I am carrying his child again, a baby, an heir to the house.
His third child, only this one will live and be part of a
family. The house is mine, and nothing will ever happen
to change that, it is there waiting for me, and one day
very soon I will be back.